Oh Crumbs

Oh Crumbs

Kathryn Freeman

Published 2019 by Choc Lit Limited
Penrose House, Crawley Drive, Camberley, Surrey GU15 2AB, UK
www.choc-lit.com

A CIP catalogue record for this book is available
from the British Library

ISBN: 978-1-78189-351-7

Printed and bound in Great Britain by Clays Ltd, Elcograf S.p.A.

To my boys (who will probably never read this)
To my husband (who was brave enough
to read the unedited version)
To my mum (who reads everything I write)
I love you all to bits.

Acknowledgements

If you know a writer, be on guard. At some point, they're bound to ask you for help with their next book. When I started writing *Oh Crumbs*, I didn't expect to need advice on martial arts. The more Doug developed as a character though, the more I realised he needed a sport to help him channel his anger. But which sport? And who did I know who could help me decide? Stand up Alex Gee, ex work colleague and captain of the GB sport jiu-jitsu squad. He was kind enough not to laugh too hysterically when I asked him which sport Doug could take up that wouldn't hurt his pretty features but would look sexy when he was fighting thugs. Alex also went on to answer my dumb questions about Brazilian jiu-jitsu, and even took the time to check the accuracy of what I'd written. So huge thanks to him and a warning to the rest of my friends. You could be next.

Now to the many other people who've helped me not just with *Oh Crumbs*, but with every book I've written. My sincere and humble thanks to the following.

My publisher, Choc Lit, who put their faith in me eight (yes, I can't believe it either) books ago. And are still showing it now.

The Choc Lit Tasting Panel of readers who were kind enough to approve *Oh Crumbs* for publication: Linda Sp, Elaina J, Jo L, Hannah M, Margaret T, Linda T, Christine Y, Sabine M, Christina G, Ester V, Paula C, Sarah B, Janine N, Kathryn B, Jo O, Susan D and Elisabeth H.

My fabulous editor, so lovely to work with,
and who always manages to add both accuracy
and pizzazz to my original manuscript.

Book Bloggers, whose enthusiasm for reading, and
amazing support of writers, is humbling. Thank
you for taking the time to help this author.

My husband, who bravely reads and critiques every
one of my manuscripts before I submit them (yes,
incredibly, we are still talking to each other).

Family and friends, who still ask about
my next book. It's coming!

And finally, but most importantly of all, you. Thank you
so much for buying and reading *Oh Crumbs*. I hope you
enjoy the story of Abby and Doug. I recommend reading
while eating a biscuit, but please watch those crumbs...

Prologue

Twelve Years Ago

Abby clung onto her baby sister who was wriggling in her arms, trying to get down. Ellie didn't understand that she was supposed to be quiet; she was only one. But still, Abby didn't like it that Ellie was starting to make a noise and kick her feet. They were in a church, after all, and the priest was talking while everyone bowed their heads – a sea of black. Black suits, black coats, black hats. Outside there had even been black clouds. Abby hated black. She liked pink best, but she was told she couldn't wear pink today. Not at Mum's funeral. Abby had wanted to disagree – her mum would have let her wear pink, she was sure – but for once she'd kept quiet. A pity Ellie wasn't doing the same.

'Here, I'll take her. You look after the others.' Her dad leant across and pulled Ellie out of her arms. Sagging with relief – Ellie was quite heavy these days – thirteen-year-old Abby reached for the hands of her second and third youngest sisters, Holly who was three and Sally who was five. There was also Mandy, nearly nine, but she was too grown up to hold hands.

The priest droned on and even though it was her mum's funeral, Abby wasn't listening. The words were funny – and not in a make you laugh kind of way. Why didn't the priest use words they could understand? And anyway, none of it would bring Mum back, would it? Unless she believed all that stuff about heaven. Abby wanted to, but she couldn't see how that worked. She'd seen her mum take her last breath. Watched her face go deathly pale and her body still. Now she was in the coffin in front of them. How could she get from there and up to heaven? And even if she did, how could she come back down to see them?

At the thought of never seeing her mum again, Abby started to cry. As the tears slid down her cheeks, Holly tugged at her hand.

'Need to pee. Where's Mum?'

Abby smothered a sob. 'Can't you hang on a minute?'

Holly shook her head, ringlets bouncing round her pretty face.

'Okay.' She prodded Mandy. 'Hold Sally's hand for me. I need to take Holly out for a pee.'

Mandy gave her *the look*. It meant she was cross, though Abby didn't give a flying fig. She had enough on her plate. Ducking down she dragged Holly up the aisle, uncomfortably aware of heads turning to stare as they shuffled past. Once outside she pulled her sister round to the side of the church, behind a bush.

Holly pouted. 'I want a toilet.'

'I don't know where they are. Just pull your pants down and do it here.' She wasn't sure if it was okay to pee in the grounds of the church but if there was a God, and if he was as good as people said, surely he wouldn't mind. It was God's fault they were here, anyway. He'd taken their mum away when he shouldn't have done. Mums didn't die when they still had children to look after. Mums hung around and became grandmums. So why had God decided to take *her* mum away? It wasn't fair.

'They're wet now.'

Abby glanced down to find Holly had managed to aim most of her pee into her pants. Guiltily she kissed her cheek. 'Sorry, I should have helped you. Here, let's take them off and bin them. That way you won't smell.'

'But I want my pants,' wailed Holly, her cheeks going pink. A sure sign she was going to start stomping her feet soon.

Abby felt like joining in. She didn't want to be in this graveyard, sorting out her sister's smelly wet pants. She didn't want to be inside the church either, hearing stuff about how great her mum was. She knew that already. What she really wanted was for her mum to come and put her arms around her and tell her everything was going to be all right.

But she'd never feel her mum's arms around her again.

Tears began to pour out of her eyes and Abby wiped them savagely with her hand.

Holly stared at her, her eyes growing round. 'Take pants off now. Smelly.' She held her nose and gave her a toothy grin.

The sight made Abby's tears fall faster, though at least this time she was laughing, too.

By the time she'd sorted Holly out, people were coming out of the church and her mum was being carried in the coffin to a big black car. Abby knew what was going to happen next, because her dad had told her. Her mum was going to be burnt. They called it cremated, but they meant burnt.

She clutched at her stomach, suddenly feeling very sick. Grabbing Holly's arm she pulled her out of the way and puked into the same bush.

'Abby?' Holly stared at her with wide, frightened eyes, tears once more slipping down her cheeks.

Quickly Abby wiped her mouth and plastered on a smile. 'Come on. Let's go and find Dad.'

The service at the crematorium was over quickly and Abby tried not to look at the coffin as it went behind the curtains. Instead she fussed over Ellie and Holly, while her dad stared straight ahead, tears rolling down his face.

Next it was back to their house where Dad had paid some people to make sandwiches and tea. Abby tried to help serve it out but after she'd dropped a second plate of food, sending shattered crockery flying across the kitchen tiles, her dad told her not to worry and to look after her sisters instead.

'Ellie stinks.' Mandy held her nose and nodded down at their baby sister, who gave them both a toothy grin.

'You could change her.' Abby knew their mum had shown Mandy how to do it.

'No way. You're the oldest. That's your job.'

Mandy flounced off and Abby sighed, picking Ellie up. 'Come on then, smelly pants.'

Holly, who was standing next to her, pushed out her bottom lip. 'Holly not got smelly pants. Abby took them.'

'I know. This time it's Ellie who's smelly.'

Holly started to giggle. 'Smelly Ellie.'

'That's right. Come on, let's go and change her. Where's Sally?'

Holly pointed to the kitchen, where Sally had pushed a chair up to the sink and was rubbing a cloth over her skirt, tears running down her face.

Shifting Ellie onto her hip, and taking Holly's hand, Abby walked over. 'What's wrong?'

'I've spilt something on my dress and it won't come off.'

Abby peered at where Sally was pointing. All she could see was wet. 'It's gone.'

'No. It's dirty.'

'Well, I'll come back and help you when I've changed Ellie's nappy.'

As she made her way up the stairs to the bathroom, Abby decided she'd rather have served out the sandwiches.

Eventually the last of the guests left and the house fell eerily quiet. It was a horrid, sad silence which made Abby want to cry because it didn't feel like home. That was *always* noisy.

'Come on, Holly. You can have a bath with Ellie. And Sally, you come too. You can help me and then go in after.' She picked Ellie out of her playpen and started to walk towards the stairs. 'We're going to play a game. Let's see who can make the most noise.'

Holly and Sally immediately scampered up the stairs, shouting at the top of their voices and Abby smiled to herself.

The bath time routine was one she'd perfected over the last few months, since Mum's cancer had made her so ill she hadn't been able to help much. Her dad had taken care of her mum and Abby had looked after her sisters and the house. She didn't mind the cooking. What she hated was cleaning and sorting out washing. Dad tried to help but he worked a lot, fixing other people's cars. Plus he wasn't very good in the kitchen.

When all her young sisters were washed and in bed, Abby went back downstairs to the living room where she found her dad sitting in his chair, head in his hands. He'd been doing that a lot recently and the sight made her heart hurt. He looked older than her friends' dads now, his hair greyer, his face more creased.

'Dad?'

Immediately he sat up. 'Hello, sunshine. Are the girls in bed?'

'All except Mandy who's having a bath.'

He smiled, though it wasn't the smile she liked, the one that made his eyes crinkle and showed his teeth. This was a sad smile, the only type he seemed to give her nowadays. 'You're such a treasure, Abby, thank you.' He motioned for her to come and sit, so she slid in beside him, even though there wasn't much room. When she was smaller she'd easily been able to squeeze beside him on his big armchair. Now it was a tight fit because she'd grown upwards and he'd grown outwards a bit. Still, it felt nice to have his arms around her.

'I'm sorry I've not been much help over the last few months,' he told her, stroking her hair, which Abby liked even though sometimes his fingers got caught in her curls. 'I'll try to be better, but the garage takes up so much time.'

'It's okay.'

He kissed her forehead. 'It's not really okay. A girl your age shouldn't be looking after her sisters and taking care of household chores. You should be out enjoying yourself. It's a shame we don't have any close family to help out. I'd like to get a cleaner but I'm afraid we can't afford it at the moment.'

Abby knew money was always tight. It didn't seem fair. Dad worked really hard, harder than a lot of her friends' dads, but they never seemed to have much money. 'I can get the others to help. Sally keeps her side of the bedroom neat so she could be in charge of tidying up. Ellie's too young, but Holly always wants to use the toy dustpan and brush she got at Christmas.'

'Holly's three, Abby. Last time I watched her, she emptied what she'd brushed up onto the sofa.'

'I can teach her where to put it. Mandy can fold up the laundry.' Abby frowned. 'But you'd have to ask her, 'cos she doesn't listen to me.'

'I'm not sure Mandy listens to anyone. Not even her teachers.' He gave Abby's shoulders a gentle squeeze. 'We'll see how we get on. You never know, the garage might pick up and then we can hire someone to do the cleaning and laundry.'

'And a cook?'

Again he gave her that half smile. 'Yeah, that'd be a treat, wouldn't it? But you're doing great. Really great.'

'I'm learning it at school, so it's fun to try stuff out at home.' Well, it would be if she didn't have to do it every day. At the weekends her dad helped out though, so really it was only five days a week she had to cook. 'Ellie's stuff is the hardest. She likes sloppy food or things she can eat with her fingers. Mum taught me.'

Suddenly the tears she'd been saving up for most of the day burst out of her and Abby couldn't stop herself. She cried and cried, big blubbery sobs. She hugged her dad tight and he hugged her back. She wasn't certain, but she thought he was crying, too.

'We'll get through this, sunshine,' her dad said after a while. 'Spencers are tough. If we stick together, we can get through anything. Even life without your mum.'

His voice cracked as he said the last words and Abby thought he was trying to convince himself, as well as her. 'Mum told me to always remember that the Spencer girls could do anything they wanted, if they put their mind to it. I'm to tell my sisters that, when they get older.'

She felt him kiss the top of her head. 'Aye, they can. You each have a bit of Mum inside you, and that makes you all very special.'

His chest shuddered, and this time Abby knew for certain her dad was crying.

It made her start to cry again, too.

Six Years Ago

Abby tried not to make a noise as she snuck into the house. She wasn't drunk – not very, anyway. She'd only managed a few bottles of those sickly fruity drinks with vodka in them. Three at the most – or maybe it was four? Whatever, she still knew what she was doing, even if she wasn't totally stable on her feet.

'Bugger.' She winced as she banged into the leg of a kitchen chair.

'We aren't meant to swear, and bugger counts as a swear word.'

7

Abby's head shot round to see who was talking, which was a flipping big mistake because now the whole room was spinning. 'Oh God,' she groaned, holding her stomach as she ran to the kitchen sink.

'That's disgusting. I'm going to tell Dad.'

When she'd finished retching, Abby rinsed her mouth out and turned to face her sister, Mandy. 'Don't you dare. If you do, I'll tell him what I've seen you getting up to round the back of the school.'

Mandy shrugged. 'So, I like kissing boys. It's not a crime.'

'It is if you let them do more than kiss you.' Abby shook her head at her. 'You're only fourteen, Mandy. Plenty of time for all that when you're older.'

'What, old like you? Old enough to go to a pub, come home pissed and puke in the sink?'

Okay, so she wasn't setting a very good example tonight, but Abby was fed up with having to be the responsible one. She was only eighteen, for God's sake. Why couldn't she have a few drinks and a laugh with her friends? Especially as those friends were going to be escaping soon and all Abby had to look forward to was ... what exactly? More of the crappy same. Looking after the house and her sisters. In fact it was worse, because this time she'd be doing it after a day at work instead of at school.

'I was having a last drink with my friends before they go to uni.' Abby filled a glass of water and sat down, hoping it would stop the room from moving quite so much. 'Anyway, what are you doing up? It's past midnight.'

'If you're allowed to stay up, so should I.'

'I'm four years older than you.' She willed the thump in her head to calm down a bit. 'Does Dad know you're not in bed?'

'He doesn't care.'

Abby glared at her. 'You know that's not true.'

'Isn't it? He spends more time in his garage than he does at home with us. I reckon he loves it more.'

'He's not there because he wants to be, Mandy.' Though in the early days after their mum had died, it had felt that way.

'You're always banging on at me to help you. Why don't you tell him to come home earlier instead? He's the parent. He should be doing the stuff around the house. Not making the kids do it.'

'He tries to, but you know how clueless he is.' Abby smiled fondly as she remembered all the times the smoke alarm had gone off in the kitchen over the last few years thanks to his efforts at cooking. 'Do you know how your school shirts ended up grey last week? It's because he did the washing. He shoved his black T-shirt in at the last minute, forgetting everything else he'd put in was white.'

Mandy rolled her eyes. 'Plonker.'

'Yep, but a hard working one. He stays late at the garage because we need the money, Mandy. It's only fair that his daughters try to make life easy for him when he comes home.'

'You'll be earning money soon, when you start work.'

Yeah, lucky her. Abby sighed and put her head in her hands. Sometimes life really sucked.

When she'd done her minute of feeling sorry for herself she glanced up, only to find Mandy's dark Spencer brown eyes staring at her.

'What?'

'Aren't you looking forward to going to work?'

Abby tried to smile, but she could feel tears welling in her eyes. 'Not especially.'

'Would you rather be going to university, like your mates?'

'It would have been nice, yes.'

'So why don't you?'

Abby bit down on the hysterical laughter threatening to escape. Mandy had no flaming clue how her clothes were

9

washed, her tea made. How food appeared in the fridge. 'If I went away, who'd look after you and your sisters?'

'Dad.'

'And we know how well that would work, don't we?' For once Mandy didn't have a quick reply. 'Exactly. So I guess this Cinders isn't going to the ball.'

'I suppose you can do one of those Open University things, you know, if you really want to get a degree.'

Abby had already looked into that, but it wasn't going out into the big world by herself, mixing with people her own age. It was working as a secretary during the day, coming home, doing the chores and then working on a computer in the evening. 'I guess I could, if I have time.'

She rose carefully to her feet, grabbing at the table for support as her legs wobbled. Her stomach felt restless, as if it had only done half the job. It was going to be a long time before she'd be able to face drinking again.

'I suppose I could help a bit more,' Mandy said hesitantly as they made their way up the stairs. 'Maybe clean my room and make some meals.'

Abby's foot slipped and she stumbled. Was the alcohol playing tricks with her, or had Mandy, for the first time since their mother's death, actually stopped fighting her? 'That would be great. Thanks.'

Mandy nodded, holding on to her arm to help her up the last few steps. 'Anyway, it's a good job you aren't going to uni because all they do there is drink and you're crap at it.'

As she stepped gingerly onto the landing, Abby started to giggle. A second later Mandy joined in and pretty soon they were both leaning against the wall, tears streaming down their faces.

'What's all this racket?' Their dad's sleep crumpled face appeared from behind his bedroom door.

'Abby's just realised why she'd be rubbish at university.'

Mandy glanced sideways at her and they burst into giggles again.

He stared at them as if they were certifiable. 'I thought we agreed you weren't going?' A smidgen of panic raced across his features. 'We need you here, Abby. I'm sorry but I don't think I can manage—'

'I know,' Abby cut in quickly, pushing herself away from the wall. 'And it's okay, I'm not going to uni. I've just got a secretarial job in the town hall.'

Relief washed over his face but then he frowned, rubbing at his chin. 'Being a secretary is good, honest work but you were such a bright thing at school. Is it going to be enough for you?'

'Of course it will, Dad. Of course it will.' She wasn't sure if the repeat was to convince him, or herself.

He gave her a tired smile. 'I hope so. Now do you think you can make it to your beds without waking the rest of the household up?'

Abby went to kiss him on the cheek. 'We'll try. Night, Dad.'

When he'd disappeared back to his room, Mandy grinned at her. 'We'll soon be off your hands, Abs. Just think, only another twelve years before Ellie is eighteen.'

It was Mandy's idea of a joke, but this time Abby couldn't smile. As she threw off her clothes and slumped onto the bed, her chest felt heavy, and tears stung the back of her eyes.

She loved her family with all her heart, but was she really supposed to wait until she was thirty before starting to live her own life?

Chapter One

Abby was running late. She was always running late, but today it was really, really important she wasn't.

'Oh crumbs, come on you three, get a move on. You're going to miss the bus if you dawdle like this.' With lightning speed she cleared the breakfast bowls off the table and into the dishwasher.

'Hey, I hadn't finished,' Holly moaned.

Though she was fourteen, at times she still reminded Abby of the little girl who'd peed her pants in the churchyard at her mother's funeral.

'Tough. You can grab a cereal bar.' Equally there were times Abby felt so much older than her twenty-four years. Times when she could barely remember life when she'd had a mum, instead of trying to be one. Twelve years she'd been doing this. And it wasn't getting any easier.

When nobody moved, Abby began to pull the chairs away from the table, resulting in a chorus of protests from all three of them. 'Come on, come on.'

'What are you in a tearing hurry about? You're always late for work.' Sixteen, going on sixty, Sally was meticulous in everything she did. Schoolwork, tidying her room, even organising her schoolbag, like she was now. Placing one neat, scrupulously labelled folder in after another.

'I'm not always late.'

'You are.' Ellie thrust her hands on her hips. 'You told us it's a good job the guy you work for fancies you, 'cos otherwise you'd be out on your ear by now.'

'I don't believe I said it quite like that.' That was Ellie for you. Still only twelve, she saw far more, knew far more – at least she thought she did – than most girls her age. 'Look, I'm in a hurry today because I've got an interview for another job.'

'Is this now you've got that degree you've been working on *forever*?'

'Thanks, Ellie, and yes. It's still secretarial, but it's for a personal assistant to the managing director, so a step up from my current role.'

'Does that mean you'll get more money?'

'If I get it, yes. If I'm late, no.'

Ellie clapped her hands. 'Come on, come on. We need to get moving so Abby can get a better job and we can afford pizza.'

Abby swallowed down her laughter as she watched the flurry of bag packing. If she'd known pizza would work as a bribe, she'd have used it earlier.

As the three sisters raced outside to catch their bus, Abby sagged against the door. Her respite was short-lived though, as Mandy barrelled down the stairs towards her.

'Hey, Abs, will you take George for a minute?'

The wriggling eight-month-old was thrust into her hands and Mandy dashed back up the stairs. For a second Abby stared down at the gorgeous face of her nephew. He was so cute, with pink cheeks and big blue eyes. What a shame he was the product of a brief, ill-advised relationship with a local waster, leaving Mandy a single mother at twenty. And still living at home.

George held out his chubby hands and pulled at Abby's fringe. 'Hey, turnip, none of that. I need to look smart for this interview.' She made a few faces at him, making him grin and revealing two bottom teeth. Adorable as he was though, time was marching on. 'Will you come and take your son, please?' she shouted up at Mandy. 'I need to get ready.'

'I'm on the loo,' her sister's voice echoed back. 'You've got no idea how hard it is to take a pee these days. Just bung him in the high chair and give him a rusk. I'll be there in a minute.'

Sighing, Abby hitched the still grinning George – who was certainly no lightweight – into his chair. 'So, my interview's at nine o'clock,' she told him as she hunted down the rusks. 'And it's a ten minute drive away. It's now twenty to nine. To give me time to park the car and walk into the building I need to leave about ...' She glanced down at her watch. '... now. And I still haven't decided what to do with my hair. Up and tidy, or down and natural?' Which, as she had crazy curls, was a polite way of saying unruly. George gurgled and grabbed at the proffered rusk. 'It's no laughing matter,' she told him, which simply made him gurgle even more.

He was happily gumming the rusk when his mother finally made it back down the stairs.

'At last. Right, I've got to go ...' Abby trailed off as George's rusk covered hands shot out and grabbed her blouse. Clearly delighted with himself, he kicked his feet and waved his arms around, managing to flick yet more rusk gunge over her. 'Shit. Dirty, crumpled and on time, or clean and late?'

Mandy halted mid-stride. 'What?'

She pointed at her baby goo enhanced blouse. 'Should I go upstairs and change? If I do it'll make me late for my interview.'

'God, I don't know.' Mandy walked into the kitchen and blew a raspberry at George. 'Which is more important in your world, tidiness or punctuality?'

'At this rate I'm going to be late *and* messy. Oh crumbs.'

Manically she tore out of the kitchen and into the living room where she grabbed her handbag. 'Where are my good luck wishes?' she yelled as she lunged for the door.

'Right here.' Mandy blew her a kiss. 'Knock 'em dead, girl.

Just keep your arms crossed – that way they'll never notice the blouse.'

Doug rolled his shoulders, loosening up muscles that had seized after he'd left the gym that morning. He was only thirty, for crying out loud. Surely he shouldn't be feeling this stiff? It wasn't as if he wasn't fit. His training bordered on the obsessive.

It had to be this chair. This office. This damn company.

With a sigh he glanced down at today's diary. The one helpfully put together last Friday by his personal assistant before she'd dropped the bombshell that she was leaving. And no, she wouldn't be able to work her notice because she was flying to Australia the next day.

It was now Thursday, and already he'd interviewed more potential PAs than he ever wanted to see again in his lifetime. Any one of them would have done, but the agency had insisted he see all of their top candidates, which apparently meant squeezing this final one, Abigail Spencer, into his morning.

'Time for a word?' Geraldine, director of marketing, glided into his office on a cloud of expensive perfume. Walking straight up to his desk she fisted her hands in his jacket lapels and kissed him.

Off balance, he pulled away. 'What was that for?' He wasn't a fan of public displays of affection, hell he wasn't even sure about private ones, and he especially didn't appreciate them in his office.

Clearly not put off by his brusque tone she slowly trailed her tongue across her blood red lips. 'That was a taster for tonight. What time do you want me?' Her eyes told him the double entendre was deliberate.

'What happened to texting or phoning? We agreed, Geraldine, this is just sex.'

She arched a sculpted dark eyebrow. 'You think I'm looking for anything more? Why do men find it so hard to understand that not all women are made for marriage and babies? I mean, do I look like anybody's mother? Really?'

She had a point. Dressed today in bright red heels and a matching skirt that hugged her hips, she didn't look like any mothers he'd met. Nor, he thought, did most mothers undo quite so many buttons on their blouse. At least not while at work. 'No,' he conceded. 'You look like a woman I'd like to see in my bed at nine o'clock tonight.'

Her sultry red lips curved in reply. 'Good answer. And remember, the only part of you I'm interested in is the part between your legs.'

She pivoted on her killer heels and sauntered back out of his office leaving him to stare after her, half aroused, half ashamed. He enjoyed sex, particularly the wild, pounding sex he had with Geraldine, but he wasn't proud of what they had together. Yes, it was a mutually satisfying encounter, but after the passion had been spent he felt soiled, somehow. Hollow. He wasn't a man for cuddling up afterwards, but still, he wanted to believe the act should be about more than two selfish people trying to get off.

'Your nine o'clock is here, Mr Faulkner,' the agency temp droned in her bored, *why isn't it five o'clock yet* voice.

Doug glanced at the clock on his wall. Three minutes past nine, if he was going to be pedantic. He'd wait and see what she was like before he made that call. 'Okay, send her in.'

While he waited for Bored Temp of the Year to show his interview candidate in, he took a look at Abigail Spencer's CV. It was pretty impressive. A secretary for six years, she'd also just completed a business degree via the Open University.

'Mr Faulkner?'

God, she looks like ruddy Bambi, was his first impression as he stared at the girl in the doorway. Huge brown eyes in a cute face. Blonde hair that surely hadn't been combed today tumbled round her face and over her shoulders. A pair of slender legs appeared from beneath her knee length skirt. He could see they were trembling, even from across his office.

'Abigail? Please, come in. Take a seat.' And for goodness' sake take some weight off those legs before you keel over, he thought. While she walked to the chair he noticed a few other things, like the way the knuckles on her hands, currently holding her jacket stiffly together, were almost white with tension.

As she neared the chair she put down her handbag and then almost tripped over it, making her entry onto the chair more of a thump than a graceful slide.

He smothered a smile. 'Did you have any difficulty finding us?'

'Umm, no.' She bit into her lower lip and smiled. 'Actually, maybe I should say yes, then you can put my lateness down to an inability to read directions which obviously isn't a good thing but it might be better than thinking I couldn't get out of the house on time.' Finally she took a breath. 'Sorry.'

'You were five minutes late because you left your house late?'

'Three minutes late, actually.' Her cheeks flushed. 'Sorry, that sounded rude. I was just trying to point out that I wasn't quite as late as you said, but, yes, I was late. I'm sorry.'

His brain was struggling to keep up with the flow of her words. 'Apology accepted, though I don't think you answered my question.'

'Sorry.' Her eyes flicked briefly up to the ceiling. 'Oh crumbs, I think I've said that three times now. I doubt that's in the How To Impress At An Interview handbook.'

'Four times, actually.'

'Four?' He didn't think it was possible, but her eyes widened even further. 'Wow, now I really am sorry.'

Doug didn't have the faintest clue what to make of her. It had just taken her nearly five minutes to bumble her way through a question he'd only asked to relax her. And she hadn't even answered it properly yet.

She must have realised this because she launched into another of her eye popping replies. 'It's not that I didn't plan to leave the house on time. I deliberately woke early so I could get my younger sisters on the school bus but then my eldest sister – there are quite a few of us – anyway, she asked me to look after her baby while she popped to the toilet.' Abruptly she halted, giving him a sweet, embarrassed smile. 'I don't think you really need to know any of this, do you?'

Feeling dazed, Doug shook his head. 'It won't make the difference between hiring you or not, no.'

'Oh.' Her face seemed to lose some of its ... joy, he supposed was the word. 'Perhaps you'd better ask me another question?'

He'd ask her another twenty-five minutes worth of questions, he decided, and use up all the appointed time, but the end result would be the same. He'd already made up his mind. 'What qualities would you bring to the role of my personal assistant, Abigail?'

Abby guessed now wasn't a good time to tell Douglas Faulkner that actually the only person to have ever called her Abigail was her headmaster. Five minutes into the most important interview she'd ever had and so far she'd literally catapulted herself into the hot seat, and then gone on to inform her would-be boss that she was late because her sister had gone to the toilet. Why oh why did she have her muppet head on today?

Opposite her there was a deep rumble as Douglas Faulkner cleared his throat. A pointed reminder she hadn't answered his latest question. Smiling apologetically she looked into his incredibly blue eyes ... and instantly lost all train of thought.

'You were going to tell me the qualities you'd bring to the role?' he prompted.

Don't look at him. He was way too attractive to be sitting in an office. His face was surely designed for magazine covers or films. Not a biscuit company. Strong jaw, high cheekbones, dark hair that curled over his collar, there was something poetic about him. Something wild and untamed that was totally at odds with the expensive suit he wore. He looked like he should be riding a black horse across high cliffs, not constrained by a suit and four walls of an office.

Risking another glance, her eyes skimmed over broad shoulders that strained against his jacket. Beneath it was a starched white shirt. Hastily she drew her own jacket more firmly across her wrinkled blouse. 'I'm organised, reliable, honest and able to think quickly and flexibly. I'm also passionate about what I do,' she added, remembering that enthusiasm featured high on the list of qualities companies looked for.

'You're passionate about typing up minutes?'

Was he laughing at her? It was hard to tell because though his eyes were sinfully blue, they were also heavily guarded. 'Maybe passionate is the wrong word to use in that case, although it can depend on the meeting. I've been in some where the minutes could be classed as fruity. At least they would have been if I'd not removed some of the more, umm, juicy remarks.'

When he didn't comment on her garbled response she waded straight into the conversation gap. 'I'm passionate about helping my boss.' Did that sound too soppy? Too slutty? 'I mean, I enjoy making his life easier, smoother. Ironing out the wrinkles for him.'

His eyes flickered towards her blouse. 'Good to know.'

Self-consciously she tugged at her jacket again, feeling the beginnings of a traitorous blush.

'Are you too warm? If you are, feel free to take your jacket off.'

Oh no. Her skin was now so hot it prickled but there was no way she could reveal her crumpled, baby goo blouse to this man and his oh-so-immaculately-ironed white shirt. 'Thanks. I'm okay.'

Though he went on to ask her a few more questions, Abby knew he was simply going through the motions. She'd blown it.

Finally he picked up the large paperweight on his desk, rolling it round in his elegant, long fingered hands. Yes, she'd noticed them. 'Is this role one of many you're applying for, Abigail, or is it this job in particular you're after?'

'This one,' she blurted quickly, truthfully.

'Why?'

Oh crumbs, she thought, then felt a very untimely desire to laugh.

'Have I said something funny?'

'No, sorry.' Heck, she'd already ballsed this up, might as well be honest. 'It's just Mum didn't like us swearing so I try to say other words instead, like *"Oh crumbs"*, and it occurred to me that if I got this job, which clearly I've blown all chance of getting now, but, well, I just thought it would be funny to work for a biscuit company called Crumbs and say, *"Oh crumbs"*.'

'I see.'

His face remained inscrutable and for a second she wanted to stand up, grab him by the lapels of his pristine suit and shake him. It might be the lamest joke he'd ever heard but surely he could attempt a flipping smile? As the silence grew, she realised he might still be waiting for an answer to his *why*.

'I want this job because I want to be stretched. I've just gained my business degree which took me *for-ever*, as my little sister would say, though that's probably another piece of information you don't need to know.' She paused to take a breath. 'I thought if I was a personal assistant to the managing director of a large, respected international company it could be mutually beneficial. I'd learn about how big companies work in real life rather than on paper, and equally some of what I've learnt on paper I could use to help the company I worked for.'

He nodded, some of his dark locks falling over his forehead. With his dynamite good looks and bright blue eyes, it was probably just as well she'd mucked up this interview. She'd never be able to concentrate on work with such a wildly sexy boss.

Suddenly he rose to his feet, which Abby guessed meant the interview was over. His body seemed to go on forever so she stood up too, though even with her heels on he towered over her.

'Thank you for taking the time to see me.' She held out her hand.

His lips curved slightly as he shook it. 'My pleasure. It was an ... interesting experience.'

'But one you'd like to quickly forget?'

This time he actually smiled, flashing a set of straight white teeth. Of course they were. 'I doubt I'll forget this in a hurry.'

Well, she'd certainly made an impression. Such a bugger it was the wrong one. A small sigh escaped her as she picked up the errant handbag she'd tripped over when she'd first arrived. Things could have gone worse, she guessed. Her arse could have landed on the floor, rather than the chair.

'When can you start?'

Her legs buckled and she clutched at the chair for support. 'Start?'

'Yes. I'm offering you the job. When's the earliest you can start?'

'Are you sure?' He stared at her silently and Abby kicked herself. 'Forget I said that. Of course you're sure. You're the managing director. Well, I'm only temping at the moment … when I say only, I don't mean it in a derogatory way, because I actually enjoy it …' Oh my God, she was going to talk herself out of the job at this rate. 'I can start on Monday,' she stated firmly. And quickly shut her mouth.

He gave her another of his small but perfectly lovely smiles. 'I'll look forward to it. Nine o'clock sharp.'

Chapter Two

After Abigail left his office, Doug collapsed back on his chair. He wasn't sure whether what he'd just done was incredibly clever, or monstrously stupid. She would drive him round the twist, that was a fact. He liked order and calm, yet he'd just recruited messy and chaotic.

Even the thought of that made him smile. Was he having a turning thirty crisis? He found he didn't care. There was enough misery in his life without adding to it by appointing some po-faced super efficient PA. Okay, maybe he could do with the efficient part, but Abigail couldn't possibly be as disorganised in her work as she was in her train of thought. Belatedly he realised he should have asked for references but even that thought didn't bother him as much as it should. The agency had recommended her and anyway he'd formed his own opinion. He didn't need one from anybody else.

Straightening up, he eyed his computer screen with the usual reluctance. Finger poised to click open his dreaded inbox, the torture was postponed by the sound of his phone. His personal mobile, which meant it was worth answering.

'Faulkner.'

'Wilson.'

His face split into a grin. 'Luke. Good to hear your voice. What can I do for you?'

'I'll get to that. First tell me why you're sounding almost … hell, if I didn't know you better, I might be tempted to say happy.'

'Bugger off.'

'That's the greeting I expected, not all this *what can I do for you* stuff. So, spill.'

Doug wasn't sure he knew the answer. 'I've just made a

mad recruitment for my new PA. Employed a girl who turned up late, though she tried to argue that one, tripped over her handbag when sitting down, refused to take off her jacket even though she looked roasting hot, no doubt because she hadn't ironed her blouse, and answered each question during the thirty minute interview with more words than I manage in a day.'

'What did she look like?'

'Ha ha. Believe me when I tell you she's not my type. I go for the thoroughbred mare and she's more a ... well, a Shetland pony, I guess. Cute but pretty useless.'

'Which begs the question – why?'

Baffled with himself, he sat back in his chair and absent-mindedly ran a hand through his hair. 'I don't know. I think because she made me smile. I have a job I hate, working for a father who likes to make my life as miserable as possible. I figured I was owed a bit of light relief.'

'As long as she's still making you smile at the end of next week when she's double-booked all your meetings and lost your minutes.'

'Hey, you're the one who keeps telling me I need to have more fun.'

'And on that subject, are you up for a beer later? You can fill me in on the Shetland pony.'

'Not tonight.'

'Oh?'

'I do have other friends, you know.'

'Name me one.' Doug heard laughter down the phone. 'Oh, I know, it's booty night, isn't it? You're seeing Gerri.'

Doug winced. 'Geraldine and, yes, I'm seeing her tonight.' Did Luke have to make it sound so sordid?

'Okay, mate, I guess I'll see you at training. We'll see if you're still smiling after a few days with your new PA.'

'Sometimes I wonder why you and I are friends.'

'Because nobody else would put up with your grumpiness. Enjoy tonight.'

Slowly Doug put down the phone, no longer quite so certain of his rash recruitment.

Abby spent the rest of the day in a daze. She'd mucked up the interview and yet she'd got the job. It was only just sinking in when she made a detour to the supermarket on her way home.

'Pizza,' she said to herself, pulling three large boxes off the shelf and into her trolley. Ellie would be chuffed.

Hastily she hunted down the rest of the items on her list, the foolish grin from this morning still on her face. She was going to work for the managing director of a large international company. As of now she wasn't a temp in a two bit courier company. She was personal assistant to Douglas Faulkner, son of Lord and Lady Faulkner. Heir to the Crumbs empire. And owner of a face she definitely wouldn't mind staring at five days a week.

It was after six by the time she turned her beloved twenty-year-old Beetle into the drive, pleased to see her dad's van already there. As she eased Rodney (the Beetle) in next to it, she smiled at the sight of the pots by the front door. Middle of March and her tulips were finally making an appearance. Maybe they, like her, could sense better, sunnier days ahead. God, she was getting soppy. Then again, good news could do that to a person.

Rodney made the usual splutters as she turned off the engine and she patted his dashboard in sympathy.

'When are you going to get rid of that heap of junk and let me find you something decent?' her dad asked as he opened the front door.

'Rodney is decent. At least he would be if you'd look under his bonnet sometime and tune him up.'

'I can fiddle around under the bonnet all you like, but the engine's in the boot and that's the bit that's had it.'

'In your opinion.' She hauled the shopping bags out from the back seat and handed them to him.

'In my *professional* opinion,' he emphasised. 'It's a wonder the garage gets any business at all when my own daughter drives around in a deathtrap. Let me find you something newer and quieter and—'

'Soulless and boring,' Abby cut in. She'd heard all this before, but because she knew he only had her safety in mind, she kissed his cheek to take away the sting of her words. 'No thanks, Dad. But I'd be grateful for that tune up.'

He grunted as they took the shopping into the kitchen. It was a hive of activity there, with Ellie, Holly and Sally all at the table doing their homework and George in his high chair, waiting expectantly for Mandy to feed him. He was a proper little man, Abby thought with a smile.

'Ooh, pizza!' Ellie exclaimed as she watched her unpack. 'We always have pizza when something good happens. Did we win the lottery?'

'I'm afraid not, but, yes, something good did happen. At least for me.'

Mandy glanced up from shovelling a spoonful of goo into George's ever open mouth. 'You got the job?'

It only took a nod and suddenly she was swamped by warm hugs and sloppy kisses. Her family were noisy and chaotic ... and she loved every single one of them. The feel of fur against her leg and the sound of a sharp bark reminded her there was one more family member. Laughing, she squatted and fondled Pat's soft black ears. He thumped his tail in reply.

'So when do you start this snazzy new job?' her father asked.

'On Monday.'

'Wow, that's fast. And your title?'

'I'll be personal assistant to the managing director of

Crumbs. They make most of the biscuits we have in our cupboard.'

'Does that mean we'll get free ones?' Ellie piped up.

'I'm not sure. I guess I'll find out on Monday.'

'And what does a personal assistant mean?' Ellie again, as usual far more interested in what was going on around her than doing her homework. 'Will you have to help him with personal stuff like cleaning his teeth and getting dressed?'

Abby laughed and kissed Ellie's tousled hair. They'd both inherited the messy hair gene from their mum. 'Not quite. I'll organise his diary for him, arrange meetings, take notes from the meetings, sort out his travel.'

'What's he like then, your new boss?' Mandy asked as she scooped up another spoonful for the waiting George. 'Short, balding and ugly?'

'Try tall, dark and handsome.'

Mandy paused, spoonful in mid-air. 'You're flaming kidding me.'

George thumped his little fist on the high chair tray and eyed her balefully, making everyone laugh.

'Google Douglas Faulkner and see for yourself.'

'I'll do it.' Sally had her computer open already on the kitchen table. 'OMG, we're talking major league hottie. You lucky cow.'

Immediately all her sisters crowded round the screen, cooing at the images, while her dad stood, shaking his head. 'Like bees round a honey pot. I thought my girls were more discerning than that.' When Abby simply smiled at him, her father dumped the bag he was halfway through unpacking onto the worktop. 'Okay, okay. What's all the blinking fuss about then?' He leant over Sally's shoulder and scrutinised the screen. 'Seems a bit fancy to me. All looks and no substance,' he declared dismissively.

Abby tucked her arms around her father's waist. 'I'm only

27

going to work for him, Dad. I'm not planning on marrying him, so you can stand down.'

'He doesn't look like he smiles much,' Mandy remarked. 'Sad eyes, unlike this little man, eh?' She cooed at her son and delivered him another monster spoonful.

Abby thought back to the morning. Mandy had a point. Though he'd not been unfriendly, her new boss certainly hadn't come across as Mr Fun. 'He employed me even though I made a right hash of the interview so he must have a sense of humour lurking somewhere.'

'Or he's desperate,' her father added dryly.

At which point her large, messy, crazy family fell about laughing.

Doug sat on his ridiculously expensive Italian leather sofa – an attempt to bring some joy to his life – listening to music on his Bang & Olufsen, another part of the attempt, and waited for the doorbell to ring. His mind kept flitting back to Luke's words earlier: *booty night*. The description made him feel uncomfortable. What he shared with Geraldine was perfectly normal, he reasoned for the umpteenth time. Man needed the release that only sex could provide, and he was lucky enough to have found a woman who not only understood his needs, but matched them.

Thankfully the doorbell interrupted any further soul-searching and he leapt up to answer it.

'Come on in.' She looked sophisticated and sexy but just a little bit hard, he thought as he let her in. World weary. 'Would you like a drink?'

For a split second she seemed surprised, and he felt ashamed that he hadn't asked her before. Didn't even know what she favoured, even though they mated like bunnies several times a week.

'Thanks, a small whisky.'

While he fiddled around with the drinks she wandered round the sitting room. 'It's nice.'

'What is?'

'Your place. I've not had a proper look round before. You usually drag me straight up to bed.' He must have cringed because she laughed.

'I'm sorry.'

'Why? I'm not complaining. It's what I'm here for. You don't need to date me first.'

'Jesus.' He ran a hand through his hair as he handed her the tumbler of whisky. 'You should expect more from me than that. Why don't you want dinners and candlelight?'

She shrugged and sipped her drink. 'I tried that once. It didn't work out.'

She wasn't as casual as she appeared, he noted. She might want a relationship based solely on sex but he wondered if, like him, it was starting to feel too empty.

But then she swigged back her drink and marched up to him, standing so close he got a waft of something wild and exotic. In her towering heels she stood nose to nose with him, mouth to mouth. Groin to groin. 'Are you coming upstairs?'

The husky tone, the lick of her lips, the possessive touch of her hand on his fly. In that moment he didn't care about how hollow he'd feel afterwards. All he wanted was to writhe around on his bed with this sexy woman and forget all about his shitty life for a while.

He followed her upstairs and slammed the bedroom door shut behind him. Instantly it was a blur of tongues and hands. They both knew what they wanted and it wasn't the soft kisses or gentle caresses of lovers. It was wild, pounding, animal sex that pushed everything out of the mind for a while.

When the passion was spent they lay side by side, regaining their breath and their strength. Until it was time for another round.

Chapter Three

The Crumbs headquarters was something to behold. Not a modern concrete building in an industrial estate but a beautiful old one, nestled in a leafy part of Surrey. Sadly though the outside had once been an impressive Georgian house, the soul of it had been hacked away, replaced with all the high tech expected of a major global headquarters. In the place of fireplaces and oak panelled walls was modern functionality. At least they'd kept the sweeping staircase in the entrance hall, Abby thought as she raced up it.

She made it to Doug's office with two minutes to spare.

Of course her boss was already there, jacket off, shirtsleeves rolled up.

Glancing through his open door she used up the spare two minutes gawping at him.

Suddenly he looked up, the clarity of his blue eyes visible even from across the expanse of his modernly furnished office.

'Good morning, Abigail.' He glanced at the clock on the wall. 'On time today.'

'My sister didn't need to go to the toilet this morning.'

'I'm glad to hear it.' Rising to his full, impressive height he walked over to her, nodding to the alcove just outside his office. 'That's your home now. I hope you'll find it to your liking.'

She'd noticed the room to the left of his office when she'd come for the interview. It was like an office within an office. Sitting there she'd be able to view everyone who came to see him, but he could shut his office door and have privacy. Wordlessly he indicated for her to take a look so she popped her head through the archway, grinning when she saw the space.

'As a temp I'm used to sitting in an open plan office at the draftiest, gloomiest desk that everyone else has rejected. Having my very own space is awesome.' Unable to resist she went to sit at the desk, running her hands over the surface. Too bland perhaps, designed for function rather than show, but *hers*. Looking through the alcove she could see an intriguing bold canvas on the wall just outside Doug's office. It would give her something to stare at if she was ever bored.

'Before you start you'll need to—'

'Talk to HR and the IT guys, I know.' She rose from her chair and walked back out of her alcove. 'I'm booked to see them at nine-thirty and ten.' Surprise flickered across his handsome face, so she gave him a smug smile. 'I sorted it out last Friday.'

'Right, okay.'

She rolled her eyes. 'Oh boy, you didn't think I'd be efficient, did you?'

He blinked, long dark lashes descending briefly over his eyes, then walked slowly back to his desk and perched on the end of it, his actions controlled and deliberate. 'The agency recommended you.'

'Is that why you gave me the role?' He didn't immediately reply, so she ploughed on. 'It's just I've been dying to ask, because you didn't see me at my best at the interview. I'm not saying my best is amazing but it's a lot more convincing than the shambles you saw. Some of my answers were all over the place.' Once again her words were met with silence, though this time she bit on her cheek to stop from filling the gap.

'I interviewed six people,' he said eventually. 'All of them appeared highly capable.' His shoulders twitched in an almost imperceptible shrug. 'You were the only one I liked.'

Her heart rate spiked. 'Liked?'

Two startlingly blue eyes gazed back at her. 'Yes. Liked.'

Even as a rush of warmth ran through her she realised she was being daft. Look at him: athletic body, movie star face. He meant liked, not *liked*. Still, it meant she was here, and the other five candidates weren't.

'Well, that's a great start. I only hope you still like me at the end of the week. Or perhaps that's a bit optimistic. Let's say the end of the day.' Jeeze, she really had to stop prattling so much. He wasn't a talker, so when he left a gap he didn't intend her to keep on filling it. 'My first job is to fetch you a coffee, yes? White, no sugar.'

Another flash of surprise crossed his face, though he didn't say anything.

'It's okay, I haven't got special psychic powers,' she reassured, her mouth running away from her again. 'I had a chat with my predecessor, who, by the way, told me I was lucky because you were a great person to work for.' *Shut up, shut up, shut up.*

'You spoke to Joanne?'

He seemed to be having trouble keeping up with her. 'We didn't exactly speak because she's moved to Australia, as you know. At least I assume you do. Anyway, your HR team gave me her contact details and I emailed her because I thought it would help to find out more about you. Not in a stalkerish way,' she added quickly, seeing his body still. 'Just how you preferred to work, how she'd organised things for you, what you liked and hated. That sort of thing. When I checked my emails this morning she'd replied. So now I know you don't drink tea, prefer to work with the office door open and will eat anything except asparagus, which I kind of understand so I won't hold it against you.'

His face relaxed marginally. 'That was very ... diligent of you.'

'Yep, that's me. Diligent. Bet you're glad you chose me now, eh?'

He gave her a ghost of a smile and moved to sit back at his desk. Taking it as her cue she left to find her alcove. The poor guy was probably reeling from her verbal barrage, wondering whether he'd made a huge mistake. He obviously liked quiet, yet he'd knowingly hired a chatterbox which didn't make any sense. Finding him some caffeine would probably help. Then perhaps leaving him alone for the rest of the day.

Just as she stepped foot outside her alcove to hunt down the coffee, she heard a crash. Glancing into his office she found he'd toppled his in tray onto the floor.

'Here, let me.' She scooted inside and started to pick up the scattered files.

'It's okay, I've got it.' He bent to grasp the remaining sheets, then caught his back on the corner of his desk as he straightened up. 'Ouch.'

Abby watched in horror as small stains of blood bloomed through his white shirt. 'Oh heavens, you're bleeding.'

'I'm fine. It's just a scratch.'

If she'd been thinking properly she'd have realised he was acting even more stiffly than usual. That he was, in fact, shifting warily away from her. But her nurture instincts were in full flow. 'Scratches can get infected. Let me take a look. I'm good at dealing with this type of thing. You should see the trouble my sisters get into sometimes.' Without further ado, she lifted the back of his shirt and scanned the wide expanse of his back. 'Well, look here, there's more than one scratch. Whatever have you been doing? Crawling under blackberry bushes?'

Silence echoed around the room and slowly the pieces started to sink in. His rigid stance. The flush blooming across his cheeks. The scratch marks covering his skin not in a random fashion, but in the way she imagined a woman with long fingernails might scratch at her lover's back.

'Oh. Probably not blackberry bushes then.' Immediately she let go of his shirt. 'I'll just, umm, go and get that coffee.'

The moment Abigail left the room, Doug staggered back to his desk. Bloody hell. This is what it must feel like to be invaded by a tornado. Just listening to her was exhausting. And, holy cow, she'd only been in the job five minutes and she was lifting the shirt off his back. Copping a stare at the scratches he knew Geraldine had gouged into his back during their latest sexual soirée.

Recalling the expression on his new PA's face when she'd finally guessed what had caused the bleeding, he started to smile. At least it had shut her up for a few minutes. And he reckoned she wouldn't be lifting up any more of his clothes for a while.

He was beginning to pull himself together when she appeared again, carrying two mugs. Joanne had always insisted on bringing his coffee on a silver tray complete with a cup, saucer and bowl of sugar lumps, even though she knew he never took sugar. Abigail was different to the formal, prim, matronly Joanne in every imaginable way.

'There you go.' She plonked the mug straight onto his desk, happily avoiding the coaster sitting expectantly next to it. 'Is there anything you need me to do at the moment?'

Calm down? Stop talking for a few blessed minutes? 'Not right now, no.'

'Okay then. I'll have a fiddle around the filing system for a bit and then go to my meetings. After that you should take me through your diary so I know what's going on.'

'I should, should I?'

Big brown eyes blinked back at him. 'Oops, did I start telling you what to do? Sorry, I've got a bad habit of doing that. Probably because I'm so used to having to order people around at home.'

'Are you married?'

Her face lit up with the laughter he'd already come to associate with her. 'Heck no, though that's really funny, you associating me bossing people around with having a husband. I like that, but actually I only have sisters. They're bad enough.' She took a sip of her coffee. 'Am I allowed to ask if you're married?'

'No.'

'I'm not allowed to ask?'

'I'm not married.'

'Ah.' Her ready smile appeared again.

Uncomfortable with the intimacy he shifted, the scratches on his back rubbing against the back of his chair. 'You were going to check out the files?'

His tone was rather sharp and immediately the warmth flooded from her face. 'Yes, sorry.'

As her neat figure retreated into her alcove he kicked himself. Bubbly and chatty, surprisingly efficient, but also easily hurt. He'd have to remember that if he was going to avoid losing a second PA.

The private phone on his desk sprang into life and the sigh Doug let out came all the way from his size twelve, neatly polished shoes. There was only one person who used that line.

'Father.' Saying the word grated, implying a relationship that wasn't there.

'Is everything sorted for the meeting with Taylors?'

'Of course.' The lie came easily. Doug really had no clue if the meeting was organised or not. He'd have to put Abigail on the case when she came back.

'It's important we get what we want out of this. Don't screw things up.'

'Thank you.'

There was a heavy pause. 'What for?'

'For showing such confidence in me. It's touching.'

Doug figured the sound of the dial tone was his father's way of saying goodbye.

With a heavy heart he set about sifting through his emails. God he hated this job. Hated every bloody second of every minute he wasted in the place. He was managing director in name only, his father saw to that. Even worse though, he didn't care. The company made biscuits, for pity's sake. It was hardly earth-shattering, or creative. It certainly wasn't how Doug wanted to spend his life.

He thought wistfully of the studio back at his house. The new set of canvases waiting patiently to be filled with paint.

It was getting harder and harder to sit in this blasted office every day, pushing paper clips around his desk when his heart was in that studio. Painting in the evenings and weekends wasn't enough. It didn't satisfy the craving to create, a craving that grew ever stronger as his mind worked out exactly how he wanted the next canvas to look.

Suddenly an image of his father's sneering face flitted through his mind. The bastard would have a field day if he cocked up this meeting with Taylors. Gritting his teeth, Doug shifted through the mess of files in his in tray. The ones he'd accidentally knocked onto the floor in his shock at finding his cute Shetland pony of a PA was actually, so far at least, staggeringly efficient. Pulling out the one marked *Taylors,* he opened it up and started to read about the intricacies of the biscuit business.

'Time for another drink?'

His head shot up. Abigail was standing in front of his desk clutching another mug of coffee. Joanne had always knocked on the door or coughed. Anything so she didn't give her boss a ruddy heart attack.

'Thanks.' He watched as she withdrew his empty mug and placed the fresh one next to the coaster. 'Abigail, do me a favour. Make some sort of noise before you come into the office next time. Please.'

She nodded, her hair bouncing in her ponytail. 'In return, would you do me a favour? Call me Abby. Abigail reminds me of my headmaster.'

'You had a headmaster called Abigail?'

She rolled her puppy eyes. 'No. I was called Abigail when I was in trouble at school.'

He had no trouble picturing her as a rebellious schoolgirl. 'You dislike it because it was overused when you were a child?'

'Whatever gave you that impression?' She ruined the whole nonchalant look by adding a laugh. 'I wonder, is it a good thing or a bad thing to find you have me sussed already?'

Sussed? He didn't have a flaming clue what to make of her, though he knew enough to avoid answering the question. 'When you're ready, I need to go through the details of a meeting with you.'

'Okay, boss. I'll just ...' She nodded at the wedge of files she was carrying rather precariously under her left arm.

Fearing they were about to fall he stood to help her. 'Let me take them.'

'No, don't worry. I've got them.' She dumped the empty mug down and tucked them more securely under her arm. 'We don't want you scrambling round under the desk again. Not with your ... err ... scratches.'

Briefly her eyes caught his. Then she blushed scarlet and picked up the mug. 'I'll be back in a jiffy.'

He sat down with a thump, utterly bemused, but before he could gather his thoughts she was back again, sitting opposite him, notepad at the ready. Every inch the efficient PA.

'We're scheduled to meet with Taylors next week,' he told her, looking at the sparse notes he'd made. 'They're an established biscuit company like us, though a lot smaller. My father's been sounding them out to buy some of our older, poorer selling brands. I'm not sure what arrangements have already been made for the meeting.'

'Joanne booked ten rooms at ...' She glanced down at her notepad. '... the Langston Spa. Very fancy. She also booked a meeting room.'

'And you know this already because?'

'I'm diligent and super efficient. Plus Joanne left a file with all the paperwork in it.' She grinned over at him, a schoolgirl's smile in a woman's body. 'Let me guess, you want me to check who's been invited, confirm they're still coming, work out an agenda, prepare the slides?'

'Well, yes.'

She leant forward, her action giving him a tantalisingly brief flash of lacy white bra. 'Am I allowed to ask which brands you're planning to sell?'

He should know. Of course he should bloody know, but Doug didn't. One biscuit sounded pretty much like another to him. Frankly he didn't even like the damn things. Flicking through the file he'd opened, he caught the names at the top of the memo. 'Dream Delight, Crunchy Crunch and Wafer Wonders.' Jeeze. How was he supposed to drum up the enthusiasm to sell them when even their names made him cringe?

Her jaw dropped. 'You're joking.'

'Err, no.'

'But they're the best ones. The brands that made the company what it is today.'

'They also sell the least.' And why was he defending his decision to his PA? Then again, it wasn't his decision, it was his father's. If it were up to Doug, he'd leg it out of here as fast as he could and sell the whole flaming business, never mind three poxy biscuit brands.

'They only sell the least because you've not put any effort

into them recently.' She was looking at him earnestly now, all trace of the schoolgirl vanished. 'Instead of getting rid of the brands you should re-launch them. You know I read somewhere that young consumers enjoy the more traditional brands ...' She trailed off and though he was pretty certain he wasn't showing what he was feeling – incredulity, with a dollop of WTF – maybe his mask wasn't as good as he thought because she bit at her bottom lip. 'Sorry. You don't need a lecture from me, do you? I'm the PA, you're the MD. I'll sort out the meeting.'

She lunged to her feet – literally. There was no grace to the movement, nor was their any fluidity in her stride as she almost stumbled back to her desk.

And yet, he thought as she disappeared out of view, she was like that proverbial breath of fresh air. A session with her cleared his senses, made him smile. Made him think.

Chapter Four

Abby looked at the kitchen clock, shook her head and yelled up to her sister for the third time.

'Come on, Ellie. You'll miss the bus at this rate.'

'I'm not waiting for her to get her bum out of bed,' Sally remarked snottily, pouring out her cereal. 'I don't see why I should miss lessons because she can't be bothered being ready on time.'

'Nobody's going to miss any lessons.' Abby mentally crossed her fingers. If they missed their bus, she'd be late for work. And it was only day two.

'Ellie wasn't looking too great when she woke up,' Holly remarked, sneaking the dog a handful of the disgusting cereal hoops she still insisted on having for breakfast. 'I think she might be sick.'

Abby's heart sank. No. She wasn't going to miss her second day at work. 'It's Pat who'll be sick if you keep feeding him those things. I'm going to check on Ellie. You two make sure you're ready to go in ten minutes.'

She bounded up the stairs to the room Ellie shared with Holly. As usual the floor was strewn with so many clothes she could barely get through the door. I'm their sister, she reminded herself. I'm not going to nag them about keeping their room tidy. Dragging her eyes away from the mess, she focused on the small figure sitting on the bed. She was dressed apart from her socks – hallelujah – but that was the only bit of good news.

'Hey, Ellie.' She ran a hand across her pale forehead. Warm but not hot. 'Are you feeling okay?'

'No. I feel like I want to puke.'

'Have you been sick?'

'Not yet.'

Okay, she thought, trying to keep calm. School rules said you couldn't go in if you'd been sick in the last twenty-four hours, but Ellie hadn't. Feeling sick didn't count. 'It might just be a passing phase. Get your socks on, go downstairs and have a piece of toast. If you keep it down, you can go to school.'

Leaving Ellie to finish dressing, Abby tapped on Mandy's door. 'Are you awake?'

'I am now,' the voice grumbled from the other side of the door.

Abby pushed the door open to find Mandy lying in bed and rubbing her eyes, George fast asleep by her side. 'What are your plans today?'

'Well, unlike you, my day started at five when George woke up,' she answered testily. 'He's only just gone back to sleep.'

'Oh crumbs, sorry. It's just Ellie's not looking good and I'm only on day two of my new job. I could do without having to stay at home with her.'

'Don't look in my direction for help. I've got my assessment today.' Mandy was doing a childcare qualification at the local college.

'Damn. I don't suppose you could—'

'Rearrange it? Not on your nelly. I've worked bloody hard for this. What about asking Dad?'

Abby let out a resigned sigh. She loved her dad, they all did, but he was the archetypal chocolate teapot. Very sweet, but bloody useless, at least during working hours. The garage sucked all his time. 'I'll just have to put her on the bus and hope she's okay, I guess.'

'Is he a bit of a tyrant then, your new boss? I didn't get a chance to quiz you yesterday.'

'Not a tyrant, no. At least I don't think so. Then again, I don't want to give him cause to become one.'

'And is he as hot as his photos?'

Despite the panic she was feeling, Abby felt her mouth curving into a smile. 'God, yes. Hotter, I'd say.'

Mandy sat up suddenly, all grouchiness vanished. 'Hotter how?'

For a few seconds Ellie was forgotten as Abby leant against the door frame, picturing her new boss. 'The photographs don't really give a sense of his height, his big, powerful frame. Or the depth of his eyes.' Bright blue eyes that seared the recipient with their intense, watchful gaze. A gaze that would fall on her turning up late if she hung around chatting any longer. 'I've got to go. See you later.'

'Umm, Abby,' Mandy's voice stopped her as she turned to dash out. 'You're not going to fall for him, are you?'

'God, no.' She wasn't *that* stupid.

'Good, because the PA falling for the boss. It's such a cliché.'

Abby ignored the jibe, knowing Mandy already thought she was a walking cliché. Yes, she'd lost her virginity to the most popular guy in school – only for him to dump her a week later. And, yes, her only other relationship had been with her first boss, Tony. Now the owner of a highly successful ad agency. It didn't make her stupid. Just easily swayed by handsome men.

'Are you girls ready?' she shouted as she raced back down the stairs, throwing up a silent prayer of thanks when she found all three of them putting on their coats.

'What if I puke?' Ellie stared mutinously up at her and Abby felt a twinge of guilt. If their mum had been alive Ellie would have been able to stay at home, cosseted until she felt better.

'If you feel sick, tell the teacher and I'll come and get you.'

'Promise?'

She wrapped her arms around her youngest sister. Usually

the cheeky, smart-mouthed one, today she looked small and vulnerable. 'I promise, sweetie.'

By the time she arrived in the office Abby felt she'd already done a day's work. She was about to sneak – technically she wasn't late, but she certainly wasn't early – through to her desk when she spotted a tall, slender woman leaning over Doug's desk. Tight black skirt, long stocking clad legs, black stiletto shoes, her manner was – familiar was a posh word for it. Rude was how Abby would describe it.

'Are you looking for something?'

The creature turned round and it was only then Abby caught sight of Doug sitting behind his desk. Whatever this woman had been doing leaning over, and boy was her mind racing over *that* image, especially considering how few buttons she'd bothered to do up on her blouse, she'd been doing it with the full permission of her boss.

Looking slightly uncomfortable, Doug cleared his throat. 'Abby, meet Geraldine, our marketing director. Geraldine, this is Abby, my PA.'

'Sorry, I thought ... well, I couldn't see you behind Geraldine.' *Please let me go and slink quietly to my desk,* she silently pleaded. Something I should have done in the first place.

'I didn't realise I was that wide.' The dark haired, exotic looking Geraldine gave her a small, tight smile.

'Oh God, you're not. Not at all. It must have been the angle, or the way you were bent over ...' Yikes. 'You're very slim,' she added lamely.

She didn't miss the veiled look Geraldine gave Doug. A private message that probably said *why on earth did you pick this one?* Geraldine gave her one final, dismissive glance before returning her dark-eyed gaze back to Doug.

Yes, rude had been exactly the right word. *Overly* familiar might have done, too. Doug must be getting a real eyeful

43

of whatever it was Geraldine was at pains for him to see. Feeling totally put in her place, Abby trudged off to her little alcove, firmly shutting the door to Doug's office behind her.

If that's the type of woman he liked – bony and cold – good luck to him.

Doug stared back at his marketing director.

'Rudeness isn't a particularly endearing quality,' he told her mildly, though inside he was fuming. He was getting pretty fed up with the way Geraldine kept turning up at his office with items other than work on her agenda.

'She implied I was fat.'

'She thought you were rifling through my desk and apologised. You know perfectly well you're not fat so you can cut out the attitude. Abby is an employee and we treat everyone in Crumbs with respect.'

'Got a soft spot for your new PA, have you?'

Doug sighed. He had enough angst in his life without adding a melodramatic female to it. 'I won't have anyone who works here being treated so carelessly. Abby's working on the agenda for the Taylors meeting next week. Go and make friends. If you're not careful she'll put you down for the after lunch slot.'

'Ah, so the perky blonde wields the power, does she?'

He turned his attention to his computer, not bothering to reply. It was a toss up whether the sex he was getting was worth the grief.

For the rest of the morning he ploughed through the Taylors proposal, trying to get up to speed with the old brands. Abby's words from yesterday kept floating round his head and he phoned Geraldine for the promotional spend on them over the last ten years and any recent market research reports.

At the sound of a light cough he glanced up to find Abby

standing in the doorway in what he'd nicknamed her Bambi pose, all awkward and hesitant. And cute.

Also worryingly quiet.

'What is it?'

'I, umm.' She shuffled and twisted her hands.

'Geraldine hasn't been rude again, has she? She's not so bad when you get to know her.'

'I need to go,' she blurted. 'I'm so sorry but the school phoned and Ellie, she's my youngest sister, she's been sick. I knew she wasn't feeling well this morning but I didn't want to let you down so I pushed her into school, but now ...' She paused, took in a deep breath. 'Sorry, but I have to pick her up.'

'Is there nobody else who can help?'

She gave him a small smile. 'I wish there was, but my other sisters are at school or college and my dad, well, he runs this garage business so he can't really drop everything and pick Ellie up.'

Though he clearly expected his eldest daughter to do that. Doug leant back in his chair and decided to ask the obvious question. 'And your mum?'

'She died twelve years ago.'

Doug winced. He'd like to bet Abby had been the stand in mother ever since. 'I am sorry. I hope Ellie gets better soon.'

Her brown eyes widened, appearing impossibly large in her small face. 'Does that mean I can go?'

'Of course.'

She showed no signs of moving, though. 'Is that it? Aren't you going to get cross? At least raise your voice? Tell me to finish what I'm doing before I go?'

A rare desire to laugh bubbled inside him. 'I can if you want me to.'

'I've finalised the agenda for next week's meeting with Taylors and sent it round to everyone for comment. I'm still waiting on two people to confirm they're coming but I can chase them up this afternoon from home. I'll also work on formatting the slides I've been given so far so they all look consistent.'

'I guess that means I can't get cross.'

A small frown appeared between her eyes. 'Are you always this calm?'

'Is that how I appear?'

'Yes. You have this air of control about you. A composure, I guess, as if nothing ever upsets you. It's only my second day on the job and already I'm going off early. You should at least be a bit annoyed.'

'Maybe I am, inside.'

'Are you?' Her eyes swept over his face, as if trying to read his thoughts. 'I'd rather know if you are. I hate having to second guess.'

Annoyed he could rule out, but he was beginning to feel frustrated. 'I'm not angry with you, Abby. Are you lying about your sister being sick?'

She looked horrified. 'Of course not.'

'Did you make her sick?'

'No.'

'Then why should I be cross?'

She shuffled on her feet and let out a loud sigh. 'Okay, I'm not going to argue with you, because then you really will be cross. Besides, you look like a tricky customer to argue with. So I'll say thank you and nip out quickly before you change your mind. I hope to be in tomorrow but I'll let you know if I can't make it. I'll also be on email and you've got my number if you need me for anything.'

'Go and rescue your sister, Abby.'

'Right.' She gave him a crooked smile and ducked back out, appearing in his doorway a few moments later with her bag and a few haphazardly shoved together files. 'I'm not pinching anything,' she told him, shuffling the files so they were slightly less likely to fall out from her hands and onto the floor. 'These are the notes behind the slides I'm going to work on at home—'

'Go.' He must have said it with the right amount of authority because she finally scuttled out, the files pushed awkwardly under her arms.

He'd wager a tenner they tumbled onto the floor before she made it out of the building.

Doug worked through his lunch and by four he reckoned he had a good enough handle on the Wafty Wafer, Crappy Crunch and Dubious Delight – or whatever the hell the stupid biscuits were called – to not make a fool of himself at next week's meeting. After stretching out his neck muscles he turned off the computer, dumped it into his briefcase and sauntered out of the office.

He was just climbing into his car – a slate grey Aston Martin Vantage, one of the few perks of being Charles Faulkner's son – when his mobile rang. Noting the caller, he slumped against the cream leather seat with a resigned thud.

'Father. What have I done now?'

'I don't pay you to bugger off at four o'clock.'

Doug clenched his jaw, rubbed a hand over his face and drew on the control he'd spent a lifetime honing. 'No, you pay me to be your son,' he countered, glancing up at the Crumbs building to where his father had an office.

'Get back inside and set a proper example.'

'Or what? You'll fire me?'

'You think I won't?'

'I think you care too much about what others think to fire your own son.'

'Then think again. I won't be taken for a fool, not by the likes of you. You drive a fancy car, earn a decent wage and live in a nice house, all thanks to me. I can take it all away from you any time I like.'

Doug leant forward, resting his head on the steering wheel. Did the old bugger really think he was bothered about any of that? 'Take it away then.'

'Don't tempt me.'

The desire to tell him to go to hell snapped at Doug, as it always did, burning a hole in his gut, but he bit his tongue. As he always did.

'Thank you for the chat. As I was in the office at seven fifty-two, and you've just spent the last eight minutes talking to me, I've completed my contracted hours.' He jabbed at the disconnect button and threw the phone onto the passenger seat. He was now in the perfect mood to beat the shit out of someone.

Shoving the Aston into gear he screamed out of the car park and headed for the gym. It wasn't a place most people would associate with a man who carried the title of Managing Director, Crumbs – even if it was only in name – and drove an Aston Martin. The men and women who joined didn't go to pose in lycra and drink energy drinks at a bar. They came to work out and to fight. Instead of fancy machines there were punchbags and rubber mats.

It was exactly the type of place he needed to let off steam after an altercation with his father. At university he'd taken up boxing and been pretty good at it. Too good, he recalled with a shudder. Now he preferred rolling around on the floor, grappling. It felt more physical, more skilful. *Safer*.

Pushing away his thoughts, he drove down the narrow alley and parked up outside the old brick building beneath the railway bridge. Hauling his bag onto his shoulder he marched inside, wincing as he read the fresh graffiti on the wall near the entrance. Was that anatomically possible?

Luke was already in the changing room. He took one look at Doug's face and came to the wrong conclusion. 'Told you you'd regret hiring a PA based on looks and not talent.'

'I don't regret hiring Abigail.'

Luke peered more closely at him. 'If it isn't the new PA who's put that glower on your pretty face, it must be your father. Have you two exchanged words again?'

The downside of having a friend who'd known him all his life was that he saw too much. 'Shut up and get changed.'

Luke shook his head and pulled on a workout vest. He was shorter than Doug by a few inches but, though Doug hated to admit it, he filled out a vest more impressively.

'You know it's about time you sorted out this crap with your father,' Luke muttered. 'You're getting more and more miserable working in a place you hate when you could be making us both lots of money doing the thing you love.'

'Thanks.' Doug threw his work clothes into his holdall and yanked on his shorts. 'When I want your advice, I'll ask for it.' He knew he was being a git, but he couldn't shake himself out of it. Only a session in the gym could do that.

'So how is it going with the new PA?' Luke had dealt with his foul temper for too many years to be bothered by it.

'She's pretty good, actually. Surprisingly efficient.' He stood and bounced on the balls of his feet, adrenaline fizzing round his system, every inch of him ready to pulverise a punchbag.

Apparently Luke hadn't finished the conversation though. 'And?' he asked, his dark eyes alight with mischief.

'And now it's time to do what we came here to do.'

'Which, translated, means *I think she's hot but I'm not discussing it*.' Doug glowered, which only made Luke laugh. 'Well, well. I wonder what the gorgeous, though rather scary, Geraldine is going to make of this new addition to Crumbs?'

'And I wonder when you're going to stop gossiping and get your arse into the gym. I'm itching for a fight and right now you're top of my people-I'd-like-to-thrash list.'

Luke nodded and rose to his feet, though the smirk remained on his face. Doug looked forward to wiping it off.

Chapter Five

Abby had often wondered what the phrase 'Running around like a blue-arsed fly' actually meant. Now she knew. She'd arrived at the swanky hotel, the venue for the off-site meeting with Taylors, at seven a.m. A full two hours before the attendees were scheduled to arrive. So where had the time gone? Of course it hadn't helped that the hotel had tried to shoehorn them into a meeting room so small they'd have been sitting on each other's laps. By the time Abby had complained and had it changed, then emailed and texted everyone with the name of the new meeting room, the early start she'd given herself had practically disappeared. Now she was sitting in the coffee area outside the new meeting room, and feeling like she'd done a day's work already.

'Is it safe to assume the latest room name you've sent round will actually be the meeting venue? Or will you be changing it again in half an hour?'

Abby looked up from her to-do list to find the immaculately dressed Geraldine staring down at her. Today she wore a fitted bright fuchsia suit which, Abby was forced to admit, looked pretty amazing with her dark looks. She also wore deep purple nail varnish on nails Abby knew, because she'd seen the evidence, were not only long but sharp.

'The original room they gave us was too small, so I had to change it.' She wasn't going to apologise to this woman. She wasn't.

'I suppose I'd better go and collect the handouts I'd put in the first room and move them to the second room, then.'

'I'm sorry, I didn't realise.' Oh bugger, looked like she was going to apologise then. 'Do you need any help?' And worse, she was going to grovel.

Geraldine gave her a tight smile. 'I'm sure I can find a strong male to help me.'

As she watched her saunter away, hips wiggling sensually in a way Abby knew she'd never be able to mimic, she bet Geraldine would have no problem finding that man. No problem at all.

With a sigh she returned to the next item on her list. Food. Somewhere between yesterday, when she'd checked up on them, and this morning, the catering department had managed to lose her lunch request. Honestly, were they trying to make her look inefficient?

Shifting through the suggested menu packages she'd been given she became aware of someone walking up to her. The hint of fresh male aftershave told her it was a tall, dark, handsome someone.

'Everything okay?'

'Doug, hi. Yes, it's all fine, thank you. Everything is fine. Just … fine.'

He frowned. 'That's reassuring to hear. I think.'

Another of those silences followed. A week into the job and Abby was still trying to get her head around them. Silence meant either he was thinking, or he'd found out all he needed to know. It didn't mean she had to fill it. 'For lunch would you prefer the healthy buffet, the lighter sit down meal or the eat-until-you-burst sit down, and maybe never get back up again, option?' she blurted.

His lips curved into the small smile that was fast becoming a high point of her day. Generally his face showed very little emotion so when she managed to tease a smile from him, it was a personal triumph. 'The first or second options might be more conducive to a successful meeting,' he replied, easing his hands into the trouser pockets of his immaculate charcoal grey suit. 'Though right now I'm thinking the third has its merits.'

She tried not to stare at him. Tried to ignore the way her

blood seemed to hum in his presence. 'Are you not looking forward to the afternoon?'

'I'm not looking forward to any of it.'

'Oh.' She risked a glance at his handsome face. As usual it didn't give much away. 'Do you not get on with the Taylors people?'

He looked like he was on the verge of replying, though she couldn't be sure because his *keeping quiet* expression was pretty similar to his *about to talk* one. At that precise moment though, Charles Faulkner swanned into the coffee area – she recognised him from the photographs on the company website. Instantly the atmosphere changed from congenial to antagonistic.

Doug's spine stiffened, his shoulders straightened and his jaw tensed.

'Everything set?' Charles' voice boomed over to them. Loud and pompous, his question wasn't directed at her, but at his son.

'Of course.' Doug's quiet, controlled voice held a frosty edge. 'Have you met my new personal assistant? Charles Faulkner, Abigail Spencer. Abby's the one who's pulled everything together today.'

Abby felt a deep flush scald her cheeks. 'Well, I wouldn't put it quite that strongly. I've arranged the room and ...' She trailed off when she realised Faulkner senior wasn't taking the blindest bit of notice.

'Teddy and Stanley are in the foyer,' he snapped at Doug. 'When you've finished flirting with your admin, I suggest you go and greet them.'

Abby knew her jaw was hanging as she watched Charles Faulkner's stocky figure disappear out of the room. 'Flipping heck, you're nothing like your father.'

A muscle twitched in Doug's otherwise expressionless face, but he didn't reply.

'Is he always that rude?' It was only when he turned to stare at her Abby realised she should hardly be saying that to him. 'Sorry, please forget I said that. Sometimes my mouth runs away with words my brain hasn't had a chance to sanction.'

'Sometimes?'

Glacier blue eyes held hers and for several nerve wracking seconds she thought she was in trouble. Then his lips twitched, making her heart flutter wildly.

'Okay, maybe more than sometimes,' she answered a little breathlessly.

Doug turned to leave, presumably to do as he'd been told and greet their guests, but just before he started walking he glanced over his shoulder. 'The answer is yes, he is always rude, so ignore him. I do.'

The sound of Abby's giggles reverberated around his head as Doug walked back to the foyer. He couldn't remember the last time he'd made a woman laugh like that, the sound filled with fun and joy. And innocence, for God's sake.

When he reached the foyer, the Taylors company representatives were out in force. He glanced quickly at his watch; still fifteen minutes before the scheduled start of the meeting. Clearly Taylors were far more eager to get the meeting underway than his team were. So far he'd only seen Geraldine, and Abby of course, though she looked like she'd already been here too long.

A sigh slipped from him, a usual occurrence when faced with a whole day of meetings with his father. The sooner he cracked on with it though, the sooner he'd escape. Pushing back his shoulders, he went to say hello.

The morning slipped by quite harmlessly, with presentations from his Crumbs team setting out the facts on the brands under discussion. Following the light lunch – which went on for two hours, so thank heavens they hadn't gone with the gut buster option – the Taylors team took to the floor to give what was supposed to be a quick run down of their capabilities.

They went on, and on. And on. Several times Doug shifted forward in his chair, ready to tell them to get a move on, but each time his father shot him a warning look.

Taking a pen out of his inside pocket Doug started doodling on his pad, feeling closer to old age and death with each passing minute.

He nearly cried in relief when the arrival of fresh tea and coffee signalled another break. As everyone shuffled out for some much needed caffeine, he caught Abby trying to stifle a staggeringly large yawn.

'I take it you've seen more interesting paint drying?' he remarked under his breath.

She flushed scarlet, slapping a hand to her mouth. 'No, it's very interesting. Very, very, umm, interesting. I just had an early start, that's all.'

'Liar.' She looked so shocked he almost laughed. 'That was a bored yawn, not a tired one.'

'How can you tell?'

'If you weren't yawning through boredom after the last two hours of monologue, I'll start to think there's something wrong with you.'

Her answering grin was infectious. Damn, this woman brightened up his days. 'I think my agenda's just gone down the toilet. We're meant to be finishing at five-thirty and it'll already be five o'clock by the time we start again.'

'Is that a problem for you?' he asked, aware now of her situation at home.

'No. As you're all staying the night I took your advice and booked myself into a room, too, in case there are any issues with the evening meal like there have been with the meeting room and then the lunch.' Thankfully she took another breath. 'My father promised he'll be home early but

54

he's pretty useless at keeping those sort of promises so I also asked Mandy to make sure she would be there when the girls got home from school.' She bit her lip and gave him an embarrassed smile. 'You didn't need to hear all that, did you?'

'No?'

She laughed. 'Sorry. Truth is, I've been kind of looking forward to a night to myself. No teenagers, no crying toddlers, just me and a big bed in a hotel room.'

A mental image of her lying on that big bed flashed through his mind, hair released from its ponytail, leaving a trail of soft blonde curls tumbling across the pillow. The image continued past her face, down her slender neck and onto plump, curvy breasts with taut pink nipples. 'I think I'll nip outside for a bit of fresh air.'

It was after six when Doug finally climbed to his feet to begin the negotiations. 'There's been a lot of talk today about the declining sales of the three brands under discussion, particularly when viewed against the positive growth of our other biscuits, so it isn't hard to understand why Crumbs are thinking of divesting. But before we talk money, I want to show you a couple more pieces of information.' He clicked onto his first slide. 'This is data you've already seen, but instead of showing you it separately, I've chosen to align the sales graph of these brands with the promotional spend on them.' Unsurprisingly, there was a correlation. 'The next graph shows the same idea with three of our growth brands.' Again, there was a correlation. 'Now what happens if you look at sales per amount of promotional spend on the brands?' When he showed that graph, there was an audible intake of breath from Teddy, Taylors' Chairman.

'Interesting, isn't it, that the three brands we're planning on divesting are actually, if you consider the small amount we spend on them, the most profitable. Then again, if you look at the latest piece of biscuit market research conducted by Mintel, it's not so surprising. It's the plain biscuits that are preferred by the younger generation. The market of the future.'

He glanced over at Abby and could tell the moment she realised that he'd basically repeated to the meeting what she'd told him last week.

'What are you trying to say?' his father growled.

With a sigh he dragged his gaze from Abby's startled face to his father's irate one. 'I'm not trying to say anything. Merely showing some further data to inform our thinking.'

'It sounds like you don't want to sell,' Teddy blustered, tossing his pen dramatically onto the desk. 'So why the bloody hell have you invited us here?'

'Of course we want to sell. Don't listen to the boy's twaddle.' His father again, charming as ever. 'We're here to make a deal.'

Doug fought for his control. 'And all I'm doing is making sure the deal is appropriate, considering the brand value of the items we're discussing.'

'You're trying to screw more money out of us, you mean,' Teddy countered, folding his arms across his flabby, overweight chest and reminding Doug of Toad of Toad Hall.

'I'm trying to secure a fair price,' Doug countered mildly, sitting back down.

'This is outrageous.' Teddy hauled his body onto his feet. 'Your father and I already have a gentleman's agreement on this. Now you're trying to gazump me.'

The venomous glare his father levelled at him washed over Doug, as had the contemptuous way he'd called him a boy. Both had been served up so often they now failed to inflict any real pain.

'Let's take a break,' Charles told the group, eyes fixed ominously on Doug. 'I'm sure little Goldilocks can arrange for some more tea and coffee outside.'

Abby's expression froze and Doug immediately felt the surge of anger he'd failed to feel a moment earlier. 'My personal assistant is called Abigail. As she's also the one who's worked tirelessly over the last week to ensure we're all here today, sitting round this table, have the decency to show her the respect she deserves.'

Silence. It was as if everyone in the room stopped breathing, stopped moving. As his father's face turned puce, Doug knew he'd end up paying for his outburst someway or another. Still, whatever the old guy was going to dish up, it would be worth it for the look on Abby's face. It was clear she didn't know whether to thank him or be terrified for him.

'Abby, would you please ask the catering team to put together a few refreshments.'

She blinked, then lurched clumsily to her feet. 'Sure, no problem. I'll call them now. They won't be long.'

'Let's reconvene in twenty minutes.'

As the group straggled out, his father marched menacingly towards him. 'You're not going anywhere.'

Abby peered anxiously through the small window in the meeting room door. Father and son were still talking. Or rather Charles Faulkner was ... shouting? He certainly looked no less angry than he had when the meeting had adjourned. Doug, of course, was simply standing there, hands in his pockets, looking bored. It seemed like he didn't do strong emotion, whether that be happy or angry.

She let out a slow breath. He probably didn't actually need her to go in and protect him, but still, it didn't seem right to abandon him when he'd only been sticking up for her.

'Young lady.'

She turned to find Teddy, the overweight, bombastic head of Taylors. Embarrassed to be caught spying on her bosses, Abby hastily moved away from the door. 'Can I help with anything?'

'Yes. I've got a complaint about my room and I want you to handle it for me.' He took her arm and started to push her towards the lift. 'Come with me now and I'll show you the problem.'

The way he was almost manhandling her, it looked like she had no choice. Abby didn't feel entirely comfortable as they moved into the empty lift. Several times she'd caught the man's gaze on her during the meeting, and not always on her face. It was broad daylight though, in a busy hotel and they were all due back to the meeting in ten minutes. She could put up with this weasel until then.

'What's a pretty little thing like you doing in one of these dreary business meetings then, eh?'

His mouth twisted and her discomfort levels rose a notch further. Smiling usually involved a pleasant lifting of facial features but in Teddy's case his face morphed into an image of Shrek on a bad day. 'I'm finding the meeting interesting, actually.'

The doors pinged open and when he signalled for her to go ahead she had no choice but to walk down the corridor towards his room, knowing full well he was leering at her backside. Why oh why had she put herself in this position? 'Mr Taylor,' she began, turning round and narrowly avoiding barging into him, 'we probably don't have time for this now.' Please let her not sound as nervous as she felt. 'Why don't you tell me what the issue is and I'll go down to reception and deal with it from there?'

His mouth shifted into another sort-of-smile. 'You wouldn't be scared to come into my room by any chance, would you? Because that's not particularly flattering to a gentleman like myself.'

'Of course I'm not.' *At least I wouldn't be if you really were a gentleman.*

'Good.'

It only took three further strides before he halted, slipping his key card into the slot. Her pulse tripped but even as the unease she'd been feeling switched to full blown anxiety, she knew she had to follow him inside. Any other action would be considered rude – and the end of her fledgling career at Crumbs.

The door shut with a thud behind her and instantly the atmosphere felt stifling, her heart hammering so fast it was hard to breathe. 'About this complaint?'

'What complaint?' He raised his eyebrows and took a predatory step towards her. 'You followed me to my room, you naughty girl.' His voice was an octave lower now and rough enough to send prickles of fear running up and down her spine. 'It would be a shame to waste the happy coincidence of you, me and a bed all in the same place, don't you think?'

Abby's heart thumped so hard it bounced off her ribcage. 'I think it's time to go back to the meeting.'

'Don't you worry your pretty little head about that, they won't miss us. Damn things never run to time, anyway. So tell me, Miss Abigail, where did Doug find a cute thing like you?' He started to stroke a finger down her cheek. It was like being prodded with a cold sausage. 'I've not been able to take my eyes off you all day.'

'Don't touch me.' The tremor in her voice undid her demand.

'Why not?' He leered down her open neck blouse. 'Why wear something like that if you don't want a man to look or touch?'

With trembling fingers she attempted to do up her top two buttons but he swiped her hands away. 'Oh no, lovely. We're undoing buttons here, not doing them up.'

He plunged his fat fingers into her cleavage and Abby screamed. 'Get off me.' As his hand clenched over her breast she grabbed at his shoulders and tried to push him away. When that didn't work, she thrust up her knee. She must have made some contact with his sensitive parts because he yelped.

'You bitch.' He bent over, groaning so loud she almost didn't hear the knock on the door.

'Teddy?' The handle rattled. 'Open the door.'

Abby froze as Doug's quiet, deep voice resonated through the woodwork. Oh God, she didn't want him to see her here. It would be mortifying.

'Open up now, or I'll knock the door down.'

He hadn't raised his voice but the steel running through it must have convinced Teddy it wasn't an idle threat because he pushed himself upright and yanked the door open. 'What the bloody hell do you think you're doing, barging in on a man in the privacy of his room?' he thundered.

Abby plastered herself against the wall in the vain hope Doug wouldn't notice her. Fat chance. His cool blue eyes skimmed the room and though his face showed no emotion when he registered her, she knew what he saw. Hastily she straightened her blouse, doing up another button for good measure. Her cheeks burnt with both embarrassment and anger. All she wanted to do was escape.

Ignoring the blustering Teddy, Doug directed his gaze at her. 'Are you okay?'

'Yes, I'm fine.'

'Why wouldn't she be? What sort of man do you think I am? Abby and I were just enjoying a little alone time.'

'I know exactly what type of man you are.' Doug's voice was hard and flat but it softened when he spoke to her. 'Abby, would you mind going downstairs and telling everyone I'll be down in a few minutes?'

Nodding quickly, she fled the room as fast as her shaking legs could manage.

Chapter Six

Doug was seething. The anger that was always with him, coiled in the far reaches of his soul, controlled and rarely vented, lashed at his insides. The moment he'd seen Abby's terrified face he'd wanted to thump his fist hard into Teddy's bloated, flushed one. What a shame that years of putting up with his father's insults, of learning to bite his tongue and not betray his feelings, had made him too good at reining in his temper to lose it with this oaf. Still, he imagined the satisfaction of pummelling his knuckles into the florid flesh.

'The deal is off,' he told Teddy as the flabby prick tried to square up to him; half his height, twice his weight, twice his age. Arrogant as well as stupid. 'Pack your bags and get out of here. I never want to see you again.'

'What do you mean off?' Teddy snapped. 'You have no authority to say that. Your father would never allow it.'

Doug relaxed his jaw. Kept his hands unclenched. 'I'm the managing director of this firm. The deal doesn't go ahead without my agreement.'

'We all know who carries the power in Crumbs,' Teddy sneered, 'and it sure isn't the patsy son.'

The barb bounced off him. There was no insult this man could throw at him that Doug hadn't already hurled at himself. 'This can go one of two ways. I go downstairs and tell them the deal's off because you're not prepared to meet us anywhere near the price I've told you. Or I go downstairs and tell them the deal is off because I caught you assaulting my personal assistant. What's it to be?'

'They wouldn't believe you.'

Doug thrust his hands into his pockets and narrowed his eyes. 'You sure about that?'

Teddy let rip a crude oath and slumped onto the bed. 'Fine, we'll do it your way. But I won't forget this, and your father's not likely to, either.'

Doug smiled at the last statement. Considering his father already believed everything Doug did was monstrously stupid, this misdemeanour would be a mere ripple in the already tempestuous waters of their relationship.

Doug left the room without another word and made his way back down towards the meeting room. Before entering he glanced through the small glass window to check who was there. Everyone, it seemed, apart from Abby.

A knot of worry formed in his stomach and he found he couldn't stride into the room without knowing where she was. *How* she was.

Ignoring the room full of people waiting for him, he walked to the reception desk. 'Can you put me through to Abigail Spencer's room, please?'

Two rings and she answered. 'Hello?'

'It's Doug. What room are you in?'

'Oh, sorry, I'm coming down—'

'No, you're not. I'm coming up.' Suddenly he realised how threatening he sounded. 'Look, if you don't want to meet me in your room, I understand. Perhaps you can come down to the reception and we'll find somewhere quiet to talk?'

'It's 224.'

'Okay then. I'm on my way.'

When she opened the door he knew immediately that she'd been crying. Her chocolate eyes were puffy and the end of her nose glowed red. Something in his heart stirred. 'Are you okay?'

'I'm fine, thanks.' Her lips wobbled as she tried to smile. 'I was just, err, phoning home to check up on everyone. I'm sorry I wasn't in the meeting.'

'Jesus, Abby.' He inhaled, searching for his calm. 'I'm not

here for an apology. I know exactly why you needed to hide out in your room for a while. I'm here to ask if you want to press charges, because if you do, I'll support you. I'm happy to tell the police what I saw.'

'Press charges? God, no, I don't want to cause any trouble.' She indicated for him to come into the room and closed the door behind him.

Doug felt pinpricks of awareness ripple through him. They were alone, in a hotel room. Then he remembered that's exactly how Teddy had reacted and guiltily he pushed his inappropriate thoughts aside. 'That bastard molested you, Abby. He's the one causing trouble, not you.'

She lowered her eyes and went to sit on the bed. 'I was worried you might think that I ... you know.' Her fingers fiddled nervously with the button on her cuff. 'That I was in his room because I wanted to be.'

Two lungs full of air rushed out of him. 'Of course I thought an incredibly attractive twenty-four-year-old would want to be in the same hotel room as an overbearing, overweight sixty-year-old. Why wouldn't I?'

At last she looked at him, a hint of a smile flitting across her wan face. 'How did you know to come and find me?'

'I asked where you were and someone said Teddy had asked you to sort out a problem with his room.' The desire to sit next to her, to hug her slight frame against his, became almost overwhelming. He raked a hand through his hair and moved himself away from temptation, leaning against the door. 'Immediately I sensed trouble. He's got a reputation for preying on young ladies.'

'Well, no surprise there. I guess it's a relief to find out I'm not special.'

'You are special.' For a man who always thought carefully before speaking, the words slipped out far too easily.

As her dark eyes widened his body tingled with an

awareness he could no longer ignore. He found his personal assistant attractive. Not necessarily a bad thing, he reasoned. Since her arrival his working day had become a heck of a lot pleasanter. And it wasn't like he was going to act on the feeling. God forbid he dragged a sweet, happy woman like Abby into his shitty life.

The room still echoed with his words. *You are special.* 'Everyone who works for me is special,' he added hastily. Inaccurately. 'Do you feel okay to come back down? The meeting's almost over and I could do with you recording the last minutes.' She hesitated and he smiled. 'Teddy won't be there, I promise.'

Abby checked her face in the bathroom mirror for the second time, very aware that Doug was waiting for her outside. She looked, frankly, terrible. And that was despite washing her face with cold water and refreshing her make-up. Yet her handsome boss had told her she was special. A warm, mushy feeling settled in her stomach and it didn't seem to matter that he'd hastily corrected his statement. The mushy feeling remained.

Oh heavens, please don't let her fall for her boss.

There was a cough on the other side of the door. 'Abby?'

Taking a deep breath, she walked out. 'I'm ready.'

His eyes skimmed over her face. 'Better.'

He held the door open and Abby slipped out, her heart racing. Doug's nearness, or the thought of bumping into Teddy again?

They didn't speak in the lift, though she was hyper aware of him: the warmth of his big body, the physical power she sensed beneath the polished suit. And heaven help her, he smelt as delicious as he looked – expensive, subtle. Sexy.

The moment they opened the door to the meeting room the lively chatter stopped and all eyes turned their way. Abby felt acutely self-conscious as she walked to her chair. Did she look like she'd been groped? Or been crying?

'Taylors have backed out of the deal,' Doug announced baldly into the silent room. 'Let the minutes state that Edward Taylor spoke to me directly during the break and told me he felt the price we were looking for was too high.'

Shock shot through Abby. After all this, Taylors had backed out?

'What do you mean, it's off?' Charles Faulkner shot a death stare first at his son, and then at her.

Dread pooled in her stomach and Abby wanted to slink under the table. Please God, let this be nothing to do with her. How could it not be, though? And the way Faulkner senior was staring at her, as if he wanted to put his hands round her neck and squeeze really hard, he guessed she had something to do with it, too.

Ignoring his father, Doug addressed the room. 'This meeting is now officially over. Anyone with a room registered for tonight is welcome to stay and dine at our expense. I wish you a pleasant evening.'

Charles hauled himself to his feet and stared darkly at his son. 'You will stay right where you are. I've not finished with you.'

Flinching at the harshness of his tone, Abby darted a glance at Doug. His face held a carefully blank expression, giving no hint as to the humiliation he must surely be feeling. How could his father talk down to him like that? In front of not just Crumbs employees, but Taylors, too.

And it was all her fault.

She tried to catch Doug's eye to offer a silent apology but his attention was fixed on his father. Hurriedly she collected her things and began to follow the others out.

'And where do you think you're going, missy?' Abby's heart thumped as she turned to meet Charles' glare.

'Abby's finished for the day,' Doug cut in. 'This is between you and me.'

'Protecting your little floozy now, are you?' he thundered at Doug. 'You think I don't know she must have had something to do with all this? One minute we're about to start negotiations, the next the pair of you waltz in late and tell me the deal I've been nurturing for months is off. Oh, and Teddy is nowhere to be seen. What has that trollop done to screw this up?'

Anger flashed through her and Abby's hand twitched with the urge to slap Faulkner senior hard around the face. But Doug was speaking again.

'I advise you to watch your language,' he told his father coldly. 'You're embarrassing yourself. As for what Abby has done, she made the mistake of going to help a man who only wanted to get his grubby hands on her. I have no desire to negotiate with people like that.'

'You believe the words of a jumped up secretary over a long time friend and businessman?'

'I believe what I saw with my own eyes,' Doug countered evenly. 'You can disagree with my decision, go over my head as I know you want to, but be warned, I won't let this drop. If you continue to work with Teddy, I'll take this matter straight to the police.'

Abby stifled a gasp. Oh God, this was all getting so out of hand. 'I told you, I don't want to cause any problems,' she began, but Doug shook his head.

'Teddy is the one who's caused the problem.' He glared at his father. 'Are we done now?'

Charles let out what Abby could only describe as a growl before swinging round and stalking out.

As the door clicked shut and the adrenaline seeped from her system, Abby felt her knees tremble. 'I'm such a stupid cow,' she said, clinging to the table for support. 'If I hadn't been dumb enough to follow Teddy up to his room, none of this would have happened. You'd still have your deal. Your father wouldn't be angry with you.'

Doug glanced sideways at her. 'He's always angry with me.'

'I'm starting to see that and I'm trying really, really hard not to ask you why. The trouble is, as well as being a stupid cow I'm also a nosey one, so the question might jump out anyway.'

He dipped his head slightly, his bearing so very poised, so in control. 'Consider me forewarned.'

She shifted so her bum was resting on the table, supporting her jelly legs. 'I'm still sorry I mucked up your deal. I expect deep down you're pretty annoyed, aren't you?'

He didn't reply, just shot her a gorgeously bemused look.

She shook her head at him. 'How on earth does anybody ever work out what you're thinking?'

He let slip a small sigh. 'Right now I'm thinking I could do with a drink. Would you like to join me?'

Her heart gave a huge thump. It's casual, she told herself. A wind down after a long, crappy day. Still, it carried on thumping. 'Yes.' It came out like a whisper so she coughed and added a slightly louder, 'Please.'

For a few moments he stared down at her, the blue of his eyes swirling with a myriad of emotions she had no clue how to decipher. Then he raised a hand and gently touched her cheek. 'Are you really okay, Abby? What that man did to you, I can't bear to think about it.'

It was the first time she'd seen any real emotion on his face and her heart began beating even harder. 'He only had a quick grope. Nothing that hasn't happened before.'

For a split second Doug's jaw tightened. 'If he, or anyone else, ever tries that again, I want you to tell me.'

'Why, are you going to beat them up?'

She meant it as a joke. Of course this mild-mannered man wasn't going to attack anyone, but his eyes flashed. 'Something like that.'

There was enough menace in his voice to make her wonder if his quiet demeanour was actually all an act. That beneath the outward calm lurked a far more turbulent personality.

They found a seat in a corner of the bar and Doug ordered a large whisky for them both. He'd been shocked when Abby had asked for one, but then he'd laughed at himself. As if he could possibly ever second guess what she was about to say, or do.

When they were settled with their drinks he asked her the question that had been bothering him. 'Are you enjoying the job so far?'

'Of course.' A small frown settled on her face. 'Why, don't I look happy?'

'Looks can be deceptive. I'm aware that you're overqualified for this role. I want to make sure you get out of it what you need.'

She seemed to take in a breath, an unusual occurrence because in his experience she said what she wanted without pause or thought. 'I'm just settling in, which is fine. In time though …' Another hesitation. '… in time I'd like to get more involved. Only in the areas you think I can manage, obviously. I don't want to muck up anything important.'

The humour in her eyes tugged a smile from him. Usually he found it hard to smile. When talking to Abby, he seemed to find it hard not to. 'I'll bear that in mind.' Taking a long sip of whisky he searched for another topic. 'How is your family? No more sickness, I hope?'

'No, we're all good, thank you. Ellie's up to all her usual tricks again. She's the precocious one, which I guess comes from being spoilt because she's the youngest. She was only one when Mum died, so she doesn't remember her.'

'It must have been really tough for you all, losing your mother so young. I'm sorry.'

She shrugged, as if it was just one of those things, rather than the devastating, life defining trauma it must have been. 'It was a long time ago now. We managed to get through it and mostly we've grown up okay.'

'I'm guessing you're the oldest?'

'Yep, that's me. Big sister and mother figure all rolled into one. Not that I'm much good at the mother part, or the big sister part sometimes, come to that. Still, you muddle through, don't you? Work with what life throws at you and hope you come through the other side. In my case life threw me a curve ball when I lost Mum, but I have a dad and sisters I love to bits, and living through Mum's death made us all a lot closer, so how can I complain?'

Doug was mesmerised by her attitude. He was so bitter, but really, what had life done to him other than give him parents who didn't care much? Nobody had died. He'd not had to struggle to bring his siblings up. He had a snazzy car, more money than he knew what to do with, a prestigious job. In most people's eyes he was bloody lucky.

'I think you're amazing.' When she looked like she was about to choke on the whisky she'd just swallowed, he amended his words. 'What you've done is amazing. Being a mother figure to your siblings when you were only, what?'

'Thirteen when Mum died, but please, I'm not amazing at all. Dad was around so it's not like I had to do everything myself.'

Considering that same father had left Abby in charge of collecting her sick sister from school last week, Doug had a feeling Abby did do most things herself. 'You haven't talked much about him. What does he do?'

'He's a mechanic and he owns a garage which demands a lot of his time, though we're all used to that by now.'

Suddenly she stopped and eyed him suspiciously. 'You're good at this, aren't you?'

'What?'

'Asking lots of questions so you don't have to answer any yourself.'

'Ah.'

She grinned playfully at him. 'Yes, ahh.'

'So this is where you've been hiding.'

The hint of expensive perfume heralded Geraldine's arrival before her words reached him.

'We're not hiding anywhere,' he replied, annoyed that he sounded defensive. 'Just enjoying a quiet drink.'

'It looks very cosy.' She deliberately looked from one whisky glass to the other. 'I don't remember you ever sharing a drink with your last PA. Joanne, wasn't it?'

He gave Geraldine a warning glance. 'Don't presume to know everything about me.'

Reaching over, she gave his shoulder a proprietary pat. 'Oh, I don't. But I do know that what I have in mind for you back in my room is something you'll enjoy.' She whispered her room number into his ear and then glided away, her hips swaying provocatively.

He was a single man, he reminded himself. Geraldine a single woman. He had nothing to feel ashamed of, and yet ... and yet. A flush worked its way up his neck. He darted a quick glance at Abby, who was staring at Geraldine's retreating back, all laughter gone from her face. He wanted to forget the interruption and carry on talking to her because she didn't just intrigue him, she made him smile. The atmosphere had changed though, shifting from relaxed and easy to uncomfortable and awkward the moment Geraldine had come into view.

'You can do a lot better,' Abby said after a while, her eyes still fixed ahead, though Geraldine had long gone.

70

His pulse tripped, but he had no answer to her softly spoken words. Was she simply speaking without thinking again, or was there a hidden meaning behind her statement?

In one motion she swigged back her whisky and stood. 'Well, I'd better go. I've a quiet room with a big television waiting for me. No sisters, no crying babies. I need to make the most of it.' Finally her eyes swung to his. 'Enjoy your evening.'

Doug wanted to reach out and stop her. Tell her to spend the evening with him instead, but his hand remained firmly clenched round his glass. She was his employee. Warm and loving, where he was cold and bitter.

Besides, he had enough on his plate with Geraldine.

Long after Abby had left Doug remained at the bar, sipping at his whisky, trying to drum up the enthusiasm to knock on his lover's door.

Chapter Seven

It was the end of April, and Abby had been at Crumbs for two months. It didn't seem possible that time could zip by that quickly. She felt she had a pretty good handle on the processes and the people now. Well, most of the people. She still didn't know much more about her boss than she had eight weeks ago. He was polite, considerate and ... quiet. She'd worked with bosses who ranted and raged, and bosses who laughed and joked. Doug was simply – there. A handsome but distant face at his desk.

He did listen though, and today she was due to present back to him on a project he'd given her, looking at updating the current packaging. That's if she managed to get to work on time.

She raced down the stairs and into the kitchen. After hurrying Ellie and Holly up, and almost tripping over the dog, she packed the computer she'd been working on last night into her briefcase.

'You look tired, Abs,' Mandy observed as she jiggled the weighty George on her hip. 'What time did you get to bed last night?'

'After the two phone calls and the midnight visit from Roger.' Abby frowned at her sister. 'What are you doing, giving that good for nothing waster the time of day?'

'He's George's father. What do you expect me to do? I can't just wipe him out of my life. He has rights.'

'Only if he earns them,' Abby countered. 'The sole contribution Roger's made to fatherhood so far is the donation of his DNA. Thankfully George was created from the good bits.' She waggled her eyebrows at her nephew and he let out a gorgeous chuckle. Yes, the boy certainly had his father's good looks and charm. Please God, let it be all they shared. Turning her eyes back to her sister, she noticed Mandy fussing with George's sleepsuit. 'What's wrong? What happened with Roger?'

'Nothing. It's cool.' She blew a raspberry against George's cheek, making him giggle again, then manoeuvred him into his high chair. All the while avoiding Abby's eyes.

'You know I can read you like a book, don't you, Mandy? Tell me what's going on.'

She heaved out a sigh. 'Lately Roger's been a bit ... moody. I know he's not good for me, that I should leave well alone, but it's easier said than done. He's been pestering to see me and last night ...' She dropped a gentle kiss on her son's head and lowered her voice. 'I'm worried he's got in with a bad crowd. When he came round last night he was wild eyed and out of it.'

'All the more reason to keep well away from him.'

'Says you, who's never been in love.'

Abby frowned, studying Mandy carefully. 'And that's what this is? Love?'

Instantly Mandy shook her head. 'Of course not. I'm not going to fall for a douchebag. I'm not totally stupid.'

The way she chewed at her lip and wouldn't hold her gaze told Abby something different though. 'I don't like the sound of this, Mandy. We need to tell Dad about it tonight. Meanwhile I want you to promise you won't open the door to Roger if you're by yourself.'

Mandy let out a snort of dismissal. 'Come on, Abs, I can take care of myself.' She eyed the clock on the wall. 'Isn't it time you were going to work, anyway? You spent most of the night putting that stuff together. Better make sure you're there when your boss wants to see it.'

Abby was torn, the sister in her wanting to talk more but the professional needing to leave. 'We'll catch up later,' she promised.

She had one foot out of the door when Mandy called her back. 'Hey, wait a minute.' Mandy ran after her, clutching at a slightly forlorn looking plant in a bright yellow pot. 'We bought this a few weeks ago but totally forgot to give it to you, which is why it's looking so sad. The girls wanted you to have something for your desk. Sally chose a plant, because she said it would give off oxygen which would help you concentrate. Plus she knows how obsessed you are with the pots outside the house. Holly chose yellow because it looked happy and Ellie picked a Peace Lily because she said it would remind you of her. I think she was being funny. Oh, and I paid for it.'

Unbelievably touched, Abby stroked the slightly drooping leaves. 'It's lovely, thank you.' She started to laugh but the emotion clogged at her throat and the sound came out strangled. 'I'll think of you all every time I look at it.'

'At least it will stop you thinking about how hot your boss is. Now scoot before you're really late. I hope what you've done impresses the heck out of him. You never know, he might take you out to dinner.'

'I don't want dinner.'

'Liar. You so fancy the pants off him. Come on, admit it.'

Mandy gave her a big, fat, knowing grin, but Abby simply smiled and walked out to her car. Lying to a sister wasn't a good idea. They had an uncanny ability to ferret out the truth, and Abby wasn't ready to face it yet.

Back in his office, Doug cast an eye over the caller ID on his phone and grudgingly accepted the call.

'Haven't you got anything better to do than pester me?' he asked the man on the other end. The same one he'd already spoken to twice this week.

'Apparently not,' Luke replied dryly. 'I'm showing this pain in the butt artist at my gallery next week but he's still not confirmed which paintings I can exhibit.'

74

Doug sighed. Luke wasn't just his best – and only – friend. He was also his manager/agent/person responsible for his current, and rather improbable, rise in the art world. 'Okay, okay. I'll sort it out tonight. Or maybe tomorrow.'

'Great. Well, when you do, remember this hobby of yours is impacting on my reputation. My livelihood.'

Doug heard and understood the irritation in his friend's voice. 'I know, and I'm sorry. I will get the list to you by the end of tomorrow. Better than that, I'll arrange for the paintings themselves to be dropped off.'

'Okay.'

'And, Luke, it's not a hobby for me, either. It's my heart, my soul, my passion.' An unexpected knot of emotion stuck in his throat, making his next words come out scratchy. 'Some days it's the only blasted thing that keeps me sane.'

He heard his friend huff out a breath. 'I know, mate. I know. I'm just a bit stressed. Exhibitions do that to a man.'

'Especially when the artist is belligerent and disorganised.'

'Yep, especially that. Still, he's also brilliant, so I'll forgive his idiosyncrasies if he gets the paintings to me tomorrow and turns up to the show with a damn smile on his face, ready to charm.'

Doug's tie felt as if it was strangling him so he pulled it down and loosened his top button. 'I can promise the former.'

'Done. I realise the second is asking for a miracle, but I live in hope.'

A swish of a door, followed by a thud and a muffled curse signalled the arrival of Abby. Doug's eyes swung eagerly over to where she stood and his lips involuntarily twitched upwards as she rubbed at the spot on her elbow where she'd obviously collided with the door frame. His very organised PA was also surprisingly clumsy. And had he mentioned very, very cute?

He cleared his throat and spoke down the phone. 'Well,

much as I've enjoyed talking to you buddy, I've got to go now.'

'Your PA's just walked in, hasn't she? It's the only explanation for why your voice is now that of a sixty-a-day smoker.'

Abby waved over at him, rolling her lovely eyes and pointing at her elbow with a hand that held a dead looking plant. His face burst into a fully-fledged smile.

'Are you staring at her now? Does she have a short skirt on?'

'I believe our business is over. Goodbye, Luke.'

As he put down the phone he could hear his so-called friend chanting *Doug's got the hots for his admin* at the top of his voice.

'Good morning, Abby. How's the elbow?'

She poked her head around his door, having relieved herself of her handbag and the dead plant. 'It's sore. The door frame must have moved when I opened the door. Either that or I'm a total klutz, which can't possibly be true.'

He rose from his chair and walked over to look at her elbow. The moment his fingers touched her soft skin though, he forgot what the heck he was supposed to be doing. He was aware only of Abby. Of her intoxicating floral smell, her pretty face. Her vitality. Her slightly flushed cheeks and deep brown eyes, now looking up at him with a puzzled expression.

Hastily he removed his hands. 'It doesn't look like it needs major surgery.'

She took a step away, which both relieved and disappointed him. 'Easy for you to say. You can't see the shattered bones beneath the skin.' When he darted her a look of concern, she laughed. 'Maybe I exaggerate slightly. The only thing that's shattered is my image of cool and grace and I don't expect either of those terms have ever been used to describe me.'

'Perhaps not.' Safer to leave it at that, he told himself as he walked back to his desk. More deserving descriptions – those like warmth, sparkle, vivacity – were best left unsaid.

'I've put my thoughts together on that packaging project,' she announced when she returned a few minutes later carrying two cups of coffee. 'Just let me know when it's a good time to go through it with you.'

He reached for the mug, rescuing it from its precarious landing position half on, half off the coaster – progress, he guessed. 'Give me an hour to get through a dull finance meeting. If I'm still alive at the end of it, I'm all yours.'

It's just a saying, Abby told herself as she watched Doug stride out of the office, tall and handsome in his dark navy suit, white shirt and muted green tie. A man who looks like that will never be yours. Still, a girl could dream, she reasoned as she attacked her inbox. And working for a man who made her body tingle every time she looked at him was a dream in itself. She knew herself well enough to admit the bounce in her step when she walked into work wasn't all to do with the job. But having a bounce, even if it was a fruitless one, was better than no bounce.

Just over an hour later the soft shuffle of feet across carpet announced that her boss was back. She glanced up in time to see him stride past her alcove, his jacket now thrown casually over his shoulder. She wondered what he'd look like in casual clothes. The suit seemed to restrain him somehow, taming the wildness she sensed at his core.

Jeeze, listen to her. She was sounding like something out of a Jane Austen novel.

She heard a light thud as he dumped something onto his desk. A moment later he appeared in her archway, knocking her off balance with his brilliant blue stare.

'I'm ready when you are.'

'Right. I'll be there in a tick. I just need to find my report.'

She scrambled around on her desk, all fingers and thumbs and racing pulse. Really, she had to get this crush thing under control or she'd be sacked for inefficiency.

Having at last secured the errant report, and grabbing at the drink she hadn't had time to finish yet, she strode into his office only to find him on the phone. He indicated for her to take the seat opposite and she listened with half an ear to his quiet, measured voice before her attention was caught by the doodle on his notepad. Doodle wasn't the right word for what he'd drawn, though. It was a work of art, an intricate landscape with lots of hidden spaces where he'd drawn funny little cartoon people. In fact ...

As he ended the call she pointed to the doodle. 'Did you paint the large canvas on the wall outside your office? The style looks remarkably similar.'

'Very observant.'

'So I'm right then,' she pushed. 'You did paint it?'

'I did.'

'It's really good. At least I think it's good. I'm not an expert on art or anything, so I don't know if it's technically good but, well, there's a lot of detail which must be really hard to draw.' He darted one of his secretly amused looks at her and she knew she was rambling. 'I like it,' she added finally.

'Thank you.'

Flipping heck, how could she not ramble when he stuck to two word answers? 'Do you sell them?'

'Sometimes.'

Wow, two words had been a luxury. 'How much would the one outside be?'

'Around ten thousand.'

Her hand jerked and the coffee she'd been holding skimmed dangerously close to the rim. 'Pounds?'

'No, Smarties,' he replied dryly, then nodded towards her mug. 'Are you sure that's safe?'

She blew out a breath and hung onto the mug with both hands. 'It was perfectly safe until you came out with a statement deliberately meant to shock me.'

He shrugged. 'I didn't.'

She gulped a steadying mouthful and tried to absorb what he'd said. 'So when you're not masterminding a biscuit empire, you're like this ... famous artist?'

'It depends on your definition of fame.' His face was guarded now, devoid of the smile she'd hoped for. 'And my father masterminds the empire.'

'He's gradually handing it over to you, isn't he?'

He gave her a loaded look. 'You think so?' The question was clearly rhetorical because he immediately transferred his attention to the report she'd placed in front of him. 'So, what are your recommendations regarding the future of Crumbs packaging?'

She swallowed hard, feeling blind-sided by the rapid switch in conversation. She might have come in ready to discuss packaging but right now her mind was stuck on his previous, heavily-laden comment. Was it possible Charles wasn't planning on handing Crumbs over to his son?

'Abby?'

Guiltily she shifted her mind back to her job. 'Currently you pack all your biscuits into tins,' she began, reciting the introduction from memory. 'That's both uneconomical and unfriendly towards the environment.'

'It also underpins the Crumbs brand values of classic and traditional.'

'Agreed, though I hope to show you that those values can still be upheld in greener, more cost-effective packaging.'

He quirked his left eyebrow.

'I presume the eyebrow lift is you wondering how I propose to do that?'

A nod and a small curve of his very fine, remarkably soft looking, infinitely kissable lips. 'Go on.'

She scrambled for her thought thread. 'Changing to cardboard packaging would save the company a considerable amount of money.' She cringed at the vague word, knowing that's not what she'd written. 'Sorry, I know considerable isn't very accurate but I worked up some figures in the report, dependent on the different sales forecasts.' She fumbled around for the right page and while he scanned it through, she took a breath and told herself to calm the heck down. 'You can see from the examples that we can emboss the card; make it heavy and posh looking. That will give it a similar look and feel to the tins.'

'But cardboard doesn't say quality.'

His expression told her diddly squat. Did he hate it? If so she couldn't blame him. She was making such a pig's ear of this. When she'd rehearsed it last night she'd been cool and professional, not the ditzy blonde she was now. 'I think cardboard says more than quality, especially to the younger generation who value the environment they live in. It says *responsible*. Besides, I have another idea for the dinosaurs who like their tins.' The eyebrow quirked again and she froze. 'Oh God, you're not a dinosaur, are you?'

His lips twitched. 'I like to think not.'

Relief rushed out of her. 'Good. So, I can see you're dying to ask what I'm planning for the ... well, I think I should call them tin lovers now, just in case not all the dinosaurs are extinct.'

Her heart flip-flopped slowly in her chest as a twinkle of amusement snuck into his eyes.

'Abigail, what are you planning for the tin lovers now you've shoved their precious biscuits into soggy cardboard?'

She accepted the jibe. It was a worthy exchange for his nearly-there smile. 'We'll sell the tins separately. Not the same tins obviously, because customers will think it's a cheek. The new tins will be stronger, better quality. The type you'd like to put on display in your home. The cardboard packs should be made so they can slide into the tin. If you don't like the idea of selling the tins, we could do offers with them. You know how the older generation like their coupons. Buy three packets and get a free tin. That sort of thing.'

'Got a blue tint, get a blue tin?'

The giggle burst out of her with no warning. It wasn't so much the joke, but the unexpectedness of it. 'I didn't realise you did humour.'

'Oh?'

Damn, she wished she could read him better. Had she just pissed him off? 'I don't mean you're dull or boring. Just that you seem very ...' She trailed off, aware she was in danger of deepening the hole she'd dug.

'Very?' he prompted.

'Quiet. Reserved. Sometimes you're like this castle surrounded by a big moat with the drawbridge up.' Flipping heck, what was she saying? As his eyebrows shot into his hairline she knew she'd need a stepladder to get out of the hole now. 'I don't mean for that to sound like a bad thing,' she added quickly. 'It's just you're the opposite of me. You're probably wondering what possessed you to recruit such a chatterbox, huh?'

'Not when she's just solved my packaging dilemma.'

Abby jolted upright. 'I have?'

He gave her one of his rare but absolutely stunning smiles. 'You have. I knew we needed to change the tins, but neither I or the packaging team could find a way to make it work for the traditionalists. You've just solved the issue.'

'Oh, wow.' She felt giddy, and it wasn't all down to his praise. 'It was worth all those late night candles I burnt.'

A frown furrowed his brow. 'You were supposed to do this during office hours. I didn't want you working late on it.'

'I didn't, well, not much. And anyway, if it helps, it was worth every minute just to hear your reaction.'

He leant back a little, making a steeple of his hands. 'Do you have a boyfriend, Abby?'

Her heart jumped. 'No.' Could it really be possible that he was starting to—

'I thought not. Why else would you choose to spend your evenings writing a report on biscuit packaging?'

Of course he wasn't starting to see her like that. She buried her disappointment. 'I spent time on the report because I found it interesting.'

'You did?'

'Yes.' Unconsciously she leant forward. 'I really enjoyed attending the meeting with Taylors and listening to the presentations on the three brands you were going to sell, though you didn't sell them in the end because ... well, because I was stupid enough to go into that man's room. But still, I found the discussions fascinating.'

Doug watched the colour bloom across Abby's cheeks and the fire light her eyes as she talked to him. She loved the business, he realised with a jolt of surprise. She hadn't seen the packaging project as a chore but a challenge. A puzzle she wanted to solve. He wished he had half her enthusiasm for it all.

'Did you need me for anything else?'

He shifted on his chair. 'No, that's all.' As she climbed unsteadily to her feet, a fact perhaps connected to the height of the shoes she was wearing today, he cleared his throat. 'About your comment earlier. Every day I've come to the office during the last two months I've thanked God I was clever enough to recruit you.'

Ping. Her cheeks flushed scarlet and she beamed at him for one long, captivating moment before turning and walking back to her desk. As his pulse struggled to return to normal he was forced to admit that her efficiency and business sense were only part of the reason behind his statement. He might be dull and humourless – yes, her words had stung – but he didn't want to be. When she came into his office he didn't feel that way, either.

In fact when he saw her he wanted to smile.

And damn it, he wanted to kiss her, too. He wanted to kiss her until they were both breathless, and then kiss her again.

Chapter Eight

By four o'clock, Doug had had enough. Strictly speaking he'd had enough at ten, but considering how his father watched his every move, he'd forced himself to work until lunchtime. A meeting from one till three had held his attention for a while but now he was back at his desk and staring into space. When he heard the soft hum of his mobile phone he grabbed at it, almost cheering when he saw who it was.

'You're still alive then?' he asked, feeling a rare pull on his heart as he pictured his sister Thea's face. He had two sisters, Margaret who was eighteen and still lived at the Faulkner home and Thea who was twenty-two and at university. Because of the age gap, he was closer to Thea. Margaret had only been six when he'd left home, and because he hated going back there, he'd rarely seen her since.

'I'm only just alive,' she countered. 'I'm back home for the Easter holidays and I hate it, Doug. This place is like a mausoleum and Mum and Dad are like Mr and Mrs Grim. Please come and see me. Or meet me somewhere. Anything to stop me going round the twist.'

It wasn't hard for him to see how a lively twenty-two-year-old medical student would feel frustrated back at home. 'How about a trip to an art gallery next week?'

'You've got another show? Wow, what's that, your fourth?'

'Yes. It helps when the gallery owner is your best mate.'

'It helps if you have talent, too. Where on earth do you get the time to paint?'

'You forget, I'm a miserable git with no social life. I work at Crumbs by day and paint by night.'

'I can't believe you still work in that horrid place. It's no wonder you're miserable. Why don't you tell Dad you've had enough? You've served a longer sentence than most prisoners.'

Thea was by far the smartest Faulkner he knew, but even she hadn't sussed out the complexities of his relationship with his father. 'Thanks. I hadn't thought of that.'

'Very funny. You think I don't know there's something going on between you two? If you won't tell me what it is though, how am I supposed to help?'

'There's nothing you can do, Thea.'

She huffed. 'How do you know, if you don't tell me what the problem is?'

For a brief moment he considered telling her the truth, but when he strung together the words in his head they sounded so lame. A sordid tale from a different century. He often wondered how weak and gutless it made him that he allowed this man to trample all over him. That instead of finding a way to fight him back he simply succumbed. Rolled over.

'Doug?'

He drew a weary hand across his face. 'There's no problem, Thea. If you want to be a help though, you can turn up at my show next week and say wildly complimentary things in a very loud voice.'

'Okay, but your evasive crap is really starting to piss me off.'

Her terse goodbye told him she wasn't just annoyed, she was hurt. He was debating how he was going to make it up to her, when Abby walked in, her face unusually tense.

'What's wrong?'

She struggled to keep her composure. 'I'm afraid I've got to go home.'

'Fine, but why?'

He watched as she wrung her hands together. 'My sister phoned, that's the eldest one, Mandy. Her ex has come round to the house, which by itself isn't an issue because I know she can handle him, but he's not on his own. He's come with two friends and I'm worried that three men looking for trouble isn't a good combination. Not with Mandy on her own with the baby. That's George, my nephew.' She heaved in a breath. 'Plus Mandy said they've been drinking and ...' She bit her lip and looked down at her shoes, tears creeping down her cheeks.

'And?'

Finally she looked up at him, her eyes like large brown pools. 'She didn't let on that she was, but she sounded scared.'

He'd heard enough. Shooting to his feet, he grabbed at his jacket and keys. 'Right, let's go.'

She faltered. 'You don't need to come.'

'You're going to sort out three menacing men by yourself, are you?' He ushered her to her desk and bent to pick up her bright yellow bag. 'Is this all you need?'

'And my coat. I'll be fine on my own though. Really.'

He looped the purple coat over his arm and pushed the bag onto her. There were limits to his acts of heroism and he wasn't about to sit astride a white charger carrying a yellow handbag.

'We'll go in my car,' he announced, dashing down the stairs ahead of her. 'We can come back for yours later.'

'There's no need. I told you, I can handle this.' Her voice was slightly breathless as she tried to keep up with him. 'Anyway, I'm probably just making a big deal out of nothing.' She fidgeted with her hands, continuing her protest even while he eased her none too gently into his Aston. 'I'm going to be so embarrassed when we get there and find them all sitting down drinking tea.'

'You'll be relieved, not embarrassed.' He started the engine, which throbbed reassuringly into life.

'I'll be both. Relieved yes, but now I'm dragging you away from the office I'm going to be mightily embarrassed, too.'

He slid her a look. 'When did the dragging happen? I must have missed it.'

'You know what I mean. Just because I work for you, it doesn't mean you should feel responsible for me.'

'I don't.'

'Sure you don't. How else can you explain why you practically pushed me out of the office and into your car.'

'So that's where the dragging came in.' Her eyes flashed with annoyance and he relented. 'I like you,' he told her quietly. 'If I felt responsible for you, I'd have sent one of the security guards. Because I like you, I'm sending myself.'

Her mouth opened, closed, then opened again but the only sound that came out of it was muted. 'Oh.'

'If I'd known saying I liked you would shut you up, I would have said it on your first day.'

She gave him one of her special smiles then. At least that's how they felt: as if he, and he alone, was entrusted with a rare gift.

Their eyes met and the atmosphere in the car shifted. At first the change was subtle. He became aware of her light perfume. Of how close she was sitting to him. Of the warmth radiating from her skin.

But then his eyes touched on her soft pink lips. The curve of her breasts.

It took a huge effort to drag his attention away from her and onto the road.

Abby's heart was pounding, and not all through fear over her sister which made her feel instantly ashamed. Mandy could be in all sorts of trouble and yet her big sister had just spent the last few seconds thinking of kissing her boss.

She swallowed a few times and tried to refocus on the road ahead. 'Take a right here.'

Smoothly he moved to the outside lane and pulled to a

stop at the lights. Abby was so conscious of how strong and tanned his hands were on the wheel. Of the curls of dark hair on his forearms, revealed by his turned-back cuffs. Inside the office, sitting at his desk, he was a handsome man. Here in the small confines of his luxurious car, he was so much more. A potent male whose citrus aftershave drugged her senses, whose athletic body tugged at that almost forgotten place between her thighs. Whose proud profile pulled at her heart.

'Take the second road on the left. Our house is at the end of the cul-de-sac.' She smoothed down her skirt and reminded herself why she was in his car. She didn't mind being embarrassed in front of him, as long as Mandy and George were okay.

He brought the car to a stop and Abby immediately pushed open the door.

'Wait for me.' His quiet voice held a ring of authority she found hard to defy so she waited until he fell in alongside her.

'Shall I press the bell or use my keys?' Oh God, she'd turned into a trembling, indecisive wreck.

'Here, let me.' He took the keys from her and strode up to the front door.

Did he notice the peeling paint on the window frames her father still couldn't afford to replace? Their house, a five bed semi-detached extended over the garage as the family had grown, must look shabby and small compared to what he was used to. Even his gleaming sports car was totally out of place amongst the vans and seen-better-days hatchbacks parked along the close.

Then Doug opened the door, and Abby could think of nothing but what might be waiting for them.

'Who the fuck is that?'

The angry male voice made the hairs on the back of her neck stand on end. And that was before the smell of alcohol hit her senses.

'Mandy, it's me. Where are you?' Pushing past Doug she ran through the tiny hallway and into the open-plan kitchen/living area.

Mandy stood in the kitchen holding George, her face almost white and her eyes, oh God. Her eyes looked terrified. Next to her was Roger whose panicky expression suggested he wanted to be anywhere else but where he was.

A quick scan of the living room found an upended coffee table and a broken vase. Standing over the table, hands on hips, was a man with tattoos on his arm and a gold ring in his eyebrow. Sitting on the sofa was another guy, slightly smaller, though the scar along his cheek and the snarl on his face made him appear no less threatening.

Heart hammering wildly, she turned back to face her sister. 'What's going on here?'

'I'm okay.' Mandy's shaky voice wasn't very convincing. Warily her sister's eyes darted towards Doug who waited patiently, solidly, *reassuringly*, next to Abby. 'Who's that?'

'Hi, Mandy, I'm Doug Faulkner. A friend of Abby's.' He nodded over to the two men in the living room. 'Have they outstayed their welcome?'

'Butt out, white collar man.' Mr Tattoo curled his lip dismissively at Doug. 'This is none of your business.'

His threatening tone sent a shiver down Abby's spine. 'Mandy's my sister and this is my house, too.' Her legs trembled as she moved to stand by her sister. 'So whatever's going on here is my business.'

Roger shuffled out of the kitchen. 'Come on, Quinn, let's go. We don't want trouble.' Sadly his whole demeanour – the way he hung his head, didn't look his friend in the face – indicated he wasn't the one in charge here.

'I suggest you take your friend's advice.' Shoulders back, hands resting loosely by his sides, Doug brimmed with a quiet, disciplined confidence.

'You can suggest all you like, mate. I ain't going nowhere. 'Specially not on your say so.' Mr Tattoo man – Quinn, Roger had called him – smirked again and started to sit down.

Abby wasn't sure how it happened. It was all too quick. One minute Doug was by her side and the next he was twisting Quinn's arm behind his back and marching him towards the door. 'Let's take this outside, shall we?'

'Oh my God.' Mandy breathed next to her. 'Did you *see* that?'

Suddenly Scarface flew off the sofa. 'You fucking leave him alone.'

Now at the front door, Doug halted. 'Come outside and make me.'

'Wayne, stop.' Roger's plea fell on deaf ears as the guy with the scar jumped over the upended coffee table and scrambled out of the house behind Doug and Quinn. 'Shit, they'll murder him.'

Fear making her breathless, Abby rounded on Roger. 'What do you mean?'

'Quinn and Wayne are high as a bleeding kite. Two on one, your stuffed shirt doesn't stand a chance.'

'Well, bloody come and help,' she yelled, pushing past him and bursting onto the front drive.

Abby's mouth fell open as she watched Doug quickly and cleanly grab Quinn from behind and throw him to the ground. They grappled for a few seconds and though the younger guy was mean and strong, Doug was quick and clever. All it took was a few quick, well-aimed punches and Quinn was writhing on the floor in agony. There was no respite for Doug though because Wayne leapt forward then, shaping to hit him. Rather than retreating from the flailing fists, Doug ducked and moved in tight against Wayne's chest, blocking his ability to punch. In a flash Doug shifted his arms, angled his body and felled Wayne just as he had Quinn. One sharp, backwards jerk of his arm and Doug had Wayne yelping in pain.

'Stop,' Wayne whimpered.

Doug nodded and slowly backed off. 'Just as long as you sit there quietly and don't move until I tell you to.'

Abby stared in shock at the men on the floor.

'Are you okay?' Doug twisted round to face her, his face, his whole demeanour, totally unruffled.

'Me? Of course I am.' She felt dazed, but who wouldn't be after seeing their mild-mannered boss take down two thugs?

'What about the other guy, Roger?'

Doug looked ready to sort him out, too, so Abby hastily shook her head. 'He's not a threat. I think this has frightened him as much as it has Mandy.'

Abby took a step towards Doug, overwhelmed by a sudden urge to hug him. He wasn't looking at her though. His attention was fixed on Mandy and Roger as they appeared in the doorway.

'What happens now?' he asked them. 'Did these guys do anything the police might be interested in?'

Mandy darted a look at Roger and shook her head. 'No police.'

Abby surveyed her sister's agonised face and knew exactly what she meant. Police would mean questions and inevitably Roger would be embroiled in the fallout. Mandy didn't want the father of her child to end up with a police record.

Doug hauled the two men up by their collars. 'Then these guys need to say thank you for saving their sorry asses. And they need to know if they ever show their faces here again they won't be able to walk away like they're doing now.'

'Get your fucking hands off me.' Quinn wrestled away from Doug's grip, rounding on him with venom in his eyes.

Very deliberately Doug wiped his hands on his expensive

wool trousers. 'Happy to, as long as you keep your hands off this family.'

For several long, pulsing seconds Quinn glared back. The cold threat in Doug's voice must have got through to him though because Quinn nodded at Wayne and the pair of them set off down the road. Quinn clutched at his stomach and Wayne held gingerly onto his arm, their hard image now well and truly dented.

As shock slowly gave way to anger Abby marched up to Roger, shoving at his chest. 'What the hell were you playing at, bringing those thugs round to our house?'

Roger held up his hands. 'Hey, I'm sorry, right. They kept saying they didn't believe I had a son. I thought if they saw George, it would shut them up.'

'Stupid.' Mandy glared at him.

Roger hung his head. 'Yeah, I know. I didn't realise how wasted they were. Not 'til they started asking Mandy for money. By then it was too late.'

'Is that why the coffee table was tipped over?'

Roger avoided Abby's eyes. 'They threatened to loot the place if Mandy didn't give them what they wanted.'

Suddenly there was a wail from inside the house and Mandy put her hand to her mouth. 'Oh God, that's George. I dumped him in the high chair before I came out.'

She darted back inside, Roger in her wake. As silence descended, Abby stared at the flourishing tulips in her beloved pots, for once at a loss how to put into words the emotion churning inside her.

'You were incredible,' she told Doug finally. 'Thank you.'

He shrugged and she thought he was going to say nothing, but then he gave her a small, slightly bemused smile. 'First time I've been called incredible.'

A hot blush stung her cheeks, the heat spreading rapidly through her body as his eyes flickered down to her lips before coming back up to hold hers. *He's going to kiss me.* Her heart hammered wildly and she prayed she wouldn't say anything stupid to muck up this moment. 'I'm glad I was the first to tell you. Are you some sort of ninja?'

He let out a soft laugh. 'I'm a brown belt in BJJ. Brazilian jiu-jitsu,' he added at her puzzled look.

'I've heard of a Brazilian, but I'm pretty sure the one I'm thinking of wouldn't take out two men.' Bugger, bugger, talk about a mood crusher ... then again, maybe she was okay because a full-blown smile slid across his face, bathing her in its warmth.

'You'd be surprised how easily us men can be floored.' All the smoothness had vanished from his voice; it sounded hoarser, deeper.

Her heart accelerated into overdrive, thumping so hard she felt her chest vibrate. Was he talking generally, or was this about him? Being floored by *her*?

He took the one step he needed to be right beside her and suddenly she could no longer think. As his head dipped the air left her lungs and when she inhaled again there was only him. Filling her senses, making her body tingle, drugging her mind with his strong, quiet presence.

The touch of his lips against hers was tentative, as if asking a question, seeking permission. She answered fully, parting her mouth and leaning in so it wasn't just their lips touching but their bodies, too. Instantly his hands flew to cradle her face and the kiss grew hungrier. He nibbled at her lips, driving her crazy before sweeping his tongue into her mouth. She was lost.

Chapter Nine

Doug was in heaven. Surrounded by warmth and softness, the taste of sweetness and innocence running over his tongue and pulsing through his lips. If he could just block out those voices he could hear. And those damn giggles.

'He's eating her.'

'Don't be silly. That's kissing. It's what grown-ups do.'

His mind didn't want to leave the dream but the voices were getting louder.

'Well, I don't want to be kissed then.'

Reluctantly he pulled away, his hands still holding Abby's face, his eyes drawn to her swollen lips and dark unfocused eyes.

'Who are you?'

Aftershocks of pleasure still hummed through his system as he turned towards the voices. And found two pairs of young brown eyes staring at him unabashed.

Abby let out a shrill squeak. 'Oh heavens, is it that time already?'

Since he didn't have a clue what *that* time was, he kept quiet. Besides, he wasn't sure he could find his voice. Not after that kiss, and not now he was being studied as if he was a circus attraction.

'Ellie and Holly. Meet my, err, Doug. I mean Mr Faulkner.'

'No, Doug.' There, he hadn't lost his voice after all. Just mislaid it while he'd been kissing the life out of his warm-hearted, funny, sweet-natured PA. Shit.

'Why was he kissing you?'

Abby's eyes darted towards him, then quickly away again. He didn't think he'd ever seen her so flushed and flustered.

'Was it nice, being kissed like that? It didn't look nice.'

The questions were being haphazardly fired at them from the youngest one. Was it Ellie? Thankfully she didn't seem to require any answers.

As Abby flushed even deeper, Doug felt his heart stir. God, she was adorable. And he was so utterly, utterly wrong for her. It wasn't just that his cynical thirty seemed a world away from her sweet twenty-four, or even that he was her boss, though neither sat comfortably. It was more that despite the trauma she'd lived through, she was untainted by the world. A bright, shining star in a gloomy sky. Abby deserved frivolity, fun, romance. Love. He wasn't up to providing any of those things.

What the hell had he been doing, starting something he had no right to pursue?

'Where's your sister?' Abby's eyes darted down the road.

He gaped, his mind thankfully diverted from his personal angst. 'There's another one of you?'

'Yes, Sally. She's sixteen.'

'Doesn't your family do anything but girls?'

The youngest one, presumably Ellie, giggled. 'We have a boy dog. He's called Pat.'

'Pat?'

'Yes. Pat the dog.' She started to snigger again and Holly joined in.

'Hey, I asked you both a question. Where's Sally?'

Doug watched, fascinated, as Abby gently scolded her younger sisters. This is what her life must be like, continually trying to straddle the line between older sister and surrogate mother.

'She's coming. She went to pick up a book from her friend's house.' Holly pointed down the road. 'Look, there she is.'

The quiet one, Doug mused as he studied the older girl walking towards them. Brown hair in a tidy plait, blazer done up, carrying a sensible brown satchel. Ellie, to his left, with her skirt rolled up over her knee and her direct questions was, he guessed, the precocious one. Holly, socks falling down and blonde hair in untidy pigtails, was the sweet one.

Beside him Abby's shoulders relaxed a little. 'Right then, we'd better get inside. You two need to get on with your homework.'

'Is Doug coming in?'

He'd forgotten how straightforward children were. 'Thank you, but I don't want to get in the way.'

'You wouldn't be.' Abby flushed again, though this time she was able to meet his eyes. 'Besides, the least we can do after all your help is give you a cup of tea. No, you don't do tea, do you? Coffee. We can make you a coffee. That is if you want a drink. Of course we've probably taken up too much of your time and if you need to go back to the office—'

'A cup of coffee would be great. Thank you.'

She bit her bottom lip. 'Good. Well, come on in.'

Doug followed the troop inside the house and made his way into the sitting area, straightening up the coffee table. The room seemed to reflect the family. Bright, buzzing with energy, cluttered but clean. As he settled onto the tomato red sofa all he could hear was a wall of noise. A dog barking, a baby crying, girls chatting away at the top of their voices with nobody listening.

'Here you go.' Abby walked towards him carrying a large pink mug. 'Sorry about the colour. I guess that's the trouble with having a house full of girls.'

'One of the lesser troubles,' he murmured, trying not to wince as Abby put the cup straight onto the wooden table. 'Don't you ever use coasters?'

'What, those stupid little things that get in the way and collect dust? Why would I?' She perched her neat backside on the back of the armchair. 'Furniture is meant to be used. What's the point of a table if you can't put anything on it?'

He couldn't fault her logic.

As he went to pick up the mug a furry object with a wet nose plonked itself between his legs and Abby laughed. 'Sorry, you'll have to excuse Pat. He's so grateful for a male visitor he sometimes forgets his manners.'

Doug scratched the dog's black ears and received a sloppy lick in return. 'So this is home life for you?' He nodded in the direction of the open plan kitchen where the noise level was surely over the advisable decibel level.

'It certainly is. Though usually without the thugs. And by that I meant the two guys you scared off. Not my sisters.'

He felt his lips twitch. 'I imagine Ellie might pack a mean punch when she's older.'

Abby gave him a flash of the grin that always brightened his day. 'You've got her worked out already.'

From the kitchen came a loud hissed whisper. 'You ask him.'

A glance confirmed it was the dynamic duo of Holly and Ellie. 'Ask me what?'

'Will we get free biscuits now Abby works for you?'

'Ellie.' Abby cut in sharply. It was the first time Doug had seen her looking cross. 'That's rude. You don't ask questions like that.'

To her credit, Ellie looked chagrined. 'Sorry.'

'Hey, it's fine,' he reassured. 'I should have told Abby this at the start. We don't give biscuits away but if your sister goes to the staff shop she can pick up some cheap misshapes that didn't pass quality control. Wonky Wafer Wonders, Duff Dream Delights and Not Very Crunchy Crunches.'

The girls let out a satisfying peal of sniggers and Doug found he was smiling again. It was almost as if, having rediscovered the art since Abby had joined the firm, his mouth now expected to smile.

'I was wrong before,' Abby told him when the girls had disappeared back to the kitchen. 'You do have a sense of humour. It's actually pretty funny, too.'

He wasn't sure what to say to that so he swallowed back the rest of his coffee. 'Well, thanks for the drink.' He was about to stand when he had a thought. 'I've just realised your car's still at work. Do you want a lift back now?'

'Heavens no, you've been put out enough already. I'll catch the bus in tomorrow, or get Dad to give me a lift.'

He felt a tug of disappointment at not being able to spend some more time alone with her, then thought back to their kiss. Better this way. Safer. 'Right then. I'd better leave you to your evening.'

As he stood, so did Abby. Their bodies almost touched, might as well have done from the zing that rushed through him. Damn he wanted to hold her gorgeous face and kiss her again. Wanted it so, so much. Did she know what was going through his mind? Maybe she did because her tongue crept out and licked at her lips, which did nothing to quell the desire pulsing through him.

Playing with fire wasn't in his nature though so he took a deliberate step back, making sure there was no danger of them actually touching.

'Mr Faulkner? Doug?' Mandy's voice from the kitchen was a welcome distraction. He glanced up to find her elbowing Roger sharply in the ribs.

Roger coughed. 'Err, can I walk out with you?'

'Sure.' Doug shot Abby the quickest of glances – he didn't want his libido firing again. 'I'll see you tomorrow.' He followed it by a longer glance at the girls in the kitchen who were staring at him thinking God knows what. *Supply of cheap biscuits. Creepy boss man who snogged their sister.* 'Nice to meet you. Have a good evening.'

They were halfway down the drive before Roger spoke. 'I, umm, well, thanks for what you did. You know, sorting out Quinn and Wayne. I dunno what would have happened if you hadn't come round.'

As he wanted Roger to think about what might have been, Doug made a play of taking the fob out of his pocket and unlocking the car. Opening the door. With one arm resting on the car roof, he finally looked at the gangling half-boy, half-man standing awkwardly next to him. 'How old are you?'

'Twenty.'

Doug felt ancient beside him. 'Young to be a father.'

'I suppose.'

'George looks to be quite a kid. Handsome face. Good set of lungs.'

A brief smile flitted across Roger's face. 'Yeah. Looks are his mother's. The lungs are probably mine.'

'Being a dad is about more than supplying DNA though. It's about being a protector and provider. A role model.' Doug thought of his own father, all too aware of the irony of his statement.

'Yeah, I know.'

'When you decide to man up to your responsibilities, give me a call.' He slid a business card out of his wallet. 'I'll find you a job.'

Roger's jaw dropped. 'You would? After all that shit … sorry, the stuff that just happened?'

'I know what it's like to think there's no way out. That this is your lot in life. But it isn't. There are always other options. Other directions you can go in. As long as you're prepared to take a leap of faith.' He nodded to his card. 'Your son needs a father. Show him, and his mother, you've got what it takes to fulfil that role.'

With that he eased into the driver's seat and started up the engine, wondering where the hell his own leap of faith was going to come from. Right now he felt so cornered he wasn't sure he'd see a way out even if it was labelled 'Exit' in big flashing lights.

* * *

Abby stared out of the window as the sleek, grey car shot off down their road, wondering what Doug had said to Roger. Wondering too, how such a mild-mannered man had managed to dispatch two thugs in less time than it took her to make a cup of tea. Most of all though, she wondered about ...

'Oh my God, Abs. The girls tell me you and Doug shared a hot smooch on the driveway.'

Exactly that. Abby wondered why he'd kissed her. 'We did, yes.'

Mandy shifted George onto her hip. 'And that's it? Can't have been much good if—'

'It was everything.' For a second Abby closed her eyes, remembering. It had been a kiss of gentle persuasion. Of heat and lust. Of dreams and fantasies.

When she blinked her eyes open again, Mandy's own eyes were nearly popping out of their sockets. 'Oh crap. You're doing what I told you not to, aren't you? You're falling for him.'

'I'm not.' *Liar*. 'What was all that with Roger?' she asked, deflecting the focus. 'I saw you dig him in the ribs.'

'I told him he needed to go and thank your boss for helping him out of a hole. Bringing those twits into our house. What the hell was he thinking? Oh, wait, he wasn't thinking, was he?' Her voice rose and she stared sadly down at her son. 'He never flaming thinks, does he, George? Sometimes I wonder why I still bother with him at all. He's such a loser.'

Abby studied her sister carefully. 'Maybe because you still have feelings for him.'

Mandy raised her eyes to the ceiling and let out a half-sob, half-sigh. 'Yeah, probably. So what does that make me?'

'Warm-hearted though slightly foolish?'

'I guess I should thank you for the slightly.' She planted a kiss on George's head. 'I hope this little man grows up better than his father.'

Abby remembered Roger's face when she and Doug had first entered the house. He'd looked terrified. Stunned and shocked by what he was witnessing. 'You know I've never been sure about Roger but maybe this has been a wake-up call for him. A sharp reminder of how he'll end up if he doesn't pull himself together.'

'We can only hope.' Once again she jiggled George. 'It's your man we should be talking about, though. All those quick, deadly moves. I couldn't believe it. He had those two gits on the floor without breaking sweat. I know they say still waters run deep, but wow.'

'Umm.' Abby flicked at a bit of fluff on her skirt, trying not to act like the girl with a big fat crush. 'I don't think he's as quiet as he first appears.'

'Especially not if he can kiss like you say.'

Oh God, she daren't go there again. 'I'm sure it was just a reaction to the moment. They say adrenaline can fire a man up. By the time he'd calmed down and had a drink he was pretty anxious to escape.'

'So would you be if you'd stumbled into this oestrogen-laden mad house for the first time.'

Abby had a sudden image of Doug being thrown into a den of lionesses, complete with frilly pink tutus, and burst into laughter. 'You're not wrong there.' She reached out to her nephew. 'Come on, little man. Let your aunt have a cuddle while your mum sorts out the tea.'

George threw his dumpy arms out and Mandy handed him over with a sigh of resignation. 'I guess that's fair. You and Batman did swoop in and save the day, after all.'

As Abby snuggled down onto the sofa with George, cooing over him and making him giggle, she wished men were as easy to fathom as babies.

Chapter Ten

The following day Doug bid Abby a rather formal good morning, and a further brief thanks when she delivered his coffee. In between those two high spots he was quiet and distant. As if the day before had never happened. As if he hadn't pulled her to him and kissed her until she'd been panting and breathless.

Each time she snuck a look into his office he had his eyes glued to his computer screen. While that was usual for most bosses, it wasn't for hers. She had a strong feeling Doug didn't like his job. When he spoke about it his eyes turned flat, a direct contrast to the way they'd lit up when she'd mentioned his paintings.

With a small sigh she crooked her head around the corner. There he was, still engrossed in his computer. Was he playing solitaire? Gambling? Watching porn? She'd like to bet he wasn't working. More like keeping his head down so she wouldn't go in and mention THE KISS.

Well, she'd given him a night and a morning to stew over it. Now it was time to talk.

Standing in his open doorway, she cleared her throat. 'Have you got a minute?' Her pulse scrambled as she became the focus of a pair of direct blue eyes.

'Sure.' He minimised whatever he'd been staring at on his screen.

'Do you mind if I close the door?'

His lids lowered a fraction, blocking whatever he was thinking, though Abby was hard pressed to read him even when he was looking straight at her. 'Be my guest.'

The atmosphere in the office changed from formal to crashingly intimate as the door clicked shut. Because she was terrified he might think she was about to jump him, Abby spoke quickly. 'I wanted to talk about yesterday.'

He leant back slightly on his chair. 'What about it?'

She took the coward's way and started off on the easy topic. 'First I wanted to thank you again. The way you took on those two guys, it was like something off the television. Even more shocking coming from someone ... umm.' She cursed her big mouth. She should have stopped at thank you.

He frowned. 'Someone?'

'Someone like you,' she blurted. 'And before you get all twitchy, I actually meant it as a compliment. You seem too calm and controlled to be a fighter.'

'Maybe it's the other way round.'

'What do you mean?'

'I'm calm and controlled because I let off my steam elsewhere. Like the training gym.'

An image of his back, complete with Geraldine's scratch marks, pinged unwanted into her mind. She bet that was another way he let off steam. 'Okay then.' She paused, inhaling a deep breath. 'Now we come to the second thing. Are we going to talk about that kiss? Or are you planning on pushing it under the carpet and forgetting about it?'

He cleared his throat. 'The latter.'

'I see.' It was what she'd expected, she reminded herself. 'So I don't even warrant an *I'm sorry, Abby, it meant nothing. It was a mistake.*'

'I can't say I'm sorry when I'm not.'

'You're not?'

'No. And a kiss like that can never mean nothing.' Her heart went into free fall as his eyes met and held hers. 'But it was still a mistake.'

'Because you're with Geraldine.' She could barely force the words from her throat.

'No. Geraldine and I are no longer … meeting up.'

Oh boy, this conversation was littered with bombshells. 'Why not?' Hastily she shook her head. 'No, sorry, that's none of my business.'

'Considering I kissed you yesterday I would say it is your business. Geraldine and I had run its course. I realised the night of that fateful offsite meeting.'

'Seems it was the day to call things off then. Deals and relationships.'

'Yes. Both had turned sour.'

Abby twisted her hands together, thinking about whether to say what was on her mind.

His eyes captured their movement and he gave her a tolerant smile. 'You don't normally hold back on giving me your thoughts.'

'No, I don't, but this is … well, it's very personal. I enjoy working here. I don't want anything to ruin that.'

A muted curse left his lips and he dragged a hand through his hair. 'Nothing you say will ruin our working relationship. I'm the one at fault here. I shouldn't have pushed myself onto you like that. I'm your boss. How could you say no?'

'I didn't want to say no.'

A slight twitch of his lips. 'I'm glad. But it doesn't make what I did right.'

'It does if I enjoyed it. Especially if I wanted you to do it again.' Hastily she bit her tongue, but of course it was too late. The words were out there.

It was several nerve wracking, ego busting seconds before he finally replied. 'I'm not going to do it again, Abby.'

'Oh.' Well, that told her. And what had she been doing, thinking he might, anyway? He was the startlingly handsome heir to a multimillion pound business. He was hardly going to make do with her when he was bound to have much better offers.

'Don't get me wrong,' he added. 'It's not that I don't want to. Just that it's better for you if I don't.'

Her heart stuck on the words *it's not that I don't want to*. 'Better for me?'

'I'm not the man you think I am.'

He looked so serious, she was hard pressed not to laugh. 'You mean you're really an axe wielding psychopath masquerading as the son of Lord and Lady Faulkner?'

Immediately his face slammed shut. 'Something like that. Now, if you've finished, I need to get on.'

Doug watched Abby make her way back to her desk, her stiff body language telling him all he needed to know about what she thought of his curt dismissal. Damn it, she had no idea how close to the mark she'd come with her throwaway comment. Masquerading as the son of Lord Faulkner was spot on, and though he'd never wielded an axe, he had used his fists. As for the psychopath, he might not be one, but he was a long way from the level-headed boss she believed him to be.

Turning back to his computer screen, Doug maximized the window he'd been looking at. He'd spent most of the morning going through photographs of his canvases and deciding which would go best together for his exhibition at Luke's gallery. As he clicked through his nearly-final selection he dimly heard female voices in the background.

Moments later Abby reappeared in his doorway. Reluctantly he minimised his screen again.

'Geraldine's here to see you. She hasn't got an appointment but she says you'll know what it's about.'

He winced at Abby's cool tone. 'Thank you.'

Her eyes gave away her feelings. She was annoyed Geraldine hadn't told her what it was about and suspected the matter wasn't work related. The devil in him couldn't help but feel oddly chuffed at her small display of jealousy. Though he wasn't going to encourage any relationship it was an ego boost knowing the attraction wasn't one-sided.

Geraldine swept into his office, instantly filling it with the scent of her perfume. As always she was dressed like sex on legs. He found he could appreciate the view without feeling any desire to re-kindle what they'd had. Sex for the sake of sex was no longer what he wanted. It wasn't really what she wanted either, he suspected.

She perched on his desk, giving him a full view of toned thigh wrapped in silk stocking. He knew she was wearing stockings not because he could see them, but because he knew her.

'Missing me yet?' she asked, her voice thankfully quiet.

'How can I be, when here you are?'

'Ah, but we both know what I meant.'

'And we both know we'd run our course. You deserve more, Geraldine.'

For a moment she lost her cool edge and her cheeks flushed. Then she chuckled and reverted to femme fatale again, slowly tracing his cheekbones with her manicured finger. 'Now where am I likely to get more than the sexy heir to the Faulkner empire?'

'Is that what I was to you?'

Finally she dropped her act, slipping off the desk and pulling over a chair so she could sit opposite him. 'You know you weren't. The sex was important, but the rest wasn't.'

'I thought so. You know one day you'll forgive yourself for falling in love with whoever broke your heart. Then you'll be ready to be swept off your feet by a man who deserves you.'

'But it won't be you.'

'No. You and I are too alike. We're both too bitter. Too obsessed with holding onto past wrongs.'

'I know who's done me wrong, but what about you? Who are you angry with?'

Doug shook his head, annoyed he'd let the conversation get this far. 'It's not important. What is important is that you wake up to what's happening and make some changes. Go and find yourself a man who wants you for your brain, your beauty, your bolshie personality. Not just sex.'

'I like the first two, but bolshie?'

He grinned. 'Some men will see it as an asset.'

'And what do you see as an asset, Doug? Big brown eyes and a ditzy personality?'

He'd spent a lifetime masking his feelings, so why this time did he fail? Geraldine zeroed in on his frozen face. 'Oh my goodness, I'm right, aren't I? You've got your eyes on Miss Disney out there.'

'I'm not discussing this,' he replied tightly, fumbling for his control. 'Not now, not ever. Tell me what you came here to say.'

Being the smart lady she was, Geraldine immediately got down to business. When they'd discussed and agreed her proposal she stood and ran a finger lightly down his arm. 'You know I won't say a word to anyone, Doug. I hope things work out for you, I really do. I may have been a bit harsh on Abby earlier and I'm sorry for that. You deserve someone, too.'

Doug tried to put his female issues behind him and finalise his canvas selection but his mind wasn't really in it. Though he was relieved he and Geraldine had sorted themselves out, he was terrified that if she could see his thing, for want of a better word, for Abby, then so could everyone else. Including Abby.

'I wasn't sure if you wanted a drink, so I brought you one just in case.'

She plonked the mug down in front of him.

He glanced at the coaster to his right, and then up at

her. With a huff she picked up the mug and placed it on the coaster.

'Thank you.'

She started to walk back to her desk.

'Abby, have I upset you in some way?'

She came to a halt and slowly turned round. 'No, of course not. Why?'

'Because you haven't smiled once today.'

'Neither have you.'

'Smiling isn't a usual part of my repertoire. It is yours.'

'Maybe I've not had very much to smile about today.'

He clearly wasn't going to get anything out of her using the indirect approach. 'Are you upset about Geraldine? Because she came to discuss a work issue. Nothing more.'

'Fine.' She shuffled her feet a little and scratched at the side of her nose. 'Actually, that's better than fine. You and she … well, you didn't seem to work together as a couple. She didn't make you happy.'

'No.' He wondered if happy, like smiling, was even in his repertoire. 'Before you go I want to talk to you about a couple of things. First I'd like you to set up a meeting next week with the heads of department you think need to be involved in the implementation of your packaging proposal.'

She blinked up at him. 'You're going to go with it?'

'Looks that way, though we need approval from the board, and in order to gain their approval we need to put a bit more flesh on the bones, hence this meeting. I'd like you to kick it off by going through your report.'

'I … well … that's good. I think.' She scribbled something onto her notepad. 'I mean, it's good you're considering the work I did. Great even.'

'But?'

'I'm not sure about the advisability of me delivering a presentation.'

'It's your work, Abby. You should take the credit.'

'Okay. In that case I'm going to take a deep breath and thank you for the opportunity. I'm sure it'll be fine. Everyone will be very happy to listen to your PA, who by the way has only been with the company just over two months, present her ideas on how Crumbs should change the packaging that's been the hallmark of the company for the last hundred years.' She bit into her bottom lip. 'Yes, it'll be just fine.'

'It will be. I'll be there, Abby. You won't be going into the vipers' nest alone.'

'Good to hear you calling it a vipers' nest. Very reassuring.' Her head bobbed and she gave him a wonky smile. 'And the second thing?'

'It's the item Geraldine came to discuss with me. I should have asked you to listen in, because it was actually all your idea, so I apologise I didn't.'

'What idea?'

'You told me on day one not to get rid of the three brands Taylors were keen to get their hands on. We didn't, though I confess my decision to abandon discussions wasn't entirely down to a desire to keep them all at Crumbs.' His mind flashed up an image of her terrified face when he'd burst into Teddy's room and his fist clenched automatically. 'Geraldine and I were discussing the revised marketing strategy for the brands, targeted at the younger generation who, I'm reliably informed, value traditional biscuit brands.'

Her face paled. 'Oh no, please don't tell me you've devised a whole campaign on one of my throwaway comments. I'd read it somewhere but I haven't looked into it properly. It might have been rubbish—'

'Relax, I'm not that naïve. Geraldine and the team have gone through all the previous research and conducted new research. They're convinced a focused campaign will prove beneficial.' He grabbed at a pen and Post-it note. 'I'm going to give you my log-in for the sales database. You can keep an eye on it and see for yourself if you were right.'

She stared at the paper for a few moments before taking it from him, careful not to touch his fingers. 'Wow, well thank you.'

'No, thank *you*. If you were right, and I highly suspect you were, then sales will go up and I'll look good.'

'And if I'm wrong?'

'It'll be one more stick for my father to beat me with, though I doubt he'll find it amongst the forest he's already gathered.' He nodded towards the log-in details he'd given her. 'Guard that with your life. Otherwise it won't just be my father breathing fire down my neck. It will be the IT department, too.'

Finally, *finally*, she smiled. The warmth from it seeped into every part of his body. 'I'll memorise it, then I'll eat it.'

His face cracked into a responding smile, proving smiling *was* in his repertoire. At least when he was with Abby.

Chapter Eleven

Abby warily opened the door to the meeting room. The moment she was spotted conversations stopped and all eyes turned on her. Though she recognised the faces there was only one person she knew to talk to. Geraldine. And the seat next to her was empty. Better to sit next to someone she didn't know, or someone she knew but was downright hostile? Oh, and who'd slept with her boss. She started to walk towards the grey-haired male head of packaging when Geraldine cleared her throat.

'Hello, Abby. Why don't you take the seat next to me and I'll introduce you to this motley crew.'

Realising there was no way she could refuse the olive branch, Abby slipped into the seat beside Geraldine while she made the introductions. Following a few curt greetings the others – all men – went back to their conversation. Geraldine, though, seemed determined to talk to her.

'Is our leader showing any signs of gracing us with his presence?'

'He'll be here in a minute. He's just finalising something.' She'd overheard him on the phone discussing arrangements for some do he was going to tonight. It crossed her mind that Geraldine might know where he was going – might even be going with him. Not that it bothered her, of course, because she and Doug weren't an item. Even though he'd given her the best kiss of her life.

'How are you getting on with him?' Geraldine's voice cut through her wayward thoughts. 'In your role it must be so important to get on with your boss. The rest of us only have to deal with our managers now and again but as Doug's assistant you must practically work on top of each other.'

Please, don't let her blush. 'He's very easy to work for but I don't see that much of him. He spends a lot of time in meetings.'

'Would you like to see more of him?' Abby felt the sting to her cheeks but before her shocked brain could think of a reply Geraldine put a hand on her arm. 'Sorry, rude question. It probably seems very catty of me to ask that considering Doug and I ... well, you know.'

'Yes.'

'We're no longer together, though. In fact we never really were, not in the true sense of the word. Does that help with your answer to my question?'

Thankfully Doug chose that moment to walk into the room. As Abby's heart gave its habitual lurch she almost laughed. It must be highly obvious to anyone who bothered to look at her that she wanted to see more of Doug in *every* sense.

'Sorry I'm late. Have you all met Abby?' When the room nodded, he continued. 'Good. Abby isn't here today as my PA, she's here as the brains behind the packaging proposal we're about to discuss.' Unconsciously Abby shrunk several inches down in her chair. 'Abby has a business degree and is keen to learn about how Crumbs operates, which is why I asked her to look at this project.' For the first time since he'd entered the room he looked directly at her and though his face was expressionless, his eyes were warm and encouraging. 'Abby, if you could please bring everyone up to speed with your ideas? Then we'll move on to how we should implement them.'

Before she could move, hard to when her muscles were frozen with nerves, one of The Three Stooges, as Abby had privately named the respective heads of packaging, manufacturing and sales, stirred in his seat.

'Just to clarify, there will be no discussion on the ideas themselves? Just the implementation?'

'That's correct, Richard. Your packaging team has already looked into this and the board turned down your proposal.'

Richard looked less than happy. 'No disrespect,' he said, flicking a brief, impolite glance in her direction, 'but we're being asked to accept the findings of a personal assistant on an area she has zero experience in, compared to our collective fifty odd years?'

As Abby died a thousand deaths, Doug narrowed his eyes. 'We're going to listen with an open mind to Abby's suggestions. After that, if there are any legitimate concerns we'll talk through them in a considered, non-judgmental fashion. If you see Abby as anything other than an astute businesswoman at the end of her presentation, you have prejudices that have no place in modern business.' He nodded again in her direction. 'Abby.'

He's not trying to big you up so you'll fail. She reminded herself of that as she pushed back her chair and walked to the waiting computer, willing her rubbery legs to function properly. He was showing them all he had confidence in her. It was up to her to prove it wasn't misplaced.

'After an introduction like that I'm almost afraid to open my mouth.' Taking a breath she gripped onto the table so nobody could see how much her hands were shaking. 'As those who know me will testify though, I can never go for too long without talking.'

Her gaze swept over her small audience. Three stony-faced men, a marketing head who appeared to have decided she wanted to be friends, and Doug. As her eyes met his she read the message loud and clear. *Show them what you're made of.*

Clearing her throat she clicked onto her first slide.

Doug listened to the way Abby handled the sometimes antagonistic questions and worked hard to suppress a grin. The three chauvinists were clearly out to prove that sweet looking young blondes had no place driving big business decisions. They'd yet to realise that behind the cute exterior

Abby was sharp and tough; Red Riding Hood maybe, but with the cunning of the wolf and the strength of the huntsman, too.

Only when the questions and objections finally petered out did he speak. 'Now we're all in agreement on the way forward, let's take a ten minute comfort break before we discuss implementation.'

As the men trooped out he touched Abby lightly on her arm. 'Wait a minute, please.'

Geraldine caught his gesture and gave him a sly smile before firmly shutting the door behind her.

All ready to tell Abby how well she'd done, the words died on his lips as he stared at her. She was loving this, he realised. It was there in her wide smile and pink cheeks, but even clearer in her dancing eyes. He'd never wanted to kiss a woman more, so he deliberately stepped away and went to turn off the computer. If only turning off his attraction was as easy.

'You enjoyed that, didn't you?' he finally asked.

'Would you think I'm crazy if I said yes?'

'No crazier than I already do.'

Her giggle bounced round the room and into his heart. This time Doug wanted more than to kiss her. He wanted to touch, hug, enclose her in his arms and let her vibrancy, her enthusiasm for life seep into his cynical bones.

'In that case I'll admit I enjoyed every minute. No, hang on, I enjoyed every minute after the bit when I nearly died from nerves while you were saying all those wildly flattering things.'

'All true.'

Her smile grew even wider. 'If you say so, Mr Boss. But wow, when they were firing off all those questions and I knew, just knew I had the answer. It was incredible. More satisfying than pizza, more enjoyable than a romcom, more of a buzz than a roller-coaster ride. It was like a sword fight and a chess game all rolled into one. And I think I came out on top.'

Her statement was without guile or arrogance. In fact there was a hint of wonder to it, as if she couldn't believe she'd handled it so well. 'You definitely came out on top. You handled the presentation and the questions like a true pro. I'm delighted you enjoyed it. Amazed, but delighted.'

'Why amazed? Because I'm only a PA—'

'Don't,' he cut in harshly, causing her to jump. 'Don't ever put yourself down like that,' he expanded more calmly. 'I'm amazed you enjoyed it the same way I'm amazed anyone would enjoy this business.'

'Because you don't.' It wasn't a question.

'You're right. I don't.'

'Then why do it?'

Good question. He kept quiet.

'Does it have to do with your father?' She was too sharp to lie to but really, what could he say? Thankfully she slapped a hand over her mouth. 'Sorry, I ask far too many questions. I really am a nosey bitch sometimes.'

'I've met a few bitches, and you're not one.' He glanced at the clock on the wall. 'If you don't escape now, you won't get that break.'

'Question neatly avoided because you're right, I do need to pee. My bladder is about to burst ...' She threw a hand over her mouth. 'Oh crumbs, that was too much information. I'm leaving now before I say anything more stupid.'

Once again, she left him smiling.

The meeting had gone better than she'd dared to hope. Well, apart from the bit during the break where she'd decided to discuss bodily functions with her boss. Again. Ten weeks after that mortifying interview though she'd not only presented her ideas to change the Crumbs packaging, she'd done so like a real pro, according to that same boss.

So why couldn't she be happy with that? Why did she

want Doug to be impressed by Abby the woman, as well as Abby the PA? If only he hadn't kissed her. Then she could have told herself it was all one-sided and she didn't have a hope of catching his eye.

Stop thinking about it!

Figuring a blast of fresh air would do her good, and hopefully take her mind off the fact that she fancied her boss, she took a stroll to the local deli in her lunch hour.

Gripping onto the sandwich, drink, apple and bag of crisps – why hadn't she paid for a flipping carrier? – she was legging it back to the office when she collided with a man walking down the corridor in the opposite direction.

'I'm so sorry … Roger? What on earth are you doing here?'

'Hey, Abby.' He nodded down to her, his fringe falling into his eyes. 'I wondered if I'd see you. Mandy said I was bound to, seeing as you're the boss man's secretary, but I guess you were at lunch when I went up.'

'You went up? To see *Doug*?'

'Well, yeah.' He scratched at the back of his neck. 'I mean I phoned him first. It's not like I just turned up.'

'But why did you need to see him? You're not in any trouble are you, because if you are you really can't go running to—'

'He told me to call him,' Roger cut in, looking miffed. 'After that day at your house. He said when I decided to man up to my responsibilities I should give him a call. So I did.'

'Right.' Abby's mind was about to blow. 'And? What did you talk about?'

'He's gonna give me a job.'

She stared at the lanky, tattoo-riddled father of her nephew. 'A job?'

'That's what I said.'

'Doing what?'

'I'll start in production, just basic stuff. If I'm any good he

116

said I can do a rotation in other departments to see what I enjoy most.' Her expression must have betrayed her because Roger gave an agitated shake of his head. 'Look, I won't let you or him down, I promise. I know you don't like me much and I can see why. I've been a total loser, but that's gonna stop now. I'll work hard and prove to Mandy I can be a good father. Maybe even a good boyfriend, husband, whatever, if it all goes well.'

Abby stared into his earnest eyes and wondered if maybe, just maybe, she could believe him. She desperately wanted George to grow up having a father he could at least like. 'I hope you mean what you say. If you do, you're welcome round for dinner anytime.'

'But by myself, yeah?'

'Exactly.' She studied him, trying to work out what their mum would have thought. Was he good enough for Mandy? He was good-looking with long fair hair and clear grey eyes. Average build but with a wiry strength. And a nice smile, she realised. One he was now using to good effect. If he managed to drag himself out of the hole he'd fallen in, perhaps he would be worthy of her sister. 'I guess I'll be seeing a lot more of you then.'

'I guess you will.'

After she'd said goodbye she walked slowly back to her desk, wondering about the man she worked for. A man who'd offered a job to a virtual stranger. Peeping her head round the corner to check he was free, she walked up to Doug's desk.

'Can I have a word?' The apple started to slip from her hands. Why the heck hadn't she had the sense to put her lunch on her desk before barging in on him?

He swung his eyes up from his computer. 'Of course.'

The apple slipped and bounced onto the floor, rolling under his desk. 'Oh crumbs, I'm sorry.' As Doug rose to his feet to pick it up she blurted. 'Why did you just offer Roger a job?'

'Ah.' Calmly he took the sandwich, drink and crisps from her hands and put them next to the apple on his desk.

'Yes. Ah. You can't give him a job just like that.' She clicked her fingers for emphasis.

Doug eased himself back into his chair. 'I think you'll find I can and I did.'

She let out a hiss of frustration. 'What I meant is you should think really carefully about this. He's been in trouble ever since I've known him and has never knuckled down to a proper job. Plus, if this is just you being charitable you need to know Spencers don't need or accept handouts. We can manage on our own.'

'I know you can.' His eyes remained direct and steady on hers. 'This isn't a handout. It's an honest day's pay for an honest day's work, with a probation period should either party not be satisfied.'

There was nothing there she could argue with. 'Okay.' Realising how churlish she sounded, Abby sighed. 'Sorry, I didn't mean to come across as an ungrateful cow. It's very kind of you to give him a job. I hope he doesn't let you down.'

'I'm sure he won't.'

'Right then.' She gestured awkwardly to her lunch. 'Time to enjoy my squashed sandwich and bruised apple.' As she picked them up, she glanced at him. 'And is it okay if I say thank you again? What with helping at the house last week and now with Roger ... it's really good of you.'

'It's no problem.' She nodded and was about to turn and leave when he surprised her with his next remark. 'If you feel the need to express your thanks in some way, you could always come to the gallery tonight.'

'You're showing some of your paintings?'

He gestured to the lunch she was clutching. 'Do you want

118

to put that down again?' When she dumped it all back on his desk he handed her an invitation card. 'My best mate, Luke, runs a gallery and he's foolish enough to exhibit my paintings from time to time. Only a select few will know they're mine, though. I paint under D. Winters and I'm a recluse. My alter ego, Douglas Faulkner, attends because he enjoys art.'

'So you go incognito and say gushing things about the paintings, while at the same time listening out for any nasty comments so you can bash those unappreciative punters over the head after they leave?'

His lips twitched. 'That's about right. Only I omit the head bashing. Too obvious.' Bright blue eyes found hers. 'Will you come? I should warn you, in the spirit of openness, that my sister Thea will be there. And Geraldine.'

'Oh.'

'Thea will be there because she's home from university and bored out of her mind. Geraldine will be there because I invited her weeks ago when I didn't think there would be any friendly face to talk to.'

'I see. But now you'll have two friendly faces. Plus your best friend. You don't really need me.'

'I may not need you but I'd very much like you there, if you'd like to come.'

Her heart gave a couple of loud thumps. 'In that case, I'd love to look at your etchings ... sorry, paintings.'

He let out a soft chuckle and she almost fainted with delight. 'Good. The invitation is for plus one so feel free to bring a friend. Oh, and you should know that Thea is one of the select few I mentioned who will know I'm the artist, along with Luke and yourself.'

'And Geraldine—'

'Isn't,' he cut in.

She walked back to her desk with a grin on her face.

Chapter Twelve

Doug stood in the gallery surrounded by his paintings and a bunch of pretentious people who thought they knew a lot about art. The things some of them had supposedly read into his paintings made his mind boggle. Did they really imagine he was that clever? He painted from instinct, from the heart. He didn't think about what he was going to paint next, it just came to him.

'You're supposed to be mingling,' Luke hissed as he brushed past him. 'Would it kill you to say hello to a few people? Maybe even encourage them to spend a stupid amount of money on one of your sodding paintings?'

'Feeling a bit tetchy, are we?'

Suddenly Luke's dour features brightened into a charming smile as he waved to someone over Doug's shoulder. 'So would you be if your major artist was a damn recluse who only managed to get his paintings to you a few measly days before the show.'

'Wow, you said all that with a smile on your face.'

'Some of us have learnt the art of smiling. You should try it some time.'

'You know what, Luke, you're turning into a real bitch.'

'I'll morph back into your mate if you convince a few of these people to buy a damn painting.'

He was about to move away but Doug held his arm. 'Don't dash off now. Geraldine's just arrived.'

'Has she now.' Doug watched as his friend eyed up the dark-haired lady sauntering towards them. 'You and she are definitely finished, yes?'

'Yes.'

'Finished as in it wouldn't cut you up to see her with another man?'

Doug shot Luke a glance. 'Don't tell me you've got the hots for her?'

Luke waggled his eyebrows. 'Hard not to fancy a woman who wears tight clothes and sexy red high shoes.'

'Well, I'll be damned.' Doug didn't have a chance to say any more as Geraldine was by his side, drowning him in her scent as she locked her arms around him and kissed his cheek. 'Doug, good to see you.' She took a step back and studied the man by his side. 'You too, Luke. It's been a while.'

And just like that, his mouthy friend suddenly didn't have anything to say. Smiling inwardly, Doug took a glass of champagne from a passing waiter and handed it to Geraldine. As she and Luke silently assessed each other he studied them. Would he be cut up if they started something? Was Luke a better fit for her than he'd been?

His friend finally found his voice. 'I seem to recall we last saw each other at the Crumbs Christmas party.' He flashed Geraldine a wicked smile. 'I gatecrashed.'

She held his eyes, her tongue darting across her blood red lips. 'We danced.'

'Yes.' Luke cleared his throat. 'I don't have any trouble remembering that.'

The air between them fizzed more than a shaken bottle of Coke and Doug decided to make his move. 'I'll catch you both later.' Neither of them so much as glanced in his direction.

He walked towards the window so he could keep a look out for Abby – yes, he was becoming besotted, yes all he'd done since he'd arrived was watch the door. He wondered if Luke would be feeling like this soon. If so, he hoped to God the man knew what he was getting himself into. Luke wasn't bitter and twisted like he was, but warm and open-hearted. Easily hurt. He'd be a much better match for Abby than Geraldine.

Doug watched in horror as the stem of the champagne flute he'd been holding snapped in his hands. Hastily he dropped the pieces into a nearby bin and grabbed a serviette to wipe the small cut on his palm.

'At last I find my brother.' Thea reached up to kiss his cheek. 'Hello there ... oh my, what have you done?'

He clenched his hand round the serviette. 'Nothing, just a small cut that keeps bleeding.' Refusing to think about his extreme reaction to the thought of Abby with Luke, Doug studied his favourite sister. 'You're looking good, Thea. No, better than that. You're looking happy.'

'And glamorous?'

'Of course. That's taken as read.'

She squeezed him round the waist. 'That's why you're my favourite brother.'

'Your only brother.'

'Details. So,' she said, leaning in so she could whisper in his ear, 'how many have you sold?'

Doug shrugged. 'Not a clue.'

Thea rolled her eyes at him. 'That's not the attitude. You should be circulating, watching out for those sold stickers. Where's Luke? I'm sure he'll be able to tell us.'

Doug glanced across the sea of heads to where Luke and Geraldine were still talking, their bodies so close they almost touched. 'I think he's busy at the moment.'

'Oh well, never mind.' She reached for a drink from one of the ever present waiters. 'You can entertain me instead with tales of espionage and cut-throat dealings in the biscuit industry.'

'Better still, you can tell me all about university.'

She immediately pounced on the subject, as he'd hoped.

And he kept his eye on the gallery entrance, waiting for the arrival of a slight blonde figure.

'Are you sure I look okay?' Abby asked her sister for the fifth time in five minutes.

Mandy looked up from the sofa where she was cuddling a dribbling George who didn't look anywhere near ready for bed yet. 'You don't look okay, Abs, you look great. A black trouser suit will take you anywhere and the pink silk blouse shouts *I'm glamorous* and perks it up for the evening.'

'I hope so.' She glanced down at herself, feeling more dull than glamorous. 'I've never been to an art show in a gallery. I've no idea what the dress code is. Doug should have told me.'

Mandy snorted. 'Sure, because men are so interested in discussing clothes.'

'He didn't have to discuss it. Just tell me what to wear.'

'He's a bloke, Abs. He'd have said *as little as possible.*'

'No, he wouldn't. Doug's not like that.' She could picture him now in his expensive suit, studying her with his cool blue eyes. 'He's more mature than that. More classy.'

'He'd have thought it then. Same difference.'

'He doesn't think of me that way.'

Mandy let out a sharp laugh. 'You told me he kissed you, right? Trust me, when a man kisses you he's already imagined you naked.'

'Oh God. Maybe that's why he said he won't kiss me again.'

Mandy laughed again, placing the squirming George on the floor, along with what looked to be half the contents of Toys R Us. 'Don't be daft. Doug fancies you, but he's struggling because he's your boss, that's all. If you really want to take it any further, you'll have to make the next move.' She eyed her speculatively. 'Is that what you want?'

The thought of taking things further with Doug, of kissing him again, made her legs so weak Abby had to sit down. 'My body is screaming yes. My head is telling me to stop being a stupid bimbo and set my sights on someone more attainable. A man who won't break my heart.' She pulled a funny face at George before focusing back on her sister. 'What about you, Mandy? How does your head and heart feel about Roger these days? You know he's got himself a job at Crumbs?'

'Yeah, I know. Thanks to your Doug.'

'He's not mine.'

'Maybe.' Mandy stared down at George, who was now grabbing at every toy he could lay his chubby hands on and shoving them into his mouth. 'For this little fella's sake both my head and my heart are in agreement. We hope Roger sorts himself out and comes back to us.'

'Then I'll wish for that, too.' Getting back to her feet, Abby bent to hug her sister. 'I'd better go. I'm half an hour late already.'

It was a fifteen minute bus ride to the gallery and Abby spent the entire journey riddled with nerves, wondering why she was putting herself through this. She had no clue whether what she was wearing was appropriate. She wouldn't know anyone when she got there, other than Doug and Geraldine. She didn't even know the first thing about art so if she was forced into a conversation, she'd end up looking like a total muppet.

She paused at the entrance to the gallery. Luke Wilson was written in silver across a graphite background and in the window discreet spotlights highlighted two large canvases. Even to her uneducated eye, she could see they were painted by the same artist she'd seen on Doug's office wall. Tentatively she pushed open the door and immediately caught Doug's eye. Right there in the blue of his gaze was the answer to why she was putting herself through this. It was because Doug had said he'd like ... no, he'd *really* like her to be there.

Her eyes flew over the crowd, bouncing from strappy dress to sequined top to plunging neckline, and she felt the blood slowly drain from her face. Oh no, the women were wearing party gear. Snazzy dresses and towering high shoes.

'Abby, thank you for coming.' Appearing magically at her side, Doug bent his head and planted a soft kiss on her cheek, enveloping her in his sophisticated aftershave.

He looked amazing in his tailored charcoal suit, but all she could think was how stupid she looked. 'Why didn't you tell me this was like a party?' she hissed. 'I'm dressed like I'm going to the flipping office. I should have worn a dress. I would have worn a dress, if you'd told me.'

'Hey.' He took hold of her hands and clasped them inside both of his. 'Calm down. You look perfect.'

'You're just saying that.'

His bright eyes flashed into hers. 'I don't say things I don't mean.'

Instantly heat scalded up her neck and over her cheeks. 'Then thank you. Though now you've made me blush, which is going to clash really badly with my pink shirt.'

His responding chuckle had her heart fluttering like a bag of butterflies. 'Come on.' He led her inside, clasping her hand and sending a bolt of awareness through her. 'Let's find you a drink before I introduce you to my sister. Then I expect the pair of you to wander round the paintings and gush in loud voices.'

He's good at doing that, Abby thought a few minutes later when she was studying his canvases with Thea. Able to calm a situation with little observable effort. He'd done it with Teddy the groper all those weeks ago, and again last week with Roger's thuggish mates. Tonight he'd taken her from nervously hyper to smoothly relaxed in the blink of an eye.

'I think this one's the best,' Thea declared in a loud voice. 'The juxtaposition of the dramatic, rising cliffs with the tiny figures makes a startlingly vivid contrast. This D. Winters is a genius. Don't you agree?'

She darted Abby a look full of mischief, forcing Abby to bite her cheek to stop from giggling. It was hard to believe this bubbly, fun-loving girl was Doug's sister. 'Absolutely,' Abby replied in as cultured a voice as she could manage. 'He takes the art of the juxtaposition to a new level.'

A warm hand clasped her shoulder. Startled, she turned to find Doug looming over them. 'Enjoying yourselves, ladies?'

'Oh yes,' Thea replied enthusiastically. 'We're extremely lucky to have this opportunity to see such rare talent close up. We were just expounding on the clever juxtapositioning—'

'Thank you, Thea,' Doug cut in dryly. 'Let's go and find Luke. Maybe he can keep you both out of trouble.'

They crossed the gallery and Abby nearly gasped out loud when she spotted Geraldine giving a more than cursory kiss to a good looking guy of average height and stocky build. Wow, she'd moved on quickly.

Behind her, Doug coughed and immediately the two lovebirds sprang apart. 'Abby, I'd like you to meet the gallery owner, and my occasional friend, Luke. You both know Geraldine.'

She'd been snogging Doug's *best friend*? This time Abby couldn't contain her gasp, and immediately Doug squeezed her hand. 'It's fine,' he whispered.

But how could it be? If that had been her best friend making out with her ex, and at her show to boot, Abby would have been spitting mad. It made her want to shake Doug. Tell him to stop letting people walk all over him. First his father. Now his lover and best friend.

With a coolness Abby could only dream of, Geraldine carefully wiped the traces of her lipstick from Luke's mouth. Then she gave them all a small smile. 'Actually, I was just leaving, so I'm afraid it's hello and goodbye from me. Thea,

Abby. I hope you enjoy your evening.' With a nod of her head and an elegant swish of her silk crimson dress, she was gone. Leaving behind her a waft of scent, and an awkward silence.

It was Doug who broke it. 'I take it she bought a painting, Luke. Or do you kiss all your customers like that?'

Luke didn't quite have Geraldine's sangfroid and he gave Doug a sheepish smile. 'Only the seriously hot ones.' He gave Thea and Abby a fake leer. 'So you two had better watch out.'

They all laughed and the atmosphere finally lost its strain. 'Look at you, all grown up now,' Luke said to Thea, giving her a hug. 'Last time I saw you must have been when you turned eighteen. All gangling arms and skinny legs. Oh and zits.'

Thea's elbow contacted sharply with his ribs. 'I didn't have that many spots, you rude man. And at least I never kissed my best friend's ex in front of him.'

'Ouch.' His eyes slid from Doug, to Abby and back to Doug. 'I accept the dig, though I have a feeling your brother isn't at all bothered by what he just saw. In fact, if I read him correctly, he's more relieved than anything.' Turning to Abby, he gave her a broad smile. 'Delighted to meet you. I hope this guy isn't giving you a hard time. He can be a real unsociable bugger at times.'

'Thanks,' Doug interjected dryly.

Though she'd taken an instant dislike to Luke when she'd seem him lip-locked with Geraldine, it was hard to maintain it now he was smiling directly at her. He looked friendly and easygoing; a direct contrast to Doug's quiet formality.

'I think I have the measure of Doug,' she replied, giving her boss a sly look. 'Furnish him with lots of coffee in the morning, don't get upset when he doesn't talk to you because that's his usual m.o. and don't expect a smile more than once a week.'

Luke burst out laughing. 'Oh boy, I think you've finally

met your match, my friend.' After giving Doug a hearty thump between the shoulder blades, he turned his attention back to Abby. 'I look forward to seeing a lot more of you, Abby Spencer, but right now I'd better go and drum up a few more sales.' He bent to whisper in her ear. 'We have to keep his Aston Martin on the road somehow.'

Thea excused herself to tag along with Luke, leaving Abby finally alone with Doug. 'Well.'

'Well,' he repeated.

'Are you really okay with Geraldine and Luke?'

'Yes.'

'Is that all you're going to say?'

'On that subject, yes.'

'Okay then, let's change it.' She cast her eyes around the room. 'I can't believe you painted all of these. When do you get the time?'

'Evenings. Weekends. As has already been pointed out, I'm an unsociable bugger.'

Unthinking she put her arm through his. 'Then treat this as the first stage in your social reintegration training. You can take me round each painting and tell me what you think the artist was trying to achieve.'

'I can tell you that now. He was trying to paint.'

'Ah, but why?'

'Because it's an escape.' When she looked at him questioningly he added quickly, 'And because he enjoys it. Still, if you want, I can give you some claptrap and you can nod knowledgeably.'

'Excellent. I'd love a chance to look intelligent. Take me to the first painting, maestro.'

Chapter Thirteen

Abby's arm was warm and comforting nestled through his as they took a tour round the gallery. He felt so at ease with her, he'd even tripped up and admitted he used painting as an escape. No wonder she'd looked so confused. The heir to the Faulkner estate hardly needed a blasted escape. He had everything he needed in life.

'When did you know you wanted to paint?' Abby asked, peering up at him.

'I've always known. As a child it was all I wanted to do.'

She laughed softly. 'I bet your parents have a huge collection of your early works they can't bear to throw out. Mum kept all mine and Mandy's stuff from school and I kept up the tradition for the others. All of which were seriously rubbish, I might add. Yours must have been awesome.'

Unconsciously he stiffened, squeezing Abby's arm harder than he'd intended. 'Sorry.' He forced his muscles to slowly relax again.

'It's okay.' She moved away a little so she could watch his face. 'It seems I hit a nerve though.'

'Yes.' He stared over at the sea of people, here to look at his art, and wondered what his parents would think if they knew. 'Suffice to say there is no collection of early works.'

'But why? Didn't you show any to your mum and dad?'

She had no clue, he thought, then wondered why he was so surprised. She came from a loving family. A normal family. They might have lost their mother but that bond, that sense of togetherness was still so strong even he'd felt it. 'My parents weren't interested, Abby.'

'I don't understand. How could they not be?'

'My father didn't like me painting.' He left it there, not

wanting to discuss old wounds; how his father had banned him from the art, forcing him into painting under the damn bed during the school holidays.

'How ridiculous.' Abby snorted. 'I know he's your father but seriously, he's like one of those dinosaurs we spoke about.'

The vision of Charles Faulkner's face on the body of a T-rex almost made him smile. Almost.

They stopped in front of another canvas. His personal favourite, it was a stormy scene of waves crashing against rocks. In the background, barely visible, were a series of cartoon-like figures in a cave, huddled round a roaring fire.

'This one reminds me of you,' she told him, staring at the painting. 'At first glance it's dark and severe but actually, if you look closely, it's quite sweet. Cosy.'

He blinked. 'Sorry?' He had no problem seeing the dark part, it was who he was so it was no wonder that's what he painted, but *sweet*?

'You heard me. You're not nearly as grumpy as you think, you know.' While he reeled from her statement her eyes followed a waiter holding a tray of canapés. 'I'm going to snag myself a few of those,' Abby said, pointing in the direction of the salmon blinis and other assorted, ridiculously small, fancy delicacies. 'Do you want any? Or were you stuffing your face with them before I arrived?'

'I might have carefully, and politely, nibbled a few.'

'In which case you'll probably still be hungry so I'll grab some for you, too. It'll look better if I spread it across two plates rather than load up one.'

As she headed for the tray with the focus of an Exocet missile, Luke appeared by his side. 'If you let that woman go, you don't deserve to be happy.'

'Let her go? I haven't even got her.'

'Oh, you have. I've seen the way she looks at you, all starry-eyed. Like a kid eyeing up a present under the Christmas tree and daring to hope it might be meant for her.'

'I'm a thundering long way from being any girl's dream gift.'

'Hey, you don't need to convince me of that, but beauty is in the eye of the beholder, or some crap like that. I'm telling you, she more than likes you, mate.'

'And I'm telling you, concentrate on your own sex life and keep out of mine.'

'Happy to. Speaking of which, I'm catching up with Geraldine after I close up here. Any tips you'd like to give me?'

'What?' Doug spluttered.

Laughing loudly, Luke patted him on the back. 'Only kidding. I'm not going to think about you and her together. Time we both looked forward, not back.'

'She'll eat you alive,' Doug muttered, feeling distinctly uncomfortable with the entire conversation. Him and Abby. Luke and Geraldine. Hell's teeth.

'I'm up for anything,' Luke replied cheerfully. 'And I see your Shetland pony – who, by the way is one heck of a lot sexier than I imagined – is heading this way so I'll make myself scarce. Don't balls this one up.'

Luke darted off, giving Abby a mock salute as he passed her, and Doug tried to unscramble his brain.

'He's funny, your friend,' she remarked as she handed him a plate overflowing with daft food items. 'And I mean funny ha ha.'

'Oh, he's a riot all right,' he replied, sticking a mini hamburger into his mouth. What was the point of these things? If you wanted a burger, you wanted a proper burger. Not one designed for Action Man.

'Umm, these are brilliant. I love all this finger food. You can experience lots of different flavours and tastes without piling in loads of calories.'

'My thoughts exactly.'

She levelled him a look, then burst into giggles. 'You hate them, don't you? Typical male. Not happy unless you've got a real mouthful.'

He nearly choked on his filo prawn. It wasn't hard to imagine the mouthful he really wanted, not when he gazed at Abby. Her eyes shone, her mouth laughed and her curves screamed at him from beneath her neatly-tailored suit.

By the time Abby had dragged him round all the canvases, the room was thinning. No doubt helped by the fact that Luke was almost shepherding people out. Doug didn't need to think too hard to work out why. His bet was on a dark-haired femme fatale with a penchant for wearing red.

Finally there was only him, Abby and Luke.

'Not a bad night's work,' Luke remarked as he set about his closing shop ritual. 'Only two unsold, and they've got people interested. Did you enjoy it, Abby?'

'Surprisingly, yes.'

'You weren't looking forward to it?'

'Oops.' She shook her head. 'Sorry, I didn't mean that to sound so negative. I was just a bit nervous, that's all. It's my first gallery showing.' She pointed at her suit. 'Hence my inappropriate clothing.'

'Not inappropriate at all. I think you look a knock out.'

'It's time we were going,' Doug cut in sharply. Too sharply, he realised as Abby flashed him a startled look.

'Oh, right, I'll just fetch my jacket.'

When she was out of earshot he hissed at Luke. 'Geraldine you're welcome to. Abby isn't up for grabs.'

Luke, the bastard, simply smirked. Then went on to make a great show of helping Abby into her jacket. Thanking her for coming. And kissing her goodbye.

Doug almost marched her out of the gallery.

'Phew,' she exclaimed when they hit the cool evening air. 'That's better. It was getting pretty hot in there.'

He didn't think she was referring to Luke's overdone charm, but he couldn't be sure so he stuck with a noncommittal grunt.

'I guess this is where I say goodnight. Thanks for inviting me and, well, I'll see you tomorrow morning.'

She took a step away before he managed to tug her back. 'Not so fast. I'll walk you to your car.'

'That'll be hard, because I came by bus. I didn't know how easy it would be to park, what with all these people flocking to see your art.'

'Then I'll take you home.'

'No, don't be silly. I'm fine with the bus. It's not far.'

Putting his arm around her waist he propelled her towards his car. 'I'm not fine with you catching the bus.' He flashed his remote and the Aston winked at them. 'My car's a lot more comfortable.'

Doug held the door open for Abby and she slid in as gracefully as she could. For the first time that evening she was grateful for her trousers. A dress would have ended up round her ears by the time she'd wriggled into the luxurious but very low seat.

She watched the handsome man walking round the bonnet to the driver's side. Her boss, but was there more between them than that? The way he'd greeted her tonight, as if he'd been waiting for her to arrive, gave her hope there could be, but the man who climbed into the driver's seat was too hard to read. She'd only just met Luke and yet she felt she already knew him. She'd worked for Doug for nearly three months and still didn't know him at all.

'It's safer, too,' he remarked as he eased into the road.

'What's safer?'

He glanced sideways at her. 'My car is safer than taking the bus.'

'The bus is less likely to be car jacked by gun-toting thieves or be involved in a high speed collision.'

'I don't speed.'

'Good, you've halved my chance of getting hurt.'

'Abby.' Frustration throbbed in his voice.

'Yes?'

'I don't like to think of you catching a bus late at night.'

He came to a stop at the traffic lights and she snuck a glance at him. He looked more unapproachable than ever, cool eyes and a face made sterner by the effect of the shadows hollowing out his cheeks.

'I'm used to taking care of myself, Doug. You don't have to worry about me.'

For the rest of the journey he remained quiet and Abby stared out of the window, acutely aware of him. At times strong and silent, others more dark and brooding. Always impossibly attractive.

When he pulled into her drive and turned off the engine, the car descended into a still silence. Now she could hear herself breathe. Feel the warmth from his body as he sat, motionless, next to her. 'Right then, thanks for the lift.' Reaching down, she clasped her handbag. 'You really didn't need to bring me home but you were right, this was a lot more comfortable than the bus. Plus I'm back earlier, so I might even get into work on time tomorrow.' She was jabbering. 'Anyway, thanks again.'

'Abby,' he said heavily.

'Sorry, I'm talking too much. I can't seem to help myself. I talk a lot anyway, which I'm sure you've noticed already, but it gets worse when I'm nervous.'

He shifted in his seat so he was facing her. 'Do I make you nervous?'

She opened her mouth, closed it, then took in a deep breath. 'When we're in the office no, but right now, yes.'

'Because you're afraid I might kiss you again,' he stated softly.

'Yes. But I'm more afraid you might not.'

He let out a low groan and placed a hand on either side of her head before drawing her towards him and planting a tender kiss on her forehead.

'You can kiss me on the lips, if you want to.' She felt the heat of his breath on her face as he exhaled deeply. 'Of course if you don't want to, that's fine, too.'

'I do want.' But he dropped his hands and leant back in his seat.

'Just to be clear, because I know I'm incredibly subtle, that was an invitation.'

His lips curved but his expression remained guarded and his eyes ... oh wow, his eyes looked so sad. 'I appreciate the invitation, you've no idea how much, but I can't accept. I'm sorry.'

'Okay then.' And though as rejections went, it was a kind one, it still stung. 'Well, thank you again for inviting me.'

'That's the third time you've thanked me this evening.'

'Third, huh? I must have had a good time.' Because she couldn't help herself, she reached out and trailed a finger down his cheek, slightly rough with stubble, and then over his lips, achingly soft. His eyes fluttered closed before he halted her progress with his hand. 'You're a hard man to understand, Doug Faulkner.'

'I know.' His eyes opened again, the blue of his gaze making her breath catch. 'I'm sorry.'

Unable to hold his look she glanced down at their entwined hands. Long and slender, the fingers wrapped around hers held both strength and artistry. 'At least now I can see why you don't enjoy being the man in the suit in the office. Not when your heart and soul are tied up with your paintings.'

He gave her a tired looking smile. 'I get far more pleasure out of painting, yes.' Drawing her hand towards his lips, he kissed it. 'Though recently I've begun to enjoy going into the office, too.'

Her heart jumped against her ribs. 'Recently?'

'The last few months.' After giving her hand a final kiss, he let it go. 'Goodnight, Abby.'

She didn't want to leave. Talking to him, cocooned in the intimacy of his car, was far more appealing than going back to her empty bed. But the finality of his tone told her the evening was over. Reluctantly she opened the door. 'Goodnight, Doug. And—'

'Thank you?' He shook his head, a glimmer of a smile playing around his lips. 'I'll see you tomorrow.'

She walked to the front door and undid the lock but didn't go in. Instead she stood on the doorstep and watched as his tail lights disappeared down the lane. For a man who kept telling her he wasn't going to kiss her again, he sure sent out mixed signals.

Chapter Fourteen

Doug knew he was holding himself too tensely so he took in a deep breath and tried to relax his shoulders. It was only a board meeting. His father would be there as chair, plus the cronies he'd made directors, but there would be some friendly faces: the head of finance; his mother; Abby, who'd be taking minutes when in reality the packaging idea he was about to propose was all hers.

Abby. She'd unknowingly caused him no end of sleepless nights since the evening of his show a few weeks ago. Nights spent tossing and turning and dreaming of scorching hot sex ... with his personal assistant. How many times had he woken up sweating, hugely aroused and utterly disgusted with himself?

'Are you ready?'

Abby appeared from her alcove and God help him, it wasn't just his groin that stirred when he stared into her big brown eyes. It was his heart. She wasn't another tough-as-nails Geraldine, though. Abby was a woman who looked for love, not sex. A woman easily capable of being hurt.

He pushed back his shoulders and rose to his feet. 'I'm as ready as I'll ever be.' After shrugging on his jacket, he slipped his pen into his pocket and followed Abby out to the boardroom, trying not to imagine he was walking to the gallows. Still, if he was, there was no finer last sight in this world than Abby's cute backside.

'I sent the proposal to them all last week so there shouldn't be any grumbles about not having had enough time to read it,' she told him, all efficiency as they entered the room and she opened up her laptop. 'I'll set the presentation up on the computer. When you're ready I'll go and collect our visitors from the coffee area. Oh, bugger.'

Her exclamation was a reassuring blast of normality. 'Anything I should worry about?'

She gave him a sheepish smile. 'I may just have left the stick containing your presentation on my desk.'

'Nothing serious then.'

'Good job I'm so efficient there's time for me to dash back and get it, load it up and still collect our visitors on time.'

'It's why I employed you.' She was about to dart off when he called her back. 'Abby, I'm sorry it's me presenting your work today.'

She rolled her eyes at him. 'Blimey, I'm not. It was bad enough talking your team through it. Presenting to your father? Oh no, you're very welcome.'

'Still, it's your work and I'm not giving you credit for it. It rankles.'

'If you told him it was my idea he'd throw it out on principle. At least this way it will stand on its own merit.'

'I hope so.' Doug had a horrid feeling his father would shoot it down for the same reasons Abby had given. Because he'd think it was his idea.

A nanosecond after Doug had uttered his concluding sentence, his father threw his pen onto the table.

'I've never heard anything so preposterous,' Charles Faulkner announced loudly.

Doug inhaled slowly and counted to ten. 'Which aspect, in particular, was preposterous?'

'All of it. Haven't we already thrown out a proposal on changing the packaging? Or did you think we're so senile we'd forget that little fact?'

Doug straightened the notepad in front of him, only returning his attention to his father when he was certain he wasn't going to leap up and grab the old man by his blasted tie. 'Just so we're all clear, which aspect of changing our packaging for something less expensive to buy and ship is preposterous?'

Silence echoed round the room and as he flicked his eyes over the group he wondered how many were metaphorically licking their lips, sensing a fight. His father's cronies definitely, his mother he wasn't so sure. Abby, definitely not.

A flush crept up his father's neck. 'The aspect of you meddling in nearly a century of tradition is preposterous.'

'Is it the meddling in tradition that riles you, or the fact that it's me doing the meddling?'

'Don't get smart with me.'

'I'm trying to understand what the objections are.'

'You're trying to act the big guy in front of this group, when we all know you don't hold any real power,' he snapped. 'You're my puppet. A younger face to prove to the outside world we're a dynamic company with a future. I still hold the majority of the power and I make the decisions.'

By his side, Doug heard Abby's sharp intake of breath. How wonderful to be humiliated not only in front of the board, but also the woman he liked. Really, really liked.

But he bottled his anger, as he always did, and placed a hand in his trouser pocket, feigning nonchalance. 'Then tell me this. How can you prove to the world that Crumbs is a dynamic company if you won't change to more modern packaging?'

Abby watched the interplay between father and son with mounting incredulity. How could Charles Faulkner talk to his son like that? Though from the look of the faces round the room, it wasn't the first time they'd heard Doug being called a ... puppet. She winced. A managing director without any power? It just didn't make sense why Charles would do that. Then again, why was Doug *letting* his father treat him like this?

'You think putting our biscuits into crappy cardboard is a dynamic move?' Charles thundered. 'What poppycock. Customers want a biscuit packet that matches the quality of the contents. They want packaging that ensures when they open it, the damn biscuits are still whole.'

'And not in crumbs.'

A dozen pair of eyes instantly swung in her direction and Abby realised she'd said the words out loud. *Please God, open a hole in the floor so I can jump into it.* When it didn't happen, she tried to smile. 'Sorry. I just thought it was funny that the company is called Crumbs, yet you're anxious to avoid them.'

'You think this discussion is *funny*?'

Bugger, bugger, bugger. 'No, I think the packaging choice for Crumbs is a very important, serious issue. Which is why Doug has spent so long researching into it. Talking everything through with the teams invested in this decision; marketing, sales and manufacturing, before presenting the results to you today. What seems odd to me, though certainly not funny, is why you're so opposed to his proposal?'

Charles's face changed from red to purple but Abby was too fired up to care. How dare the pompous twit belittle all their efforts?

'Market research has shown that the most important people, the current and future customers, prefer the cardboard packaging Doug's just outlined to the old-fashioned tins.'

Charles thumped his fist on the table. 'If I want the opinion of a glorified typist, I'll ask for it. Otherwise, if you value your job, I suggest you shut that motor mouth of yours.'

Abby held his gaze and nodded, once. She wasn't scared of him. Guys who thought they could get what they wanted by bullying didn't faze her because she knew them for what they were. Men terrified of losing their power. Of getting old. But as she did want to keep her job and, more importantly, didn't want to embarrass Doug any further, she kept quiet.

Gradually Doug steered the discussion onto a more productive footing and by the end of the session he'd even gained agreement to trial the new packaging on some of the more low profile brands.

There was another tedious half hour of board business before the meeting was officially called closed and everyone began to drift away. As she cleared up she saw Doug give his mother a very formal goodbye kiss on the cheek.

Then he closed the door, and it was just the two of them.

'Well, that was a real eye-opener. Are board meetings always this much fun?'

The man walking towards her didn't look like he thought anything was fun. She'd never seen him looking so furious. Oh the cool mask was still in place, but there was no hiding the fury in his eyes as they glared at her. 'Don't ever do that again. If I need you to come to my rescue, I'll ask you.'

His words were so clipped, so cold, she felt telltale pinpricks at the back of her eyes. 'Okay, fine. I apologise for sticking up for you.'

She grabbed blindly at the stack of papers she'd collected, determined not to cry in front of him. Not over something so stupid. Biting at the inside of her cheek she collected everything she needed before walking over to where he stood waiting by the door, jacket slung over his shoulder.

'I can understand why your ego doesn't want a girl defending you,' she said as she drew close, 'but why didn't you do it yourself? Why let your father bully you?'

He flicked her a hooded look. 'It isn't wise to comment on matters you don't understand.'

His frosty tone sparked her temper. 'Do you ever get really angry, Doug? So angry that you scream and shout? React instinctively, without thinking?' When he continued to stand impassively, his hand on the doorknob, she carried on. 'I do, lots of times. I did today, when your father tried to belittle me. At that moment I didn't give two hoots who he was, or where we were. I wasn't going to let a man like that intimidate me, or make me look a fool. Nobody should allow another human being to talk to them like that. Nobody.'

'Your sermon is much appreciated.'

The urge to shake him, to ruffle his composure, bubbled inside her. 'Come on, drop the guard for once. Stop standing there like a stiffly starched shirt and react like a real man.'

The twitch in his jaw muscle told her she was getting to him. 'Are you trying to bait me?'

'Perhaps. How am I doing?'

'Too well.'

'Good. Maybe I should keep going.'

'That's enough,' he interrupted shortly, yanking open the door, tension fizzing off him. 'I need to go. I'm late for an appointment.'

She glanced at her watch. 'It's half five. I don't have a record of anything in your diary.'

'It's outside work.'

As he charged off down the corridor Abby struggled to keep up with him. 'Look, I'm only trying to help. It would do you good to shout a bit, get everything off your chest. It's not healthy to keep it all festering inside you. It's like a boil, ready to erupt.'

'First the sermon, now the psychological assessment. It would appear you're on a roll.' He marched into his office, unplugged his computer and slid it into his bag, before swiping his car keys off his desk and heading back out.

'Doug, wait, please.' Her heart pounded as she looked at his tense face, the strain of all that control evident in every one of his beautiful, rigid features. 'I'm worried about you. Are you sure you're in the right frame of mind for going out?'

The edge of his lip curved upwards in something closer to a sneer than a smile. 'For where I'm going, my frame of mind is exactly right. Have a pleasant evening.'

As the door to his office banged closed Abby trudged slowly back to her desk. And burst into tears.

Doug knew his curt dismissal had upset Abby but he couldn't stay in that bloody building a minute longer. Besides, he was still reeling from the way she'd marched to his defence in the meeting. It mortified him that she'd felt the need to face up to his father, clearly believing he didn't have the guts to do it himself. There'd been a time when he had done, but he wasn't going to drag that memory out again in a hurry.

Slowly the shame of the way he'd spoken to Abby washed through him. He'd let his self-disgust morph into anger and then directed it at the one person who'd been on his side. It wasn't her fault that in standing up for him she'd made him appear pathetic. Not her fault that it was precisely because he *was* pathetic that he was in this shitty situation.

When he pulled up outside the gym he found Luke already waiting against his car, arms crossed. 'Too much of a hot shot to make it here on time, eh?'

'Don't you bloody start,' Doug muttered, hauling his bag out of the boot. 'I'm ready to throttle someone and it might as well be you.'

'Had a fight with the Shetland pony?'

Doug shot him a look. 'Shut it.'

Luke strode ahead and stopped at the doorway, blocking his path. 'Either you drop the pissy attitude and we train like we planned, or I take you on right here, right now. Your choice.'

Doug clenched his fists, itching for a fight. But it wasn't the guy who stood in his way that Doug desperately wanted to thump. Slowly he let the air out of his lungs. 'Let's train.'

They entered the locker room in silence and began to get changed.

'You ready to talk about any of it yet?' Luke asked finally as he secured his belt round his judo style gi.

'No, but I might be when I've choked you into submission.'

'Not in this lifetime, buddy.'

Doug followed his friend out of the changing room and onto the mats. 'How did it go with Geraldine? Enjoying yourself with my cast off?'

And suddenly Luke was barrelling into him.

A punishing hour later, the heated sparring session – or rolling as they called it in BJJ – being followed by a more disciplined training session, they sat next to each other on the bench getting their breath back. Doug felt drained. Drained not just of energy but also of the burning fury and resentment that had propelled him here. Right now, for a short while at least, he felt at peace.

'Do you think you're ready for next month?' Luke asked, after glugging back half a bottle of water.

In a moment of utter madness, Doug had entered the Surrey BJJ open. 'No, but we could train every night between now and then and I'd still not be ready.'

Luke chuckled. 'Yeah, well, I told you at the time you were nuts. You're too competitive, that's your trouble.' He glanced at him. 'So what happened with your father today?'

'How do you know it was him?'

'Because every time you see him you turn into a boorish thug.'

'Thanks.' He wiped at the sweat on his face. 'He did his usual let's-humiliate-my-son act.'

Luke snorted. 'He's done that plenty of times before. Why were you so wound up this time?'

'Abby was in the meeting. And rather than sit and listen to him quietly—'

'She stuck up for you.'

'Yes.'

'Which made you feel even worse.'

'Score another point. It wasn't humiliating enough that my father told the board my preposterous idea would never get approved because he holds all the power and I'm just his puppet. No, I also had to have my twenty-four-year-old, five foot nothing PA sticking up for me because she clearly thinks I haven't got the balls to do it myself.'

'Ouch.' Luke leant forward, his eyes swimming in sympathy. 'I don't suppose you've considered telling Abby about what's going on, have you?'

'Of course I haven't.'

'No, because that would mean letting someone in, and you can't have that, can you? You are Douglas Faulkner the recluse. The man who walks alone.'

'Bugger off.'

Luke gave him a long, considering look. 'You know that none of what you've just told me would hurt so much if you weren't falling for her, don't you?'

Doug glared back. 'Bollocks. You've got enough on your hands with your own love life. Don't go meddling in mine.'

Grinning, Luke got to his feet. 'You're not wrong there. Geraldine is ... well, quite a girl. Not as tough as she appears, though. I think the bravado is a front and I'm looking forward to knocking it down and finding the real woman underneath.'

'Good luck with that.' Doug swiped his towel off the floor and followed Luke into the changing room where he went through the mechanics of showering and getting dressed. All the time his mind kept playing Luke's words over and over in a loop in his head. *None of it would hurt so much if you weren't falling for her.* What if the guy was right? What was he supposed to do about that?

Chapter Fifteen

She'd begun working at Crumbs in early March, when frost had still been an occasional visitor. Now it was summer. An unbelievable sixteen weeks had come and gone, during which she'd got to grips with her job, and fallen hard for her boss.

The first she was proud of. The second, not so much.

With a sigh she sat back on her chair and shut her eyes, her mind instantly conjuring a mental image of the man sitting round the corner. Wildly handsome face, dark slightly dishevelled hair, striking blue eyes. She shouldn't have fallen so quickly, so easily, but surely it was hard for any woman to resist that combination? Especially when the man beneath the dramatic looks was every bit as attractive. Kind – giving Roger a job was proof of that. Brave, at least when it came to protecting others. Funny, when he allowed himself to relax. He was also deeply unhappy, working in a job he didn't like, for a father he also didn't seem to like. All for reasons he clearly didn't want to share.

What hope did she have of getting close to him when he didn't want to let her in?

Since their altercation in the boardroom, Doug had become even more distant. In fact his manner had been so excruciatingly polite that if he said 'would you mind' to her one more time, she was going to scream.

The sound of a polite cough made her look up with a guilty start. Straight into a pair of cool blue eyes.

'Is now a convenient time for you to discuss the line extension project?'

That's a new one. With a sigh she reached for the report she'd spent the last two weeks working on and followed him into his office. As she took the seat opposite him she stared mutinously at his expressionless face and thought, sod it. 'Aren't you going to ask if I *mind* taking you through the report now?'

His eyebrows shot up to his hairline. 'Sorry?'

She flung the report onto the desk. 'For the past few weeks you've preceded every request with a *would you mind*. It's been *would you mind* setting up this meeting. *Would you mind* phoning Mr Blogs. *Would you mind* peeling me a grape.'

'I'm pretty certain I didn't say the last one.'

'Not yet, maybe.'

Slowly he reached into his jacket pocket for a pen, taking so long that Abby's teeth actually began to ache. 'Do you have a problem with me being polite?' he asked finally, setting the pen down in front of him.

'Yes. As a matter of fact, I do.'

Surprise flared briefly in his eyes. 'Why?'

'You've never treated me like a PA, Doug. Not even from day one. You've always treated me more as ... well, a person you liked. Except for the last few weeks.'

He steepled his fingers as he considered her question in his frustratingly slow manner. 'So am I not allowed to like you *and* be polite?'

She resisted – barely – the urge to strangle him. 'You're missing the point. You don't have to mind your p's and q's around people you're supposed to like. *Abby, I'm ready to go through the report now.* That's what you'd have said a few weeks ago. Not the cringe-inducing *is now convenient*, or the dreaded *would you mind.* You know I'd be really happy with *Abby drag your fat arse in here and take me through that damn report.* Though I'd prefer if you dropped the fat part.'

'I see.'

'Do you? Do you really?'

He let out the ghost of a smile. 'No, not really. I was just saying that to shut you up.'

147

Finally, a glimpse of the old Doug. 'That wasn't very polite.'

'I was told off for being polite. Now, sit on your definitely-not-fat arse and take me through your damn report.'

Laughter burst from her and when she looked up she found Doug was laughing, too. And oh boy, if she could fall for the distant, sad man, how was she supposed to hold back when the relaxed version showed up? Her eyes drifted to his mouth and all she could think was how much she wanted to kiss him.

He caught her eye and everything seemed to go into slow motion as they stared at each other. She was dimly aware the laughter had stopped. Acutely aware of the blue of his eyes as they burnt intensely into hers. But just when she was sure he was going to do something about the sexual energy that fizzed between them, he broke the contact.

'So.' He cleared his throat and started again. 'What are your recommendations?'

Just like that, he was all business again. *But you know he's still attracted to you.* There could be no mistaking the heat in his eyes just now. He might not want to acknowledge it, but it was there and they both knew it.

'Abby?'

'Oh crumbs, yes, the project.' With a huge effort of will she unscrambled her brain. 'As, umm, as you can see, I considered the usual line extensions a biscuit company might consider. The healthy option ranges, which could be low sugar, low calorie or less fat. The low-cost budget range and the luxury range. I'm not convinced any of these fit with your current market position, though. When people think of Crumbs they think of fine ingredients, which already puts it at the luxury end of the market. Bringing out a budget brand wouldn't align with that, nor would a healthy option line because consumers look to Crumbs for an indulgence. In my opinion

Crumbs should bring out a range of savoury biscuits that fit with its current brand values of quality and excellence.'

'Cheese biscuits.'

'Yes, but I'm not talking crackers,' she added hastily. 'These would be high end savoury biscuits. Olive and sundried tomato. Parmesan and rosemary. That type of thing.'

Her words trailed off and the room descended into silence. Though it wasn't unusual in her dealings with Doug, it was unnerving. Her heart began to thump and she found she was twisting her hands. Oh God, maybe he hated it ...

'Wow.'

Her head shot up. 'Wow?'

'I believe that's what I said.'

'You mean you like the idea?' How could she tell when his face was so devoid of any expression?

'That is generally what the term wow implies.'

Jeeze, even when he was paying her a compliment, he was frustrating. 'Well, I'm glad you feel that way.' Torn between relief that he liked it, and irritation that he was so flipping tight-lipped, she pushed her chair back and stood up. 'Perhaps when you've had a look through the report you'll have a few more questions. I mean, that is usually what happens in these situations, isn't it? Questions asked and answered, a bit of a discussion.'

When he still said nothing, Abby gave up. It was only when she reached the door that he finally spoke. 'I don't have the questions, Abby.'

She halted and glanced back at him. 'What do you mean?'

He shrugged awkwardly. 'I mean you're so much better at this than I am.'

Her jaw dropped. 'Oh, no—'

'Oh, yes,' he interrupted. 'I can manage the negotiations, the people and the day to day stuff, but when it comes to marketing or long term strategy I'm like the carp dumped by the side of the lake, flapping his tail and desperately hoping someone will shove him back where he belongs.'

'In front of a canvas.'

He gave her a resigned smile. 'If I'm honest, yes.'

She took a few steps back into his office. 'Then why work here?'

His eyes fell to his desk where he picked up the pen and started to play with it. It was a habit, like steepling his fingers, that Abby presumed gave him time to think. 'It's a family business, and I'm family.'

'You don't have to manage it to be involved. Your mum doesn't. Thea doesn't.'

'They don't have a Y chromosome.' He held up a hand. 'You don't need to lecture me on equality, but it's also fair to add that they aren't interested in the business, either.'

But neither are you. Abby wished she knew what was going on because whatever it was, it was making Doug extremely unhappy. Each time she'd asked though, she'd received an evasive answer so there was no point pushing on a locked door. 'Well, thank you for the compliment. Coming from someone whose opinion I value, it means an awful lot.'

'You know you're wasted as a PA, don't you?'

Her heart thumped. 'Are you trying to get rid of me?'

He let out a sharp laugh. 'Of course not. You're my ace up the sleeve. As long as you keep giving me your ideas, I look good.' His expression sobered. 'It's not right though. I'm happy for you to get as involved as you want here, gain some experience, but you should be working in an environment where you get credit for your ideas. I'll do what I can, but my father is a chauvinist. He tolerates Geraldine because she came from a rival company with a stack of references.'

'And I'm a secretary who's already pissed him off, twice.'

'You're a very bright woman with a business degree and a

rare ability to think outside the normal parameters. Pissing off a small-minded misogynist is a credit to you.'

A warm rush of pleasure flooded through her. Nobody had ever told her she was clever, or had such belief in her ability. Mum had loved her, but had been too busy bringing up a family, and then tackling cancer, to talk about school or careers. Following her death the focus had been on keeping the family together and muddling through. Her dad had tried hard, but between the garage and her four younger sisters – one of whom had become a single mum – his time, and his attention, had been spread very thin.

Yet here was this man, an extraordinary artist and, despite what he thought, a damn good businessman, telling her she had what it took. 'Thank you.' Somehow she squeezed the words past the ball of emotion in her throat. 'I've missed this.'

'What?'

'You and me, talking. We used to have such a good rapport before ... before ...'

'Before I started acting like a prick.'

His wry, self-mocking smile caught at her heart. 'You were cross with me. I understand. Having your PA mouthing off to your father wasn't cool. Neither was that same PA winding you up afterwards. I'm sorry.'

'Don't be. I was angry at myself, not you. You were an easier target. *I'm* sorry.'

She grinned. 'So, we're good then?'

He inclined his head and she caught the twinkle in his eyes. 'We're good.'

Feeling fuller somehow, more energised, she walked back to her desk and focused on her work.

Doug was finding it hard to concentrate. Instead of the reports he was supposed to be reading, all he could see was

Abby's face when he'd told her how bright she was. As if he'd given her a rare and expensive gift, rather than simply telling her the truth. He hadn't even mentioned her other qualities: exuberance, warmth, kindness and the most phenomenal strength of mind. He'd tried hard to put their relationship back on a more professional footing these last few weeks, and she'd not shied away from letting him know what she'd thought of it.

What was he going to do about his, at times overwhelming, need to put his arms around her and kiss her? It was like a nagging ache, always there.

He was knocked out of his self-absorption by the buzz of his mobile phone. A quick check of the caller ID, and he grimaced. 'Mother.'

'Hello, Douglas. I'm calling to remind you of the arrangements for Friday.'

'Friday,' he repeated dumbly.

'Don't tell me you've forgotten. It's the Faulkner Foundation Ball. I told you to put it in your diary months ago.'

'Yes, I'm sure you did.'

'You are coming.'

It wasn't a question but Doug automatically flicked through his diary, even though he knew nothing short of the words *end of the world* would save him. And even that would result in a heated debate his mother would probably win. 'Of course I'm coming.'

'And will you be bringing anyone?'

Last year he'd been so desperate for company he'd invited Geraldine. A bad idea all round. She'd found it utterly tedious, which of course it was, and Doug had found spending the evening with his disgruntled sometime lover even more deadly than going alone. 'No, I—'

'Doug, I've got a Robert Langstone on the line but before I put him through ...' Abby appeared in the alcove, slapping a hand over her mouth when she realised he was on the phone. She rolled her eyes, mimed cutting her neck and dashed out of his vision.

A smile slowly settled across his face. 'Actually, I've changed my mind. I will be bringing someone.'

'Does this someone have a name?'

'Abigail Spencer.'

'Do I know her?'

'Yes. She was at the last board meeting. She's my personal assistant.'

'Oh.'

As he imagined the displeasure on her face his smile widened. 'Do you want me to come, or not?'

'Of course I do. It's the Faulkner Foundation. All the family should be there.'

The charity, or to be more exact the prestige that came with being the charity patron, was all his mother lived for. 'Then seat me next to Abby.'

'Abigail.'

Clearly it was one thing to have a lowly PA coming to her fancy do. Another entirely to call her Abby. 'Fine. She'll answer to either.'

'I want the family there for 7 p.m., before the guests arrive. Don't be late.'

'I wouldn't dream of it.'

He ended the call and thrust the phone onto the desk. What on earth had he done? He had no time to wonder because Abby was poking her cute nose back in his office.

'Sorry for interrupting just now. I'm such a klutz. I know I should tell you who's on the line over the phone, but it always seems so silly when you're just round the corner.'

'It's fine. Is Robert still there?'

'No. I told him you'd call him back.' She scuttled in and stuck a yellow Post-it note onto his desk. 'He seemed very nice.'

'He is, to the ladies.'

'Ah.' She giggled. 'Is that why he wanted to know all about me? He told me to tell you that on his next visit he was going to take me out to lunch.'

'Did he now.' Doug fought against an irrational spurt of jealousy. Abby wasn't his and Robert was a chronic flirt. 'What are you doing Friday evening?'

She blinked. 'Is this still about Robert? Because I'm sure he was only joking when he talked about taking me out.'

'I'm sure he wasn't, but that's not what this is about. My mother is patron of a charity she helped to found: the Faulkner Foundation. Its annual ball is on Friday when frighteningly pompous people gather and have toe curlingly dull conversations over artfully displayed, utterly bland food. I'm required to attend, and though it's all in a good cause I'd rather watch paint dry while having my fingernails removed without anaesthetic.'

'Oh boy.'

'I wondered if you'd like to come with me?'

For a split second she looked stunned. Then she started to laugh. 'How many people have you asked so far?'

'You're the first. Why?'

'I just thought with an invitation like that you might be struggling to find a willing victim. Which is why you've turned to me.'

'The description is true, though possibly on the generous side. As for why I'm asking you …' He paused, looked her in the eye and went with the truth. 'I can't imagine anyone else I'd rather suffer it with.'

She hiccupped out another laugh. 'Is that because you want to see me suffer, too?'

'No. It's because when I'm in your company I forget everything else going on around me.'

Shit. For once in his life he'd talked without thinking,

154

and now she had the look of a shocked Bambi. There was nothing he could do to take back the words though, and he was amazed to realise he didn't *want* to. She deserved to know how he felt about her, even though he wasn't going to act on it.

A flush stained her cheeks and she actually seemed lost for something to say.

'So, will you come?' he asked gruffly.

'Yes.' He thought he was in for one of the shortest replies on record, but then her hands flew to her cheeks. 'Oh my God, I've got nothing to wear. How fancy is this do, exactly? Will I need a posh dress? And will there be loads of courses that'll require locating the right cutlery? And who's going to be there because if it's a bunch of rich people I won't have a clue what to say. They'll be talking Barbados and The Ivy and I'll be more Cleethorpes and McDonald's.'

He chuckled. 'Relax. I'll buy you something to wear.'

She shook her head furiously. 'Oh no, absolutely not.'

'Absolutely yes. You're doing me a massive favour. The least you deserve from it is a new dress. As to the rest,' he continued, railroading over her further protest, 'I'll talk you through the courses, point out the cutlery and the only person you have to talk to is me.'

'Is that a promise? I mean about the cutlery and talking only to you. I can find a dress.'

'It's a promise about all of it. Including the dress,' he added firmly.

Slowly the bright smile that was so much a part of her slid across her face. 'All righty. In that case, I'm sold.'

And just like that, something he would usually dread was now something he was looking forward to.

Chapter Sixteen

Abby stared again at the deep purple velvet dress draped over her bed. She'd never owned anything as beautiful – or expensive. She'd guessed, even before Mandy had googled the designer, that Doug had spent a small fortune on it. More on one dress, for one occasion, than her annual clothes budget. It felt criminal to accept it, but as her fingers skipped over the soft velvet she knew she couldn't give it back. With a sigh of pleasure she slipped it on and studied herself in the mirror. She'd never felt so special. Or so slim. And that was before she'd managed to do it up.

'Mandy? Will you help with this zip?' she shouted through the closed door. Why did designers put zips on the back, when only a disjointed woman with extra long arms had any hope of doing the flipping thing up?

There was a knock on the door. 'Mandy's gone downstairs to let Roger in. Will I do instead?' Her father popped his head round and whistled. 'Well, don't you look a knock out.'

'Thank you, kind sir.' She wriggled round so her back was towards him and he grasped the zip.

'It's been a long time since I've been anywhere near a lady's zip,' he muttered, and Abby tried not to wince as he jerked it up. When he'd finished he drew her round to face him and studied her with soft brown eyes so similar to her own. 'Your mother would be so proud of you if she could see you now.'

'Oh, Dad.' Abby felt her eyes well. At times, with all the chaos that Spencer life entailed, it was easy to forget that it hadn't just been her and her sisters who'd lost someone important when their mum had died. Her father had lost the love of his life.

'Hey, I didn't mean to make you cry. Here.' He drew a

wrinkled old hanky from his pocket. 'Wipe your eyes with this. It looks reasonably clean.'

'Thanks.' She dabbed at them carefully, both to protect her make-up and to ensure minimal transfer of engine oil onto her face. 'You must be the only person in the world who still uses handkerchiefs.'

'Bloody sight more sensible than a tissue which shreds the moment you touch it.' He smiled at her, his face looking older than it should for his age, but comfortingly familiar. 'I meant what I said, you know. You look smashing. That bloke of yours certainly knows how to pick a dress.'

She glanced down at the soft velvet which fell over her curves like a violet waterfall. 'He's not my bloke, but yes, he's got great taste.'

'In my day, when a guy took a woman to a fancy do and bought her a dress it meant he was keen on her.'

'I wish.' The words tumbled out without her thinking and Abby quickly shook her head. 'No, forget I said that. Doug is a really good boss. That's the most important part.'

Her father frowned. 'I assumed, as you went to a gallery with him, and as he's been to the house and met your sisters, that he was chasing my girl.'

'If only he was.' She slumped onto the bed, then immediately leapt up again. 'Oh help, I don't want to crush the dress. Then again, does expensive, silk blended velvet even crease?' She smoothed a hand down the front, letting out an hysterical laugh. 'Oh God. How am I supposed to spend an evening with a bunch of rich people when even the dress I'm wearing is too posh for me?'

Her father took her hand and squeezed. 'You're worth a hundred stuck up Felicitys. Come here.' He did something then that he hadn't done in a long while. He put his arms around her. Instantly Abby forgot about the dress, threw her arms around his neck and hugged him back.

'Sorry,' she sniffed, trying to control her tears because she really, really didn't want to meet Doug with eyes that clashed with her dress. 'I'm having a mini meltdown but I'll be all right in a minute.' She tried to laugh. 'Truth is, I'm terrified about tonight. Terrified I'll embarrass Doug in front of his family.'

'Poppycock. Any man who walks into a room with you on his arm would feel ten foot tall.'

'Oh, Dad.' After giving him a watery smile she kissed his weathered cheek. 'Only a father could say that.'

'I mean it.' He tucked his hand under her chin. 'Am I allowed to ask what's going on here? Are you falling for this Doug fellow?'

Glumly she nodded her head. 'I'm very afraid I am. I know he likes me, but I also know he won't take it any further.' She exhaled a long, deep breath. 'Why is it when it comes to men I always punch above my weight?'

'If you're referring to that bastard Tony, excuse my language, then you're talking rubbish. He wasn't good enough to clean your shoes.'

'He was the owner of a successful advertising agency who dumped me to marry a rich, glamorous heiress. His business is now three times the size it was and he hasn't looked back since.'

'But is he happy?'

Abby burst out laughing. 'We can pretend he isn't.'

Her father stroked a finger down her cheek. 'You're a beautiful young lady. One who's single-handedly raised this family for the last twelve years.' She opened her mouth to contradict him, but he interrupted her. 'Don't think I don't know what you've done for us. There isn't a man alive who wouldn't count himself as incredibly lucky to have you.'

'Jeeze, Dad.' She swallowed, then swallowed again. 'You're going to make me cry again and I can't go to this stupid ball with puffy eyes.' After taking a moment to get herself together, Abby glanced back up at him. 'You know, I can't remember the last time we had a proper talk like this.'

He gave her a sad smile. 'That's on me, lass. I've not been around as much as I should have. The garage sucks up too much of my time. It annoyed your mother, too.'

She kissed his weathered cheek again. 'It doesn't annoy me, Dad. You said I raised this family by myself but I didn't. You were always at the heart of it. I just want you to know you still are. And that we all still need you.' Afraid she was going to cry again, she struck an exaggerated model pose. 'Who else is going to tell us we're beautiful?'

He chuckled. 'Well, at least I have some use. I'll leave you to do whatever it is that women do before they go out. I'll wait downstairs, ready to give this man of yours a grilling when he rings on the door.'

Her heart lurched. 'Please tell me that's a joke.'

His brown eyes twinkled. 'How else am I going to know if I can trust him with my precious daughter?'

Doug parked on the street just by the Spencer house. The drive was fully occupied with a truck, which he guessed was her father's, and a clapped out old Beetle. Abby's? As he walked up the path he smiled at the pots by the front door. Not arty, or sophisticated, they brimmed with flowers of all colours and description. Abby's again, he'd like to bet. He reached for the bell but even before he'd pressed it, the door swung open and a fifty-something male of average height and build greeted him. The instant he looked into his eyes, Doug knew who it was.

'You must be Abby's father. Hi, I'm Doug Faulkner.' He held out his hand. 'Pleased to meet you, sir.'

'Good God, can't remember the last time I was called sir. Come on in, lad. And the name's Derek. We don't stand on ceremony here.'

Cursing his boarding school manners, and uncomfortably aware he'd already been pigeonholed as a pompous ass, Doug followed him inside. A wall of noise greeted him. The baby was screaming and two of the girls, Doug couldn't remember their names, were in the middle of a heated argument.

He nodded over to Mandy, but she was bouncing her son up and down, trying to get him to calm down, so he tried Roger instead. 'How's the job going?'

Roger opened his mouth and Doug knew words were coming out of it but he had no clue what they were because the two younger sisters had, unbelievably, upped their yelling by a few decibels.

'Holly, Ellie, that's enough,' their father thundered. 'We've got a posh visitor. Let's show him we know how to behave.'

The two girls stopped and turned to look at him. The younger one grinned. 'That's Doug, Abby's boss. He's the one who beat up those guys and snogged Abby on the drive.'

Oh boy. Feeling utterly unhinged, Doug glanced desperately around the room but there was no Abby to help him out. Only Mandy and Roger, who were both clearly struggling to hold back their laughter. Oh and Derek, who looked like any father would on hearing his darling daughter had been snogged by an unworthy male. 'I admit to the last point but I'd like to argue the first. I didn't beat anyone up.'

'From what I heard you did turf two unwelcome visitors out of our home.' Derek's face relaxed sufficiently to give him a small smile. 'The jury is still out on whether that makes up for what happened on the drive.'

As Doug struggled to find a reply, Abby appeared on the landing. The moment his eyes caught hers he felt all the breath leave his lungs. 'You look stunning,' he managed.

'Tell me when I reach the bottom.' She eyed up the stairs as if they were part of a complicated assault course. 'I'm not used to wearing a long dress, or such high heels. It's a potentially lethal combination.'

Uncaring of the very interested eyes fixed on him, Doug ran up the staircase. 'Here, take my hand. I won't let you fall.'

Her small hand curled around his, making him feel like a prince as he guided her carefully down the steps. On reaching the bottom her hand slipped from his and immediately he missed the intimacy.

'You can tell me how good I look now.'

A laugh ripped out of him. 'Okay then.' He took a step back and gave her a deliberate once over. 'I've never seen anyone look as beautiful as you.'

She raised her eyes to the ceiling. 'That was over the top. Try again, but make it more believable.'

'Ignore her, Doug,' Mandy piped up from the open plan kitchen. 'She has a habit of telling you what you should be thinking.'

'She has a habit of not believing a compliment, even when it's the truth,' Doug countered, his eyes still on Abby. 'I meant it. You're beautiful.'

As Abby's cheeks flushed Doug became aware that once again he was the centre of attention. Though he was comfortable complimenting a woman, he wasn't comfortable being watched while doing it. 'Are you ready?'

'Yes.' She sounded as eager as him to escape. 'We should probably go before my family says anything more embarrassing.'

'I haven't done the *look after my daughter* speech yet,' her father announced, walking up to them and putting his arm around Abby's waist. The gesture was so natural, so familiar, Doug found himself absurdly envious.

'You're not going to give that speech because I'm going to give you a *look after your daughters* speech instead.' Abby hugged her father, giving him a kiss on the cheek. 'The stew is in the slow cooker, the oven chips need another ten minutes and Holly still has to finish her homework. Don't wait up.'

As he watched the easy affection between father and daughter, Doug felt in the way so he went to stand by the door while Abby said her goodbyes and gathered her black shawl from the back of the sofa.

'Enjoy yourselves,' Derek called out as they were leaving. 'If there's any snogging to be done, make sure you do it on the sofa and not the drive. We have standards round here.'

The door closed with a bang behind them, but not before Doug had heard the burst of laughter.

Abby groaned. 'Oh God, could my family be any more embarrassing?'

'Wait till you meet mine. It will take embarrassment to a whole new level.'

'I doubt that, though your father is kind of scary.' He opened the passenger door for her but before she climbed in she looked down at her dress. 'Before I forget, thank you so much for this, though you really shouldn't have spent so much.'

'Do you like it?'

Her eyes snapped up to meet his. 'Are you kidding? It's the most incredible thing I've ever owned.'

'Then it was worth every penny.'

She gave him a shy smile and shuffled down into her seat. Geraldine had a way of slipping in that made the process appear seamless. Abby sort of flopped in, then jiggled a while. But heavens, her method stirred something inside him that Geraldine, with all her sophisticated elegance, never had.

'How did you know what size to buy?' she asked, when he'd reversed out of the drive.

'I have a fair bit of experience with the female form.' Hearing her sharp intake of breath, he slid her a wry smile. 'I have sisters, too.'

'Oh, yes, right. Though I suspect your knowledge comes from elsewhere, too.'

'I've had my moments.'

Abby bet he had. She cast another look in Doug's direction. A tux did wonders for a man, and when that man was already drop dead gorgeous, it took him off the scale. It wasn't just the way Doug looked that sent a flush of awareness shooting through her, but the way he carried himself. He was born to wear an expensive tuxedo and drive a classy sports car. It made her realise she wasn't only going to a posh do with the boss she was falling for. She was going with the movie star handsome heir to Lord and Lady Faulkner.

Groaning inwardly she hugged her arms around her waist. Now she wasn't just anxious, she was shitting bricks.

His gaze flickered in her direction. 'Are you okay?'

'Yes. I'm fine. Just a bit nervous.' Like Everest was a bit of a mountain. The Arctic a bit cold.

'Don't be. Other than a cursory hello you won't need to talk to anyone other than me. I promise not to make you nervous.' He gave her his rare, heart dropping smile and she didn't have the heart to tell him he was already making her nervous because of how he made her feel. 'If at any point you want to go, you only have to say the word and I'll take you straight home. We can grab some of the stew you made your family.'

'Oh no, I wouldn't be that cruel. I'll force myself to stay at least until we've finished the meal.'

'There's always McDonald's.'

She spluttered out a laugh. 'Oh sure. I can just see me sitting in Maccy D's with this dress on. I'll look like a right twit.'

He turned to her, a rare intimacy in his eyes. 'You'll look like you do now. Unbelievably sexy.'

She felt her tummy dip and then a swarm of butterflies take up residence. Earlier he'd called her beautiful, now sexy. Was he finally going to do something about this attraction between them?

She snuck another glance at him, but his expression told her nothing.

Chapter Seventeen

Doug turned the car through a pair of imposing gates and into a long, gravel drive. Abby squinted, making out a grand brick building in the distance. The closer they got to the building, the larger and grander it became. And the more her heart thumped.

'Is this where you grew up?' she squawked, unable to keep the awe from her voice.

'It's the Faulkner family home, yes.'

'So it's where you grew up.'

'It's where I lived when I wasn't at boarding school.'

She'd sensed his unease as soon as he'd turned into the drive. Now his expression was so tight all the questions she was itching to ask died on her lips.

Doug brought the car to a halt outside the front entrance and immediately a smartly dressed gentleman swooped to open her door. She didn't have a clue how to make an elegant exit from a low slung sports car so she concentrated instead on making a safe one, gathering up her dress so she didn't trip over it.

Doug was waiting and she clutched gratefully at his outstretched hand, both for stability and reassurance.

'Thanks, Edward.' Doug threw the valet – or crikey, who knew, perhaps it was the butler? – his keys and nestled her hand into the crook of his arm. 'Are you ready for this?'

'I thought you said I shouldn't be scared?'

'You shouldn't.'

'Then don't ask me if I'm ready in the same way a skydiving instructor might ask just before he pushes you out of a plane.'

His features relaxed a little and his vivid blue eyes scanned her face. 'I'm so glad you're here, Abby. You've no idea how glad.'

'I hope you're still saying that at the end of the evening.'

He laughed softly, keeping hold of her hand as they walked towards the entrance, a highly glossed green door, surrounded by columns and reached by a set of sweeping steps.

'I feel I should show someone a ticket.' When he gave her a puzzled look she realised he had no clue how gobsmacking his family home was to someone like her. 'This house is like something out of a National Trust brochure. The only other time I've gone into a place looking like this I've had to pay for the privilege. I hope it's got a good tea shop.'

His soft laugh helped disperse some of her nerves, though they returned with a vengeance when she came face-to-face with the woman waiting for them inside. She'd met his mother at the board meeting, but they hadn't been introduced. In her late fifties, at a guess, she was elegantly dressed in blue silk with a matching sapphire necklace. Her shrewd brown eyes were cold and assessing. 'You're late.'

'Nice to see you, too, Mother.' Doug's voice was clipped as he turned to Abby. 'As you've no doubt guessed, this is my mother, Belinda. Mother, I'd like you to meet Abigail.'

'Ah yes, the secretary.'

Still holding his arm, Abby felt every one of Doug's muscles stiffen. 'No. My date for this evening.'

Belinda nodded. 'Of course. Charmed to meet you, Abigail.' Before Abby could work out whether her words had been ironic (probably), perfunctory (possibly) or heartfelt (no chance in hell), Belinda turned to the slight figure standing behind her. 'This is Margaret, my youngest.'

Margaret gave her a very small, very shy smile. 'Hi.'

'Good evening is a more dignified greeting,' Belinda admonished, before turning her attention back to her son.

'We've been waiting for you so we can take the family photograph. Abigail can wait out in the hall.'

She turned, effectively dismissing them, but Doug held onto her arm. 'You can be rude to me. I expect it. Abigail, on the other hand, deserves as much respect as any of your other guests this evening.'

The coldness of his words sent a shiver down Abby's spine. She'd never backchatted her mum like that. Then again, her mum hadn't been a bitch. 'I'll be fine waiting here.' Anxious to avoid any further unpleasantness, Abby nodded over to a fancy chair. 'There's even a seat for me. Come and find me when you're finished.'

A muscle twitched in Doug's jaw. 'No, I'm not having my guest sitting in the flaming hall. We'll find Gwen.' He paused to send a brief smile towards Margaret, who'd slunk back against the wall, before giving his mother a dark look. 'I'll be with you in a few minutes.'

Doug marched off down the corridor and Abby teetered behind him. Damn these stupid shoes. Why did she ever think she could carry this look off? Abruptly he halted and looked over his shoulder. 'Christ, sorry.' Three strides later he was back with her, threading her arm through his. Abby was pathetically grateful for the contact. 'I forgot to warn you how much I hate coming here. Or how much my family winds me up.'

'Margaret seems sweet and Thea is lovely.'

He darted her an amused look. 'Very tactful and yes, Margaret is sweet and Thea is lovely. As is the lady I'd like you to meet.' He pushed open the door to a kitchen the size of her house. 'Gwen?' he shouted. 'Where are you hiding?'

'Doug!'

Abby's eyes skimmed across the expanse of shining tile floor and gleaming granite worktops, over the crowd of people in chef's uniforms, and onto a short, dumpy lady with grey hair and a dazzling smile, bustling towards them.

As Abby watched, fascinated, Doug was swallowed by a pair of plump arms.

'Now, who is this gorgeous lady?' Gwen asked, when she finally released him.

'Abby, I'd like you to meet Gwen, who's been here for as long as I can remember. I can't understand why she's not putting her feet up and enjoying a well-deserved retirement.'

Gwen gave him a hefty shove. 'Oh, you. Doug knows very well I can't abide not being busy. Besides, this is my home.'

'You do have another one,' he countered, his expression suddenly serious.

The older lady squeezed his arm. 'I know, and I'm very grateful.' Her voice caught as they exchanged a look. 'One day, when I'm ready.' She dived into the pocket of her apron and dragged out a tissue which she used to wipe at her eyes before giving Abby a bright smile. 'Pleased to meet you, Miss Abby.'

'Oh please, it's just Abby. Otherwise I feel I should be on the set of *Downton*.'

Gwen's ample chest vibrated with laughter. 'I can see you and I are going to get along famously.'

'I hope so,' Doug interjected, 'because I'm going to ask you to look after Abby for me while I do my family duty.'

'Tush, no problem, it will be my pleasure. I'll entertain her with stories of you in short trousers. No need to hurry back.'

Abby giggled as Doug shot them both a wary look. 'I think you can safely guarantee my quick return.'

The moment he disappeared Gwen pulled out a stool. 'Now, my dear, you sit yourself down here and we can talk while I pretend to be busy.'

'But you are busy,' Abby protested, noting the hive of activity around them. 'I don't want to cause any problems. Just ignore me.'

'Good heavens, I'm lucky enough to meet Doug's girlfriend and you expect me to ignore you? Impossible.'

Flustered, Abby shook her head. 'I'm not his girlfriend. I work for him.'

Gwen considered her. 'Well, he didn't bring that Geraldine to see me. Kept her well out of sight.'

Abby bit back on what would have been a rather smug smile.

'Now I'll find you a drink and you can tell me all about what he's like as a boss.'

Having done his duty and had his photograph taken – another happy Faulkner family portrait for the album – Doug went to collect Abby. Pushing open the heavy oak door to the kitchen his heart lifted at the sight of her and Gwen chatting away, then stilled when he considered what Gwen was filling Abby's ears with. Gwen didn't know The Big Secret, but she knew enough to embarrass the heck out of him. Tales of him in short trousers, indeed.

'And what are you doing back so soon?' Gwen exclaimed when she caught sight of him. 'We've only just got started.'

'Then my timing is spot on.' He nodded over to Abby whose face told him she'd been laughing a lot. Whether it was at his expense or not he wasn't sure he wanted to know. 'Time to enter the lion's den.'

Immediately her face fell and Gwen swatted him with her tea towel. 'Don't make the poor girl nervous.' She patted Abby's arm. 'Any big cats out there are old and toothless by now. Just you go and enjoy yourself.'

'I'll try, thank you.' Her big brown eyes swung his way. 'Is there a, umm, what do you call a loo in a place like this? A powder room?'

Gwen chuckled. 'We call a loo, a loo. Use the one round the corner. That way you won't bump into any toothless cats.'

As soon as Abby was out of sight, Gwen turned to him. 'Doug, my dear boy.' She peered up at him, her grey eyes searching his face. 'You look less strained than when I last saw you. Are you happy?'

He clasped her hands in his and smiled. 'I'm getting there.' It was what he always said, but this time it felt like there was some truth in it.

'Because of Abby?' Gwen's face lit up, her eyes shining. 'She's a rare drop of sunshine, that lady. You'd do well to grab hold of her.'

'I'm her boss, Gwen,' he said softly.

'Aye, I know that. But you're also more than halfway in love with her.' He opened his mouth to deny it, but she gave him another of her legendary shoves. 'You can fool a lot of people, young man, but you can't fool me.'

Emotion clogged in his throat as he stared down at this woman who'd been more of a mother to him than his own ever had. He didn't know what to say; deny and he'd disappoint her, admit she was right and he'd scare the hell out of himself. Unable to do either, he bent to kiss her wrinkled forehead.

When he straightened he saw Abby walking towards them, a soft smile on her gorgeous face. 'I'm ready to face those lions now.'

'Off you go then.' Gwen's eyes glistened as she looked first at Abby and then at him. 'And come and see me again soon. Both of you.'

That lump was still in his throat as he watched her disappear back into the hubbub of the kitchen.

'You and she have something special. She's lovely.' Abby grinned. 'And boy is she a great source of info on the enigmatic Douglas Faulkner.'

A shiver ran through him. Did he dare ask? Deciding he had enough on his plate just getting through the evening,

Doug wimped out and took her hand. As they walked down the long hallway towards the ballroom he heard her chant *please don't let me trip up* and had to smother a grin.

When they reached the entrance to the already crowded ballroom, she pulled up sharply. 'Oh my God. It *is Downton Abbey*.'

Doug tried to see the large, fussy room through her eyes. An over-the-top chandelier, gold embossed wallpaper. Large French windows, open to let in the balmy summer evening, leading to an expansive patio overlooking carefully maintained grounds. 'I guess there is a resemblance.'

'Are all the rooms as grand as this one?'

'No.'

She narrowed her eyes at him. 'How many rooms are there?'

He shifted awkwardly. 'I don't know.'

'Seriously?' Those big brown eyes were now saucer-like. 'I bet it was dynamite playing hide and seek. Our house was pretty useless for it. Once we'd tried under the bed and in the wardrobe all the good hiding places were exhausted. Here we could have hidden for days.'

He decided there was no point telling her there were times he had. Not hidden exactly, just stayed in his room and not seen a soul.

Suddenly her hand gripped his arm. 'Oh, bollocks.'

Doug followed her line of vision and saw his father striding towards them. *My thoughts exactly*, he thought grimly.

His fears were soon realised. Five minutes into the conversation and his father still hadn't acknowledged Abby, even though she'd tried to talk to him.

'Abby asked you a question,' he said coldly, before turning to the woman hanging onto his arm as if it was the only thing keeping her anchored. 'Perhaps you could ask it again, Abby. I don't think he heard you.'

She bit her lip, something he knew she did when she felt embarrassed or awkward. Damn his family for making her feel that way. 'I wondered how long your family has lived in this house. I mean how many generations.'

Charles gave her a derisory glance. 'Four. Why, have you set your sights on being part of the fifth?'

She paled. 'Crikey, no, of course not. I was just making conversation. I'd never dream, I mean, it didn't cross my mind ...'

As her voice trailed off, anger coiled inside Doug. 'Ignore him. He's trying to make you feel awkward. It's his speciality.' His hands twitched and he briefly imagined the satisfaction of shoving his fist into his father's face. Then he remembered the last time he'd had such a strong urge. Burying his anger he led Abby away to the other side of the room.

'I'm not sure I like your father,' she said, when they were out of earshot.

Her understatement almost made him smile. 'I'm not sure I do, either.'

'Still, I'm sorry I've caused bad feeling between you.'

He spun round to look at her. 'Abby, Abby.' Her expressive eyes stared up at him and he felt his heart clench. 'Do you really think the bad feeling is because of you?'

'Not all of it, no, though I'm clearly not helping. He's hardly my number one supporter.'

'He's only attacking you to get to me. I'm the one he has the issue with.' Gently he traced his finger down the side of her face. And then over her soft, soft lips. As he gazed into her eyes he felt the floor move beneath his feet. It was like drowning in a vat of warm, velvet chocolate.

'Why does he treat you like that?'

The softly voiced question snapped him out of his trance. 'It's a long story.' Sighing, he dropped his hand back down to his side. 'I'd love to leave now, but we can't. Apart from anything else, Gwen would tan my backside if we missed her meal.'

'Did she really used to spank you?'

'What do you think?'

'I don't think she did. I can't imagine anyone spanking you.'

He quirked an eyebrow and immediately she started giggling. 'I didn't mean it like that.'

As her cheeks grew pinker and pinker, he smiled. Time to shove his family out of his head and enjoy this funny, beautiful woman.

From that moment on, the evening picked up.

'Abby, how brilliant to see you again.' Thea's warm greeting was a sharp and welcome contrast to the rudeness of his parents. 'I can't believe Doug's persuaded you to come to this. I hope whatever he's bribed you with will be worth the tedium.'

He cleared his throat. 'Perhaps I used charm, not bribery.'

Thea roared – yes, flaming *roared*, with laughter. 'Of course you did. Charm is exactly what you're renowned for. That and sparkling conversation.'

That set Abby off too, though she was clearly trying – failing adorably, but trying – to keep her laughter to the demure end of the scale. Doug conceded that having the piss taken out of him was worth it to see two of his favourite women sharing a giggle.

When it was finally time to eat, Doug found he and Abby had been put on a table with the Crumbs board members and their wives. As the older guests all knew each other, Doug was only required to nod his head and smile now and again. At each course Abby's eyes darted questioningly towards him as she pointed to her choice of cutlery. When he nodded, yes, she grinned and drew a tick on the tablecloth with her finger.

'I've so got the hang of this,' she whispered, when they reached the dessert course. 'You can officially put me on your *suitable for Buckingham Palace* list.'

His chest rumbled with laughter. Here he was, attending another of his mother's fusty balls, in the home he hated, yet he was actually enjoying himself. Bloody hell.

The table was cleared and the coffee brought out. Moments later the small chamber orchestra began to play. Smiling, Doug held out his hand. 'Miss Spencer, do you dance?'

'I've been known to shake my butt a time or two.' Her eyes travelled down to his outstretched hand. 'Oh, you mean you want to dance now?' She glanced over her shoulder. 'To *that*?'

He stifled a laugh. 'What's wrong with *that*?'

'Nothing, if it's background music. If you expect me to dance ... well, jeeze, I need a beat.' She wrinkled her forehead. 'But you want me to do that ballroom dancing, don't you?'

'Well, we are in a ballroom.'

'And that's instantly going to make me into a waltzing diva, is it?'

'Maybe not instantly, though a good teacher will help. Come on.' He tugged at her arm, but she remained seated.

'Seriously, Doug, no. I've never done this sort of dancing before.'

'Don't worry. I have.'

He tugged again and she reluctantly rose to her feet. 'I'm going to make a total arse of myself,' she hissed. 'And if I fall over and break my neck you'll have to explain to my family that I can't look after them any more.'

'Relax,' he told her softly as he led her smoothly onto the dance floor. 'I've got you.' He took hold of her left hand and placed it on his upper arm. An involuntary tremor ran through him as her fingers clasped hold and the tremor grew stronger as he placed his right hand on her shoulder blade, his fingers touching her bare skin. When her other hand snuggled shyly into his left hand, Doug knew he was sunk. He could no longer see his personal assistant. All he could see was the woman he'd once kissed and whom he desperately wanted to kiss again. And again.

Gently he nudged her leg with his, pushing her back a step. 'Just follow my lead,' he whispered into her ear. 'We'll keep it simple.'

But as he carefully guided a very pliant Abby around the floor, Doug knew the time for keeping things simple was fast slipping away. It was impossible to ignore the throb between his legs as her curves brushed against him. Or the ache in his chest as he stared into her eyes.

Chapter Eighteen

Abby felt like a princess. She was dancing in a swish ballroom, in front of a real band, and in the arms of an incredibly handsome man. For a few minutes she allowed herself to imagine she wasn't Abby Spencer the secretary but Lady Spencer, a woman with impressive connections who could glide easily into Doug's world.

A woman he'd want to take home, peel out of her fancy dress and carry up to his bedroom.

She stumbled and Doug caught her, his arm tightening round her shoulder. 'Oh bum, I'm sorry. I knew it was going too well.' She tried to get back into the swing of it again, but her body wouldn't relax. It was far too conscious of the muscular thighs pushing against hers. The strong hand that spanned her back.

'Are you ready to go home?'

The warmth of his breath as it fanned against her neck.

Words that usually came so easily eluded her, so she nodded. Immediately he led her off the dance floor and back to her seat where he picked up her bag and shawl.

In a matter of minutes they were in his car and driving away.

'Was it as bad as you expected?' he asked as he turned onto the main road.

She stared at his strong profile, illuminated by the street lights. 'It wasn't bad at all. In fact, I enjoyed it.' *I enjoyed being with you.*

His lips twitched. 'Seriously? Even the dancing?'

'Yes.' *Especially the dancing.* 'I loved talking to Gwen.'

'Ah yes. You never did tell me what you spoke about.'

She smiled at the wariness in his voice. 'Nothing too

incriminating. Unless you count how you were bullied by your baby sisters.'

'I let them bully me,' he muttered. 'There's a difference. Is that it?'

'She told me how obsessed you were with your painting. How when your parents tried to take your paints away you snuck them under your bed. Is that really true?'

A muscle ticked in his jaw. 'My father thought painting was cissy. He wanted me to undertake more manly pursuits.'

'Oh.' Her mind conjured a picture of Doug as a boy, painting furtively in his room, unable to show his parents his creations, and she felt the squeeze on her heart. 'Gwen said she promised you you'd be the next Leonardo da Vinci, but privately she thought your paintings were a bit odd.'

'She did, did she?'

He sounded so offended, Abby spluttered with laughter. 'Oops, maybe I shouldn't have told you that, though she did say she loved the painting you did for her last year.' Her laughter faded as she studied his profile. 'She said you'd bought her a house to put the painting in, but that she's not ready to leave your family just yet.'

Doug's shoulders dropped as he let out a deep sigh. 'Gwen's seventy years old and has worked there for over fifty years. I want her to enjoy a well-deserved retirement, but while Margaret's still at home she wants to be there.' He indicated to turn into her road.

'She likes being busy, Doug. Maybe she doesn't want to rattle round a new home doing nothing.'

'I know.' He eased to a stop and turned off the engine. 'But I can't bear the thought of her being at the beck and call of my parents for very much longer.'

His face looked strained and Abby's heart went out to him. 'She'll retire when she's ready, and knowing she has a place she can retire to will make that decision much easier.

It was a very kind, thoughtful thing to do, but then that's not surprising because you're both those things. Kind and thoughtful.'

'Thank you.' Slowly he angled his body to look at her. 'And if now is the time for sharing what we think of each other, I need to tell you you're warm, funny, off the scale smart, strong.' His eyes blazed into hers. 'And so beautiful my breath catches in my throat each time I look at you.'

Her heart bounced beneath her ribs as her own breath disappeared. 'I ... wow. That's you being kind again.'

'No. That's me being truthful.'

Dazed, she shook her head. 'I try to be warm and funny and strong. I'm quite smart but I'm definitely not beautiful.'

He traced his finger over the planes of her face, making her shiver. 'Your mouth, your smile, your eyes. They're all beautiful.'

'My eyes are brown.' Her voice was no longer her own. It was lower, huskier. 'Who's ever heard of a brown eyed blonde? It doesn't work.'

He lowered his head and planted a delicate kiss on each eyelid. 'Works for me.'

The touch of his lips was feather-light, but Abby felt the zing of it all through her system. She could barely breathe, definitely couldn't swallow. When she lifted her eyes to stare into his intense blue ones all the desire she was feeling, every pulsing, aching, throbbing ounce of it, was reflected back at her.

Throwing caution to the wind, she flung her arms around his neck and kissed him.

For a split second she felt his whole body stiffen. *Oh crap, she was jumping her boss.* But just as she was about to pull away he relaxed and then, thank you God, he began to kiss her back.

As his tongue dived into her mouth and his hands

wandered restlessly over her back, Abby tried to push herself closer but the gear knob kept jutting into her hip.

She let out a groan of frustration and he instantly pulled back, his breath coming out in short, sharp pants. 'Sorry, are—'

'Don't you dare apologise for kissing me,' she cut in, smothering his face in further kisses. 'I'm just having a little trouble with your knob.'

His eyes glittered. 'I don't get many complaints.'

'I'm going to ignore that appalling joke.' Taking his gorgeous face between her hands, she gave him a long, soft kiss. 'Would you like to come inside?'

He stilled and she shrank back, slamming her eyes shut, as if that would prevent her from hearing his next words. *I'm sorry. We can't do this.*

But when she opened them again he was walking round to her side. Before she knew it he was helping her out and pinning her back against the car door. 'Abby, Abby,' he groaned and then he plundered her mouth again, grinding his hips against her so she could feel every hot, tantalising inch of him.

Doug had lost his mind the moment Abby had turned those stunning dark eyes his way and told him she wasn't beautiful. Hell, he'd probably lost it months ago, when she'd first set foot in his office, though he'd tried hard to do the right thing. Now he didn't know what the right thing was any more. He only knew she'd kissed him and he didn't have the will or the strength to turn away.

Which was why he was now ravishing her against his car bonnet, on her driveway. Classy.

She wriggled her hips, pushing against his arousal and making him ache even more. Realising he wasn't far from exploding, he exhaled sharply and drew back. 'I think you said something about going inside?'

She gave her swollen lips a quick lick before straightening up and tottering towards the front door. Doug followed behind her, his body throbbing in places he didn't realise could throb. As she fumbled with the keys he couldn't resist cupping her breasts, squeezing them over the velvet bodice. Christ, what he wouldn't give to see them.

'You're not helping,' she gasped, then moaned as his fingers snuck inside the bodice and traced round her nipple.

'Here, let me do it.' He made to grab the keys with his free hand but she shooed him away.

'No. I'd rather you kept your hands where they were.'

He did as he was told, leaning against the door so he could use his spare hand to pull down her zipper slightly, allowing him easier access.

Abby chose that moment to unlock the door and it suddenly swung open, propelling them both, stumbling, inside.

Abby let out a little shriek and immediately there was a bark, followed by a scamper of feet.

'Pat, shush.' She bent down to stroke the dog, her dress falling off her shoulders. The sight of all her exposed skin made Doug suck in a breath. 'It's only me and Doug,' she soothed, fondling the dog's ears. Doug imagined her hands fondling him and his crotch throbbed so much it was painful.

She stood, the bodice of her dress falling down around her waist and exposing her full, naked breasted glory. 'Now, where were we?'

His eyes greedily took their fill but just as he reached out to touch, a small voice came from the stairs. 'Abby, is that you?'

Abby froze and Doug hastily grasped at her dress, lifting it up to cover the twin globes of perfection that would be forever imprinted in his mind.

'Umm, yes, Ellie. It's me and Doug.' The sound of him zipping up her dress echoed round the room.

'What are you doing?'

'I've just invited Doug in for a cup of coffee.'

Doug swallowed down his laughter as he glanced over at Abby. Her hair was wild, her dress looked like she'd shoved it on in a hurry and her mouth as if it had been thoroughly kissed. As Ellie walked slowly down the stairs he wondered how long it would take her to work out that sharing a drink with Abby hadn't been on his agenda.

'Why has Doug got lipstick on his mouth? Have you been kissing?'

Slowly the night that had offered such promise began to shrivel and turn to dust. It was for the best, of course. He shouldn't be leading Abby on, starting something that had no future. But God, the frustration, the crushing disappointment. He couldn't even let out the stream of oaths circulating in his mind because Ellie was standing in front of them now, her eyes like saucers.

Quickly he wiped his hand across his mouth. 'I was trying out your sister's lipstick. It doesn't look as good on me as it does on her.'

Beside him, Abby let out a snort.

'What's all the noise about?'

Another sister. The place was riddled with them. Mandy stood at the top of the stairs, her eyes skimming with unabashed interest over Abby's not-quite-straight dress.

'It's like Piccadilly flipping Circus,' Abby muttered under her breath.

Her words, together with the absurdity of the situation, finally took their toll on him and Doug started to laugh.

Abby stamped her foot. 'It's not funny, you know. The one time I bring a man home and the whole bloody house decides to hold a midnight party.'

Reaching the bottom stair, Mandy began to snigger which set Ellie off, too. Pretty soon they were all bent over with laughter.

It wasn't the ending to the evening he'd envisioned, but as he tried to get his breath back Doug knew it had been a long time since he'd laughed that hard.

'I'm sorry we woke you,' he finally managed.

'You didn't wake me,' Mandy replied, walking into the kitchen to boil the kettle. 'That was George's fault. So it's only nosey Ellie you have to apologise to and I suspect catching you two making out has more than made up for her disturbed sleep.'

'That's gross.'

'Only if you're not doing it right.' Mandy finished making up the bottle for George and then clasped Ellie's hand. 'Come on you. Time to go back to bed.' She glanced at Doug and winked. 'I promise you won't be disturbed again.'

After hearing the sound of two doors clunking shut, Abby let out a long, deep breath. 'So, on a scale of one to ten, how embarrassing was that? Twelve?'

Doug shook his head. 'No. Twelve was the last time I kissed you. On your drive in broad daylight with two of your sisters watching. This only rated an eleven.'

She raised her eyes to the ceiling and gave him a wry smile. 'We haven't had much luck on that front, have we?'

'No.' He moved to stand in front of her, clasping her gorgeous face in his hands. 'But it's probably for the best.'

'Oh no, don't you start pushing me away again.' She reached up and covered his hands with her own, anchoring him in place. 'There's a reason why we end up kissing each other. It's called mutual attraction. I know I started it today and I'm probably being horribly presumptive, but you must feel something for me or you wouldn't have kissed me back.'

'I feel far more than something, but just because I do, doesn't make this right.' He inhaled slowly, trying to find his composure. His balance.

'If you tell me it's because you're my boss, I'm going to scream.'

'It certainly doesn't help.' Her lips, thanks to those heels she was wearing, were just a few short inches away. Add to that the feel of their entwined hands against her face, and it felt so, so intimate. And way too tempting. He closed his eyes and searched for the words. 'Abby, you're light; I'm dark. You're warm and open; I'm cold and closed off. You're also six years younger than me.'

When he dared to glance at her, she shoved his hands away. 'I'm twenty-four, not bloody fourteen. And I know you think you're cold, but you're not. As for being closed, that's a choice, not a personality trait.'

'Maybe, but it's my choice,' he retorted, his words sounding too sharp, too defensive. 'Based on my experience of what relationships have to offer.'

She regarded him pityingly. 'Your parents have an unhappy relationship so you assume that's the case for everyone? How cynical. And how sad.'

Her words bit into him, icy shards that stung. 'Yes,' he countered, his voice sounding tight and clipped. 'So you're better off finding someone who believes in the Disney version of life, like you do. Not the over-eighteen version.'

'Is that what Geraldine gave you?'

'She gave me sex, yes,' he replied bluntly. It was time she saw the real him, not this fantasy she had in her mind.

Abby flinched and her eyes darted to the wall behind him. 'I see.'

He exhaled on a curse, knowing he'd hurt her. What the hell had he been doing leading her on, inviting her first to the gallery and now to the ball? It was no wonder she'd started seeing blasted hearts and rainbows. 'Abby, I'm sorry. I can't be the man you need me to be.'

Her eyes welled with tears. 'You big numbskull. Who are you to tell me what *I* need? Clearly you've decided I'm not the woman you need though, so I guess I should let you go. Thank you for tonight. I enjoyed most of it. I'll see you on Monday.'

She moved to open the door and stood beside it, waiting for him to leave. As he walked out, his heart felt unbearably heavy. He was used to feeling angry and frustrated, but all that seemed petty compared to the feelings washing through him now. Abby *was* everything he needed, but how could he take when he couldn't give back?

He knew when he saw her again on Monday she'd still be his highly-efficient personal assistant. But not his friend.

Soon, when she found a job worthy of her, she wouldn't even be his PA. She'd be gone, and his miserable life would be back to the steaming pile of shit it had always been.

Except that this time, he'd know how different it could have been.

Chapter Nineteen

It had been two days since Abby had pounced on her boss in his car, snogged him by her front door and then been told she was too childish/innocent/naïve for him.

It still hurt like a bitch.

Who did he think she was, Mary flipping Poppins? She wasn't a virgin. She knew that sex didn't automatically lead to love and marriage, nor did she need it to.

Liar. You're falling for him.

She sighed, picked up the basket of dirty laundry and trudged downstairs. Sundays sucked.

'Give that here.' At the bottom of the stairs her father held out his hands for the basket.

'Do you even remember where the washing machine is?'

He grunted. 'Less of your cheek. I plumbed the damn thing in. I know where it is.' His eyes fell on the washing. 'You might need to remind me what setting to put it on, so the colours don't run.'

As they threw the clothes into the machine, more footsteps echoed down the stairs. Not echoing, Abby realised. *Clomping.* She turned round just in time to see Mandy giving a sandy-haired male a goodbye kiss. 'Was that Roger I just saw leaving?' she asked as Mandy wandered towards them, holding George. Abby stared pointedly at her watch. 'At ten o'clock on a Sunday morning?'

Mandy just smiled and kissed the gurgling chap in her arms. 'Maybe.'

'Well, well. Things have certainly moved on in the last few weeks.' An unwanted stab of jealousy shot through her. Mandy and Roger were patching things up, yet her own love life had fizzled out like a reject firework.

Mandy flushed. 'Is it too quick? I don't want to seem like a total slut.'

'I won't have anyone calling one of my daughters a slut,' their father grumbled. 'Especially herself.'

'And anyway, it's hardly slutty to spend the night with the father of your child.' Abby reached out her arms. 'Oh, come here you big slag. Give your father and sister a hug. I'm delighted things are working out for you. Really I am.'

George let out a stream of giggles and kicked his legs as they shared a group hug.

'It's still early days,' Mandy said, when they broke apart. 'And I know I shouldn't look too far into the future.' She broke into a grin. 'But what the heck. It feels right this time. Roger's changed. All the bits I fell for are still there, this time in a more grown-up package. He told me he's just woken up to the fact that he's a dad and he wants to make George and me proud.'

Again Abby pushed aside the sting of jealousy. She was too young to want a husband and child. She was just starting her career.

Mandy touched her arm. 'I'm sorry you and Doug didn't work out. He seemed like a really good guy. Roger raves about him. Doug this, Doug that. It's like the man's some sort of God to him.'

'Yeah. He is amazing,' Abby sighed to herself as Mandy walked away. 'When he wants to be.'

She hadn't realised she'd said the words out loud until her father put his arm round her shoulders. 'You all right, sunshine?'

The nickname tugged a smile from her. 'You haven't called me that in years.'

'No? Then I should have done. You've always been my ray of sunshine.' He hugged her closer. 'Though right now you look like you've got a rare cloud over you. If you want a shoulder to lean on, to cry on, mine is always here. A bit arthritic now, but strong enough to bear the weight of anything my darling daughters want to throw at it.'

'Thank you.' She swallowed past the ball of emotion. 'But I've cried enough over Doug Faulkner.'

'Aye, I reckon you have. Still, it will do you good to remember this. Men are daft creatures, but sometimes they do the wrong thing for the right reason. Strikes me he's trying to protect you.' His hand shot up in defence. 'I know you don't need it, you're a tough cookie, but he's not known you as long as I have.'

'What does he think he's protecting me from, exactly?'

'Himself? His family? You've told me they're an odd bunch. Anyway, it doesn't matter. Put him behind you and get on with your life. If he's anything like the average male he won't like being told what to do or how to feel, especially by a woman. He'll come to his own conclusions, in his own sweet time, though chances are they'll be the same ones you came to months earlier. If you're still interested in him by then, maybe it was meant to be. If you've found someone else, it's his loss.' He bent to kiss the top of her head. 'Now, how about you remind me how the oven works. I'm going to make us some lunch.'

Walking into work the following morning, Abby remembered her dad's advice and pushed all foolish, romantic thoughts of Doug aside. He was her boss. Not a friend, because they'd tried and failed at that. Not a man she was falling in love with, because that would make her stupid and she was blowed if she was going to think of herself as that.

'Would you like a cup of coffee?' she enquired sweetly when she arrived. He narrowed his eyes at her.

'Do you mind showing me where you filed the forecast for the savoury range?' she asked an hour later. He scowled.

And just before lunch. 'Would now be a convenient time to take you through the week's diary?'

He finally exploded. 'No, it bloody wouldn't!'

'Oh? When would it be convenient for me to come back?'

A muscle jumped in his jaw and she wondered why she'd ever thought of him as calm. Beneath his millpond surface was a series of white water rapids that raged and churned, though only rarely broke through.

'Stop doing this, Abby,' he said finally, only the tightness of his voice betraying his annoyance.

'What, stop being the courteous PA? You know, I was wrong when I got shirty with you about doing the very same thing. It turns out I can be your PA, or your friend. I'm not sure I can be both, because then I start hoping and wishing for things that apparently aren't on the table.'

He exhaled loudly, the sound filled with anger and frustration. 'Fine.'

'Good. So, *is* now convenient for the diary walk through?'

His bright blue eyes flared. 'Don't push me. You might not like what you find.'

'Because deep down you're not Douglas Faulkner but some sort of evil monster in disguise?'

His flinch was visible. Abby watched in confusion as he shut his eyes, inhaled and let out a long, slow breath. 'What have I got on this week?' he asked finally.

She'd rarely seen him so tense, so tightly coiled. At least not when it had just been the two of them. 'I'm sorry,' she whispered, pulling up a chair. 'I didn't mean to upset you.'

Doug gazed into Abby's soft brown eyes, so full of concern, and his heart lurched painfully. Those damn puppy dog eyes of hers were going to be the death of him. She didn't know how close her joke was to the truth. In fact, she didn't really know him at all. Would she still be looking at him with such sympathy if she did?

'You haven't upset me,' he managed. 'So, about this week.'

She dumped the giant diary he insisted she use onto his desk and went to stand next to him so she could view it at the same angle. 'You do know nobody except you works from a physical diary any more, don't you?'

'I'm an artist. I like to touch and feel, not look at a computer screen.'

'You certainly have an artist's temperament.'

He was so very aware of her as she looked over his shoulder, talking him through his various meetings. Nothing she said entered his brain, though everything he sensed – her breath against his neck, her scent, her warmth – would, he knew, be forever branded there.

'Hey, buddy, I've come to take Gerri for lunch and thought I'd pop in and say hello.' Luke came to an abrupt halt as his gaze ran over Doug, Abby and then back to Doug. 'Hope I'm not disturbing you.'

'It's a bit late if you were.' Aware his friend had seen more than Doug wanted him to, he eased back, away from Abby. 'Are those for me?' He nodded at the arm Luke was hiding behind his back.

Luke's cheeks reddened and he sheepishly revealed a small posy of freesias.

'Oh, they're lovely,' Abby exclaimed. 'I bet they smell gorgeous. That's the thing with freesias. They're one of the nicest smelling flowers. Good choice.'

Luke beamed. 'Thank you. I figured it was about time I bought Gerri some flowers.' He stared pointedly at Doug. 'When was the last time you bought a lady flowers?'

'When was the last time you got thrown out of an office?' Doug countered.

Luke laughed. 'Okay, I'm off. I'll see you Saturday.' He

was turning to go when he paused. 'Hey, Abby, has Doug told you about the weekend?'

'Umm, no.'

Doug stiffened and shot his friend a few death glances but Luke ignored him.

'Ever watched the fine art of Brazilian jiu-jitsu?'

'At the risk of repeating myself, umm, no?'

It seemed his glares weren't getting through to Luke. Either that or the guy had a death wish because he carried on opening that big mouth of his. 'How do you fancy watching your boss getting trounced in a few fights at the BJJ Surrey Open? Gerri and I are going and this old man needs all the support he can get.'

'Old?' Doug gave him a withering look.

Luke shrugged. 'You're in the masters category now. A few more years and you'll be a senior.'

'I'll still be beating you.'

By his side, Abby giggled. 'It sounds like fun.'

'Oh, it will be. So, will you come?'

'I'm not sure Doug would like that.'

Luke let out his easy laugh. 'Oh, don't worry about him. Of course he'd love you to watch.' His eyes twinkled in challenge. 'Wouldn't you, Doug?'

Doug swallowed. 'Support is always helpful.'

Luke clapped his hands together. 'Great, that's sorted then.'

Apparently though, his torture wasn't finished, because Abby spoke again. 'Could I bring my family?'

While Doug died several deaths at the thought of the whole Spencer clan witnessing his potential humiliation, Luke laughed out loud. 'Of course. We'll have a Faulkner supporters group. I'll get your email address from Doug and we can work out the details.' He glanced down at the freesias. 'I'd better go and find Gerri before these start to wilt and she expires from starvation.'

'I've never worked out why I count him as a friend,' Doug muttered darkly as he watched Luke lope out of his office.

'I imagine it's because he's fun and can charm the spots off a leopard.'

He slid her a look. 'You think he's charming?'

'He's managed to persuade Geraldine to let him call her Gerri. I don't believe anyone else has managed that.'

'True.' He recalled his own pitiful attempt, and her scathing reply. 'Has he also persuaded you to go to a smelly hall and watch a bunch of sweaty people grapple on the floor?'

'I think I might enjoy it.' She picked up the diary and moved to the other side of his desk. 'Though only if you'll feel comfortable with me going.'

'You, maybe. The entire Spencer tribe, no.'

'We won't bring Pat. I suspect dogs aren't allowed.'

'God help me.' He thought he'd muttered the words in his head, but he must have said them out loud because she started to laugh.

'We're not that bad.'

'Imagining what Ellie and Holly might say sends shivers of dread down my spine.'

'We won't go then.'

And now he was faced with her not going, he realised how much he wanted her there. 'If I'm going to be humiliated, it might as well be in front of as many people as possible.' He looked straight into her velvet brown eyes. 'It won't be pretty.'

The look she levelled at him could have stripped paint. 'Dad is into boxing and wrestling, so we've all grown up watching combat sports. None of us girls are strangers to watching two people fight each other. Either on the television or real life.' His face must have registered his shock because she gave a despairing shake of her head. 'Why do men assume girls aren't up for watching a testosterone fuelled sport?' When he couldn't think of a suitable reply she sighed, her hands fiddling with the spine of the diary. 'You know you keep telling me you're not the man I think you are, but I'm not the sickly sweet, naïve young girl you think I am, either.'

With that she turned and walked out. As Doug watched her retreating figure he was certain her deliciously rounded hips swayed more than usual.

For the rest of the day he found he couldn't settle. He kept seeing images of Abby when he'd kissed her by her front door after the ball. Her velvet dress undone, revealing breasts a man would never get tired of looking at.

Right now, turning her down seemed like the ultimate in insanity.

Chapter Twenty

On Saturday morning the Spencer clan – minus Mandy and George – piled into their father's truck. Abby sat up front next to him. Holly, Ellie and Sally fought for the two window seats behind them. They were on their way to the BJJ open to watch Doug fight, though not all of them were willing participants.

'Tell me again why we have to go and watch this Brazilian jiggle?' Ellie demanded from the back seat.

Sally sniggered. 'It's not a jiggle. It's called jiu-jitsu and it's a type of martial art.'

'Okay, so why do we have to waste our Saturday watching some weird karate stuff?'

'It's not like karate,' Sally pointed out. 'It's more like judo – you fight on the floor. They call it grappling. I've been reading about it and it sounds pretty cool because fighting on the ground levels things out, taking away the advantage of being bigger and stronger. You win by being cleverer and having a better technique instead of just having more muscle.'

'So, it's a weird form of judo. I still don't see why we have to watch it.'

'Because me, your father, Sally and Holly all want to see it,' Abby replied, her patience beginning to slip.

'I could have stayed home with Mandy.'

'Mandy is spending the day with Roger and George. It's important for them to have some family time together.'

'Besides, Doug's fighting,' Holly piped up. 'We have to support him 'cos he's Abby's boyfriend.'

Abby sighed. 'No, Holly, he's my boss and ...' She trailed off. Was there an *and*? 'He's my friend,' she finished inadequately. As she'd already told him she couldn't be his friend, what on earth was she doing, dragging her family to go and watch him?

'That's what I said. He's a boy and he's your friend, so he's your boyfriend. Plus you've kissed him.'

'Twice,' Ellie supplied smugly. 'You didn't see the second one.'

Abby glanced at her father for support but his shoulders were shaking up and down with silent laughter. 'Okay, just so you know, kissing someone doesn't automatically make them your boyfriend. I kiss Roger and Dad, too. They're not my boyfriends.'

'Duh. You don't kiss them on the lips and swallow their tongue.'

All three in the back started giggling and her father snorted. With a huff of frustration Abby dug into her handbag. 'Who wants a sweet?'

She kept them quiet by feeding them boiled sweets for the rest of the journey.

The sports hall was large and echoey. The wooden floor was covered with blue mats and a series of blue plastic chairs lined two sides. Glamorous it wasn't.

'It's like our school gym,' Holly announced as they trailed in. 'Only bigger.'

'Where's Doug?' Ellie asked. 'When is he fighting?'

'I guess he's ... you know what, I don't know.' Abby scanned the chairs, about half of which were filled. 'I'm hoping his friend, Luke, will have all the answers when we see him.'

'Will he know how long we're going to have to sit here?' Ellie's lip curled as she pointed to the chairs. 'On *those*?'

'The fights are between two and ten minutes long,' Sally announced helpfully. 'It depends how old you are. Of course Doug isn't five, so his will be longer than two minutes and only the really good black belt people have ten minutes.'

'He's a brown belt,' Abby remembered.

'Then his fight is going to be five or six minutes, depending whether he's a master or a senior.'

'You mean we've come all the way here to watch a five minute fight?' Ellie asked mutinously.

'It could be six minutes,' Sally added unhelpfully.

'What a stupid waste of time.'

'Oh dear, had enough already?'

Suddenly, standing in amongst them was Doug. A casually dressed, very male looking Doug in worn jeans and a white T-shirt that hinted at the muscles beneath it.

'Ellie thinks it's a long way to come to watch you fight for five minutes,' Holly explained.

'Or six if he's not a senior,' Sally reminded them all *again*.

'Which I'm not, thank you.' Doug gave them all a small smile. 'I'm actually only just a master, though right now I feel like a veteran.'

'I didn't think there was a veteran class.' Sally looked puzzled. 'I only saw seniors.'

'You're right. I was trying to be funny.' He glanced at their faces. 'Trying being the key word.' An awkward silence descended and Abby was about to dive straight into it when Doug surprised her by continuing. 'Anyway, I hope to last through the first round at least, so you might have to watch for twelve minutes.'

'Will you get into the final?' Sally's voice held all the enthusiasm Ellie's lacked.

Abby glanced sideways at her sixteen-year-old sister, wondering at the reason behind her sudden interest in the martial arts.

Doug shook his head. 'There are better guys than me here today; a few black belts. I'm hoping for a good run but I won't make it to the final.'

'Thank God,' Ellie muttered.

Abby glanced at Doug who looked suitably bemused. 'I think what Ellie meant to say,' she clarified, 'was that she's really looking forward to watching you.'

Ellie opened her mouth, received a dig in the ribs from her father, and closed it again.

'I'm sure she did,' Doug replied dryly. 'Though I hope you haven't come here just to watch me.'

'We've not seen BJJ live before,' her father answered. 'It's a good opportunity and a rare day out for me and my girls.'

'We could have gone to the zoo,' Ellie grumbled. 'That would have been a proper day out.'

Before Abby could apologise for her sister, Doug spoke again. Quite a feat for a man who didn't usually manage more than two sentences in any five minute period. 'How about I take you all out for a meal after? Do you like pizza?'

Ellie's eyes lit up for the first time that day. 'We all do.'

Abby cringed. 'Doug, you don't have to do that.'

'I want to. That way if I fight like a muppet I've still got something to look forward to.'

'If you fight like a muppet, we get to eat the pizza earlier.' Ellie beamed her full on cheeky grin and they all burst out laughing. Even Doug, Abby noticed, the laughter looking unbelievably good on him, lighting up his face, deepening the blue of his eyes. It was like the rare burst of sun on a miserable wet day. She had a mad urge to capture it and never let it go.

Not long after Doug left to get ready, Luke and Geraldine arrived. Luke good-naturedly answered all the questions fired at him as they found their seats. By the time the fights had started even Ellie was taking an interest.

'Doug's up next.'

They followed Luke's gaze and Abby's heart gave a little jolt at the sight of Doug, dressed in a blue gi, walking towards the centre of the matting with his opponent, dressed in white.

'At least we can easily tell who's who,' Holly announced.

Ellie shifted to the edge of her seat. 'Do we get to boo the man in white?'

Luke chuckled. 'I think it's best if you cheer the man in blue.'

Suddenly the fight started.

Was it wrong of her to be more interested in the fleeting glimpses of Doug's muscled chest than it was of the fight itself? In her defence it was pretty clear, from the number of times the referee indicated points for Doug, that he had this fight in the bag.

At the end of six minutes the referee raised Doug's arm and they all cheered. Including Ellie.

And so it continued through several rounds, right up to the semi-final. By this stage they'd forgotten how uncomfortable the seats were and Ellie had forgotten that she didn't want to watch.

'Don't get your hopes up,' Luke warned. 'The bugger ...' he winced. 'Sorry, Doug's done really well to get this far. He's already beaten a guy he shouldn't have.'

Six minutes later.

'Bloody hell,' Luke announced, this time uncaring of who was around him. 'I never thought he had it in him. He's going to be unbearable to train with from now on.'

Sadly the ultimate dream, the gold medal, wasn't to be. Doug was beaten in the final, though judging from the expression on his face when he stood on the number two spot on the podium, silver was more than okay.

Doug ached everywhere. Even in parts of his anatomy he was sure he hadn't used. As he changed back into his clothes he wondered if his body would ever feel the same again.

Although he'd fought in competitions before they'd usually been within the club or between clubs. This was the first open he'd entered, done on a whim to test how good he'd become.

He tucked the silver medal into his holdall and allowed himself a smug smile. Seems he was pretty good.

The changing room door swung open and Luke sauntered in. 'Looks like you got lucky today.'

'*Lucky?*'

His mate burst into a grin. 'Okay, what can I say. You exceeded my expectations. Well done, mate, though I reckon I deserve some of the glory.'

'How's that?'

'Well, I did invite that cute little blonde of yours to watch. I'm sure she gave you extra incentive not to make a total arse of yourself. Probably gained you at least two rounds.'

There were so many words Doug knew he should pull Luke up on in that sentence. Abby wasn't his and while she was definitely cute and blonde she'd hate to be described that way. He was too damn tired to bother though, plus he was acutely aware that overall Luke's statement was frighteningly accurate.

They wandered back to find the others who clapped and cheered when they saw them, embarrassing the hell out of him. Luke, of course, bowed and took the applause as if he'd won the flipping thing. Still, Doug was grateful to his friend for hogging the attention. He felt weirdly emotional glancing round the cheery faces, especially when his eyes landed on Abby. Her face shone with something he couldn't put his finger on, but whatever it was caused a lump to settle in his throat. It was hard to remember a time when anyone had taken this much interest in something he'd done.

Luke and Gerri – though he supposed she was still Geraldine to him and all other mortals – declined his half-hearted offer to take them out for pizza, too.

Which left him with the Spencer family.

'Do you want to follow me?' he asked Abby's father, when they all finally trooped out. 'I know a good place not far away.'

'Sure.' Doug watched Derek give his eldest daughter an unsubtle nudge. 'Why don't you go with Doug and keep him company?'

Abby flushed and glared at her father, making Doug feel like the gawky kid the cool girls didn't want to be paired off with. 'It's okay, I'm used to my own company,' he replied stiffly.

As Abby and her father proceeded to have a second staring contest Doug turned away and walked moodily towards his car.

When he reached it, he heard a little cough behind him and turned to find Abby looking uncomfortable.

'You did—'

'You don't have to—'

She nodded her head. 'Winners first.'

He exhaled sharply and angled the key fob at the car. 'Don't feel you have to ride with me, Abby. I know your father was trying to be kind, but please, go back to your family. I'll see you there.'

In answer she opened the passenger door and slid inside.

'My father wasn't trying to be kind,' she said a little later as he'd steered out of the car park. 'He was trying to matchmake. He thinks the reason you keep pushing me away is because you're trying to protect me from something and if I give you time you'll eventually come to your senses and realise I'm pretty strong and I don't need your protection.'

He opened his mouth to tell her he knew she was strong, but she spoke right over him.

'What my father doesn't know is that actually the problem is you don't believe I'm right for you, and it doesn't matter how long I wait, I'll never be right.'

Doug's hands stilled on the steering wheel. This wasn't a conversation he was ready to have. Certainly not while he was driving to a restaurant to eat with her family. Probably not ever. Yet he didn't want her thinking things that were untrue.

Turning into the restaurant car park he eased between a pair of white lines and cut the engine. 'You're exactly right for me,' he told her quietly. 'Which is why you also scare the life out of me.'

Her head spun, eyes wide with shock. 'But—'

'It's me who's not right for you,' he interrupted. 'And now isn't the time to go into it.'

'When then, Doug?'

He opened the door, pretending he hadn't heard her. How could he answer the *when*, if he hadn't determined the *if* part. *If* he had the balls to forget his fear of being incapable of love and boldly dive head first into a relationship with this incredibly sweet, but he suspected easily hurt, woman who'd blazed into his life four and a bit months ago.

Thankfully by the time he and Abby were shown to a table, the rest of the Spencer clan descended on them, and the chance for any further private conversation was over. He found himself sitting next to Ellie, which also meant he didn't actually need to talk at all.

It gave him time to think. And as he let the chatter from the lively, smiling girls Abby was both big sister and mother to flow over him, he considered that maybe her father was right. He was trying to protect a woman who didn't need his protection.

In the end it came down to two questions.

Could he live with himself if he tried to love, but ended up hurting her?

Was he living at all if he didn't even try?

Chapter Twenty-One

The next few weeks stuttered by and every day it looked increasingly less likely that Doug would expand any further on the words he'd dangled in front of Abby outside the pizza restaurant. *You're exactly right for me.* A heady sentence, had it not been followed by, *which is why you also scare the life out of me.* Didn't a five foot three girl deserve to know why she scared the life out of a six foot something male who was pretty damn amazing at martial arts?

A shadow fell across her computer screen and she looked up into the bright blue eyes of that same six foot something male. He'd put his suit jacket on and tightened up the fancy tie he habitually loosened when he was working at his desk.

'Abby, I need you to do me a favour, please.'

'Well, as you pay me to do what you ask, you can pretty much guarantee I'll do it. As long as it doesn't involve breaking the law. Or anything I'm particularly squeamish of, like removing dead mice. Or live ones, for that matter.'

'No rodents are involved.' He gave her a tolerant smile. 'Only a contract with a distributor. We've done business with them for years so it will only involve a bit of polite conversation to indicate how much we value them and a quick scan through the updated contract together. I've taken a look and it seems okay to me.'

'Wouldn't it indicate their value more if you were there in person, rather than sending your PA?'

'I've already spoken to Stan and told him I can't be there, but my right hand woman will be.'

'Your right hand woman,' she repeated. 'Is that a promotion?'

He gave her another patient smile. 'Sadly, no. It's my way

of trying to butter you up. Will you sort out Stan, please? Luke wants me at the gallery. Some big American cheese seems keen to show my paintings.' He paused. 'In his New York gallery.'

'Hey, wow. That's fantastic.'

His mask slipped a little. 'It is, isn't it?'

'Of course I'll sort Stan out.' She hesitated. 'He's not another Teddy, is he?'

'No, I promise, though he is another friend of my father so you might want to treat him with kid gloves.'

Great. It was impossible to say no to Doug though, not when the excitement he was so desperately trying to hide was there in the rare sparkle of his eyes. 'Okay, I'll ferret out my kid gloves. You go and charm the socks off that gallery owner.'

She gave a start of surprise when he leant over to kiss her cheek. 'Thank you.'

He left her with a tingling cheek and a free falling heart.

Stan White was a short, slender man who wore what was left of his hair in one of those ridiculous comb-overs that fooled nobody. He also had bad breath so Abby purposefully sat on the other side of the table to him as they went through the contract in Doug's office. It was pretty standard, but she was concerned about the products listed.

'Do you usually stock all the Crumbs range?' She'd already checked on the previous contracts and as far as she could see they stocked everything.

'We sure do. Been working with you guys for years. We sell everything.'

'It's just I can't see the new savoury range listed, which I guess must be an oversight.'

'What the blazes is going on here?'

Abby nearly jumped out of her seat as Charles Faulkner

marched into the office, slamming the door behind him so loudly the whole room shook.

'Well?' he thundered, animosity positively dripping from his tongue. He had the look of a bully who'd caught a snivelling youngster rifling through his cookie jar.

Abby swallowed and tried to ignore the quick fire bounce of her heart against her ribs. 'I'm taking Mr White through the contract.'

'You're what?'

'I'm taking—'

'I heard what you said. What I'm having trouble understanding is why you're the one doing it.'

'Doug is otherwise engaged at the moment.'

'I don't care if he's entertaining the bloody Queen, secretarial staff have no place conducting contract discussions.' He nodded over to Stan. 'Go and wait in the reception a minute, would you, Stan? I'll be back out to finish this.'

Stan hastily picked up his stuff and shuffled out of the room without even an apologetic backwards glance, leaving Abby to face the angry grizzly bear alone. Charming.

'You're fired.'

Okay, she'd not anticipated that one. Willing her knees to stop knocking she rose to her feet. 'On what grounds?'

'Meddling in company business.'

'In what way is taking a distributor though their contract, under the direct orders of the managing director, meddling?' There. Her voice was hardly shaking.

'Were you suggesting revisions?'

Why hadn't she kept her big gob shut? 'I only mentioned that the new range wasn't included. I was going to check when Doug came back whether it should have been or not.'

'Then I'll save you the trouble. Meddling in affairs you shouldn't is grounds for gross misconduct. I want you out of here in five minutes.' His top lip curled in a sneer. 'Not so cocky now, eh? And don't think your boyfriend will get you your job back, because I still run this company.'

Charles Faulkner left the same way he'd entered, slamming the door so loud it rattled on its hinges.

Abby slumped back down on the chair, staring after him in shock. Had she really just got *fired*? As the reality of it began to sink in and she glanced round Doug's office for what she knew would be the final time, a sob burst from her. Damn it, she loved this job. Where else was she going to get the chance to work on such important projects with her lack of experience? Yeah right, because it's the job she was so cut up about. Not the fact that she'd never bring Doug another coffee, smiling to herself as she placed it next to his coaster because she knew it drove him mad. Never again see his eyes fill with admiration as she presented one of her ideas to him.

She'd resigned herself to never kissing him again, but not seeing him again?

Tears streamed down her face as she grabbed at her belongings with shaking hands; her handbag, the pot plant the girls had bought her, the umbrella she'd jammed into her filing cabinet just in case. A photograph of them all on pizza night when they'd celebrated her getting the job.

A final sob wrenched from her as she stuffed the photograph into her yellow bag and left her office for the last time.

Doug whistled as he climbed the stairs to his office. Whistled as he opened the door and dumped his jacket on the back of his chair. Carried on whistling as he walked back out to Abby's desk.

Then stopped.

She'd gone. Not just left early for the day gone, but gone, gone. He almost felt it before he saw the evidence. No photograph, no struggling-to-stay-alive plant.

No Abby.

Snatching at the phone he called William, the HR Director, his anger mounting the more he listened to the man's stuttering reply. Within seconds Doug was barging through the door of his father's office.

Charles's head snapped up at the interruption, but when he saw who it was a slow smile slid across his face. 'Ah, you've obviously heard that I had to sack your little blonde girl. Most unfortunate. It couldn't be helped, I'm afraid.'

Doug's hands clenched as he took two purposeful strides towards the desk. 'Call William and tell him you've made a mistake.'

Charles Faulkner leant forward. 'No.'

Doug leant forward too, bracing his arms on the desk so their faces were almost touching. 'You have no grounds to sack her and you know it. She was going through the contract with Stan under my direct orders. Sack me.'

'You'd like that, wouldn't you?'

'Yes.'

'As intriguing as that possibility sounds, the answer is no. Can't have people thinking I've got a total imbecile for a son.'

'If you're sacking the woman I hired, for doing a job I told her to do, people will think it anyway.'

'She's been sacked for meddling in company affairs. The message is already out there and can't be undone. Go back to your office and do what I pay you to do.'

Anger lashed at Doug's insides, burning a trail from his gut to his fist, bypassing his brain. He raised his right arm and grabbed his father by his collar. 'You bastard.'

His father's face started to turn red but there was no fear in his eyes, only cold amusement. 'I rather believe that term describes you, not me.'

Doug's fist tightened on the collar, turning Charles's face a shade darker. 'This is going to end,' he announced harshly, then twisted his hand just that little bit more, almost cutting off his air supply.

Charles's eyes began to bulge and his hands tore at Doug's, trying to release his hold, but Doug was too strong for him. What would it feel like to push on those carotids just a little bit more? The strangle was part of BJJ. A legitimate way of getting an opponent to submit. If it worked on fit young men, what would it do to a fat old one?

Disgusted with himself, Doug relaxed his hands and shoved his father back onto his chair. Christ, what had he been thinking, wrapping his hand around an old man's neck?

Feeling sick, Doug spun away and staggered along the corridor to the gents where he emptied the contents of his stomach into the toilet. After rinsing his mouth he rested his hands on the sink and stared into the mirror, not recognising the haggard man looking back at him. The eyes were lost. Those of a man shipwrecked in stormy waters, who'd just seen his last lifeline float away.

Splashing cold water on his face he tried to reassure his harrowed reflection that Abby wouldn't necessarily hate him for what he'd let his father do. Perhaps she'd even understand he was powerless to stop him.

Powerless to stop an old man trampling all over the woman he … he … His heart shrivelled in his chest and Doug hung his head. He'd never know what Abby could have meant to him.

What a fucking mess.

He dried off his face with a paper towel before scrunching it violently into a ball and throwing it in the bin. The sound of his mobile crashed into the silence, echoing round the stark room and for the tiniest of moments his heart lifted. Maybe it was Abby, telling him not to worry.

'Luke.'

His friend didn't pick up on the heaviness of his voice.

'Hey, not just Luke. I'm the man who's managed to persuade the God of the New York gallery scene to take eight of your paintings. You can call me Sir from now on.'

Doug shut his eyes and leant against the cold tiled wall, unable to raise a smile. What a difference a few minutes made.

'Doug?'

'Sorry, mate,' he croaked. Jesus, he sounded like he'd been crying. He ran the tap and splashed more water on his face. 'Now's a bad time.'

'What the hell happened in the hour since you left here with a bloody big grin on your face?'

'I ... that is, my father ...' He squeezed at his eyes with his thumb and forefinger. 'My father sacked Abby for gross misconduct.'

There was a beat of silence as his friend tried to process the information. 'What did she do?'

'What I asked her to.'

'And what was that?'

Doug choked on the next words. 'What I should have been doing, only instead I was in your gallery, schmoozing an art dealer. Sorting out my own future, while at the same time fucking up hers.'

There was a loud exhale of air on the end of the line. 'Stop blaming yourself, Doug. It's your father who's the bastard here, not you.'

'No.' Doug straightened up and faced himself in the mirror. 'I'm the weak shit who lets my father get away with this. I'm the one at fault.'

'Then do something about it,' Luke countered. 'You never bothered to challenge him when he was picking on you but now he's picked on Abby, perhaps it's time to ask yourself where your loyalties lie. With your mother and sisters, or with the woman you love.'

'I don't love her.' It was an instinctive reply, though the words tasted wrong in his mouth. As if they'd passed their expiry date.

Down the end of the phone he heard Luke snorting. 'Course you do, you dumbwit. You're just too stupid to realise it. Now get off this phone and go and beg her forgiveness.'

With a rush of determination Doug raced down the stairs and into his car. Luke was right. It was time to look after the woman who'd brought happiness into his life, even if she refused to talk to him again.

Even if it was at the expense of his own family.

Chapter Twenty-Two

Abby had been home for three hours and already recounted the tale of what had happened three times. The first had been with Ellie, Holly and Sally.

'Why are you home already?' Sally had asked when they'd piled through the door.

'Are you ill?' That had been from sweet, caring Holly.

'Are you skiving off?' Predictably that had come from Ellie.

When she'd told them what had happened, she'd had another three predictable replies.

'That's ridiculous. Mr Faulkner can't sack you like that. You can get him for unfair dismissal. We learnt about that at school.' Had been Sally's response.

'Oh, poor you. That's not fair.' Holly had gone on to hug her, causing Abby to tear up yet again.

The tears had turned into helpless laughter when Ellie had asked, 'Does that mean we won't get any more cheap biscuits?'

Abby had only just recovered from that bout of questioning when Mandy arrived home and she'd had to explain it all again.

'The miserable git *sacked* you?' she'd exclaimed. 'And what does Doug think of all this? I presume he's sorting his father out.'

Abby hadn't been able to reply. She didn't have a clue what Doug thought as he hadn't bothered to contact her. Before she'd been able to brood too much on that though, her father had come home and she'd had to go through the whole wretched tale again.

'Bullshit,' he exclaimed. 'If that Faulkner bloke thinks

he can treat my daughter like this he's got another think coming. I'll be round there first thing tomorrow.' He shot her a look. 'And if his son hasn't beaten me to it, he's not the man I thought he was.'

Abby's mind flashed back to the board meeting where Doug had let his father stomp all over him. He was hardly going to stand up to his father for her if he wouldn't flaming do it for himself. The thought made her angry. She'd lost a bloody good job today and it was Doug's fault, not hers. Not even Charles Faulkner really, because though he might have fired her, Doug had given him the ammunition.

The doorbell sounded and Abby jumped up from the sofa with a start. Was that Doug? She'd taken one step towards the door when her father blocked her path. 'Stay where you are. I'll get it.'

His feet sounded ominously heavy as he marched towards the door. Their house didn't have much of a hallway so anyone sitting in the living area, as Abby was, could overhear the conversation at the front door.

When she heard Doug's low, quiet voice her heart thrashed wildly. 'Hello, Derek. Is Abby in?'

'She's in, yes,' came her father's terse reply. 'Doesn't mean I'm going to let you talk to her, though.'

Abby cringed, rising to her feet but then slumping back down again. Maybe it was best for her dad to get it out of his system.

'I understand your reticence,' Doug replied, his voice so deliberate, so controlled. 'You have every right to be angry.'

'Aye, I'm that all right. Angry with your father, disappointed in you.' There was a silence and she tried to imagine Doug's face as the words hit him. Was he looking upset, or was he wearing his damn mask again? 'Are you going to make sure my girl gets her job back?' her father continued harshly. 'Though maybe she won't want it after the way your family have treated her. She's far too good to be a secretary to the likes of you, anyway.'

'I know she is.'

Abby bounded to her feet and rushed to the door. Listening to her father chew Doug off a strip was beyond painful.

Doug's eyes darted over to her and, oh God, the misery in them almost made her forget how cross she was with him. 'Abby.' Briefly he closed those sapphire pools. When he opened them again they pleaded with her. 'I'm so sorry.'

'Yes, I think you are.'

'It's no good being sorry. You need to bloody well sort it out.'

'Dad!' Abby shot her father a *shut up you're embarrassing me* look.

'No, your father's right. And I will sort it out, but ...' Doug heaved out a sigh. 'It's complicated.'

'What's complicated?' her father demanded. 'You're the flaming managing director.'

Doug thrust a hand through his hair, his expression tight.

'Dad, you're not helping here.' Abby nudged his arm. 'I love you to bits but right now I need you to butt out and go and make the tea. I've got this.'

Her father gave Doug one final hard stare before grunting and walking away.

'Hell, Abby.' Doug shook his head, his voice loaded with frustration. 'How much of a wimp do you take me for? You think I can't handle a few jibes from your father?'

'It's not *my* father who's the problem here.'

His jaw clenched and his chest rose and fell. 'I know.'

'So, do you want to come in for a drink and discuss this like rational human beings, or would you rather continue the doorstep slanging match? I'm sure the neighbours would prefer the latter. They're used to hearing a few ding dongs coming from our house though they usually involve Mandy and Roger. And never have they involved a man who drives an Aston Martin.'

'*Abby*.' There followed another deep expulsion of breath. 'Why aren't you punching me in the face right now, rather than inviting me in for a drink?'

'I'd hate to ruin such a lovely face.'

His breath came out in a choked laugh. 'Jesus.' He took a step back and shoved a hand in each pocket. 'I realise it makes me a coward but, if you don't mind, I'd rather we discussed what we need to somewhere quieter.'

'Quieter than the drive?'

'Quieter than the Spencer family home.'

'Ah.' At that moment there was a loud crash, followed immediately by a chorus of barking, a squeal from George and a cacophony of raised voices.

'What I'd really like is to take you back to my place so I can give you the answers to some of the questions you've asked and I've evaded.' His eyes sought hers and their sincerity pulled at her heart. 'Somehow I've managed to dump you right in the middle of my mess. You don't know how sorry I am about that and the very least you deserve is an explanation. Will you hear me out, please?'

She would never be able to refuse those eyes. 'As long as food is involved because my stomach's rumbling.'

His face relaxed slightly. 'I can throw something together.'

'Okay then.' Her heart jumped, clearly forgetting how much he'd let her down and focusing instead on the part where he made her a meal. In his house. 'I'll just grab my handbag and tell the noisy crew I'm going.'

A few minutes later she was climbing into Doug's car, her ears ringing with her father's last words. *If you don't get him to sort things out, I will. And he won't like my methods.*

'I might not have punched your face yet, but I am bloody

annoyed,' she told Doug as he reversed out of the drive. 'I don't want you thinking I'm a pushover.'

Abby remained quiet for most of the drive, leaving Doug to his own crappy thoughts. He didn't blame Derek for being spitting mad. He'd allowed Abby to be treated like dirt – he deserved all the condemnation thrown at him. If Abby herself had any sense she'd tell him to go to hell. He pulled up at a traffic light, his eyes darting automatically towards her, drifting over the curves so clearly outlined by her fitted blue dress. Despite the inappropriateness of the situation, he felt a flash of desire.

It cooled a little when he glanced at her face. Sombre, where usually it was so alive.

'I don't even know where you live,' she said into the silence. 'I presume it's not far, otherwise I could have taken my own car so you didn't have to drive me back.'

I don't want you going back. As the words echoed around his head he cleared his throat. 'I don't live far. I'll take you home when you've had enough.'

'I guess that's the least you can do,' she replied, eyes fixed on the road ahead, 'considering that between you and your father I lost my job today. It was a pretty good job, too. My boss needed to loosen up a bit but at least he let me get involved with the business. He was cute, too, if you like the strong and silent type.'

He shot her a quick glance but her profile gave him no clue as to what she was thinking. 'And do you? Like the strong and silent type?' he qualified when she didn't reply.

'I'm still making up my mind.'

Okay. He deserved that. Letting the comment slide he turned on some music. Time enough for talking when they were at his house.

Ten minutes later he pulled up to his gates and clicked the remote on his dashboard to open them.

'Oh my God, you live *here*?' Her hand swept over the imposing four bed detached house he called home. 'In all of *this*?' She slapped a hand on her forehead. 'Then again I expect it seems small compared to your other home. The one you grew up in.'

'I spent most of my growing up years living in a bedroom in a boarding school dormitory,' he reminded her. 'But yes, this is where I live now.'

The trappings of a millionaire's son. For years he'd hated the place but since he'd paid off the outstanding mortgage with the earnings from his paintings, he'd begun to see it as less of a bribe and more of a home.

He held the car door open for her but she refused his outstretched hand, reaching for the door handle instead as she climbed out.

It felt like a punch to the gut.

'Shall we eat first, talk after?' he asked as he walked through the front door and snapped on the lights. 'That way we don't spoil our appetite?'

'I can pretty much guarantee whatever you've got to say won't stop me eating.'

He'd noticed that about her, how she didn't pick at food like most other women he knew. 'Is pasta okay? I rarely go wrong with that. Anything else you'll be taking a risk.'

'I don't mind taking a few risks.' She looked him straight in the eye, as if she was trying to tell him something, though he wasn't sure what. 'But pasta sounds great. Do you need me to do anything, or can I take a nosey around your house instead?'

'There's nothing much to nosey, but help yourself.'

He had a full five minutes to fry the bacon and chop up the beans, tomatoes and garlic before she was back.

'You're very neat and tidy,' she told him as she walked back into the kitchen, her voice slightly breathless, as if she'd dashed through his house in a rush. 'Though thinking of your desk, and your obsession with coasters, I don't know why I'm surprised.'

'It's not an obsession,' he felt compelled to point out. 'Merely a healthy regard for my furniture.'

'If you say so.' She twirled around, eyes scanning over the open plan sitting room behind them. 'I do like your house, despite the tidiness.'

'Despite?'

'Of course, because being too tidy can make a place seem soulless. More of a show home than a real home.' She jumped up onto one of the bar stools, grimacing as she nearly toppled over. 'Oops, I've never been any good with tall stools, my legs are too short.' He wanted to point out that actually her legs were exactly right, but she was still talking. 'Anyway, where was I? I was saying you just about get away with being too tidy because your walls are messy.' When he raised an eyebrow she sighed. 'Okay, not messy exactly, but stuffed full of art. I don't understand most of it, though I love the colours.'

'And the messiness.'

'Yes.' She smiled and his heart lurched.

Sadly she wouldn't be smiling when he'd finished talking to her. Reaching into the fridge he pulled out a bottle of wine. 'Would you like a glass? It might help the pasta slip down.' And the conversation afterwards, he thought grimly.

They ate in the kitchen at the breakfast bar, keeping to small talk: how the girls were doing at school, how lucky they'd been with the summer weather so far. All the while he stewed over what he was about to tell her.

After he'd cleared away the plates he offered his hand to help her down from the stool. 'Let's go and sit somewhere more comfortable.'

This time she put her hand in his, and as she slid off the

stool she tumbled straight into him. His arms shot out to steady her and she wrapped hers round his shoulders. Then looked straight into his eyes. 'I think I'm a bit tipsy.' She frowned, wrinkling her nose. 'Remind me again why I'm cross with you.'

His arms refused to let her go. How could they when the feel of her curves darted arrows of pleasure straight to his groin? 'I lost you your job,' he said roughly.

'Oh, yes.' Her lips were so, so close to his.

He groaned, the noise coming from deep inside him, a mixture of absolute pleasure and absolute fear. The pleasure was easy to figure. The fear came from his dread of hurting her.

Still, he couldn't stop.

He bent his head and sank onto her waiting lips. Her sweetness hit him first, lip gloss perhaps, and a plush softness he remembered from before. But then she opened up for him and the sweetness was drowned out by a scorching heat that had him helpless to do anything but deepen the kiss, thrusting his tongue into her welcoming mouth. With one hand on the back of her neck, he slid the other over the round curves of her bottom.

And let out another groan.

'Abby.' God, his mind was melting with her heat. He could only whisper her name when what he should be shouting was *stop, we can't do this. Not yet. Maybe not ever.*

'If you push me away again, I'll kill you.' A fierce determination lit up her eyes even as her fingers danced across his face. 'And after that I'll never speak to you again.'

He let out a strangled laugh. 'I don't want to push you away. I want to pull you closer and wrap your body against mine, with no clothes between us.' He used both hands to squeeze her hips, thrusting against her so she knew exactly what he wanted.

This time the moan came from Abby. 'God, yes.'

He knew what he was about to do – making love to her first, telling her the truth about him later – was entirely wrong, but Doug was unable to stop.

The mind he'd spent so many years controlling was no longer functioning. His body had taken over and it knew exactly what it wanted.

Chapter Twenty-Three

How had her clothes dissolved like that? One minute Abby had been kissing the life out of Doug with her dress most definitely on. The next she was still kissing him – or he was kissing her – with her clothes off. She'd intended to stay mad at him, she really had. That was until she'd fallen into his arms and all sanity had vanished. It didn't seem to matter that she was coming across as a giddy virgin, happy to let the big alpha male walk all over her. Sod her job, sod her self-respect. She *wanted* this.

He gathered her in his arms, this tall, strong, quiet man walking her towards the sofa as if she was weightless.

'It should be a bed,' he announced gruffly as he carefully lowered her to her feet. 'But there's no way I can—'

'Carry me up the stairs,' she finished for him, clinging to his shoulders as her breath came out in short pants even though he'd been the one carrying her. 'Of course you can't. I'm an ample, if I breathe in, size ten. Okay, maybe I'm an eleven but they don't really do that size so I guess that makes me a twelve.'

He continued to stare at her, eyes alight with pure, unbridled lust, as he slowly and methodically unbuttoned his shirt and pulled it off.

'Oh my God,' she said breathlessly, her fingers desperate to trace the planes of his sculptured chest. 'Can I touch?' Immediately she realised how gauche she sounded and dropped her hand to her side.

'Please. I wish you would.' His hand clasped hers, bringing it to rest against his rock hard pectoral muscles. 'And before you interrupted me I was going to say there's no way I can wait to take you upstairs. I need to be inside you. Now.'

The saliva disappeared from her mouth. She could feel the steady thump of his heart beneath her hand; knew hers was pounding twice as fast. Faster still as she watched him open his belt, yank down his zip and pull off his trousers and boxers in one fluid, sexy, eighteen-rated movement.

When his hands were free he ran them restlessly up and down her arms, laughing softly. 'Hell, I can't believe I'm saying this now, when I'm seconds from exploding, but are you sure about this?'

In answer she reached up and threw her arms around his neck.

With a strangled groan he held onto her, pushing her back against the sofa. He didn't join her straight away – spending a few frustrating seconds fishing a condom out of his wallet and covering himself – before finally, finally, his long, hard body moved over hers. And oh God, the feel of him. She ran her hands over and over the smooth skin of his back, feeling the movement of his muscles as he shifted to settle between her legs.

His left elbow bent as he rested above her, leaving his right hand free to stroke her breasts with almost reverent movements. Then, with no warning, no let's start this gentle, he tilted his hips and thrust into her in one powerful, mind shattering movement.

His eyes remained locked on hers as her body adjusted to the incredible feel of him deep inside her. Sex before this had always happened in a dark bedroom but now she couldn't take her eyes off his. Didn't want to because then she'd miss seeing all that white-hot passion, the swirls of pleasure as he thrust deeply.

'I can't do gentle,' he warned, his expression tight as his hips continued their pounding rhythm.

She wanted to tell him she didn't need gentle. What she needed was for him to lose himself in her. To carry on doing exactly what he was doing now, only faster, but for once her mouth wasn't working. Perhaps because her mind had turned to mush and the only thing she could concentrate on was the growing pleasure between her legs.

It seemed he didn't need her words because intuitively he picked up the pace and soon they were both racing to an explosive climax.

Doug's body felt utterly boneless, as if his climax had sucked everything out of him. Sadly he couldn't continue to lie on the deliciously soft pillow that was Abby. 'I'm sorry,' he said as he hauled his wrecked body upright.

She gasped, a hand flying to her face. 'Oh my God, don't tell me you're going to *apologise*? Sorry for losing control for once in my life and having stupendous sex with you, Abby?'

He moved them both, lifting and twisting her body so she was sitting on his lap, her buttocks nestled over his naked crotch. 'I'm not sorry I had stupendous sex with you. I am sorry I squashed you.'

She wriggled, causing the part of his anatomy he'd thought must be totally wiped out to stir again. 'FYI, I enjoyed being squashed by you.'

He had to admit her beguiling dark eyes had the dazed glow of a happily content woman. 'Still, I should have taken more time, been more gentle.' He kissed the tip of her nose. 'At least made it to the bed for our first time.'

Her eyes smiled at him. 'That would seem to imply this will happen more than once.'

He glanced down at her naked body, the luscious breasts pressed against his chest. 'It will happen again right now if you don't keep still.' Very deliberately she moved up and down on him and he let out a half-laugh, half-groan. 'Abby, no. Much as I'd love a repeat, we need to talk.'

Her eyes dimmed a little and she eased off his lap. 'That's supposed to be my line.'

Reluctantly he walked over to the kitchen, picking up the clothes he'd unceremoniously dumped in the rush of desire. 'Here.' He handed her some wispy underwear – how had he not remembered her wearing *that*? – and her dress. 'For what I'm about to say, I need you dressed.'

He left her changing while he hunted down his own clothes. When he was dressed he turned to find her sitting primly on the edge of the sofa. It was so at odds with her flushed face and messy just-had-sex hair that he had trouble keeping a straight face.

'What's so funny?'

He shook his head. 'Nothing. It's just you look so ... sweet sitting neatly on the sofa.'

'I have to sit neatly in this dress. If I don't it rides right up, though really it doesn't matter now as you've already seen everything I have to offer.'

'Seen, but not sampled nearly enough.'

Her eyes went all soft and dewy eyed. 'Please don't be sweet to me. I've just remembered I should be mad at you and I can't do that if you're sweet.'

Slowly he lowered himself into the armchair, leaning forward and resting his forearms on his knees. 'I'm very afraid, when you hear what I've got to say, you'll find it all too easy to stay mad at me.'

She huffed. 'Then flipping just tell me and get it over and done with.'

'I'm not Charles Faulkner's real son,' he blurted.

'Oh.'

For once he couldn't read her expression. Was she shocked? Disappointed? 'Please say more than *oh*.'

Her eyes slid over his face. 'I guess I'm not all that surprised. For starters you don't even look alike. He's short and dumpy and pretty ugh looking. You're tall, athletic and pretty wow looking.'

221

He felt a flush creep up his neck. 'Thank you.'

'Plus he's not a very nice man whereas you're very nice. When you're not getting me fired.'

He drew in a breath and let it out slowly, watching as she tried and failed to tuck her legs up under her because her dress was too tight. In the end she yanked the hem up so it barely skirted her thighs. Reluctantly he dragged his eyes away. 'You being fired had nothing to do with you, or what you were doing for that matter, and everything to do with me.'

Her eyes remained on his. 'That's hardly an explanation.'

'No.' He'd never found words easy to come by. Even harder when what he had to say was so shaming. 'Apparently Charles long suspected I wasn't his son. I wanted to paint, not indulge in what he considered manly pursuits like rugby and hunting. But mainly it was my eyes. He comes from a long line of brown eyes, so does my mother. When I was thirteen, following the birth of a second brown eyed daughter, he had a DNA test done. I remember the expression when he told me; the vindication along with the disgust. He's never liked me and now he had a reason not to.'

'So that's what I saw in the boardroom when he was telling everyone you were his puppet. Him *not liking you*.' She rolled her eyes. 'If you're going to talk to me, Doug, you need to tell me the truth. He hates you, doesn't he? He blames you for what happened, even though it was your mum who deceived him, not you.'

Doug sat back and ran a hand over his face. Shit, she was right. It was time he manned up for once. 'Yes. Charles Faulkner, the man I call my father, hates my guts.' It was the first time he'd said the words out loud to anyone, even Luke, and he wasn't sure if he felt better or worse for admitting them. His father hated him. Had *always* hated him. 'He fired you to get at me, to punish me.'

222

Abby drew in a sharp breath and scrambled to her feet, coming to sit on the arm of his chair. Gently she ran her fingers across his arm. 'I'm so sorry.'

He stared up at her in surprise. 'What for? It's you who got fired.'

'Yes, but it's you who had the crappy childhood.' Her hand clasped his and the tenderness of the gesture did funny things to his heart. 'I'm guessing that with a father who hated you and a mum who doesn't strike me as being the least bit maternal, it can't have been much fun growing up in Faulkner Towers.'

He found himself smiling at her irreverent name for the Faulkner family home. 'Your guess would be right.'

'Have you talked to your mum about your real dad?'

He laughed, because it was such an Abby thing to say. 'We're not like your family. We don't do talking. The heated arguments I've overheard suggest my mother had a brief affair.' He sighed, leaning in to her. 'I can't condone that, but Charles is a bully. I can't imagine being his wife is easy.'

Doug was acutely aware of the warmth of Abby's body next to him. The cushion of her breast against his shoulder. One quick movement and he'd have her on his lap, and oh God, he ached to do that. There was nothing sexual in his need, not this time. Just an urge to hold onto something special. An antidote to all this dark. Yet despite the sex they'd just had, he didn't feel he had the right to ask it of her.

'That's why Gwen is so special to you.'

'Yes.' He took comfort from pressing more heavily against her. 'Thanks to her, and painting, I didn't turn into a total basket case. I'm just insecure, introverted, cynical and closed off.'

Her arm reached around his shoulders, giving them a light squeeze, and he felt a shudder of longing ripple right through him. 'You weren't closed off half an hour ago.'

'Sex isn't an emotion, Abby.'

'It is when it happens between the right people.'

The slight catch in her voice, together with the liquid brown of her eyes, at last gave him the confidence to draw her onto his lap.

'Are we the right people?' he asked, his voice tight with an emotion he couldn't place.

'I don't know,' she whispered, her hands on his face, her mouth only inches from his. 'But if we don't try, we'll never find out.'

Abby felt her heart go into free fall as Doug lowered his head and kissed her. It was gentler this time, as if he was trying to make good on his promise earlier. Softly his lips captured hers, his tongue playing lightly around her mouth, drawing away before it became too heavy.

'Before you decide whether trying is something you want to do, there's more you need to know.' His arms tightened around her, hugging her against the solid wall of his chest. 'My father – and I say that through habit – couldn't abide the thought of people knowing he'd been cuckolded so he continued to call me his son. When his longed for true male heir didn't arrive he gave me an ultimatum on my eighteenth birthday. Continue to play my role in his archaic fantasy, which included joining the family business after university, or he'd expose me as a bastard, throw my mother and sisters out and disinherit them.'

Horrified, she wriggled away a little so she could see his face. 'He's been *blackmailing* you to work at Crumbs?'

'Yes.' His lids lowered over his eyes, as if he was ashamed of what he'd just admitted. 'I've been on the verge of telling him to go ahead, do his worst, so many times but at the last minute I stop myself.' Suddenly his eyes blinked open, his expression fierce as he looked directly at her. 'I don't give a toss about the world and its dog knowing I'm not his son – it will embarrass him far more than me. It's the shame it will bring to my mother that makes me pause.' He sighed then, his expression turning sad, hopeless. 'And even if I was willing to do that, how can I risk her financial future, and that of my sisters?'

Abby swore under her breath. It was all becoming so much clearer now. 'So that's why you don't stand up to him at work. You're stuck in an impossible situation.'

'If by that you mean I've allowed him to tie me up in knots and treat me exactly like the puppet he says I am, then yes.'

He was so tense beneath her. She could feel the muscles in his legs and arms become more and more rigid the longer he spoke. 'You've done what he's asked so you can protect your family,' she told him softly. 'It's the action of an honourable man, not a weak one.' He didn't reply, merely squeezed her tighter. 'Have you told your mum about this?'

She felt his chest expand and contract as he sighed. 'No. I told you before, we don't have that type of relationship. It's an understatement to say my family is very different to yours.'

'I wish you could have met my mum.' Out of nowhere Abby's eyes began to prick.

'Hey.' Doug trailed his thumb over her cheek, mopping up the stray tears. 'I didn't mean to make you sad.'

'I'm not sad. I miss her, that's all. Miss the way she'd hug me for no reason, the way she'd listen when I rambled on about God knows what, looking so interested when really she must have been thinking *get to the point, Abby, I've got a million things to do*. I know that sounds soppy—'

'It sounds incredible,' he interrupted.

The tears began in earnest now, though not only for the memory of her mum. 'That's so wrong, you know. Every child should have at least one parent who loves and cherishes them. I've been lucky enough to have two.'

Meticulously he wiped at her cheek. 'Please don't tell me some of those tears are for me. I had a very privileged childhood. I lived in a grand house, went to an expensive school and had pretty much anything I wanted.'

'Except love.'

He stilled. 'Love isn't a concept Faulkners understand.'

Abby was smart enough to know where he was going with that particular topic. 'You've just told me you're not a Faulkner,' she pointed out.

'I've grown up with them, Abby. Your family and mine couldn't be more different.' His blue gaze riveted on her. 'We couldn't be more different.'

Her heart, moments ago feeling so full, slowly started to shrivel. She slid off his lap, feeling gutted when he didn't try to stop her. 'I guess this is the part where you tell me the sex was great, but that's all there'll be.'

The warmth and closeness of a few minutes ago had been shattered. Now he was sitting in the chair as stiff as a board, staring at her with that reserved, highly disciplined expression she was coming to loathe. And not talking.

'Fine. As I value myself too much to get locked into a meaningless relationship that only revolves around sex, I'll be on my way.' She'd taken two steps away from him before she remembered how she'd arrived. 'Damn it, I can't even storm out because I don't have my car, which is your bloody fault. I'll have to phone for a taxi but don't worry, I'll do it outside so we're not in the same room for any longer than we need to be.'

Her words were met with a crashing silence.

Oh God, she was so stupid when it came to men. Scurrying into the kitchen she found her shoes where they'd been discarded while they'd been ... he'd been ... her heart faltered and she clutched at her chest. She'd already allowed him to take too much from her – her job, her body. She was damned if she was going to let him take her heart.

Grabbing her handbag off the kitchen stool she marched to the front door.

Chapter Twenty-Four

Doug remained in the armchair, his mind throwing down restraint after restraint, keeping him immobilised. Abby was blue skies and sunshine. She didn't need a dark cloud like him in her life, dampening her spirit and blocking out the warmth. In time she'd thank him for this.

'Oh shit.'

The sound of a hard clunk, quickly followed by an anguished exclamation, snapped him out of his paralysis and he dashed into the hallway. Abby was hanging onto the hat stand by the door, her foot caught in the tassels of the rug.

'Here.' He reached out to help but she swatted his hand away, as if she couldn't bear him to touch her.

'I'm fine.'

The coldness of her tone shocked him. He wanted to feel the heat of her anger; for her to shove at him, yell, slap him round the face. Anything instead of this … indifference.

'That rug's a death trap.' She nodded to where she'd just pulled out her heel. 'Make sure you warn the next woman you bring back here to have sex.'

'Jesus, Abby. I didn't bring you here to have sex.' Why was he just standing there, so gutless, so useless? Why wasn't he on his damn knees, pleading with her to stay?

The look she threw him bordered on contempt. 'It was more a spur of the moment thing, then? Abby's upset because she's lost her job. I know how to cheer her up. I'll shag her.'

The sharp words tore through him, the trail they left so painful that for once, he spoke without thinking. 'I brought you here to explain why I'm impotent where my father is concerned,' he snapped. 'And so you would understand why, despite the fact that you're the most incredible woman I've ever met, and I'm so damn attracted to you I can't think straight when we're in the same room, I have to keep pushing you away.'

She turned to face him, hair rioting around her face, her huge brown eyes looking like those of a confused Spaniel. 'I know I'm only a PA, or at least I was one—'

'Stop it,' he barked, his anger rising. 'I've never treated you like that.'

'No.' She glanced down at her feet. 'So why do you need to push me away, if all you want is sex? Though I suppose there are plenty of women out there better at sex than me. If I had to make a guess, I'd say I'm only Brownie badge status.' She winced, finally looking up at him. 'And that sounds wildly inappropriate because unless things have changed radically in the last fifteen years, I doubt Brownies have a badge for sex.'

Her monologue was everything he found irresistible about her. Funny, honest, with a touch of crazy. Suddenly he knew he couldn't let her go. Not when she was the only bright light in his world.

Walking up to her he loosened her fingers from the door handle, placing them on his chest so she could feel the pounding of his heart. With his other hand he cupped her face. 'Stay. Please.'

She chewed at her bottom lip. 'Why?'

'When I said we couldn't be more different, I was trying to warn you that I don't know how to have a proper relationship. It doesn't mean I don't want to try.'

He pressed his lips gently to hers, hoping to convey at least some of what he was feeling.

'In the past my relationships with women have only ever been about sex. It was an ... outlet for me. A pleasurable means of working off a shitty mood. I don't know if I'm capable of anything more.'

The hand on his chest moved to hold his. 'Any man who lives through a loveless childhood yet still has the humanity to buy his ex-nanny a house and give a job to the dubious father of his crazy PA's nephew, and for that matter give a job to his crazy PA in the first place, is capable of anything he puts his mind to.'

He tilted her face so he could stare into her eyes, afraid to hope. 'Is that your way of telling me you're prepared to give me a chance?'

'No.' The yellow handbag she'd been holding landed with a thud on the floor. Then, in front of his astonished eyes, she slipped off her shoes and unzipped her dress, inching it over her hips with an unconsciously sexy movement. That was until the zip caught on her underwear and she let out a muffled curse. '*This* was supposed to be my way of telling you.' She craned her neck to glance behind her then looked at him despairingly. 'But the flaming zip is stuck and now I'm stood half undressed in your hallway and feeling like an out of practice hooker.'

He couldn't help himself. The relief, the joy, the fact that she looked so bloody adorable. He started to laugh.

'Are you going to help me?' She shot him a deadly look, one that promised all sorts of payback when she wasn't caught up in her underwear.

'I might. If you make it worth my while.'

'That's what I was trying to do, though clearly even my Brownie badge will need to be handed back now.'

She gave up pulling the dress down and wriggled it over her head instead. Once she'd dropped it on the floor she unclipped her bra and stood naked in front of him.

Doug stopped laughing. 'Christ, you're stunning,' he croaked. 'You don't just take my breath away, you suck it all from me.'

'Really?'

He allowed himself the luxury of tracing the soft curves of her breast with his finger. 'Really,' he affirmed, dipping his head to lick at one exquisite breast.

Her body trembled at his touch. 'I hope you've got enough breath left to carry me upstairs, because I'd like a bed this time.'

Abby had guessed which was Doug's bedroom when she'd snooped around earlier. Not because there were any personal effects on the highly polished mahogany drawers, or any clothes draped over the big antique armchair, but because it smelt of him.

He lowered her gently onto the immaculately made bed before sitting on the edge, his blue eyes burning with intent. 'I want to do it right this time.'

Self-consciously she nodded at her naked body and then over to his fully clothed one. 'If doing it right means you keep your clothes on, I'm going to put in a strong objection.'

Immediately he stood, shrugging off his clothes in about the same time it took her to take off her shoes. There was no show, no posturing, just a quiet dedication to the task. 'Better?'

The bed dipped and she watched in awe as he climbed over to her, the muscles of his chest rippling beneath his lightly tanned skin. Clearly grappling men on the floor was good for muscle definition. Supporting his head on his hand he lay alongside her, easing one of his legs between hers. Wiry hairs tickled the inside of her thighs, but then she turned to look at him and the only thing she could feel was heat.

'When I said I want to do this right,' he continued, eyes fixed on hers, 'I meant I don't just want to have sex with you. I want to show you how much you mean to me.'

'Oh.' Suddenly her mouth was bone dry, her heart pounding. This was really happening. Ten minutes ago she thought she'd lost him forever and now she was *on his bed*. 'I'd like that. As long as what I mean to you is something ... good.'

His reply was to trail soft kisses over her heated skin, starting at her face before spending a sinful amount of time around her central erogenous zones. By the time he crawled back up to her, lust blazing in his stunning blue orbs, she was panting.

'How am I doing so far?' The huskiness of his voice sent another ripple of desire through her.

'Pretty well.'

He cocked an eyebrow. '*Pretty* well?'

'I don't want to praise too much, too early. You need to have something to aim for.'

He chuckled, his breath fluttering across her skin, but then he bent to kiss her and all the playfulness disappeared. His mouth sought hers with a renewed urgency and it wasn't long before he was entering her again, his body claiming her in one strong thrust.

'Abby,' he groaned as his hips began to drive into her.

She was pinned beneath his hard body as he plunged into her at a punishing pace, far removed from the slow, languorous love-making she'd been used to with Toby. That had felt like being lapped by the gentle waves of a calm Caribbean sea. This felt like being tossed into the middle of a storm, leaving her helpless, unable to hold onto anything. Yet it was without fear, and with heat, not cold. Storm was the wrong word, too, because this feeling was more electric; a raw energy surging through her, making her feel desirable, invincible. And the pleasure – it was like nothing she'd ever experienced, coiling inside her, tightening with every hard thrust until she thought she couldn't stand it any more.

'Doug. It's too much. I can't ... oh God.' He continued to

pound into her until she felt like she was drowning in feeling. Moments later, she shattered.

Following a few more thrusts, Doug's powerful body stiffened and collapsed on top of her.

For a few precious seconds she savoured the solid weight of him, the heavy thump of his heart as it beat against her chest. The heat radiating off his skin, surrounding her in him.

All too quickly he rolled off her, eyes staring up at the ceiling as he lay on his back.

Just as she turned to ask him what was wrong he jumped off the bed and disappeared into the bathroom, shutting the door firmly behind him.

Doug disposed of the condom and then, arms resting on the sink, stared at his reflection in the bathroom mirror. He didn't look like an aggressive man, but looks could be deceptive.

Fuck. He'd told Abby he'd show her how much she meant to him, then taken her like an animal in heat. Trouble was, he was used to women who were sexually aggressive. The type who, like him, saw sex as an outlet rather than an intimacy.

Abby wasn't that type.

There was a tap on the door. 'Doug? Are you okay?'

His chest tightened painfully and he hung his head, cursing again. He didn't want to go out there and face the concern he knew he'd see on her face.

'I'm fine.' He closed his eyes and concentrated on his breathing. In and out, in and out. Finally he tugged a towel off the rail and wrapped it round his waist because God, he couldn't face this naked, and walked back out to the bedroom.

Abby was sitting on the edge of the bed, her body dwarfed by a dressing gown she must have taken from the back of his door.

233

'What's happening?' she asked. 'One minute I'm having the best sex of my life, the next the man I thought was enjoying it with me has stalked off to the bathroom.' Her eyes scanned his face. 'And come out with an expression on his face more suited to a dentist waiting room than a bedroom.'

'The best sex of your life.' He shook his head. 'Abby, how many men have you slept with?'

Her eyes darted away from his and onto the floor. 'Three.'

'Three including me?' When she nodded, he let out a short laugh. 'So the best sex of your life isn't based on very much then, is it?'

Her eyes flew to his face. 'Why are you doing this? Why are you trying to sully what, to me at least, was something special, though obviously I don't know anything because I'm just a naïve little girl who's only mustered three sexual partners. One took my virginity then didn't touch me again, one stayed with me for six months before finding someone better. You've managed sex with me twice.'

Her voice caught on her last words and Doug realised with horror that in his disgust with himself he was doing the one thing he'd been desperately trying to avoid. Hurt her.

Rushing over to the bed he took hold of her hands, gripping them when she tried to resist. 'I'm sorry. I didn't mean to upset you.'

She stared at him incredulously. 'Seconds after coming inside me you roll away and shut yourself in the bathroom. How did you think I'd react?'

Tears rushed down her cheeks and Doug felt wretched. He tried to hug her but she was stiff in his arms, all that joy, that exuberance, gone. Thanks to him. 'This is what I keep trying to tell you, Abby. I'm not relationship material. I'll end up hurting you.'

She jumped to her feet. 'Bollocks. You were doing just fine

until you rolled away from me. Why, Doug?' When he didn't reply she pushed her face right into his, forcing him to look at her. 'Why did you turn away from me?'

'I thought I'd hurt you,' he replied tightly. 'You said it was too much and I didn't stop. Couldn't stop.'

'I said that because it felt so amazing. That must have happened to you before.'

He leant forward and rubbed at his eyes with the heel of his hands. 'Yes, but not with someone like you.'

'Like me?'

Her eyes were huge in her face, her blonde hair a tangle over his too-large dressing gown. She looked so sexy, yet so *sweet*. Something inside him snapped. 'Yes, someone like you. Someone unique, someone special. You deserve a man who'll treat you like a princess and shower you with love. Not an emotional screw up like me.'

Her eyes flashed. 'Don't say that about yourself.'

He took in a deep breath, fighting for his calm, feeling like a rowing boat pitching about on choppy waters, desperate to make its way back to harbour. 'I've been angry for so long I don't know how else to be. The only way I can keep it in check is by fighting and meaningless sex.' His eyes held hers. 'Now tell me I'm not a screw up.'

'You're not a screw up.'

Her inability to see him for what he was stirred the anger he was trying so damn hard to contain. 'You don't think it's screwed up to punch my father so hard I knocked him out?' he demanded roughly, pushing himself up.

Her face paled. 'Oh, Doug.'

He couldn't stand to see the horror in her eyes so he deliberately turned his back on her, walking towards the door where he placed a hand on either side of the frame, dragging air into his lungs, his chest so tight it was strangling the oxygen from him. He needed Abby to leave so he could lick his wounds. He needed a damn punchbag so he could get rid of some of the angst churning in his gut.

Suddenly he felt her hand on his bare back, her small frame beside him, pushing herself into his personal space. 'How old were you when you hit your father?'

He turned to look at her. 'Nineteen. Old enough to know better.'

'Why did you hit him?'

Doug exhaled slowly, fighting for the control he wished he'd had back then. 'He was threatening my mother.' Her lips parted, ready to speak, but he cut her off. 'That's all it was. A threat. I don't know if he'd have actually hit her.'

'So it would have been better to watch him hit your mum first and *then* punch him, would it?'

'Jesus.' He rubbed at his face, his mind flashing back to the moment when his father, face red, veins on his neck pulsing with anger, had waved a clenched fist at his terrified mother. 'No.'

'So why was protecting your mum so wrong?'

'It wasn't. What was wrong was punching the lights out of my father, leaving him sprawled on the floor, knocked out cold, when I should have just restrained him.' He shuddered, reliving the moment he'd come home from university for some stuffy do of his mother's, only to find his parents having a flaming row in the study. He'd heard them argue before – and wasn't that an understatement – but this had sounded different. There'd been more menace to his father's words.

At least that's what he'd told himself, but now he wondered if he'd made it up to justify his following actions. Justify assuming that the raised fist he'd seen his father wave at his mother had held a real threat.

Justify landing the first punch on his father's jaw. Followed by the second. And the third. After which he'd watched in terror as the old man had crumpled, falling to the floor with a thud. He could still remember the rush of relief at finding he hadn't killed him, that his father was still breathing. Quickly drowned out by the horror of realising what he'd done.

'You think you could have restrained an angry man at nineteen, do you?' Abby, hands on her hips, was still pushing her point. 'One a great deal heavier than you?'

'I like to think so.' He knew he could do it now, thanks to his BJJ training. At nineteen, all he'd known was how to punch.

'You *think* so. And what about if he'd pushed you away and then hit her? How would you have felt then?'

Doug gazed down at Abby. She looked all soft and small wrapped in his huge dressing gown but that was just an illusion. 'I don't know.'

'Really? I'll tell you then. You'd have felt just as awful, just as guilty as you do now, because you're not cold and unfeeling like your non-biological father. You're emotional and sensitive.'

Her eyes blazed into his as if she could make him believe her words simply through force of will.

'You really believe that, don't you?'

'Yes.' Her reply was immediate and unequivocal. 'If it had been me in your situation mind you, I'd have hit your father years before that. Probably as soon as I was tall enough to reach his stomach. Or better still, the sensitive parts dangling below it.'

Unbelievably he felt himself starting to smile. 'You would, eh?'

'I would.' She tucked her arms around his waist, squeezing tightly. 'Where I come from, a man who threatens a woman deserves a punch in the face.'

'Even if he's knocked unconscious?'

'Yes.'

He guessed that was yet another difference between them.

In his circle men didn't punch other men. They especially didn't punch older men, father or no father.

'Did your mum thank you?'

Images of his mother's stricken face as she'd screamed at him for being a violent oaf flashed through his mind and he kissed the top of Abby's head. 'Not exactly.'

'She should have done.' Abby pulled back a little to stare up at him. 'It was your father who was at fault, Doug. Not you.'

He gave her a small smile, accepting she was partly right; his father had been at fault. But it had been his own immediate, violent reaction to what he'd seen that had scared him to death. He'd immediately given up boxing, a sport he'd taken up to help channel his anger, and shifted to martial arts. With BJJ he felt more in control. He only hoped he was.

Abby nestled against him, her warmth banishing the dark, ugly memories. With a soft groan he heaved her closer.

'Please don't push me away again,' she murmured into his chest.

His heart shifted disturbingly. 'I don't think I can any more.' He lifted a hand to point to his chest. 'You're in too deep.'

Pleasure washed over her face, bringing a tinge of pink to her cheeks. 'Good.' Taking his hand she kissed his knuckles, causing another wave of sensation to flood through him. 'Do you think we could manage that cuddle I missed out on earlier? Because if you're serious about having a relationship with me you need to know that I'm a cuddler.'

His pathetic uncertainty must have showed because she rolled her eyes. 'I'll show you. It's not hard.'

After pulling down the duvet she lay on the bed and removed her robe. With her naked body on full display, she pointed to the bed next to her. 'First you take off that towel and lie next to me.'

Biting back a smile, he did as he was told.

'Then I sidle up to you and snuggle onto your chest like so.'

Her body wrapped around him like the most luxurious velvet blanket.

'Now you put an arm around me so that should I move away, which I won't by the way, but suppose I tried, I wouldn't be able to succeed because you're holding me too tightly.'

As he moved his arm as requested she entwined her legs with his, her hair falling over his chest. He let out a long, pleasurable sigh. 'What happens next.'

'We sleep.'

Nobody was more shocked than Doug when he did.

239

Chapter Twenty-Five

Abby woke to a hot male body spooned against her back, his arm around her waist. When she tried to move the arm tightened, pulling her closer to him. For a man who didn't know how to cuddle, he'd certainly caught on quickly.

On a breath of pleasure she snuggled against him, enjoying the feel of his hard muscles against her back. And that was when she realised he must be awake.

'I hope you're not leaving just yet. I have plans for you.' His voice was gruff, that deep male timbre a woman only heard first thing in the morning. And this morning, it was all hers.

When his hand moved to caress her breast, she smiled. 'I think I might like those plans.'

He eased her onto her back, dazzling blue eyes gazing down at her. 'By the time I've finished, you won't just *like* my plans. You'll be crazy about them.'

It was only when she collapsed against the pillow a long while later that Abby glanced at the bedside clock. And squealed in horror. 'Flippety flip flip, look at the time. I've got to get back. The girls need sorting out. They should be catching their bus in ... oh crumbs ... fourteen minutes.'

She leapt out of bed, scanning the room for her clothes. Where the blazes had she left them?

'They're by the front door.' Doug eased his long legs out from the duvet. 'I'll get them.'

As she watched his naked body, and those perfect muscular buttocks, walk out of the room she wanted to say forget the girls. They could miss school for once in their life if it meant she could snuggle back into bed with him. But responsibility won and she ran into the bathroom, splashing water on her face and under her armpits.

'Your clothes are on the bed.'

She took five precious but essential seconds to ogle him again before scrambling into her underwear.

By the time she'd zipped up her dress he'd thrown on a pair of jeans and a T-shirt and was dangling his car keys in his hand. 'You can call home when we're in the car. I'll take the girls to school if they miss their bus.'

'Oh no, you can't do that.' She followed him down the stairs, out of the door and into his family unfriendly car.

'Why can't I?' With quick, precise movements he turned the car round and headed out onto the road. 'I was the one who made you late.'

When he pulled to a stop at the traffic light she turned to glance at him only to find him watching her, eyes full of heat. 'For the record, I'm very, very happy to be late.'

He gave her a small smile, attention returning to the lights as they turned green. 'You didn't even get to sample my morning special.'

His lips twitched and Abby took the hook. 'I rather thought I *had* sampled it.'

'You only sampled my morning appetizer. The special is even more filling and … satisfying.'

He gave her a quick, searing glance before putting his foot down and easing the Aston round a slow moving truck.

They were a minute from her house when she saw the school bus go past. 'Damn, we missed it.'

'Perhaps they're already on it. Aren't they old enough to get themselves to school by now?'

There spoke someone with no understanding of the young female species. 'Dad will have woken them before he went to work so there's a chance they might be awake. Mandy might even have got their breakfast ready, if she's not had a bad night with George. Plus Sally is very sensible, so she'll probably be dressed with her bag packed.'

He turned into their road. 'All good so far.'

'But I'll bet you ten pounds they'll all still be in the house. Ellie and Holly will be chatting, putting each others hair into odd styles, pulling everything out of their wardrobe to find a clean blouse. Sneaking on make-up they know they're not supposed to wear. Hunting for shoes they threw off the day before in their delight to get home. Oh and finishing off homework they forgot was meant to be handed in today.'

He slid the Aston to a stop and Abby jumped out and banged on the front door.

When Sally opened it, Abby raised her eyes heavenwards. 'Why aren't you on the bus?'

Sally's eyes widened with horror. 'Oh no, did we miss it? I told them to hurry up but they wouldn't listen. They kept giggling and throwing each other's shoes around the living room and then Holly remembered she hadn't printed off her English homework.' Abby didn't have time to give Doug an *I told you so glance* because Sally's eyes were filling. 'We're going to be really late now, aren't we?'

Abby shook her head. 'No, I don't have a job any more, remember? I can take you to school in Rodney.'

Behind her Doug cleared his throat. 'Rodney?'

'It's her rusty old car that doesn't start very well,' Sally chipped in before Abby had a chance to open her mouth. 'Yesterday Dad had to give it a jump start.'

'I've got a shiny new car that starts first time,' Doug replied, nodding to his, admittedly, shiny car. 'So round up your sisters and let's get going.'

Sally's jaw dropped. 'Cool.' She dashed into the house yelling, 'Holly, Ellie, get here now. Doug's taking us to school in his sports car!'

There was a chorus of *wow, really* and *sick*. 'Why is your car a more acceptable mode of transport than mine?'

Eyes that were so often reserved and detached twinkled back at her. 'Because it starts?'

'Yes, let's go with that.' Would her heart ever not react when he smiled at her? She placed a hand over it, willing the fluttering to calm. 'You do realise you've only got four seats, don't you?' She remarked, peering inside. 'I won't be able to go with you.'

'Worried I'll lead them astray?'

He'd never looked more sexy, she thought, with his unbrushed hair, unshaven face and clothes tugged on in a hurry. 'No. I'm worried about leaving you at the mercy of three giggling girls without a chaperone.'

'I've got sisters,' he reminded her. 'I think I can cope.' He moved towards her and gave her a quick but devastating kiss. 'We need to talk. Can I come back here after I've dropped them off?'

She rolled her eyes at him. 'Of course. I reckon I owe you breakfast.'

'Is that a reward for my school taxi service, my culinary skills from last night or my ... *other* skills?'

She had no chance to reply because the girls came out of the house like a tornado, pushing past her and towards the car.

'OMG. Look at these seats,' Ellie shrieked. 'Cream leather. I'm gonna have a car like this when I'm older.'

'It's so pretty.' Holly trailed her fingers along the bonnet, leaving smudges Abby bet Doug would be wiping off as soon as they were out of sight. 'I bet it goes really fast.'

'It does.' Sally's voice held a hint of pride, as if the car was hers. 'It's got a top speed of 205 mph thanks to its 6 litre V12 engine.'

As they clambered inside – 'It might be cool but it's tiny at the back' and 'I'm the oldest, I've got to sit at the front next to Doug' – Abby felt a twinge of guilt.

'Regretting your rash offer yet?' she asked him as he slid into the driver's seat.

'Of course not. I'll be fine.' He gave her a manful smile, though his handsome face looked a shade paler than it had a few moments ago.

Abby bet he'd keep telling himself that all the way to the school.

Doug reversed out of the drive and reminded himself the three girls were all younger and shorter than he was. He'd come to no harm. Physically, at least.

'Did Abby spend the night at your house?'

'In your bed?' Lots of giggles.

'Does that make you Abby's boyfriend now?'

The questions were being fired at him from Ellie and Holly in the back. Beside him, Sally was noticeably quiet.

'Of course he's her boyfriend,' a voice from behind proclaimed. 'Once you kiss a man he becomes your boyfriend. After you sleep with him he's your lover.'

Doug kept his mouth shut and his focus on the road. Thank God nobody seemed to require any answers.

'*Have* you slept with Abby yet?'

His eyes darted to his rear-view mirror and collided with Ellie's very interested ones. And yes, *now* they all decided to shut up. He sucked in a deep breath and prayed the school was round the corner. 'You'll need to ask Abby that.' He turned to find his front seat passenger, Sally, staring at him. She flushed bright red when he caught her eye and started to study her knees. 'Sally, I don't know where the school is. Can you direct me?'

Her eyes darted briefly up to his and she gave him a shy smile. 'Sure. You turn left at the top of this road. It's not far.'

Doug stifled a cheer.

When he pulled up outside the school gates they shouted their thanks.

'We like you,' Holly told him as she climbed out. 'You're much nicer than Abby's last boyfriend.'

'Thank you.'

'And if you split up with Abby you can go out with Sally. She fancies you,' Ellie added.

Beside him Sally inhaled sharply, her face turning a vivid shade of scarlet as she scrambled out of the passenger seat. 'I'm sure Sally will have no trouble finding her own boyfriend,' Doug countered, raising his voice sufficiently for Sally to hear. 'Now, you'd better go. It's bad being late, but even worse when you turn up late in an Aston Martin.'

They waved goodbye, Sally's eyes not meeting his, and Doug slowly let the air out of his lungs.

When he arrived back Abby opened the door, dressed in jeans and a knitted pink top. She'd obviously had a quick shower because her hair hung in damp curls around her make-up free, scrubbed-clean face. She was like an advert for all that was wholesome and good in life and he couldn't resist. He kissed her, drinking in her purity.

When he finally let her go she was flushed and breathless. 'If you're that pleased to see me, the girls must have been really bad.'

'They asked me if we'd slept together and if I was your lover. Then at the end they told me if I didn't want you as a girlfriend I could have Sally instead.'

She held her hand up to her mouth, her expression half horror, half trying not to laugh. 'Dare I ask what you said in reply?'

'I told them to ask you about the first two.'

'Thanks.'

'And that Sally was quite capable of finding her own boyfriend.'

Her eyes took on a soft, melted chocolate look. 'I've noticed Sally has a crush on you. When you're shy and sixteen it can be very painful, so thank you for being so sweet to her.'

'I was just being truthful.' He paused and sniffed. 'Is that bacon?'

'Yes. I figured you'd worked up an appetite this morning.'

She led him into the kitchen where she deftly transferred the bacon onto two waiting plates of buttered bread.

'Are there any more Spencers lurking?'

'Pat's still here.' She nodded over to the dog who was sitting with his tongue hanging out, eyeing up the bacon. 'But Mandy's in college today and Dad will be at work, so you're quite safe.'

They sat at the table and Doug allowed himself two large mouthfuls of bacon buttie, before broaching the elephant in the room. 'Speaking of work.' He pulled out a cheque he'd written yesterday. 'I want you to take this.'

She gave a dismissive glance. 'No.'

He'd expected a battle and it looked like he wasn't going to be disappointed. 'This is severance pay. It's only what you deserve and what you're entitled to.'

'When you're sacked you're not *entitled* to anything. Especially an amount that's more than my annual salary.'

'You are entitled to it if you're unfairly dismissed.' He couldn't use the word sacked, it made him too angry.

Her jaw set in a stubborn line. 'I don't want a hand-out, Doug. Don't insult me.'

'And I don't want to worry about your family going behind on bills because I wasn't strong enough to stop my bastard of a father putting you out of a job.'

'We'll manage.'

'And while you're *managing*, I'll be sick with worry and feeling like a total shit.' He leant across, placed the cheque in her hand and turned up her fingers so she was forced to accept it. 'Take it, not for your sake, but for mine. I need to know you're okay while I work out how to deal with this situation once and for all.'

She looked conflicted, clearly unsure which should take precedent: her pride or his needs. Leaning across the table he gave her a gentle kiss. 'Please. For me.'

Her shoulders slumped. 'That's not playing fair.'

'I know.'

With a huff of resignation she put the cheque in her pocket. 'I'll put it in a separate account and only use it if I need it.'

'Fair enough.' Feeling as though he'd won a small victory, he took another bite of his sandwich, carefully avoiding looking at the dog who was watching him patiently.

'What do you plan on doing?' she asked.

'I'm not sure yet,' he admitted. 'I've battled this issue since I was eighteen and I still don't know how to beat him.'

'That's because you've been fighting him by yourself, even though it isn't only about you. It's about your mother and sisters, too. If you ask me, and in case you don't I'm going to tell you anyway, you need to let them know what's going on. They have a right to know what you're having to do on their behalf.'

The bacon sandwich, delicious a few seconds ago, suddenly lost its appeal. Doug pushed the plate away. 'How's telling them going to help, other than make them feel guilty?'

Abby reached across the table and gripped his hand. 'What if they don't care about the money?'

'My mother and sisters are entitled to their inheritance whether they want it or not. I'm not about to deny it them.'

Her hand wriggled away from his and she thumped it on the table in exasperation. 'Doug, for once in your life will you think about *you* and what *you* want?'

The answer came to him immediately, with no conscious thought. 'I already know what I want,' he said quietly. 'I want you.'

Chapter Twenty-Six

Doug paced his living room floor. Where the heck was she? As far as he could remember, this was the only time in his life he'd asked his mother a favour. He was counting on her to at least turn up and hear him out. Not out of love – he'd given up expecting that a long time ago – but out of human decency.

The next ten minutes dragged by as he divided his attention between his watch and the driveway until at last he saw a dark blue Jaguar sweep through the gates. He took a few deep, calming breaths and went to open the door.

'Douglas.'

There was an awkward pause before the woman on the doorstep turned her cheek towards him.

'Mother.' He gave her a dutiful peck. 'Thank you for coming.'

'I've had to lie to your father to be here. I hope whatever you're going to tell me is worth that.'

For her it wouldn't be, but Doug had given over a large part of his life protecting her. He wanted some of that life back.

He led her into the living room. 'Would you like a drink?'

She settled herself into the armchair, crossing her legs. 'Am I going to need one?'

Choosing to ignore her statement about the drink he sat down on the sofa opposite, taking a moment to study her. With her back ramrod straight and her shoulders square, she looked almost regal. His mother was still a very elegant, attractive woman but now he'd met Abby he knew what was lacking about her. She was cold.

Leaning forward, he rested his hands on his knees and got straight down to business. 'Your husband, aka my non-

248

biological father, chose to sack my personal assistant a few days ago.'

'Is this the blonde you brought to the ball?'

He bristled. 'If you mean the lady with the blonde hair, Abby, then yes. She was filling in for me in a meeting, doing what I'd asked her to do, yet your husband's contempt for me led him to invent some trumped up charge and ruin her professional future.'

'What does this have to do with me?'

He caught her eye and held it. 'The reason he's able to throw his weight around, treat me and those close to me like dirt knowing I won't fight back, is because he's blackmailing me.'

'That's ridiculous.'

He smiled at her sadly. 'Why isn't it a surprise that you don't believe me?'

'But how?' She frowned, a hint of confusion in her expression. 'What have you done?'

'Thanks for your vote of confidence.'

'Come on, you have to admit this all sounds highly unlikely.' She re-crossed her legs, waving a dismissive hand at him. 'Tell me how Charles is supposed to be forcing you to bend to his every whim.'

Staring straight back at her, he clearly and succinctly outlined his father's threats.

When he'd finished, Doug watched closely for a reaction, but his mother was as good at hiding her thoughts as he was. Something they'd both learnt to do after years of living with a bully.

'Why are you telling me all this now?' she asked at length.

It wasn't quite as good as *I'm so sorry he's put you through this* or even *thank you so much for looking after me*, but it was exactly what he'd expected.

'I could stand working in a job I hated, for a man I loathed, as long as I was the only person affected. Now he's started on Abby and I'm not willing to let a woman I care for be trampled on.'

She gave him a puzzled look. 'You're referring to this blonde?'

'I'm referring to *Abby*, yes. I won't have her pushed out of a job she's far better at than I am.'

'She's a personal assistant.'

'She's a woman with a degree and a flair for the business that puts me to shame.'

His mother pursed her lips, running her fingers absently over the arm of the chair. And people thought he took a long time to answer, he thought grimly.

'What do you propose to do then?' she asked eventually.

'Call his bluff. Tell him to go ahead and inform the world I'm not his son. He may choose to throw you all out of the house, of course. If he does we'll have to deal with the consequences.'

Her mouth hardened. 'You mean your sisters and I will need to deal with them.'

He looked her square in the eyes. 'Yes.'

There was another irritatingly long pause before she spoke again. 'So you've decided to put this woman's career above your sisters' welfare? Above mine?'

'Yes.' He expected to feel guilt, but it was hard to when he imagined how Abby must have felt when she'd been sacked for doing her job. 'I have an ace up my sleeve though, so I don't think it will come to that.'

'As it's my future you're risking, will you tell me what the ace is?'

'You'll find out soon enough.'

With a sharp nod of her head she rose to her feet. 'I guess that's that then. I don't suppose I can stop you from doing what you plan.'

'You can't.'

Her eyes searched his, as if assessing the strength of his determination. He stared unblinkingly back at her.

'She's got to you, this girl, hasn't she?'

'Yes.' She'd done more than *got to him*. She'd buried herself deep inside him.

'Then I should probably thank you for warning me of your intention.'

He'd put his life on hold for eight years and she was thanking him for the *warning*? 'Will you tell Margaret and Thea? I'd do it myself but as they don't know I'm a half brother, it might be better coming from you.'

'Yes.'

He was pretty good at not saying very much, but his mother was a master at it.

When she reached the front door she halted. 'When will you see Charles?'

'Tomorrow.'

She nodded and he was about to open the door when she surprised him. 'You say you hate your job. What would you rather be doing?'

'Painting.'

Her face showed the hint of a smile. 'Yes. You always did love art as a child. Your father ... your biological father ... was an artist, too. Patrick O'Shea. Perhaps you should look him up one day and compare styles.'

Doug grabbed at the door handle as his knees threatened to buckle. It was the first time she'd ever mentioned his real father. 'Am I allowed to ask why?' When she looked blank he added. 'Why did you have an affair?'

Instantly her face shut down. 'That's my business.'

'It is, but as the results of it had a direct impact on my life, I think I'm entitled to know.'

Her jaw tightened, and her hands gripped at her handbag.

'I married Charles in good faith. Oh I knew he could be bombastic and domineering, and it wasn't a marriage made in love, but I thought we could make it work. He wanted a pretty wife who could make him look good and provide an heir.' She dropped her gaze to her hands. 'I was a cocktail waitress, fed up with being pawed by dirty old men. Fed up with being poor. I wanted security. Money. To be somebody.'

Doug felt his heart start to pound. He'd never heard his mother talk of her past. 'What went wrong?'

She gave him a thin smile. 'I expect you can work that out for yourself, having been at the sharp end of his temper.'

'Did he hit you?' It was a question he'd asked himself many times since that awful night.

She shook her head. 'No. His strikes were more emotional than physical, though it's hard to say which are the more damaging.'

'And Patrick?' he asked softly, already guessing the answer.

Briefly her face softened, and a hint of warmth entered her eyes. 'He was a flirt, a charmer. A man who made me laugh. Who made me feel wanted.'

'So why not leave Charles?'

She gave him a bitter smile. 'Because I wanted the status, and the wealth, too much.' Her eyes darted away and she gave herself a little shake, as if horrified at the glimpse she'd given of the real woman behind the Lady Faulkner façade. When she turned back to him, she touched her lips briefly against his cheek. 'Goodbye, Douglas.'

He watched as she stepped elegantly into the Jaguar. From cocktail waitress to lady of the manor. Had it really been worth the price she'd paid?

Abby was sitting with her father in the living room, half-watching an inane soap, when Mandy tiptoed down the stairs to join them.

'Is he asleep?' She hoped for her sister's sake that George had finally given in and closed his eyes.

'He's quiet, so I thought I'd risk it. I crept out of the room on my hands and knees. How sad a mother am I?'

'As sad as your own mother,' their father answered. 'She used to do the exact same thing to all of you.'

'Ah, did she?'

There was silence for a few moments while they all remembered the woman who'd been such an important part of their lives.

'Not seeing that man of yours tonight, Abby?' her father asked eventually.

'No, he's seeing his mum.' She stopped there, no doubt leaving them with an image of Doug having a cosy night in with a sweet old lady.

'You've forgiven him for losing you your job, then?'

Even Mandy winced at that. 'Dad,' she scolded. 'That's a bit harsh.'

'Is it? Abby does what her boss tells her and she gets the sack? Doesn't seem right to me.'

'That's because you don't understand the full picture.' Abby rubbed her father's arm. 'I told you before, I know you're being supportive but I don't need you wading in with both feet. Doug's handling it.'

Her father grunted. 'It's been two days and I've not seen Faulkner senior knocking on our door yet, begging on his hands and knees.'

Mandy giggled. 'Now that I'd like to see. Lord Faulkner pleading for our Abby to work for him.'

'And why not?'

Knowing her father was winding up for another of his *my daughter's more than good enough to work for the likes of him* rant, she kissed his cheek, hoping to placate him. 'The situation's more complicated than you think. Give Doug the time he needs to resolve things.'

His sharp brown eyes studied her. 'You're sure about this bloke, Abby? Really, really sure?'

'Yes.' She pushed against the tightness in her chest, daring to say the words she'd been thinking for the last few days. 'I'm falling in love with him.'

Her father blinked, his face going a shade paler. 'Enough that you might be thinking of leaving home sometime soon?'

Oh God. It was all there in his eyes. His worry for her. His love for her. But also his concern about what this might mean for all of them.

'Hey, don't start pushing me out yet. I've only just started dating him. We all know how easily relationships can go wrong.' *Especially when the man you're dating thinks he can't do them.* 'Besides, I'm quite happy with where I am now.'

'And how happy were you two nights ago, I wonder,' Mandy piped up, wiggling her eyebrows suggestively. 'When you stayed over at his.'

'Mandy!' Abby could feel herself blushing furiously.

The shrill sound of her phone burst into the moment.

'Thank God for that,' her father muttered.

On seeing who it was, Abby dashed upstairs, away from prying ears.

'Hello.' And crikey, where had this shy feeling come from?

'Hello, yourself.' His soft, deep voice made her almost giddy. 'Missing me?'

'Yes.' Bam. No hesitation. She sank despairingly onto her bed. 'Well, there's my chance to play cool blasted into smithereens. Moving quickly on, how did it go with your mum?'

A small pause. 'Surprisingly well. She recognised she couldn't stop me calling my father's bluff, promised she'd warn Thea and Margaret of the potential ramifications and thanked me for telling her.'

'I ... umm, well that's good.'

Another pause because, unlike her, he thought before he spoke. 'You're dying to tell me you told me so, aren't you? Why are you holding back?'

She settled further onto the bed and stared up at the ceiling. 'I thought I'd try to be more mature.'

'Don't.'

'Don't what?'

'Don't change, Abby,' he replied quietly. 'You're perfect just the way you are.'

And wow, he might not say many words but those he did say were dynamite. 'I'm not, you know, though I definitely like your thinking.'

There was another pause and she chose to imagine he was smiling. 'I'll see my father tomorrow,' he said eventually. 'I can't guarantee I'll be able to get you your job back, but I'm going to damn well try.'

'I don't care about the job. I'll get another one, though obviously my boss won't be as good.'

'Obviously.'

'The most important thing is for you to get out of your father's control, away from Crumbs. It's high time you did what you *want* to do, not what you've been forced to do.'

The silence that followed was so long Abby ended up glancing down at the phone to check if it had run out of battery. 'Will you still want to go out with a penniless artist?' he asked finally.

Ah, so that was what he was stewing over. 'Someone once bragged to me that the so-called penniless artist can sell paintings at ten thousand pounds a pop. And that he's going to be showing in New York soon.'

'I revise my question. Will you still want to go out with an arrogant reasonably well-off artist?'

'I'll always want to go out with you, Doug.' It was

probably too much, too soon, but she'd never been much good at hiding her feelings.

'I might hold you to that,' he replied quietly. 'I guess I'd better let you get back to whatever it was you were doing.'

'Watching television with Dad and Mandy. I know how to live.'

His answering soft laughter rippled through her and she wished she could see him. See those beautiful eyes shining at her. 'Can I call round tomorrow evening? Maybe take you out for dinner?'

Jeeze. She'd just told him she'd always want to go out with him. Surely he knew the answer to that question. 'Well, let me see,' she teased. 'There are a number of really good soaps on the telly tomorrow.'

'The following day then?'

What? Shutting her eyes, she flopped back on the bed. How did this man not realise what he meant to her? 'I'd love to see you tomorrow,' she told him firmly. 'I'd love it even more if instead of a restaurant you'd take me to your house, let me cook you a meal and then ...' The confidence left her all of a sudden. She wasn't used to being so bold.

He cleared his throat. 'And then?'

'And then I'd like you to take me to that big bed of yours.'

He cleared his throat more loudly. 'And then?'

Laughter whooshed out of her. 'And *then* you can decide what to do with me.'

She heard the smile in his voice. 'I'll see you tomorrow at my house then. Oh, and Abby, by the way.' He paused, his next words spoken more softly. 'I miss you, too.'

Abby held the phone to her chest and smiled dreamily up at the ceiling. She'd told her dad she was falling in love with Doug, but she suspected that wasn't quite true.

She was pretty certain she was already there.

Chapter Twenty-Seven

After parking in his usual space in the Crumbs car park Doug pulled out his mobile and scanned the screen. He'd had three texts during his drive to work.

He read Abby's first. *Hurry up and get through today. I can't wait to see what you're going to do to me in your big bed.*

Chuckling he scrolled down to Thea's. *Tell Dad to stuff his job. I can't believe you've been doing it all these years for our sake. Thanks for looking after us, bro, but time to look after yourself now.*

And finally he read Luke's. *Good luck, mate. This is long overdue. If you need any help grappling the son-of-a-bitch to the ground just shout.*

He quickly dashed off a reply to Abby. *I hope you won't be disappointed.* Then he read it back and deleted the first two words. *You won't be disappointed.* Grinning, he hit send.

A knock on his window made him sit up with a start. 'Mother? Is everything okay?'

'Yes.' She glanced around. 'I'd like a quick word.'

'Sure.' He grabbed his jacket from the passenger seat and climbed out. 'Shall we go to my office?'

'No. I don't want to bump into Charles.' She pointed to her Jaguar a few places behind his. 'Let's sit in my car.'

At her instruction he hopped into the passenger seat. It felt oddly intimate when she sat next to him and closed the door.

She must have felt the awkwardness too, because when she spoke her voice trembled slightly. 'I wanted to catch you before you spoke to Charles.' He noticed she didn't say *your father*. 'After I left you last night I went to see Sebastian, Charles's lawyer. We're … friends.'

Doug stared at her incredulously. 'Oh my God, you've slept

with him too, haven't you?' When she didn't say anything, just stared rigidly ahead, her lips pursed, he started to laugh. 'Well, well. That's certainly one way to screw your husband. Sleep with his trusted lawyer.'

'I didn't deliberately set out to do it,' she replied tightly. 'And Charles has hardly been faithful. He's dangled three mistresses in front of my face. Goodness knows how many he's had behind my back.' For a moment they were both silent, then she spoke again. 'Living with your father ... Charles ... hasn't been easy. Especially after he found out he wasn't your father.' She looked directly over at him. 'He made us both suffer. There were times I felt so lonely.'

He could empathise with that. 'Perhaps you would have felt less lonely if you'd interacted with your children more.'

He watched her flinch but didn't feel too much sympathy. She could have left Charles, but she'd chosen a title and wealth over happiness.

'I've made a lot of mistakes,' she conceded, looking down at her clasped hands. 'And I have to live with them. But you shouldn't have to suffer for them, and for that I apologise.' Briefly her eyes sought his. 'I came here to tell you that Sebastian is doing what he feels necessary to protect us all financially, should Charles decide to call your bluff. So you don't have to worry. Do what you need to do.'

The remorse in her tone left him reeling. 'That's ... good to know.'

'Good luck.'

A smile flickered but was quickly extinguished. Almost as if she was afraid to show emotion any more. Feeling a touch emotional himself, Doug leant across and kissed her cheek. 'Thank you.'

Doug peered through the glass in the door to his father's office and saw he was sitting behind his desk, as he was every

Friday. 'Don't want to encourage an atmosphere of slacking off on a Friday,' had been his explanation.

'We need to talk,' Doug announced, barging straight in without knocking. 'More accurately, I need to talk and you need to listen.'

'If this is about that blasted secretary of yours—'

'It involves Abby, yes,' he interrupted. 'It also involves the threat you made to me when I was eighteen.'

Choosing not to sit, Doug walked to the desk and put his hands on the edge, just as he had a few days earlier when he'd almost strangled the son-of-a-bitch.

'I'm here to tell you to go ahead and announce that I'm not your son. Throw your wife and daughters out.' He inched his head forward so they were almost nose to nose. 'In fact, I'll go one better than that. If you don't bring Abby back *I'm* going to announce that not only am I the product of my mother's affair, but the only reason I'm working at Crumbs is because you blackmailed me into it.'

Charles surged to his feet, gripping the desk in a mirror image to Doug's stance. 'Don't you threaten me, boy.'

'Oh, this isn't a threat,' Doug replied coldly, standing up to his full height. 'It's a promise.'

'You think anyone will care what you have to say? You're just the product of a meaningless fuck who I was gracious enough to take under my wing. I made you managing director to please my wife.'

'You really think that will stick? That your wife will happily stand by what you say?'

'She'll say what I bloody well tell her to say,' he thundered.

Doug stared at the man in front of him, feeling a surge of strength, of power. He'd been so terrified of him as a child, but actually he was nothing but an arrogant, blustering fool. Why hadn't he realised this sooner? Why had he let him trample over him for so long? 'I think you'll find your days of ruling the roost are numbered, old man, though if you want to maintain that illusion, there is a way out for you. As long as you agree to my terms.'

His father slammed himself back onto his seat and laughed harshly. 'Your terms?'

'Yes. Before I take you through those, have a look at these sales figures from the last few months. What do you see?'

Charles didn't bother to look. 'I don't need you to show me sales figures. I know exactly what's happening in my company.'

'Then you know that sales are up. In particular sales of three old brands you wanted to get rid off.'

'Your point is?'

'My point is that you wanted to sell them. It was Abby who saw their potential when nobody else did. She was also responsible for the change in packaging, which has since resulted in Crumbs being shortlisted for several design awards. Finally, she's the mastermind behind the savoury range, hailed only last week as another Crumbs triumph.'

Doug took a sadistic delight in seeing his father go ashen in shock. 'What do you hope to gain by telling me this?'

'It isn't what I hope to gain, but what you could gain. Invite Abby back to Crumbs not as a personal assistant, but as a management trainee. I'll guide her as much as she needs. When she's ready, you'll give her a department to run. Director of Development and Innovation would be a good fit.'

'That's preposterous. I'll never let that woman be a director in this company.'

'Then you're a bigger fool than I thought you were. Offer Abby the job and not only will I keep quiet, but the company your family built will continue to thrive. Don't offer Abby the job in the next twenty-four hours and I'll go to the press. I'm sure there will be quite a lot of interest in the twisted family life of Lord Faulkner.'

His father banged his fist on the table. 'I won't be threatened like this.'

A wave of calm descended on Doug and he actually found himself smiling. 'Too late. It seems I did learn something from you, after all.'

He turned and headed for the door. For thirty years he'd let the man behind that desk treat him like shit. No longer.

From this moment on, Charles Faulkner had lost the power to interfere with his life.

Abby couldn't sit still. Ever since Doug had texted to say he'd pick her up at 6.30 p.m. she'd been stalking round the house like a trapped animal trying to find a way out. Currently she was in the kitchen, watching as Mandy fed George.

'Will you just sit down.' Mandy gave her an exasperated glare. 'You're making me nervous. And why are you so jittery, anyway? It's not like this is your first date. You've already slept with the guy.'

Mandy hadn't bothered to lower her voice and over in the adjoining sitting room Abby could hear Ellie hissing to Holly. 'See, I told you. That means Abby and Doug are *lovers*.' It was followed by loud, unrestrained giggling.

Back in the kitchen Mandy bit her bottom lip, mouthed, 'Oops,' and tried to hold back her own laughter.

'Thanks, Mandy. Always good to know I can rely on you to be discreet.'

'Sorry.' She didn't look it. 'So, you were telling me why you're wound up like a spring, ready to bounce out of the door the moment your dashing escort arrives.'

'I'm worried,' Abby admitted quietly.

'About what?'

'About what will happen when he realises I'm not the pretty, insanely smart woman he's kidded himself into believing I am.'

261

'Abigail Spencer.' Mandy took two giant paces towards her and gave her shoulders a none too gentle shake. 'Stop thinking such rubbish.'

Before her sister could give her any further reassurance there was a knock on the door. Abby bolted towards it like a rabbit on speed, her heart hammering as she took in the sight of the handsome grey-suited man on her doorstep. 'Hi.'

He smiled at her more with his eyes than his mouth. 'Hi, yourself.'

'How did it go? I'm all ready. I even packed an overnight bag so I wouldn't have to come home tomorrow in tonight's clothes, which should reduce some of the questioning.' The words wouldn't stop careering out of her mouth. 'I hope that's okay. Oh, and I made a fish pie for dinner.' Her hands flapped towards the bags on the floor by the door, one holding the neatly wrapped pie. 'I hope you like fish. And that you're not allergic to seafood because I put some prawns in it and it would be an awful shame to spend tonight watching you sick it all up. Or worse, go all blotchy and I'd have to rush you to A&E.'

She'd run out of breath. As her body sucked much needed air back into her lungs she noticed that Doug's smile had reached his mouth now, curving his sensuous lips. Cupping her face, he kissed her. Not the quick peck of a man greeting his girlfriend with her family just round the corner, but a deep, slow, wrench-the-ground-from-under-her sort of kiss.

When he finally let her go he traced a finger down her cheek. 'Fine, I'd be disappointed if you hadn't, I do and I'm not.'

'Sorry?'

'The answers to your questions.'

'Oh.' Embarrassed, she dropped her eyes down to the floor. 'Sorry. When I'm excited or nervous I talk even more than usual. It's probably going to really get on your nerves.'

'You'll never get on my nerves, Abby. Never.' His finger nudged her chin back up. 'Please tell me you're excited, not nervous?'

'Yes, at least I'm far more excited than nervous but, well ...' She trailed off, annoyed with herself. Why couldn't she be cool like his other women must have been? Like Geraldine must have been? 'Sorry. This is all a bit new still. You know, dating the boss I fancied from day one.'

He smiled again, a hint of smug. 'You did?'

She shook her head, laughing. 'Of course I did. Have you taken a good look at yourself recently?'

'I'd rather look at you.' While her heart performed a series of neat somersaults he reached inside and grabbed the bags. 'Do you need to say goodbye?'

'No, I'm good. I did that half an hour ago, and then again ten minutes ago. I think they're sick of me now.'

They settled into his car but Doug didn't immediately turn on the engine. Much to her surprise he reached over and took her hand, bringing it to his lips and planting a gentle kiss on the palm.

Her insides melted. 'What was that for? Not that I'm complaining.' She shook her head for emphasis. 'Nope, definitely not complaining.'

Still holding her hand he stared at her, as if trying to work out something. Whatever it was darkened his eyes. 'You know sometimes when I look at you, my heart stops.'

'Wow.' She swallowed down the lump that had shot into her throat. 'For a man who says he doesn't do relationships, you're really, really good at this.' Tears started to prick and she had to work hard to stop them from falling. 'Is that why you kept pushing me away? Because you were worried about it not starting again?'

He let go of her hand and started the car. 'I kept pushing you away because I wasn't the man you thought I was. You saw the managing director of Crumbs, heir of Lord Faulkner. That isn't me.'

'I saw a drop dead gorgeous guy with dazzling, yet kind eyes who looked like he could do with cheering up.'

He flicked her a glance loaded with promise. 'I can guarantee whatever you've got planned to cheer me up, it's going to work.'

The nerves slipped quietly away, though the excitement remained.

Chapter Twenty-Eight

Abby woke slowly, stretching out her limbs, luxuriating in the knowledge that this was Sunday morning and, for once, she didn't have to rush anywhere. Thanks to the surprising job offer from Crumbs three weeks ago she was now a working woman again. Not only that, she was a management trainee. She was still pinching herself but Doug had been remarkably calm about it all. 'It's only what you deserve,' he'd told her in that quiet, patient voice of his.

It wasn't so quiet or patient when they were alone in bed though.

Smiling at the thought, Abby lazily reached out her arm, expecting to connect with a naked male body like it had the previous few Sundays.

Instead she found a cool pillow.

Slipping off the bed she donned his dressing gown and headed downstairs towards the back of his house. The door to his studio was open and she paused, grabbing at the rare opportunity to watch him. The man she saw in the office, dressed in a formal suit, was so different to the man standing in front of the canvas, wearing a pair of tatty jeans and a paint-splattered grey shirt. The businessman was serious, controlled and flat. The artist was dynamic and energised, his body moving as one with his arm as he brushed paint onto the canvas.

Wanting to get closer, she tiptoed inside. Her arm knocked against a jar of paintbrushes on the nearby worktop, sending it crashing noisily onto the floor.

'Oh God, I'm so clumsy. Sorry.' Frantically she began to pick up the scattered brushes.

'Leave them.' He pulled her back up and kissed her soundly. 'Good morning.'

Letting out a happy sigh, she rested her head on his chest. 'Good morning to you, too. I didn't mean to disturb you. I just wanted to watch quietly for a bit but I guess Spencers don't do quietly.'

She felt his chest rumble with silent laughter. 'I've noticed that. You aren't disturbing me though. I woke early and it was either paint or make love to you.' His hand stroked her hair. 'I wanted to do the second, but I figured you deserved a rest after last night so I came down here.'

She grinned, raising her head to look at him. 'Last night *was* pretty amazing. What happened to the man who only did sex?'

Doug bent his head and planted a gentle kiss on her mouth. 'You taught him how to make love.'

Emotion welled, making swallowing hard. 'I must be a really great teacher then,' she whispered. 'Because he's awesome and I can't get enough of him.'

Doug's arms tightened around her and suddenly she was being lifted up and carried down the hall. Letting out a squeal Abby flung her arms around his neck, inhaling turpentine and Doug. 'Where are you taking me?'

'Back to bed.'

'But what about your painting?'

'It can wait. I can't.'

By the time Doug placed Abby on his bed, he was aching with need. He'd been so tempted to wake her up this morning when he'd studied her in the dawn light. So pretty, so sweet, so very, very special. He'd lightly kissed her temple but she'd been dead to the world and though his body had been crying out to take her, his conscience had told him he needed to let her sleep.

He'd always enjoyed sex, but what he'd found with Abby was more than sex ... more than he'd ever dared hope for. It

266

was no longer about physical release, but a primitive need to bury himself inside her, connect with her. Become one with her. And unlike physical release, where once had been enough, once with Abby only made him want her again. And again.

Quickly he stripped off his clothes and joined her on the bed where she instantly welcomed him, parting her legs to invite him in. He'd never felt so cherished, so *wanted*, in his whole life.

He set an easy rhythm, teasing them both until they needed more. Then he drove them home.

'Stay,' he whispered, drawing her against him as they both caught their breath. 'Spend the day with me in bed.'

She sighed, her breath fluttering against his chest. 'As appealing as that sounds, you know I can't. I need to go home and see the girls.' She raised her head. 'We always have a roast dinner on a Sunday. Family tradition. Dad would blow the kitchen up if he tried cooking one.'

Doug made himself laugh. It wasn't her fault he lived for the days he saw her. Much as he wanted to, he couldn't expect to consume her, to take over. She still had her life to lead and he ... well, he'd spend the day painting, like he always did. That New York gallery wouldn't fill up by magic.

Her finger traced gentle circles over his chest. 'Of course you could always join us, though I won't blame you if the thought of spending an afternoon with my family has you pleading work and diving back into your studio.'

He felt his heart lift and swell, filling with an emotion he didn't understand, though he had his suspicions. 'I'd love that.'

She shifted so she could peer into his face. 'Really? Do I need to remind you of the last meal you had with my lot? It was the BJJ competition and you spent a lot of time deflecting questions.'

'I'm more prepared now. Besides, it's been a long time since I've had a home-cooked roast.'

Her dark eyes softened. 'I can't imagine you go home to your family very often.'

'Not if I can help it, no.'

She ran a hand through his hair, smoothing it down, and Doug was hard pressed not to purr. He couldn't hold back the quiet groan though, and her lips curved as she kissed him. 'You like being touched, don't you?'

'I like anything you do to me.'

'Is being touched like a home-cooked roast? Something you've not experienced very often?'

He shut his eyes, focusing on the soothing feel of her caress. 'Yes,' he admitted hoarsely.

'Then we've got a lot of making up to do, haven't we?' Kissing his nose, she sat up and pushed away the duvet. 'And it starts today with my roast chicken.'

'Oh no.' He caught at her arm and tugged her back. 'It starts now with the touching, which continues while we take a shower. After that we can get to the chicken.'

'By then I think we'll need it,' Abby added dryly, though she didn't object when he rolled her back underneath him.

If the Spencer family were surprised to have an extra person for dinner they didn't show it. Doug didn't think anything fazed them. They were so rowdy and chaotic that the arrival of an extra body didn't seem to register. It was vastly different to Sunday meals with the Faulkners, though the number of people sitting round the table was pretty much the same. Here there was laughter and mickey taking, not long periods of silence interrupted by moments of painful conversation. The Spencers sat round the table because they wanted to be there, not through force of habit. They lingered after the

268

meal, continuing to chat while they cleared up. Not fleeing to their rooms as soon as they could.

Doug attempted to take some plates to the kitchen but he was shooed away by Abby. 'No. Guests aren't allowed to clear up, house rules. Go and sit down and someone will bring you a coffee.'

'I'll do it,' Sally announced, then flushed when Holly and Ellie both rolled their eyes at her.

As he'd never had anyone have a crush on him before, at least not someone so young, Doug wasn't sure what to do. 'Thank you. White, no sugar would be great.' He smiled, hoping it came across as sincere but not flirtatious.

Abby watched the exchange with a knowing look and when Sally was out of earshot she whispered in his ear, 'You're doing just fine. When you're sixteen, having a crush on a gorgeous male is perfectly normal. At least in Sally's case the male is one I approve of.'

'Thanks,' he muttered dryly, 'but hell, I don't want to lead her on.'

'You're not. You wouldn't. She doesn't even want anything to happen. Just for you to carry on treating her as you are doing. Like somebody special.' She gave him a searching look. 'I can't believe you're so unused to female attention.'

'*Teenage* female attention,' he corrected her.

He received a playful dig in the ribs. 'Okay then Mr Babe Magnet, sit down and wait for your adoring fan to deliver your drink.'

Doug ambled over to the living room where he found Derek sprawled out on the sofa.

'I see living in a house full of women isn't all bad,' Doug ventured, taking the armchair. They hadn't spoken since the day Abby had lost her job and Doug wasn't quite sure where they stood.

'There has to be some compensation for hormones and

shrieking,' Derek replied gruffly, though Doug knew, by the way his eyes twinkled, that he wouldn't have it any other way. 'Lad, about the last time we spoke. Sorry if I came across a bit harsh.'

'You were looking out for your daughter. I'd have done the same in the circumstances.'

Derek nodded. 'I believe you would. She's cock-a-hoop with her new job, you know.'

'She got it on merit.'

'I know, but I also know what you had to do to make it happen.' Dark eyes, so similar to Abby's, flickered over to his daughter. 'Look out for her and make her happy. It's all I ask.'

'The first is a given.' He thought back to his father's threat, *I'll never let that woman be a director in my company.* He'd see about that. 'As for making her happy, I'll try every day, for as long as she'll let me.'

Derek held out his hand. 'Sounds good to me.'

Doug grasped the offered hand and they shook.

'What are you two colluding about?' Mandy asked as she came to join them, popping the wriggling George down on the floor in front of her. It seemed to Doug, from the mess still on the boy's hands and face, that he'd been attempting to absorb his meal through his skin.

'I made Doug a bet,' Derek announced, startling Doug into sitting upright.

'Oh?'

'What bet?' Ellie cried, wrapping her arms around her father's neck. 'Did you make a bet on them getting married?'

Doug wasn't just sitting straight now, he was rigid.

'Who's getting married?' Holly asked, flopping down next to Mandy.

'Nobody,' Abby replied firmly, arriving just in time to come to his rescue. The idea of spending the rest of his life with Abby sat surprisingly easy with him, but *marriage*? He wasn't sure he could make that leap, at least not yet. The thought of ending up like his parents sent cold shivers through him.

'So what was the bet you made?' Abby asked, sliding onto the armrest of his chair. Deciding she was too far away, he circled an arm around her waist and tugged her onto his lap, making her squeal. 'I'm too heavy. Especially after that roast.'

'What you've just eaten wouldn't make much difference,' Sally announced, carefully placing a too-full mug onto the table in front of him; not a coaster in sight. 'I mean, as a percentage of your overall weight, the weight of that meal must be ridiculously small.'

Doug coughed and winked at Sally. 'I believe what Sally is saying is you can carry on eating roasts because your weight is in perfect proportion to your height.'

Sally giggled. 'Oh yes. That's what I meant.'

'Well rescued.' Abby snuggled further into his arms. 'So come on then, about this bet?'

Derek grinned as his family watched him expectantly. And Doug twitched nervously.

'I bet Doug twenty quid he wouldn't change young George's nappy.'

The girls all dissolved into laughter. 'Are you going to do it?' Ellie demanded, scrambling onto her hands and knees and sniffing George's bottom. 'He's a bit whiffy.'

Doug reached into his back pocket, pulled twenty pounds from his wallet and placed it on the coffee table.

Chapter Twenty-Nine

Four weeks into her new role as management trainee and Abby was shooting down the motorway on her way to a business workshop on marketing strategy. She was running late, all thanks to George who'd managed to be so sick last night he'd kept Mandy up. That in turn had meant Mandy had been in no fit state to help get the others off to school this morning, so Abby had been forced to hang back and wait till they were on the bus before setting off – half an hour later than she'd intended. Not a great start to what was supposed to be, George willing, a residential three day course. She'd known when Geraldine had suggested it that it would be hard to get away but for once she'd put her needs first.

She prayed to God that George recovered quickly or she'd be turning straight round and heading back.

When her phone started to ring ten minutes later, her heart sank, lifting again when she looked at the number flashing on the hands-free set her father had recently installed. Not Mandy asking her to turn around, but Doug.

'Hey there.'

'Hey back.' There was a pause but now she expected it. More than that, she cherished it because it was so much a part of the man she'd fallen for. 'Are you on your way to the workshop?'

'Yes, finally. Are you at work yet?'

'No. I thought, at least I'd hoped, you might pop in before you left.'

Oh shit. Abby vaguely recalled promising she'd do that last night. 'I'm so sorry, I didn't have time. George kept Mandy awake most of the night and trust me, you don't want to know how he managed that. Suffice to say he was onto his fourth sleepsuit when I saw him this morning.'

'Is he okay?'

'Oh yes, but it meant Mandy was so tired this morning I didn't have the heart to drag her out of bed so I had to get the girls off to school. Hence I'm running late.' Another pause, but this one stretched and stretched so much it became uncomfortable. 'Doug?'

'I'm still here.'

'That's kind of hard to know, when you don't actually speak to me.'

'Sorry. I'm just … disappointed not to see you.'

She imagined him waiting alone at home, expecting her to drop in any moment, looking at the clock as the minutes ticked by. A lump balled in her throat. 'Did I mention how sorry I am? If it helps any, I'd rather have been with you than dragging mouthy teenagers out of bed.'

'It helps.' Before she had a chance to reassure him she'd rather be with him than doing *anything* at all, he changed the subject. 'Who's the guest business guru on your workshop? Anyone I know?'

'I think it might be. I remember he phoned you a while back and I had to take a message. Robert Langstone?'

She heard his sharp intake of breath. 'Yes, I know Robert. Be careful there, Abby. He's the monstrous flirt I warned you about.'

'The one who told me he was going to take me to lunch. I remember now.'

'I'm sure you do.'

He sounded just a little bit off, a little bit hurt. 'I'm not going to be having any lunches with him, Doug. At least not by myself.'

'I'm pleased to hear that.' Another pause and she began to revise her earlier opinion of them. She couldn't cherish the silence when she sensed he was upset. 'I guess I'd better get to the office and pretend to make some sharp decisions. Enjoy the course.'

'I'll enjoy it more when it's over and I'm snuggling up to you in that big bed of yours.'

At last, a pause where she could almost hear him smile. 'I'm counting the hours.'

It was well into the afternoon session before Abby spoke to Robert Langstone personally. He was exactly how she'd imagined him: handsome, hugely confident, utterly charming.

'You used to be Doug's personal assistant, didn't you?' he said as he joined her in the coffee area during the break. He sat with his legs apart, a swagger to his stance that made her smile.

'I did. I remember speaking to you on the phone. I didn't think you'd remember me.'

'Oh, I remember all the pretty girls.' Somehow he managed to say it without sounding creepy. Perhaps it was the genuine smile, or the kindness in his eyes. 'You're Doug's girlfriend, too.'

'I ...' She trailed off, flustered. 'Sorry, I wasn't expecting that. How do you know?'

He laughed, taking a swig of his coffee. 'Doug happened to mention it when he called this morning. When I say happened to, I think we both know he phoned deliberately to make sure I knew.'

'Oh.' An uncomfortable heat pricked at her cheeks and she knew she was blushing, something she absolutely hated doing in front of this hot-shot businessman she was trying to impress professionally. 'I don't know why he'd do that.'

Again Robert laughed. 'Oh come on, sure you do. He knows my type when it comes to women, and you're most definitely it.'

Her discomfort increased. 'I don't know what to say. I'm

flattered, of course, but I'm not here to impress you with my looks, such that they are. I want to impress you with my business knowledge.'

'Oh, don't you worry, you're doing that, too. The presentation you gave just now was spot on. The best I've ever seen on one of these workshops.' He sat back and studied her for a moment. 'Are you happy working with Doug?'

Carefully Abby put down her coffee, smiling to herself as she placed it on the coaster. Seems some of Doug's mannerisms were rubbing off on her. 'I'm not sure if you're asking me from a personal or professional standpoint but the answer to both questions is yes. I'm very happy with Doug, in every sense.'

Robert let out a bark of a laugh. 'Nicely handled and don't worry, I'm not coming on to you, though I may flirt out of habit because I can't seem to help myself when it comes to attractive women. What I actually wanted to find out was whether you feel you're being stretched enough at Crumbs. Or whether you'd consider a move to a more dynamic company. Like mine.'

Shock had her lurching forward – thank God she'd put her coffee cup down. 'You're offering me a job? But you've only just met me.'

'I've seen enough to know you're exactly the type of bright young talent I want in my business. Crumbs is traditional and dated. Come and work for me and I'll show you how companies of the future will operate.' He rose to his feet then, though not before giving her a cheeky wink. 'Think about it.'

Doug looked at his watch for the seventh time since he'd arrived in the office. It felt like she'd been away for three weeks, not three days, though technically for him it was four because of course she'd gone home to her family last night, not to him. He respected that, absolutely.

It didn't stop him wishing he'd been the first one she'd dashed home to.

The days had dragged with no Abby to light them up at work. The evenings had been even worse. He used to be content coming back to his haven of a studio and painting. Now every evening spent without her seemed like a waste; hollow, stark, empty. It was funny that the two things he'd always been so obsessed about – removing himself from his father's control and achieving success with his art – were now within his grasp, yet his current happiness was down to neither. It was all due to Abby.

His head turned at the sound of footsteps and then suddenly she was there, striding into his office, hair in a ponytail, body enclosed in a smart purple suit that looked amazing on her. Smile a mile wide. 'Good to see you've not been slacking while I've been away.'

'Abby.' He stood and walked round the desk to hug her, uncaring of who might be watching.

She melted against him as he drank in her smell, her feel, her warmth. 'Looks like you might have missed me,' she teased when he finally let her go.

'I did.' His eyes searched hers. 'Did you find the time to miss me?'

Rising onto her tiptoes she planted a soft kiss on his lips. 'Of course I did.' Then she arched her brow. 'Why, worried Robert Langstone might have stolen your girlfriend?'

The way she emphasised the last word sent a rush of guilt through him. 'Ah. I guess Robert told you about our … conversation.'

She smiled, fiddling with his tie. 'He told me how you'd phoned that morning to warn him off, yes.' Raising her expressive eyes up to his, she frowned slightly. 'Don't you trust me?'

'Of course I do.' She was as honest as they came, he knew

that. 'That doesn't mean I'm going to make it easy for the competition to steal you away.' He was disconcerted to find a slight pink tinge to her cheeks. 'Abby?'

'No, it's nothing, at least not in the sense you mean.'

Jealousy fizzed through him and he forced himself to take a step away before he did anything awful like grab at her arms too tightly. 'What happened?' He knew his voice was too harsh, but the control he prided himself on was hard to find where Abby was concerned.

She bit on her lip, shaking her head. 'Don't look at me like that. I told you, nothing happened. He flirted, as you'd warned me, but he didn't push. At least not personally.'

He heard the caveat, but was too focused on the more important issue to pursue it. 'Did you like him?'

'Of course I did.' He flinched and she immediately closed the gap between them, putting her arms around his waist and squeezing him tight. 'Oh my God, Doug, I don't mean like that. I liked him as a person; he was fun and charming and easy.' He didn't miss the fact that none of those words described himself. 'But I didn't *fancy* him, if that's what you're getting at. How could I, when I'm utterly besotted by you?'

Slowly he felt himself start to relax. 'You are?'

She thumped at his chest. 'Of course I am, you great muppet. It turns out I don't go for men who are cocky and easy-going. I like them reserved and complicated.' Her lips gently brushed his. 'Plus artistic and wildly attractive.' Another brush of her lips. 'And did I say athletic yet? I definitely love that in a man.'

With a sigh he drew her back against him again, kissing the top of her head. 'You've no idea how much I missed you, Abby. No idea at all.'

He felt her smile against his chest. 'I do, you know, because I felt it, too, even though I had Robert to keep me company.'

Laughing, he pushed her away. 'Okay, I deserved that. Now tell me about the part of that sentence from earlier that went *at least not personally*.'

She glanced up at him rather coyly. 'He did sound rather keen to have me work for him.'

It wasn't the same gut wrenching jealously he'd felt earlier, but his heart still gave a painful lurch. If he lost her professionally, wouldn't that be just a step towards the bigger loss? He knew damn well Robert's business was up in Manchester – at least three hours away from him, on a good run. She'd have to move and he'd hardly see her.

'Hey, don't look so worried.' Her hand cradled his face, reassuring him. 'I told him no. I'm happy, Doug. Both personally and professionally, I have everything I need right here.'

He took her hand and raised it to his lips, praying she would always think that way.

Chapter Thirty

It was October, a busy time in the Spencer family with two birthdays coming up. It was a family tradition that birthdays were celebrated together. It didn't have to be on the day itself, as long as the occasion was marked with presents, cake and candles.

'When are we going to celebrate your and Dad's birthday?' Abby asked Holly as they all sat down for dinner midweek.

Doug had joined them, as he did now and again because otherwise, between home life and her new job – she'd been a management trainee for two months now – she hardly saw him. He was perched on the end, next to Sally who still blushed every time he spoke to her, and opposite the dynamic duo of Holly and Ellie.

'This weekend.' Holly beamed, bolognaise sauce dribbling down her chin. 'Can we go out for pizza?'

'Can't do Saturday.' Mandy put a spoon in George's hand and helped him scoop up some bolognaise. He was fifteen months old now and determined to feed himself, though his co-ordination wasn't always the best. 'You said you'd look after George, remember? Dad's got his pub quiz and me and Roger have that party.'

'Damn, yes, I'd forgotten.'

'Not supposed to say damn,' Ellie reminded her, sucking a piece of spaghetti into her mouth. 'Not in front of our sensitive ears.'

Sniggering followed her comment, but when Abby glanced at Doug she saw that though his mouth smiled, his eyes were like those of a puppy who'd been accidentally kicked by its clumsy owner. And she was the bitch doing the kicking, she realised with acute shame. Only yesterday he'd asked her if she was still on for going away for the weekend. How had she forgotten her promise to Mandy? Juggling the Spencer diaries and PA work had been hard but do-able. Add in a more demanding job, and an actual social life of her own, and it was starting to seem flaming impossible. 'Sorry,' she mouthed.

He shrugged, and though she knew it was an accepting, can't be helped sort of shrug, guilt slammed through her. 'How about Sunday?' she asked the table, figuring she could persuade Doug to take her away the following weekend instead.

'I'm not giving up hockey.' Ellie pouted. 'We've got a tournament coming up and if I don't go to training I won't get picked.'

'We could go out after that.'

'But it's Tabitha's party on Sunday.' Holly gave her a I-can't-believe-you-don't-know-that look. 'I told you last week, remember?'

Oh God, she had, too. And damn it, that was a present they needed to buy. 'Okay then, how about the next weekend?'

Finally there was agreement on the following Saturday. Another weekend when she'd be tied up with family, instead of the man at the end of the table. Her heart ached when she looked over at him again. He was talking to Sally now. Freshly seventeen, nearly a woman, she was transfixed by every word he was saying. Abby knew how it felt to be the sole recipient of Doug's dazzling blue eyed focus.

It was no wonder Sally couldn't look away.

With a sigh, Abby turned back to her meal.

'That sounded as if it came from your boots, sunshine.' Her dad gave her a nudge, his eyes filled with concern. 'Everything okay?'

She smiled and touched his hand. 'Don't fret, I'm fine. Just wish there were more hours in the day, and more days in the week.'

Her eyes drifted again to Doug and her dad followed her gaze. 'Must be hard on him, sharing you.'

'Yes.' She kept her eyes on the man in question, falling for him that little bit more as she watched how careful he was with Sally. Giving her his full attention, smiling yet not encouraging. 'Trouble is, he doesn't have many family commitments, whereas I—'

'Have too many,' her father cut in, smiling sadly. 'You can't let all this ...' He nodded round the table: Ellie and Holly now shrieking at each other over boys; Mandy chatting away to George who, judging by his babbling, was convinced he was talking back; Sally who was placing her fork and spoon neatly back in her empty bowl; Pat who'd snuck his head onto her lap, his wet nose burying into her hand. 'You can't let it come between you and a chance at happiness. If you need time away, take it. We'll survive. House might not, mind, but we will.'

'I know you will.' But she wasn't cooking here on a Wednesday evening, instead of at Doug's, because she thought they'd starve without her. She was doing it part out of habit, but mostly out of love. When she was with Doug, she *missed* them. But when she was with her family, she missed Doug. Somehow she had to find a way to balance out the dual tugs on her heart.

Saturday night, and for a second Doug allowed his mind to settle on what might have been. He and Abby sipping champagne at the bar in the luxury Cotswold hotel he'd booked them into. Then relaxing together in the private hot tub, Abby sitting between his legs, his arms around her. Warm bubbles surrounding them.

'Doug.' Ellie put her hands on her hips, clearly exasperated with him. 'It's your go.'

'Sorry.' He shook himself out of his daydream and back

to the reality of his Saturday night. Playing Monopoly with two teenage girls. He supposed he should be thankful Sally was having a sleepover at her friend's, though actually he enjoyed her company. He guessed because he had more in common with the quiet, serious girl than happy Holly and mouthy Ellie. After a quick roll of the dice he moved his boot past jail and onto Regent's Street. 'Excellent. I'll buy that.'

'OMG, that's so not fair,' Ellie complained. 'You've got all three of the green ones now. And Mayfair and Park Lane. You're going to win.'

'He might not.' Holly, who was the assigned banker, handed him his property card. 'He's hardly got any money left.'

'Yeah, but we know how this dumb game works.'

'You wanted to play,' Holly pointed out. 'Doug wanted to watch a film.'

'Not any films we wanted to watch.'

Doug decided to leave them bickering and go and hunt down Abby, who'd gone to bath George.

'Hey, where are you going?' Ellie shouted as he reached the bottom of the stairs.

'Taking a break from building my property empire. Be back in a minute.'

He knocked on the bathroom door and popped his head round, his heart squeezing at the sight of Abby, arms deep in bubbles, cheeks flushed, cooing at George as she washed him with a sponge.

'Do you offer that service to more mature males?'

She gave a little start, then grinned when she saw him. 'It depends on the man.'

'I was thinking of someone say, thirty, who'd be very keen to feel your hands on him as he took a bath.'

The flush on her cheeks deepened. 'It could be arranged.'

He perched on the edge of the bath and watched as she pulled George out of the water and started to dry him, his emotions all over the place. He loved the maternal side of Abby. The warmth, the kindness that was so much a part of her. For the first time in his life he could even see a future where he might have children of his own. Blonde, brown eyed girls.

But right now it was the other side of Abby he wanted more of. The smart as hell, sexy woman who liked rolling around in his bed as much as he did. That woman was becoming an increasingly, frustratingly, rare sight.

'Abby.' She glanced up and a frown formed at whatever she saw in his eyes.

'Yes?'

Seeing George was happily playing with a toy boat, Doug took her hand and hauled her up. 'This,' he said softly, his gaze fixed on her mouth. Then he bent to kiss her. The moment their lips touched heat flooded through him and he groaned, hauling her closer, deepening the kiss, tangling his tongue with hers. His hands curled round her hips and he ground against her, desperate for the contact.

'Doug!' Ellie's loud voice pierced through the fog of his desire and he cursed, drawing back, his heart pumping. Shit, what was he doing, kissing her like that with her nephew on the floor beneath them. Her sisters downstairs.

'Sorry.'

'No.' Her lips were swollen, her cheeks rosy red. 'I'm sorry. This isn't how you planned our Saturday night to be.'

'Are you coming?' Ellie's voice screamed back up to them.

He gave Abby one final, soft kiss. 'Better do as I'm told.'

'I'll make it up to you.' She dropped down to her haunches to pick up George. 'Dad will be back around eleven. Maybe we can go back to your place then?'

The promise in her eyes was enough to add a bounce to his step as he headed back down the stairs.

The discarded Monopoly board was still on the coffee table. Ellie and Holly had just disappeared off to bed and Doug finally, finally, had his arms wrapped around Abby as they cuddled on the sofa.

'You let them win.'

He smiled into her hair. 'It seemed a small price to pay to finish the game and get you to myself.'

He felt her shoulders rise and fall as she let out a deep breath. 'I know I said this earlier, but considering you've spent your Saturday night playing Monopoly with my sisters I think it needs saying again. I'm sorry.'

His arms tightened around her. 'Don't be. I enjoyed it.' She looked up at him, brown eyes rounded in disbelief. 'Okay, I'd rather have been with you in a hot tub, but as that wasn't an option, I had a good time. Both of them have bits of you in them. Holly has your kind, smiling nature.'

She arched a brow. 'And Ellie?'

He grinned. 'You can be mouthy when you're riled.'

Laughing softly, she snuggled against him. 'I can't disagree with that.'

The television was on, some film where people did a lot of staring into the distance and looking profound, but Doug wasn't listening to it. His whole focus was on the warm, supple body draped around his. He couldn't stop touching her, stroking her arms, her legs, her back. Dipping his head every now and again to kiss her.

Eleven o'clock came and went, and still no sign of Derek. And while his body was humming with arousal, the woman nestled against him was getting more and more quiet.

'Abby?'

She murmured, burrowing deeper into his arms. With a

resigned sigh Doug lifted her up and carried her up the stairs and onto her bed. She raised her head, eyes cloudy with sleep. 'Aren't we going to yours?'

He tucked the duvet round her. 'You're beat, Abby. Go to sleep. I'll stay until your dad gets back.'

She rubbed at her eyes but he could see it was an effort. 'But I want to sleep with you.'

He eased himself onto the bed next to her. 'I'm here. Now sleep.'

Within seconds he could hear the rhythmic sound of her breathing. Kissing the top of her head he made his way back downstairs, body tight with unfulfilled need. *At least you had her in your arms for a while*, he told himself as he slumped back on the sofa to wait for Derek. It was more than he could have hoped for a few months ago.

But now he was getting greedy. The more of her he saw, the more of her he wanted.

Chapter Thirty-One

October flew by. The birthdays came and went, Abby ran two off-site meetings, watched a hockey tournament (Ellie's team came second) and even managed a Saturday night with Doug.

They hadn't managed the weekend away, but maybe November would be kinder to them.

Coming back from a meeting, Abby checked the messages left on her phone and smiled at the first. Robert Langstone was still trying to persuade her to join his company. Of course she'd considered it – a director post with her paltry experience, she'd be a fool not to – but why move to Manchester when she had everything she wanted right here? Crumbs might be old-fashioned but she enjoyed the challenge of trying to modernise it. Plus she was smart enough to know that it was having Doug as the rock behind her, the sounding board, that gave her the confidence to push her ideas.

It was also having Doug to go home to, when family responsibilities allowed, that made her day complete.

There was still one blot on the landscape, but so far she and Charles Faulkner had done a good job of avoiding each other. Several times she'd asked Doug whether Charles was still meddling but he'd simply given her one of his enigmatic smiles. 'It's all in hand. Don't worry about him.'

A tall, drop dead gorgeous man stepped into her office and her heart gave a little sigh of pleasure.

'Can you squeeze lunch with me into your hectic schedule or are you going to bail like you did yesterday?'

Though there was a smile on Doug's face, Abby sighed. Nobody had warned her how difficult it would be to juggle the needs of work, her family *and* her lover. Still, as problems went, this wasn't one she was going to complain about.

'I'm free from one till two, if that works with *your* hectic schedule.' It didn't help that Doug had a juggling act of his own. Managing director of Crumbs and artist with a rapidly growing reputation that demanded more and more of his time.

He bent over her desk and kissed her. 'I'll make it work.'

It was ten past one by the time she made it out of her morning meetings and back to her office. Doug was already there, perched on her desk, talking on the phone.

'Looks like my lunch date has finally arrived. I'll see you at the gym later.' A pause. 'No, I'm not doing that. Focus on your own woman and keep your hands off mine.' He put the phone down and eased off the desk. 'Luke,' he explained. 'He says hello.'

'It sounded like he said more than that.'

'I'm not going to give you a kiss from him. When I kiss you it will be from me.' He took three strides towards her, captured her head in his hands and gave her a deep, soul enhancing kiss. 'Come on. I've reserved a table at the Italian. We need to get a move on.'

'But I've got a meeting at two. I thought we were just going to the café?'

He let out a deep sigh. 'And I thought it would be nice to have a proper lunch with you for a change. Away from anything to do with work.'

Abby bit her tongue and grabbed her jacket. It was only when they were seated at the restaurant, having given their orders, that she broached what was on her mind. 'I know it's difficult for you to understand, because you've always carried the weight of the Faulkner name, but I need to be able to stand up in front of the Crumbs management team as a professional in my own right.'

He'd been toying with his fork, but now his hands stilled. 'What do you mean?'

'I mean I can't afford to be late for meetings. It's hard enough being the boss's lover. Already I have to be twice as good as the next person to overturn the impression that I slept my way into this position. If I start turning up late and unprepared too, what chance do I have of becoming a manager people will respect?'

'Sorry.' Carefully he placed the fork back on the table. 'Perhaps you'd prefer it if I bring you a sandwich next time so you can eat it in your meeting.'

'That's not fair.'

Doug allowed the air slowly out of his lungs. Abby was right, he *wasn't* being fair. But in the two months since she'd started back at Crumbs, instead of them becoming closer, he'd felt her drifting away from him. Sometimes he wondered if she liked her work more than she liked him.

Their lunch arrived and Doug waited for it to be served up before talking again. 'Let's not argue,' he pleaded. 'All I wanted was some precious time with the most important person in my life.'

Immediately she looked stricken. 'You're really important to me, too, you know. And I'm sorry if at times it looks like you aren't. What with my family and the job, you must spend a lot of time cursing me.'

'No.' When she tilted her head and continued to look at him, he smiled. 'Okay, I'll admit to the occasional curse.' Also the occasional time when he selfishly wished for the original Abby back. The personal assistant who'd thought he was heir to Charles Faulkner and some sort of god, rather than this Abby who knew he was only masquerading as a Faulkner and that actually she was far smarter than he was.

'Well, if we're admitting to things, I'll admit that you're

right. This lasagna is a lot nicer than a cold sandwich.' As she tucked back into it though, her phone began to ring. 'Oh bugger, I'm going to have to take this. Sorry.'

Doug slapped a smile on his face and forced himself to continue eating while Abby yakked away to the person on the end of the phone about a critical deadline that absolutely couldn't be missed.

'Sorry about that,' she said, ending the call and clattering the phone back onto the table. 'We've got another line extension to the savoury range that we need to get ...' She trailed off when she looked at his face. 'Oh crumbs, you said no work, didn't you? Sorry.' Then she rolled her eyes. 'That's all I seem to be saying lately, isn't it?'

It was, but Doug kept quiet. Part of his problem was that Abby was excited by her work, while he didn't understand what all the fuss was about. It wasn't that she'd changed since getting the promotion though, so he could hardly complain. She'd loved the business right from that very first day when she'd walked awkwardly into his office and nearly tripped over her handbag.

'Well, I'm going to try not to say it any more today,' she continued. When he looked at her blankly, she shook her finger at him. 'You weren't listening.'

'It's hard to listen to everything you say,' he countered, earning him a playful kick under the table. 'Though I did hear you say you were going to try not to say sorry any more.'

She huffed. 'Umm, okay then. Of course if I do muck up I might need to use another word instead, like apologies, or pardon, but—'

'I want us to go away together,' he interrupted. 'I'd like to take you to Florence or Venice.'

'Wow.' She dropped her fork. 'Really?'

Her excitement was so obvious he found himself smiling. 'Yes, really. When can you get away?'

As instantly as her face had lit up, it fell. 'Oh boy, I really don't know. I'll have to sort it out with work, and then there's my family to consider.' She glanced at her watch and let out a string of curses. 'I'm going to have to go. I'm really sorry ... ouch, there's that word again and I'm using it only two minutes after I promised I wouldn't.' When he put down his fork she shook her head. 'No, you finish up. It's bad enough one of us doesn't get to finish their meal.'

He swallowed down his frustration. 'Will I see you later tonight?'

'You know I can't.' She pulled at her jacket, trying to tug it off the back of the chair. When he saw the chair tilt at an alarming angle Doug shot to his feet and calmly untangled it. 'Thank you. More haste, less speed. I know.' She shoved her arms into the sleeves with alarming force, totally ignoring her mantra.

'You can't make tonight ... because?' he prompted.

'Oh, yes. I'm visiting the manufacturing site over the next two days. I have to fly up tonight.'

Doug took some money out of his wallet and slipped it onto the table. He was damned if he was going to sit there like some poor chump whose girlfriend had just walked out on him. Which she had. 'I'll fly up with you,' he decided, then checked his phone. 'Damn, I can't. Pamela's got me down for a nine o'clock.'

He held the door open for Abby as she rushed through like a blonde tornado. 'You haven't trained her not to put in meetings before ten or after four?'

'No. I shouldn't have to. She should know. You did.'

'That's because I was super efficient. Or, to be more accurate, I could see you were a man who didn't particularly like being in the office, so I tried to make it as painless as possible.' She came to an abrupt halt. 'Please, Doug, go and finish your lunch. You're making me feel bad.'

'I told you, lunch wasn't about the food. It was about seeing you. So how about the night you get back? We can go to a restaurant and try and eat a complete meal together.'

She was almost running, her slender but short legs having to work overtime to keep up the punishing pace she'd set herself. All to get to a meeting on time. Finally they entered the Crumbs building and Abby scampered up the stairs to her office. There she threw down her handbag and picked up the file on top of her desk. 'I'd love to see you then, you know I would, but I'm away from home tonight and tomorrow. I can't go out again as soon as I get back. It's not fair on my father, or my sisters.'

'Fine.' He was certainly getting the message. Loud and blindingly clear. 'Perhaps, when you've got a spare moment, you could let me know when I *can* see you.' He gave her a cool peck on the cheek and turned to walk away but she gripped at his arm.

'Don't be like this.' Her large brown eyes pleaded with him but he was too hurt to be mollified by them. 'You know I've got responsibilities. You can't have a hissy fit just because I won't drop everything to see you. It isn't fair.'

'This isn't a hissy fit.' God, he didn't even know what one was. 'This is me wishing you a safe trip. Goodbye, Abby.'

For a split second she looked torn. Well that and spitting mad with him. In the end work won though, and she dashed off to her meeting.

Exhaling loudly, Doug stalked back to his office, wondering why he was so damn cut up. He'd never come first in anyone's life, so why did he think he had an automatic right to come first in the life of the woman he ... he ... oh God.

His head full of uncertainty, Doug slumped into his chair. Is this what love felt like? The desire, the burning need to spend every single available moment with someone, coupled

291

with the agony of not knowing whether they felt the same way?

'Do you have a moment, Douglas?'

He dragged himself out of his introspection to see his mother hovering in the doorway. 'Of course, come in.'

'I won't keep you. I know you must be ... busy.' Considering she'd just found him with his head in his hands, slumped at his desk, he appreciated her tact. She took a few steps inside and closed the door behind her. 'I just wanted to let you know that I've spoken to Sebastian and everything is in place.'

He mustered a smile, wondering if his Great Idea was quite so great now. 'Thank you.' What she'd managed to do over the last three months deserved more than that though, so he stood and walked round to face her. 'I mean that sincerely.' He dropped a kiss on her cheek.

To his shock her hand gripped his arm. 'No, it's me who should be thanking you. It's taken a long time, but I've finally realised how much you've done to protect this family. To protect me.' She paused, looking him straight in the eye, her expression as gentle as he'd ever seen it. 'Even that time you hit your father it was about looking after me, wasn't it?'

He glanced down at her hand. 'Yes.'

When he looked back up again she released his arm, only to lay her hand on his cheek instead. 'I should have thanked you, not torn you off a strip. I'm sorry. At the time I wasn't thinking straight. Afterwards I was too keen to bury my head in the sand and forget what he'd done, how he'd threatened me.' Dropping her hand to her side, she took a step back. 'Margaret and myself are moving out tomorrow. Sebastian has our new address. Gwen is finally moving into that house you bought her.' He could swear her eyes were glistening slightly as they stared into his. 'I hope you'll keep in touch. Goodbye, Douglas.'

292

With that she walked out of his office. Lady Faulkner, a proud, dignified lady who'd let that pride, that love of title and show, rule her life to such an extent that in the end, it was all she had left.

Abby finally came to the end of her meetings. Wearily she made her way back to her office, noting that Doug had already left for the day. It seemed to be the way of things recently. Letting out a deep sigh she gathered up her laptop and the two files she needed to take a quick look at, and slipped them into her sleek black briefcase. Her heart squeezed as she recalled the day Doug had given it to her. It had been the same day she'd opened the letter from the Crumbs HR Director, inviting her to become a management trainee. She'd leapt around like a crazy person and Doug had just stared at her, his unwavering blue eyes conveying his delight and his pride. Then he'd gone to his car and brought out the briefcase, wrapped in a big red bow. He'd presented it to her awkwardly, as if he wasn't sure she'd like it.

It had only been when she'd squealed and flung her arms around his neck that he'd admitted he'd never bought a present for a woman before – at least for one not related to him – and he'd been worried she'd take offence at its practicality.

A tear dropped onto her hand as she lovingly stroked the soft leather. They'd seemed so close that day but now, three months later, she worried at the cracks she saw. He was frustrated by her inability to drop everything when he asked. She, in turn, was being driven crazy by his inability to understand how hard it was for her to treat her job at Crumbs as casually as he treated his.

'Enjoying your time at the top are you, Abigail?'

Abby's head shot up to find Charles Faulkner strutting into her office. Of all the times to come and find her he had to choose now, when her defences were down. Heart hammering, she gripped tightly onto the briefcase. 'If you mean am I enjoying working back at Crumbs as a management trainee, the answer is yes.'

He gave her a cold smile. 'You think you've won, don't you?'

'Pardon?'

'Swanning about the office using your jumped up title, sleeping with a man you think will inherit the place. You must think all your Christmases have come at once.'

Abby tightened her hold on the briefcase so he wouldn't see her hands shaking. 'I'm doing the job I'm paid by your company to do. Anything more than that is none of your business.'

'When it concerns my family, I make it my business,' he countered harshly. 'If you think for one minute I'm going to let a trollop like you insinuate herself into my company, or the Faulkner family, you must think I'm some sort of fool. Doug doesn't have the right genes, but by God I won't have the Faulkner line sullied even further by the likes of you. So have your fun, Goldilocks, but don't think you're going to get the keys to the damn kingdom. I'll never let a woman like you get any further in this company. Never.'

With that he swung his large body round and barrelled out of her office the same way he'd barrelled in, almost knocking into someone in the process. 'Mind out of my way, girl,' Abby heard him boom.

She was still reeling from the venom of his words when Geraldine knocked on the door.

'Abby? Are you okay?' Geraldine took one look at her face and shook her head. 'Please tell me you're not going to take any notice of what Charles just said? He's an angry, bitter man who's always had it in for Doug for some reason I've never grasped, though after what I've just overheard I think I'm now enlightened. He's not Doug's real father, is he?'

Abby numbly shook her head. 'It's not common knowledge so—'

'I can keep a secret,' she interrupted, then blew out a breath. 'At least it helps explain his animosity towards Doug. It looks like he's found a new way to target him though, through you. Please don't give the man the satisfaction of letting him upset you.'

Abby half-staggered to her desk where she finally let go of the briefcase, letting it fall to the floor. Her legs still trembling, she perched on the edge, trying to get her equilibrium back. It angered her that Charles's nasty words could have this much effect on her. She'd known he'd retaliate, hadn't she? The man had sacked her and then been effectively blackmailed into not just taking her back, but promoting her. That must have really pissed him off.

'Abby?'

Taking a few calming breaths, Abby tried a smile. 'Don't worry about me. I'll be fine. I just ... heck. I've never been called a trollop before.'

'The definition of a trollop is a promiscuous woman. Have you been sleeping with four other men while you've been seeing Doug?'

Abby let out a strangled laugh. 'God, I can't even find enough time to see him.'

'Exactly. Ergo you're not a trollop.' Geraldine slid onto the desk next to her. 'Don't let Charles ruin what you and Doug have. I've never seen him so happy. He's always had this sadness lurking in his eyes that I could never understand, much less do anything about. It's not there any more, and I know that's down to you. Don't let his father come between you. It will break Doug's heart.'

Abby doubted that. Doug seemed to be getting more and

more frustrated with her, rather than into her. 'I have no intention of letting Charles Faulkner get to me,' she said firmly, though the words *I'll never let a woman like you* kept racing through her mind. 'But thanks for the pep talk. I'm afraid I've got to dash now. I've got a plane to catch.' She rolled her eyes. 'And wow, I never thought I'd be saying things like that. I sound like a proper businesswoman.'

'You are proper. I've seen how amazing you are at your job.' Geraldine's gaze skimmed over her face. 'You are okay, aren't you? I mean you're not going to leave here and then sob your heart out in the taxi are you?'

'Of course not.'

The moment she stepped into the taxi though, Abby broke her promise. She felt emotionally battered. First the testy lunch with Doug, then the exchange with Charles Faulkner. For a woman who pretty much had everything she'd ever dreamed of – a gorgeous man she loved, an exciting career – she was feeling pretty damn miserable.

She was wiping away the tears when her eye caught yet another message from Robert, asking her to call him. The timing was almost uncanny.

'Robert, it's Abby Spencer.'

'Abby, thank you for phoning me back. Have you given any more thought to my job offer?'

She leant back against the seat and stared out of the window. 'I've thought about it, yes.'

'And?'

'I like Crumbs.'

'Enough to pass over the chance to be a director in a fast growing modern company? You're more forward thinking than that, Abby. I've seen the way your mind works. You'd fit right in with us. How many of your ideas get squashed in Crumbs because old Faulkner is stuck in the dark ages?'

'Doug?'

Robert laughed. 'I'm talking about Charles Faulkner. How do you get on with him?'

Charles Faulkner's angry face as he'd called her a trollop flashed through her mind. 'I don't.'

'Then at least come up and let us show you around. Even better, take a week off and get a real sense of the place. If you like it, stay.'

'I couldn't just leave Crumbs, not like that.'

'Why not? Do you owe Charles Faulkner any loyalty? And I'm sure Doug would understand. From what I've seen, he's not particularly enamoured with working for his father, either.'

'Thanks. I'll think about it.'

'Don't waste time thinking. Come up and give us a try.'

Abby ended the call with her mind buzzing. A chance to be a director, away from the ugliness of Charles Faulkner and his threats.

The way she felt right now, it sounded like heaven.

Chapter Thirty-Two

Doug turned up to his gym session in a foul mood, which wasn't missed by his friend.

'What the blazes have you got to be angry about *now*?' Luke asked as they got changed. 'You've sorted the work issue by somehow persuading your father to take Abby back. I feel I should say something like respect, dude. You've solved the Abby issue by somehow persuading her to date you – again, respect. What the hell else is there to be grumpy about?'

When Luke put it like that, Doug had to admit his life was a thousand times better than it had been, but ... 'I want more,' he admitted, throwing his shoes into his bag and hauling out his trainers. 'I want a life with Abby where I see her every day.'

'Shit.' In the middle of putting his vest top on over his head, Luke halted. 'You want to *marry* her?'

Doug hunched over, rubbing at his face. Hadn't he frozen with fear a few months ago when one of the girls had mentioned marriage? But what he'd witnessed with his parents – infidelity, callous disregard for your partner, coldness, threats and betrayal – didn't compute with how he saw his life with Abby. They'd wake up in each other's arms. Make love. She'd say something, probably say a lot of things knowing her, and make him laugh. 'Maybe,' he found himself saying. 'In time.'

'Well, wow.' Eyes almost bugging out of his head, Luke slid his top down his chest. 'That's pretty major. I thought you didn't do relationships.'

'I didn't. Until I met Abby.'

Slowly Luke's mouth turned upwards in a shit eating grin. 'Bloody hell, I never thought I'd see the day. Douglas

Faulkner, Mr Remote, turns out to be a right softy. Love, marriage. Hell, next it'll be kids.'

Doug swallowed, hard. 'Hold on. Before you have me changing nappies, you should know that's a long way from how Abby sees us. I currently lie eighth on her importance list behind her father, four sisters, nephew and her job. Actually, thinking about it, Pat might be before me, too.'

'Pat?'

'Yeah, the flaming dog.'

Luke cracked a smile. 'Pat the dog. I like it.'

'This isn't funny,' Doug snapped, then sighed. 'Sorry. Ignore me. I'm actually pretty lucky to be eighth.'

'You know just because Abby puts the needs of her work and family before you, it doesn't mean she thinks they're more important.'

'It sure feels like that.'

'So you expect her to drop her responsibilities and come running whenever you click your fingers?'

'Of course I don't.'

'Then why the gripe? How can Abby get respect from the Crumbs staff if she doesn't put all her effort into the role? And how can she suddenly drop the family she's been looking after for the last umpteen years? Isn't her loyalty and her integrity part of why you love her?'

'Okay, okay, enough.' Shame coiled in his gut and he held up a hand in surrender. 'I get the message. You're right, of course you are. I'm just feeling sorry for myself. I've been doing it for so many years it's become a habit.'

'You get to call a woman like Abby your girlfriend, you should be thanking your lucky stars, mate.'

'I am. For the first time in my life I've got something good to look forward to and I'm not going to cock it up.' He studied his friend. 'Now we've dissected my love life, how about we move on to yours?'

Luke snorted dismissively. 'What are we, girls?'

'Spill.'

He let out a dramatic sigh. 'Okay. Gerri and I are getting on just great.' Doug couldn't help but wince, which made his friend chuckle. 'You never did find out why she hated being called Gerri, did you? The first guy she fell for called her that, then went and broke her heart so since then she's hated the name. I told her I wasn't anything like that dumb prick – I was better looking and I was never going to hurt her – so I was going to keep calling her Gerri.'

'And she accepted it?'

'Don't look so surprised. She's a pussy cat who's spent too much of her life hiding her true nature behind a wall of hurt.' Luke stared pointedly at him. 'What she needed was a well-adjusted, normal, open, warm-spirited soul to patiently knock that wall down.'

'Sorry, but I don't immediately recognise that description. Who is that person?'

Luke flicked him with his towel. 'You can mock, but Abby's done the same for you, too.' His face turned serious for a moment. 'And just as Abby is the one for you, Gerri's the one for me. All we have to do now is make sure they realise it.'

Doug slowly shook his head. 'Hell's teeth. Five months ago we were free spirits. Now look at us. We're sunk.'

'Never. Not while we can still grapple a twenty stone man to the floor with our bare hands. Now get your pathetic arse out there and let me wipe the floor with you.'

The gruelling session worked out all of his remaining angst. By the time Doug was showered and back in his car he was able to acknowledge he was a lucky sod who didn't deserve Abby in the first place. So what if he didn't get her to himself very often? Having her in his life at all was a million times better than the alternative.

He could only pray his shitty behaviour this afternoon hadn't turned her off him completely.

Abby lay on the bed in her hotel room and sighed. It was one of the rare occasions when she had nothing to do but please herself. What a shame she wasn't in the mood. In an effort to pick herself up she ran a bath and ordered a hamburger from room service. After raiding the minibar – *up yours Charles Faulkner, I'll cheer myself up on the Crumbs expense account* – she took the bottle of wine to the bath and spent a good fifteen minutes soaking her body and her liver.

When that, and then the hamburger, failed to cheer her up she clutched at the final straw and phoned home.

Holly answered, immediately firing her with questions. 'How big is your bed?'

Abby stretched across it, imagining Doug lying next to her. 'Too big for me.'

'Have you had anything from the minibar? Dad says they always charge lots of money for that stuff but because you're away with work you can make the company pay.'

'Yes, he's right. Look, isn't it time you were going to bed? Can you say hello to your sisters from me and find Mandy or Dad?'

There was the sound of the phone being thrown against something hard, some muffled shouting, and finally Mandy came on. 'Hey, how's the working girl?'

Abby sucked in a deep breath and let it out in a loud sigh. 'Miserable.'

'Shit, Abs, what happened?'

Abby shut her eyes, trying not to give in to tears again. 'Doug and I had a sort of fight, then Charles Faulkner came into my office and said some nasty words. I've tried alcohol, a bath and a hamburger and I still feel crap.'

'Blimey, that's one lousy day. What do you mean, nasty words?'

'He called me a trollop and told me he'd never let a woman like me get anywhere in his company.'

'So, there are plenty of other businesses out there you could work for.'

At her sister's bolshie tone, Abby finally managed a smile. 'True. In fact, I'm sitting on a job offer from one.'

'Oh wow, you haven't mentioned that before. Who and where?'

'The who is a fast growing healthy snack company.' When she named the company Mandy squealed. 'The where is Manchester.'

'Umm, I'm liking the first part but not the second. How about the what, as in what's the job?'

'It's a director post.'

'Bloody hell, Abby. Why are they offering that to you? And I mean that in a very caring, sisterly way that in no way infers you aren't fantastic.'

For the first time in what felt like ages, Abby started to laugh. 'I can't believe it either, but I met the owner on a workshop I attended a couple of months ago. He was the external expert, there to observe, and we hit it off. He wants me to go up and spend a week there. And if I like it, stay.'

'Well, blow me. I don't want you to go to flipping Manchester, of course, but you'd be stupid not to consider it. As long as Charles is head of Crumbs you'll never get what you want there. This could be a real opportunity. And while you're chewing that one over, what about the fight with Doug?'

'The fight wasn't really a fight, because Doug doesn't do raised voices. He just gets distant which hurts even more.' She pictured his face as he'd told her to have a good trip. As if she'd been his work colleague, not his lover. 'I'm not sure how much longer I can carry on like this. I was so happy when he finally let me in but since we've been together all I seem to be doing is making him miserable again.'

'Don't be stupid. I've seen the man when you're around. He's besotted.'

'You wouldn't think that if you'd been a fly on the wall during our last conversation.' Tears pricked again and she reached for a tissue from the bedside table. 'Anyway, let's talk about something else. I phoned to be cheered up, not to continue to pick over my crappy day.'

'Well, if it won't make you feel bad, I can gloat over my domestic bliss. Roger is going to help a friend out in a shop on Saturday now so he can earn a bit more money. He says he's saving up so we can buy a place together.'

Abby's jaw dropped. 'That's fantastic news.'

'Isn't it?' And if she sounded ever so slightly smug, Abby couldn't blame her. Mandy had been through a lot, she deserved some happiness. 'Don't worry though, we won't be out of your hair for ages. Crumbs pays well, but not *that* well.'

When Abby finally put the phone down she stared up at the ceiling. Mandy was planning to leave home to start a new life with her son and partner. That was good. Really good.

But where did it leave her?

She spent the next two days having a tiring but fruitful time at the manufacturing site. It was non-stop. She didn't even get the evening off, as the site manager and a few of his crew insisted she go out for a drink with them after the meeting. A drink soon turned into a few, so obviously they then had to go for a curry to soak up the alcohol. She'd ended up crashing out in her hotel room at one in the morning. Now finally on her way home, she wasn't just tired, she was hung-over.

Her phone buzzed and she smiled when she answered it. 'Hey, Geraldine. Is everything okay?'

'Yes, it's fine. Are you all right to talk?'

'Am I ever. I'm kicking my heels at the airport, waiting for the flight home.'

'How did the site visit go?'

'Good, thank you. It was great to put names to a few faces and to see how these items we spend so much of our time talking and thinking about actually get made.'

'Yes, it is a bit crazy when you think how much effort goes into the humble biscuit.' She paused. 'I hope you haven't been dwelling too much on what Charles Faulkner said to you.'

'I'd be lying if I said I hadn't. I'm not sure how I can carry on working for a man who hates me that much.'

She heard Geraldine's intake of breath. 'Are you thinking of *leaving*?'

'Let's just say I'm considering my options.'

'That sounds intriguing. Are you sitting on some options, then?'

And for the second time in as many days, Abby talked about the job offer from Robert Langstone.

'Wow, good on you, girl. Have you told Doug?'

Guilt crashed through her. How had she managed to tell both her sister and even Doug's ex, but not the man she was sharing a bed with? 'Not exactly, no.' She could tell herself she'd not needed to because it hadn't been an option until the altercation with Faulkner senior. It didn't help that she'd not told Doug about that yet, either.

'Okay.' Geraldine, obviously reading between the lines, tactfully moved the conversation on. 'Anyway, I called because I'd appreciate your take on the new advertising concepts that have just come in. Are you around tomorrow?'

'Sure, I'd love to see them.' Abby hesitated. 'Do you and Luke ever argue about the amount of time you spend at the office?'

Geraldine laughed. 'No way. Luke's pretty tied up with the

gallery but even if he wasn't he'd know better than to get in the way of my work. I told him from the outset I was a workaholic and he had to accept me as he found me because I wasn't changing. Why, is Doug getting antsy?'

'A bit.' It felt awkward slagging him off with his ex, especially as it wasn't only her job Doug had to put up with but her family, too.

'If you want my advice, don't let anyone tell you what to do. You have to stand up for what you want. If what you want is to become a director in Robert's company, you should go ahead and take it. Chances like that don't come along too often.'

They were words that resonated with Abby more than she cared to admit. She'd scoffed at Doug for not standing up for what he'd wanted but was she any better, allowing herself to be pulled in different directions by both him and her family?

As she ended the call she noticed an unopened text message. When had that arrived? Hastily she read it.

Goodnight, Abby. Sweet dreams, D xx

Shitty, shitty, shit, shit. He'd obviously sent it after she'd checked her phone that first night. Somehow, during the whole of the following day and evening, she'd managed to miss it. Burying her head in her hands, she tried to swallow back the tears. It was hardly surprising the guy was so annoyed with her. She was pretty annoyed with herself.

After taking a few deep breaths and wiping her eyes, she fired off a hasty reply. *Sorry I missed your text. It's been a hectic few days. Talk soon xx*

When Abby arrived back home she was greeted as if she'd been away for a month rather than two nights.

'I missed you,' Holly told her, squeezing her tight round her waist.

'But you had Dad and your other sisters,' Abby reminded her gently, feeling choked.

'I know. But I still missed you.'

Ellie wasn't quite so forthcoming but she did give her a longer goodnight hug than usual. Even Sally decided to open up to her about a boy she didn't fancy, she really didn't. Though she did quite like him.

When Abby had said goodnight to them all, and checked in on George who was sleeping soundly while his parents enjoyed a meal out, she wandered back down to find her father watching television.

Well, watching wasn't quite the right word. His head was slumped forward and though he seemed to be trying to keep awake it was obviously a losing battle. For a moment Abby simply stood and studied him. He'd aged in the last twelve years since he'd lost the love of his life, his face more lined, his hair now grey, but he was still handsome. Would he ever find someone else to love? Her heart clenched as she imagined them all slowly leaving home and her father coming back to an empty house.

God, she hoped not.

She must have made a noise because suddenly his eyes snapped open and he turned to smile at her.

'Abby.' He patted the seat next to him. 'Come and tell me what has you looking so worried.'

'I'm not worried,' she protested. 'I've just got a lot to think about.'

'Then tell me. A problem shared, though probably not halved if it's shared with me, will at least seem clearer by the time you've managed to get it though my thick skull.'

'You're hardly thick.' Abby settled down and snuggled in to his chest. 'Though this is going to take some working through so listen carefully.' She sucked in a breath and let the words out in a rush. 'Charles Faulkner hates me and told me I'll never get anywhere in his company and that he won't allow me to sully the Faulkner line. That probably won't be an issue though because Doug and I had a fight and I think, no scratch that, I *know* he's fed up with me. On the plus side, I've got an offer of a director job for an up and coming health food company, though it's based in Manchester. They want me to go up and spend the week there. See for myself. And if I like it, I get to stay and run my own department. Away from Charles bloody Faulkner. But then I'd have to leave you. And if Doug and I don't even have time to see each other living twenty minutes away, I can't see how we'd manage living over three hours away. Then again, like I said, that might not be an issue because he's probably had enough of me.'

Her father didn't immediately say anything. Instead he slowly got up and walked over to the kitchen, coming back with a bottle of whisky and two glasses. 'I think it's going to be a long night.' He poured a healthy measure into both glasses and then handed her one. 'Now, tell me all that again, but at a speed an old man can understand.'

Chapter Thirty-Three

Doug tried Abby's phone for the third time, got put through to voicemail for the third time and hung up on a despairing sigh. After his boorish display the other day when he'd flounced off in a huff – damn it, yes, a hissy fit – he'd realised Luke was right. He'd lose her if he didn't shut up and put up.

Still, he was allowed to sigh, surely, because it was now Friday, four days since he'd last seen her. He'd had one text and a hasty phone call. The text had been on Wednesday, an apology for not seeing his original goodnight text. To say he'd been gutted that she hadn't thought to look at her phone to check it, never mind to send him one, was an understatement. Since then he'd received a phone call in response to a message he'd left asking if she was free Thursday. She was very sorry – and yes he could imagine her face cringing as she'd said the word – but she had to attend Ellie's parent teacher evening. Before he'd had a chance to ask about Friday she'd had to dash off because Ellie and Holly had been having a blazing row which apparently only Abby could sort out.

That was the trouble with falling in love with Wonder Woman.

The sound of the phone was a pleasant distraction from his tetchy thoughts.

'Hello, Geraldine. What can I do for you?'

'Do you know where Abby is? I've got a further ad concept I'd like her to see.'

'She's at an off-site meeting all day.' So he'd found out from her diary. 'Presumably my input isn't desirable?'

'Hey, don't be like that. I used to ask your opinion but I stopped when you couldn't drum up any enthusiasm for anything I showed you. Abby's not only interested, she's insightful.' He wanted to be offended, but it was hard when he knew she was right. 'Is Abby okay after that incident with Charles? She keeps saying she's fine, but it must have shaken her up a bit.'

Doug's heart seemed to stop beating. 'What incident?'

He heard a sharp intake of breath. 'Oops, she didn't tell you, did she? My big mouth.'

'I repeat,' he said tightly, 'what incident?' When his request was met with silence, Doug shot to his feet. 'Geraldine, please. Answer me.' If he had to beg, he would.

'There must be a reason why Abby hasn't mentioned it, Doug. If I tell you I feel like I'm betraying her trust.'

'Did she ask you not to tell me?' he demanded, starting to pace up and down.

'Well, no.'

'Then bloody tell me.' He dragged in a deep breath. 'Please.'

He heard her sigh. 'Charles was doing his usual bastard of the highest order routine. Words to the effect that he was never going to let a woman like her insinuate herself any further in his family.'

Anger raged through him, shooting hot arrows into his chest and his head. 'I don't want the pretty version,' he said, his voice hardened with the strain of his control. 'I want the gritty, true, everything you can remember version.'

As he listened to Geraldine quietly recounting exactly what Charles had said to Abby, Doug's blood started to boil. How the hell could the man possibly think *she* wasn't good enough for his dysfunctional family?

'And?' he demanded, sensing there was still something Geraldine wasn't telling him.

'He told her he'd never let a woman like her get anywhere in his company.'

'The bastard,' Doug hissed through his clenched jaw.

'Exactly,' agreed Geraldine. 'It's not surprising she's seriously considering Robert's offer ... ah, shit. I'm not sure I'm meant to say anything about that, either.'

Doug shut his eyes. 'I know Robert's keen to have her.' In every bloody sense, he thought bitterly. 'Has she decided to work for him?' And oh God, how had it come to him asking his ex-lover what his current girlfriend was thinking?

'I don't know. Robert asked her to go up for a week. Sort of a trial run. And if she liked it, to stay. I told her to give it serious thought. Chances like that don't come along very often for women as young as Abby. And she's hardly going to get anywhere in Crumbs, is she?'

After Geraldine had murmured her goodbye Doug slowly, and very carefully, ended the call and put down his phone. Then he dropped into his chair, put his head in his hands, screwed his eyes shut and practiced breathing in and out. In and out.

When he felt his anger was back under control, he dialled Abby's phone again, which predictably went to voicemail. 'It's Doug,' he said, his voice sounding raw. 'When you get this will you please, please call me back.'

Abby was exhausted. She'd had a morning meeting with the buyer of a large retail chain and then she'd spent the afternoon at home trying to stuff some clothes into a suitcase.

'Knock, knock.' Mandy popped her head round the door. 'How's the packing going?'

'Okay. I'm getting used to filling a suitcase now.'

Mandy nodded, moving further inside so she could hug her. 'Crikey, big sis, I hate seeing you leave. I'm going to miss you.'

'Oh no.' Abby shook her head, waving her finger at Mandy. 'Don't you go getting soppy on me. It's not like I'm disappearing off the face of the earth.'

'Yeah, I know.' Mandy gripped her shoulders. 'You're sure about this? It's a whopping big step.' She cast her eyes briefly downwards. 'Especially for someone with such dainty feet.'

'I'm sure,' Abby answered unwaveringly. 'Even more than that, I'm sure I'm sure. I've never *been* so sure of anything. It's not a done deal, though. Both parties have to want it. I may be back before you know it.'

'Like that's going to happen,' Mandy scoffed.

'I hope not.' She cast her eyes around the place she'd called home for the last twenty-four years. 'It's going to feel so strange not living here.'

'Strange that you won't hear the sound of George screaming with another teething episode? Ellie yelling that Holly's pinched her favourite jumper, Sally shouting at them to be quiet because she's trying to read and Dad ... well, Dad just moaning at everyone because—'

'This house has too much oestrogen!' they chorused together.

Abby felt her throat tighten. This was much, much harder than she'd thought. Providing things went well it wasn't like she was moving to the other side of the world, but still. It felt like the end of an era.

Downstairs they heard the clunk of the front door opening.

'Bagsy I choose what channel we watch.' Ellie.

'That's not fair, you got to pick yesterday. Anyway, we have to do our homework first and I've got way less than you so I'll be watching first.' Holly.

'How do you know what homework I've got?' Ellie.

'I don't, but I've not got any, so beat that!' Holly.

'God, you two are so childish.' Sally.

'Ooh, listen to you.' Ellie.

Shrieks. All of them.

'OMG, that's disgusting. Why did he do it there?' Ellie.

'Pat, you naughty dog. You have to wee outside the house, not inside it.' Holly.

'Bagsy not clearing it up!' Ellie and Holly.

Abby looked at Mandy, who started to smirk. Pretty soon they were both convulsed into laughter. 'Still feeling nostalgic about leaving?' Mandy gasped between giggles.

'Yes,' Abby admitted. 'Though I won't miss everything.'

Doug was still at the office, and becoming more and more frantic. He couldn't get hold of Abby even though he'd found out her meeting had ended at lunchtime. Where was she? Why wasn't she returning his calls? He tried not to think of what Geraldine had told him, but the more he couldn't get hold of her, the more it all started to make sense.

She hadn't told him about the job offer because she was planning on taking it. And she wasn't picking up her phone because she wanted to give him the *I'm ditching you* speech face-to-face.

It was now 6.30 p.m. and Doug had to accept that even workaholic Abby was unlikely to come back into the office now. He cast a despairing glance at the alcove where she used to sit, mentally sifting through all the things he should have told her, but had wimped out on. Like *I love you*, for starters.

Would it have helped, though? She was always destined for greater things than him.

Out of desperation he gave up on her mobile and called her home number.

'Hello?'

Doug's stomach dropped. 'Good evening, Derek. I was looking for Abby and I wondered if she was home yet?'

'Depends where you're calling home, I guess.'

He didn't know how he wrenched the next words out. 'What do you mean?'

The pause was so long Doug started grinding his teeth. 'I thought you knew. She left here with a suitcase.'

Doug's fingers clenched round the phone as he tried to make sense of the words. When they began to slip into place – Charles's threats, Robert's job offer – he sagged against the wall and slid, slowly, all the way to the floor. He didn't hear Derek shouting out his name, checking if he was still there. All he heard was the sound of his dreams as they crashed and broke into a million tiny fragments.

Chapter Thirty-Four

Abby checked her watch again. It was 7.30 p.m. and she'd been sitting on this doorstep for half an hour now.

Where on earth was Doug? These days he always left the office early, so he couldn't be at work. And it wasn't gym day. Casting a sideways glance at her case, she began to feel sick. For all she knew he was meeting up with someone.

Maybe with no plans to return home tonight.

Biting her lip, she dragged her mobile out of her bag. She'd phone him.

Bugger. The damn thing was flat.

Her head snapped up at the sound of a car engine and her heart began to thud as his sleek sports car scrunched up the drive. Suddenly the door was thrust open and a man lurched out.

It couldn't be Doug, because he was always so calm and this man was ... manic. But oh my God, it was Doug. His hair was a mess, as if he'd been jamming his hands through it, repeatedly. And his beautiful face was distraught.

Immediately she jumped to her feet. 'What's wrong?' He just stood there, gaping at her, his eyes frantically skimming her up and down. 'Doug, what is it?'

'What are you doing here?'

She froze, her heart in her mouth. 'I ... umm.' Oh God, this had been so much easier when she'd practiced it in her head.

'You've come to say goodbye.' It wasn't a question but a statement, spat out in a harsh tone. He took a couple of paces towards her but stopped a few feet away, as if terrified to touch her. Now he was closer she could see his eyes were bloodshot, as if he'd been *crying*? 'It's easier if you just ...' He shut his eyes. '... go.'

Why did he look so awful? And where on earth did he think she was going? 'But I've only just got here. What are you trying to tell me? I had this stupid notion that turning up at yours might be a nice surprise for you, but obviously I had that wrong.'

Her confusion turned to hurt as he continued to maintain that awful distance. 'I can see from the look on your face that I'm the last person you want here right now, so I'll make myself scarce.' Her voice shook, as did her hands as she reached for her bag.

'You think telling me you're going to Manchester is a *nice* surprise?' he snapped.

'Manchester? Why on earth am I going to go there?' Suddenly the penny dropped. 'Oh, you must have been speaking to Geraldine.'

'I have.' In a slow, deliberate movement he placed his hands in his pockets and drew in a deep breath. 'Why did I have to hear it from her?'

'Hear what from her? How Robert wants me to go up to Manchester and see how his company works?' She took a step towards him, noticing how he stiffened. 'You know I'm not going to work for him. Why would I when there's nothing in Manchester for me, apart from the job? My friends aren't there. My family isn't there.' Her heart raced as she gently placed a hand on his cheek. 'You aren't there.'

She watched as his face gradually began to lose its deathly expression, though his hands remained rigidly clenched at his side. 'So you're not leaving me?'

'Of course not.' He couldn't have thought ... could he? 'Doug, did you really think I'd come here to tell you goodbye?'

'Yes.' She stared into his stunning blue eyes and watched as a whole gamut of emotions flickered through them. Hurt, loss, despair, confusion. Slowly he raised his hand and placed it over hers, drawing it against his chest. As she felt the pounding of his heart beneath her fingers, his expression turned to one of cautious hope. 'So if you haven't come to say goodbye, are we still good?'

She smiled into his eyes. 'I hope so.'

And suddenly he was pulling her into his arms, clinging to her as if his very life depended on it. He showered kisses over her face and then plundered her mouth, kissing her deeply, passionately, with every fibre of his being. When he finally drew back, they were both shaking.

'I'm so sorry,' he whispered, his voice thick with emotion. 'I didn't mean to crowd you or be so demanding.'

'Demanding?'

He ran his hands up and down her arms, as if he couldn't bear not to touch her. 'I know there's so much else going on in your life and I'm incredibly grateful for whatever time you can spare me. A day a week. Even just a night a week. God, as long as I know you're part of my life, I'll be happy with anything.' He bent to kiss her and this time it was achingly gentle. 'I adore you, Abigail Spencer. When I think how close I came to losing you ...'

Abby shook her head, tears streaming down her cheeks. 'Heavens, Doug, you only came close to losing me in your way too furtive imagination. I was never going anywhere, except hopefully inside your house because I've been sitting out here for ages and I'm flipping freezing. My bum's been on that cold step so long it's gone numb.'

'Oh, Abby.' She saw the life sparkle back into his eyes before he bent to lift her into his arms and carry her up the steps.

Doug shifted slightly on the sofa, trying to get more comfortable. He was wrapped around Abby's naked body, both of them covered by a throw he'd tugged over them when the heat of passion had begun to ebb away. Satiated and happier than he could ever remember being, he was loath to disturb the woman in his arms.

Gently he stroked at the soft skin of her stomach, smiling as he heard a rather loud rumble. 'What was that? Are they digging up the roads again?'

Swatting him, Abby opened a sleepy brown eye. 'Ha ha. That's my stomach telling you I'm hungry. You need to feed your guest.'

'How about I distract you with my body for a while, instead.'

'I'm sure you could, but I tend to get grumpy the longer I go without food.'

Sighing, he gave her one final kiss before reluctantly leaving her to venture into the kitchen. Figuring naked cooking might be considered unhygienic he hopped into the trousers he'd gleefully tossed away an hour ago and opened the fridge door. Spying the lasagna Gwen had been kind enough to bring when she'd popped round two days ago to tell him how much she loved her new house, he peeled off the tin foil and plonked it with great flourish into the oven.

As he set about throwing together a salad, a pair of soft lips kissed his naked back. 'Do you mind if I take a shower?'

'No. As long as you have it with me.'

She laughed and hugged his waist. 'It's a deal.'

Abandoning the salad he followed Abby out of the kitchen, admiring the way she struggled to keep the blanket round her naked body. Smirking when he gave it one hard tug.

'Hey!'

'Just trying to help.' He found it hard not to laugh as she flapped her arms around her body in a fruitless attempt to cover herself up.

'For that you can haul my case up the stairs,' she muttered, scampering ahead of him.

It was only when the very distracting sight of her naked bottom had disappeared that Doug remembered the giant suitcase. If she wasn't going to Manchester, where exactly *was* she going?

He gave the handle a tug, then braced himself and yanked again, harder. Wherever she was off to, she'd surely packed enough clothes to see her through all four seasons.

Making a mental note to ask her about it, he shrugged off his trousers for the second time that evening and strode into his shower room. The sight of her naked body swept all thoughts of suitcases temporarily out of his mind.

'So, about your suitcase,' he asked when they were both back downstairs, Abby once again engulfed in his dressing gown. 'Where are you going, if not Manchester?'

She gave a guilty start and a deep red flush stole up her neck and across her cheeks. 'Oh, I'd forgotten about that.'

Midway through chopping a cucumber he froze, his heart plummeting all over again. 'Please don't tell me it's far.'

Her teeth nibbled at her bottom lip. 'Oh it's not far. Not far at all actually. In fact you might think it's a bit too close.'

'You could never be too close to me.'

'Not even if I was in the same house?'

The knife clattered out of his hand and onto the worktop. 'Pardon?'

Her eyes skated away from his. 'Oh God, I should have known this was a bad idea. Of course you don't want me living here. I'm messy and I talk too much. You're used to your neat, tidy space and your quiet and I'd just steamroller over it and—'

He didn't let her finish. Taking several giant strides round the breakfast bar to where she was sitting on a bar stool, he pulled her towards him and kissed her. And kissed her. And kissed her. 'You really want to live here, with me?' he asked breathlessly.

'Yes.'

The word was reassuringly absolute and at last the pieces began to click into place. 'So when I phoned your house and your father told me you'd left with a suitcase, he meant you were coming *here*.' He shook his head, starting to laugh. 'It would have saved me one hell of a lot of heartache if he'd said that.'

'He probably assumed you knew. I didn't tell him I was planning to surprise you.'

'You certainly did that, along with giving my heart a thorough emotional workout.'

She stretched her neck to kiss him again. 'Sorry.'

'Oh no, don't apologise for giving me the best surprise I've ever had.'

'Ever?'

'Yes, ever.' This time it was his turn to be absolute.

Still perched on the stool she leaned in and hugged him tighter. 'I'm glad it was worth all the trauma. I had no idea you thought I was leaving.'

'The last time we saw each other I was a prick and we had cross words. After that you kept turning me down.' He wrapped his arms round her and kissed her, stopping the response he knew she was itching to deliver. 'Then I hear from *Geraldine* about the interaction you had with my father. Why didn't you tell me, Abby?'

'Ah.' Her head dipped so he couldn't see her eyes. 'I was going to, but these last few days have been crazy busy and as time went on it started to lose its importance. I mean, he's never had anything good to say to me, so it was hardly news.'

His sigh was born of pure frustration. 'I deserve to know when my father is bad-mouthing the woman I love.'

The arms around him stilled. 'You love me?'

He groaned, bending to kiss her again. 'Of course I love you.'

Tears immediately began to fill her eyes and she gave him a tremulous smile. 'That's ... oh boy.' She swiped her hand across her watery cheeks. 'That's good. Really, really good. And to get back to what you were saying, you deserve a whole bunch of things I wasn't delivering on. Between the job and my family you've been getting shoved aside and it isn't right.'

'I told you, I don't expect to always come first. I'd like to think I was more important than your job, but I understand your priorities concerning your family.'

Tears ran freely down her cheeks as she stared up at him. '*You* are the most important thing in my life, Doug. I love my family but they aren't my future. You are. Because in case I forgot to tell you, I love you, too.'

His heart filled with such a rush he thought it might burst. 'You do, huh?'

'I do.' Her fingers trailed across his jaw in a gentle caress and he pushed more firmly against her hand in a bid to deepen the contact. 'I will still need to spend a fair amount of time with my family though,' she continued, smiling at the dopey expression he knew was on his face. 'At least for the next few years, so I figured even if I couldn't see you straight after work, if you don't mind me living with you I can at least come home to you every night and tell you how much you mean to me.'

'Yes. God, yes.' He tightened his hold on her, desperate to show her both with his words and his body that he wasn't going to let her go. Ever.

'I'm not sure how much longer I'm going to have a job mind you, after my latest run-in with your non-father.'

'Ah, about that.' He eased her away a fraction, just so he could see her face properly. 'He might not have much choice in the matter.'

'Oh?'

'I suspected he'd rather sell the company than let you become a director in it – or me now, for that matter – so we did a bit of digging.'

'We?'

'Umm, I had a surprising ally. My mother.'

'You've been working with your mother? That's, well to be honest it's almost unbelievable but it's amazing, too.' Her eyes turned soft. 'Do you think you'll learn to be friends?'

'I'm not sure, but it's been good to feel I'm not fighting my father alone any more. We found out that Charles has been slowly selling off shares in Crumbs to interested parties. What he doesn't know is that those interested parties now comprise mainly of my mother, sisters, friends of my mother and myself. Between us we've bought enough to take control.'

Her eyes rounded. 'Seriously?'

'Yes.'

A bubble of laughter escaped her. 'Oh boy. He's going to go ape shit when he finds out.'

'By then it will be too late. My mother's got it all in hand.' He grinned. 'Seems that sleeping with my father's trusted lawyer comes with a lot of perks.'

Abby arched her back, rubbing herself suggestively against him. 'Does that mean I can literally sleep my way to the top now?'

'If you sleep with me every night you can have any job you want. It doesn't need to be at Crumbs either, though we're hoping it will be.' He kissed her forehead, her cheeks, her nose and finally her mouth. 'But you need to know that if you decide to live with me, I won't ever let you go.'

Her eyes welled, turning a liquid brown as she registered his meaning. 'That's good, because I don't ever plan on leaving.'

Too choked to talk, he simply held her.

Finally he had a place he could call home. It had nothing to do with the four walls and everything to do with the woman who'd be sharing them with him.

The poignancy of the moment was interrupted when her stomach let out another loud rumble. As she glanced up at him he caught her eye.

And suddenly his home was filled with laughter.

Epilogue

Abby pushed Doug forward. 'Go on. Go in and talk to him. You don't even have to tell him who you are. You can talk about the latest oil paints, or easels or ... oh, I don't know ... palette knives. Yes, ask him about where he gets his palette knives from.'

Doug raised an eyebrow. 'You're suggesting the first conversation I have with my father, my real father, is about palette knives?'

She huffed. 'No! I'm saying you don't have to blurt out you're his son if you don't want to. You can ease into the conversation.'

'By discussing palette knives?'

'By discussing whatever the heck you want to, but you do need to actually walk into his studio in order to do that. Which means opening this door.'

She watched as he stared at the door, the handsome face she'd once found so hard to read now clearly telling her *I'm scared*. He took a step back. 'We don't have to do this now. In fact we've not really got time.'

'We're not due at the venue for another hour and a half,' Abby cut in gently, rubbing the small of his back with her hand. 'And we've been through all this. Today happens to be a really convenient time to see him. We know he's in, because I phoned this morning. We've not had to come out of our way because it's round the corner from where we need to be later. If it's a disaster it doesn't matter because you have plenty more going on today to take your mind off it.'

His broad shoulders sprung back and he inhaled deeply. 'Okay then.' His eyes darted to hers. 'You're coming with me, yes?'

'If you want me to.'

He grabbed her hand and squeezed it. 'I do.' Then he pushed his way into the studio-cum-shop owned by the portrait artist, Patrick O'Shea.

The bell tinkled as the door opened and before Abby had a chance to study the paintings that littered the front of the shop a tall, distinguished looking man greeted them.

He smiled warmly and Abby had to stifle a gasp. There was no doubt that this man was Doug's real father. The height and the body shape were similar but it was the eyes that gave it away. Doug had obviously inherited his dazzling blue eyes from his father. Irish blue eyes that twinkled when they smiled, and it was clear from the lines on Patrick's face that he'd done a lot of smiling in his life. Doug was only starting to learn.

'Mr O'Shea.' Doug stood woodenly in front of his father and Abby ached for him. What must he be thinking, coming face-to-face with the man whose genes he carried?

'Ach, we don't stand on ceremony here. Patrick is fine.' There was a hint of an Irish accent in his voice. 'How can I be of help?' He glanced towards Abby. 'If you tell me you'd like me to paint this lady, you will truly have made my day.'

Abby blushed, immediately seeing why Doug's mother had fallen for the guy. 'Thank you but I think the world can do without another version of me. Not that it wouldn't look fabulous, I'm sure,' she added hastily, then realised how that sounded. 'I mean it would look fabulous because of your skill, not because of the model.' She caught Doug's amused glance and slammed her jaw shut. So much for the promise she'd made him that she'd keep quiet.

Patrick chuckled softly. 'You've found someone special here all right, Douglas Faulkner.'

Doug's face paled. 'You know who I am?'

'Of course I do. I've been taking a keen interest in you ever since I found out Belinda was pregnant. She denied I was the father but the dates we'd been ...' He coughed delicately. '... seeing each other and the date you were born ... well, they both matched up.'

'You've been in touch with my mother all this time?'

'Oh, I wouldn't put it that strongly. I've tried to, though she cut me off at every attempt.' Patrick's vivid blue eyes stared straight into Doug's matching ones. 'I wanted to know what was happening to the boy I believed could be my son. When I heard whispers about a hot new artist who some believed was actually Douglas Faulkner, I googled you. Your age, your looks. Let's just say I put two and two together and figured I'd made four. Your visit today suggests my maths were right.'

Doug stared at the man with the bright blue eyes. His father. He didn't know what to think, what to say. He'd never been any good at the emotional stuff and meeting his father for the first time surely came under that category.

Suddenly he felt the squeeze of the small hand wrapped inside his. Glancing sideways he saw Abby gazing at him, her dark eyes full of compassion and understanding. Most of all though, full of love. It was she who'd patiently coaxed him this far. Surely he could manage the last few steps himself.

Holding out his hand he offered it to Patrick. 'Your maths were right. I'm pleased to meet you at last.'

The hand that shook his was firm and strong. 'You don't know how much this means to me.' The grip held for a few more moments before Patrick finally released his hand and turned to Abby. 'And this must be the young lady who called earlier, asking about my prices. I could tell from your voice you were a beauty.'

Abby ignored the offered hand and put her arms around

Patrick's neck, kissing his cheek. 'And you're a flatterer. Hello, I'm Abby Spencer.'

Patrick's face lit up as Abby hugged him and Doug smiled to himself. Clearly his biological father and he had more than eye colour and painting in common.

'Can you spare the time for a drink and a chat? I can lock up the shop and put the kettle on.'

Before Doug had time to glance at his watch, Abby was threading her arm through Patrick's. 'That sounds fantastic.'

Doug raced to his car, flinging open the passenger door for Abby. 'We're going to be late.'

Abby giggled as she slid inside. 'We're late, we're late. For a very important date.'

He threw the car into first and zipped out onto the road. 'I believe a wedding does come under the banner of *an important date*.'

She sobered slightly, but her eyes were still dancing. 'Umm, it does, but we aren't going to be late. Not if you drive quickly. Besides, being late is a Spencer family tradition.' She put her hand on his thigh and squeezed. 'If we are late, will it have been worth it, to finally meet your father?'

It was a question he didn't have to consider for long. 'Yes.'

'What did you think?' she asked. 'Did you like him?'

'As fathers go, he hasn't got much to live up to in my book.' She dug him in the ribs which he took to mean she wasn't happy with his flip answer. 'Yes,' he told her as he screeched into the small car park of the pretty waterside hotel. 'I liked him.' He flicked her a gaze. 'And one of the best things I liked about him was that he took a shine to you. Now come on, lady. You might be used to being late but I'm not.'

They flew out of the car and into the lobby. Balloons were dotted everywhere, silver and pink to match the bridesmaids' outfits. Doug started to feel all hot and cold as he took in all the wedding regalia. The carefully dressed tables and chairs in the adjacent restaurant, complete with large pink bows. The artfully arranged pink roses. The three tier cake that stood in pride of place near the top table. God, he wasn't sure he was up to this. There was only so much emotion a mere male could manage on one day. Seeing his father for the first time had already pushed him outside his limit.

'You're looking a bit pale,' Abby whispered into his ear as she waved frantically at her arriving sisters. 'Cheer up, it's only a wedding.'

Sally, Ellie and Holly piled out of Roger's car and rushed towards Abby who was wearing a very similar, but more elegant, version of their pink dresses. Roger followed behind, carrying a wriggling George.

'Dad has already gone once round the block with Mandy,' Ellie said breathlessly. 'They'll be here any minute. Can you put my hair up? I asked Dad but he was useless, and Mandy was too busy doing her own and Sally started but she took so long we had to go.'

Abby took the proffered clip and with a few swift snaps of the wrist had Ellie's hair neatly up. 'There you go, all done.'

'Oh no. I can't believe it.' Doug looked over in alarm as Holly's face crumpled. 'My nail varnish is smudged.'

'Nail varnish,' he muttered to nobody in particular.

Abby being Abby didn't tell Holly that smudged nail varnish wasn't a disaster. She simply glanced at the offending nail, then at the rest of Holly's fingers. 'Nobody will notice because the rest of your nails look amazing, Holly. You'll have to give me a manicure some time.'

'A manicure is more than just painting your fingernails.' Sally waved her hand in the air. 'I had my nails done after school yesterday. The woman massaged my hand, filed my nails, pushed back my cuticles—'

'Mandy and Dad are coming round the corner,' Ellie

screeched. Doug had never been so grateful for one of Ellie's interruptions.

'Okay then,' Abby clapped her hands. 'Here's how it's going to work. Best man Doug is going to escort the groom and his son – aka Roger and George – into the stateroom, where the other guests are waiting. As chief bridesmaid I shall wait here with my fellow bridesmaids for the bride. We will then follow the beautiful bride and her father down the aisle, gliding elegantly towards the handsome groom and best man.'

The girls burst out laughing. 'OMG, I can't glide,' Holly squawked.

'Yes you can,' Abby told her firmly. 'We're all going to practice now while we wait for Mandy.' She glared at Doug and Roger. 'When we lose the men.'

Doug took the hint and draped a reassuring arm around Roger. 'Come on, mate. Time to go and meet your fate.'

'Shit, don't say it like that. I'm bloody terrified enough as it is.'

Doug gaped at him. 'You've had a child with Mandy, lived with the Spencers for the three months since Abby left, faced weeks of intense questioning about your honeymoon plans from those three sweet-faced monsters you're soon to call your sisters-in-law and yet you're terrified of *this* part?' Shaking his head, he gently pushed him forwards. 'This bit's a doddle. You only have to stand at the front and repeat a few lines. I'm the one who should be terrified.'

Roger stared at Doug, then down at the squirming George. When he looked back at Doug a grin split his face. 'Oh yeah. I'd forgotten.' Laughing now, he maneuvered his son into Doug's rigid arms. 'Good luck, mate. He's all yours.'

'Just for the ceremony,' Doug reminded him, but Roger only laughed again. At least he'd made the guy forget his nerves, which Doug guessed was part of a best man's duty.

Immensely touched at being asked, he was anxious to fulfil his role properly, though he hadn't realised babysitting a restless toddler would be one of his duties. It did go to prove how much a part of the Spencer family he'd become, though. And if the privilege of being part of their big, loud, loving family came at the expense of the occasional child-minding duty, he'd gladly suck it up.

He followed Roger into the rather grandly named stateroom. Decorated with pink bows, green foliage and lots of flickering, romantic candles it looked like wedding heaven, and babysitting horror.

Perhaps George would be okay just sitting on his lap.

Abby stifled another giggle as she watched Doug yanking George's pudgy little hand back from yet another candle. She'd never seen George looking so happy, or Doug so harassed. From the moment George had seen his mum and not been able to go to her, Doug had had his hands full. He'd found a way to distract him by letting him think he was going to touch the candle, then pulling him back at the last minute. A high risk strategy, though it seemed to be working so far.

'If any person present knows of any lawful impediment to this marriage, he or she should declare it now,' announced the registrar.

There was silence, interrupted by a screech of toddler giggles. Doug winced and shrugged apologetically as he bounced George up and down on his knee. Abby's heart, already full to capacity, threatened to burst. To think she'd once believed he was lacking emotion. That *he'd* believed he was cold. The Doug she was living with was far from cold. He was fun-loving and compassionate. Sexy, kind, generous and absolutely adorable.

Finally the ceremony finished, the groom kissed the bride, much to the delight of the bridesmaids, and Abby caught up with Doug. As George looked on with great interest, she gave Doug a big, soppy kiss.

'What was that for?'

'For being the most handsome man in the room and the best babysitter of all time.'

His eyes glittered. 'I'll accept the first, but I'm not sure playing with candles is in the top ten list of recommended ways to entertain a toddler.'

'If it works, it gets in my list.' She held out her arms. 'You can relax now for a bit. Dad and the girls will look after George.'

'Relax?' He looked at her with a pained expression. 'I've got to deliver a heart-warming yet funny, short yet descriptive, thoughtful yet entertaining best man's speech.'

She laughed. 'You'll ace it. Go and get yourself a drink to settle your nerves. I'll be back when I've palmed this little monster off on Dad.'

It wasn't hard to spot her father. He was the one watching the photographer take photos of Mandy and Roger with a part proud, part dazed expression on his face.

'Time for some grandson, granddad bonding time.' She lifted the heavy toddler into her dad's arms. 'When he gets too much, come and find me. Better still, find Sally, Holly or Ellie.' She was about to go when she noticed his eyes had misted over. 'Hey, are you okay?'

He touched a hand to her cheek. 'Just being sentimental. Your mother would have loved today. She'd have been so proud of you all.' He swallowed and gave her a sad smile. 'I wish she was here to see how beautiful her girls have turned out.'

'Oh, Dad.' Abby gripped his hand. 'You know she is here, in a way. You told me when she died that part of her is in each one of us.' She nodded over to where Ellie was trying to persuade one of the waiters to give her a glass of champagne.

'I'm not so sure about Ellie, mind. I think she may have come from another planet altogether.'

As if she'd heard them, Ellie turned round. 'He won't give me a glass.'

Her father looked down at George, and then over at his youngest daughter. 'No, but he'll give me one. And if you help me take care of George, I'll let you have a sip.'

Ellie beamed. 'Deal.'

Doug's speech was exactly as he'd promised. When he sagged back down on his chair to the sound of laughter and loud applause, Abby squeezed his hand. 'I told you you'd ace it.'

'I think that's pushing it, but I'm glad it's over.' He turned to give her a dazzling smile. 'Our turn next.'

Her heart skipped a beat. 'Our turn? Was that … is that …'

'A proposal?' he cut in, shaking his head. 'No. Even I can manage something more romantic than that.' Taking her hand he stared deep into her eyes. 'It was a warning though, so you might want to start thinking about your answer.'

Abby had told herself she wasn't going to cry today, but it seemed she was wrong. 'Okay.' She dabbed at her eyes. 'But there are only a few ways a girl can say yes.'

His eyes brimmed with joy and for a few seconds they simply grinned inanely at each other.

'Here, it's your turn.' Ellie unceremoniously dumped a flushed, pungent smelling George onto her lap. 'I think he needs changing.'

'You *think*?' But when she turned to reprimand Ellie, she'd scarpered. Abby turned to Doug. 'I don't suppose …?'

Her lover gave her a dashing smile. 'My babysitting duties were only procured for the ceremony.' He darted her a quick kiss. 'But hurry back and I'll save the first dance for you.'

'Who gets the second?'

'Ellie.'

'The third?'

'Holly.'

'The fourth?'

'Sally.' He gave a slightly awkward shrug of his shoulders. 'What can I say? I seem to be a hit with the Spencer ladies.'

Laughing, she stood up, holding her whiffy nephew down wind. 'Okay, but from dance five onwards, you're all mine.'

He leant back against his chair and gave her another slow, heart-stopping smile. 'Abby, I was all yours from the first day you launched yourself into my office.'

And with her heart overflowing with happiness, Abby went off to deal with her nephew's nappy.

Thank You

I get so much pleasure out of writing a book – spending months in a fantasy world with my perfect hero, what's not to love?! The greatest pleasure though, comes from hearing that others have enjoyed the fantasy I've created. I'm not alone in that. Authors love feedback – it can inspire, motivate, help us improve. It can also help spread the word. So if you feel inclined to leave a review, I would be really grateful. And if you'd like to contact me (details are under my author profile) I'd be delighted to hear from you.

Kathryn

x

About the Author

Kathryn was born in Wallingford, England but has spent most of her life living in a village near Windsor. After studying pharmacy in Brighton she began her working life as a retail pharmacist. She quickly realised that trying to decipher doctor's handwriting wasn't for her and left to join the pharmaceutical industry where she spent twenty happy years working in medical communications. In 2011, backed by her family, she left the world of pharmaceutical science to begin life as a self-employed writer, juggling the two disciplines of medical writing and romance. Some days a racing heart is a medical condition, others it's the reaction to a hunky hero ...

With two teenage boys and a husband who asks every Valentine's Day whether he has to bother buying a card again this year (yes, he does) the romance in her life is all in her head. Then again, her husband's unstinting support of her career change goes to prove that love isn't always about hearts and flowers – and heroes can come in many disguises.

For more information on Kathryn:
www.twitter.com/KathrynFreeman1
www.kathrynfreeman.co.uk

More Choc Lit

From Kathryn Freeman

Do Opposites Attract?

There's no such thing as a class divide – until you're on separate sides

Brianna Worthington has beauty, privilege and a very healthy trust fund. The only hardship she's ever witnessed has been on the television. Yet when she's invited to see how her mother's charity, Medic SOS, is dealing with the aftermath of a tornado in South America, even Brianna is surprised when she accepts.

Mitch McBride, Chief Medical Officer, doesn't need the patron's daughter disrupting his work. He's from the wrong side of the tracks and has led life on the edge, but he's not about to risk losing his job for a pretty face.

Poles apart, dynamite together, but can Brianna and Mitch ever bridge the gap separating them?

Too Charming

Does a girl ever really learn from her mistakes?

Detective Sergeant Megan Taylor thinks so. She once lost her heart to a man who was too charming and she isn't about to make the same mistake again – especially not with sexy defence lawyer, Scott Armstrong. Aside from being far too sure of himself for his own good, Scott's major flaw is that he defends the very people that she works so hard to imprison.

But when Scott wants something he goes for it. And he wants Megan. One day she'll see him not as a lawyer, but as a man ... and that's when she'll fall for him.

Yet just as Scott seems to be making inroads, a case presents itself that's far too close to home, throwing his life into chaos.

As Megan helps him pick up the pieces, can he persuade her that he isn't the careless charmer she thinks he is? Isn't a man innocent until proven guilty?

Search for the Truth

Sometimes the truth hurts ...

When journalist Tess Johnson takes a job at Helix pharmaceuticals, she has a very specific motive. Tess has reason to believe the company are knowingly producing a potentially harmful drug and, if her suspicions are confirmed, she will stop at nothing to make sure the truth comes out.

Jim Knight is the president of research and development at Helix and is a force to be reckoned with. After a disastrous office affair he's determined that nothing else will distract him from his vision for the company. Failure is simply not an option.

As Tess and Jim start working together, both have their reasons for wanting to ignore the sexual chemistry that fires between them. But chemistry, like most things in the world of science, isn't always easy to control.

Before You

When life in the fast lane threatens to implode …

Melanie Taylor's job working for the Delta racing team means she is constantly rubbing shoulders with Formula One superstars in glamorous locations like Monte Carlo. But she has already learned that keeping a professional distance is crucial if she doesn't want to get hurt.

New Delta team driver Aiden Foster lives his life like he drives his cars – fast and hard. But, no matter how successful he is, it seems he always falls short of his championship-winning father's legacy. If he could just stay focused, he could finally make that win.

Resolve begins to slip as Melanie and Aiden find themselves drawn to each other – with nowhere to hide as racing season begins. But certain risks are worth taking and, sometimes, there are more important things than winning …

Available in paperback from all good bookshops and online stores. Visit www.choc-lit.com for details.

Too Damn Nice

Do nice guys stand a chance?

Nick Templeton has been in love with Lizzie Donavue for what seems like forever. Just as he summons the courage to make his move, she's offered a modelling contract which takes her across the Atlantic to the glamorous locations of New York and Los Angeles. And far away from him.

Nick is forced to watch from the sidelines as the gawky teenager he knew is transformed into Elizabeth Donavue: top model and the ultimate elegant English rose pin-up, seemingly forever caught in a whirlwind of celebrity parties with the next up-and-coming Hollywood bad boy by her side.

But then Lizzie's star-studded life comes crashing down around her, and a nice guy like Nick seems just what she needs. Will she take a chance on him? Or is he too damn nice?

Available in paperback from all good bookshops and online stores. Visit www.choc-lit.com for details.

A Second Christmas Wish

Do you believe in Father Christmas?

For Melissa, Christmas has always been overrated. From her cold, distant parents to her manipulative ex-husband, Lawrence, she's never experienced the warmth and contentment of the festive season with a big, happy family sitting around the table.

And Melissa has learned to live with it, but it breaks her heart that her seven-year-old son, William, has had to live with it too. Whilst most little boys wait with excitement for the big day, William finds it difficult to believe that Father Christmas even exists.

But then Daniel McCormick comes into their lives. And with his help, Melissa and William might just be able to find their festive spirit, and finally have a Christmas where all of their wishes come true …

A Little Christmas Faith

Is it time to love Christmas again?

Faith Watkins loves Christmas, which is why she's thrilled that her new hotel in the Lake District will be open in time for the festive season. And Faith has gone all out: huge Christmas tree, fairy lights, an entire family of decorative reindeer. Now all she needs are the guests ...

But what she didn't bank on was her first paying customer being someone like Adam Hunter. Rugged, powerfully built and with a deep sadness in his eyes, Adam is a man that Faith is immediately drawn to – but unfortunately he also has an intense hatred of all things Christmassy.

As the countdown to the big day begins, Faith can't seem to keep away from her mysterious guest, but still finds herself with more questions than answers: just what happened to Adam Hunter? And why does he hate Christmas?

Available in paperback from all good bookshops and online stores. Visit www.choc-lit.com for details.

A Little Christmas Charm

Would you swap sea and sunshine for tinsel and turkey?

Gabby Sanderson is used to being let down – even at Christmas. Which is why she's happy to skip the festive season completely in favour of a plane ticket and sunnier climes.

But this Christmas could be different, because this time she might not be spending it alone. Can Owen Cooper charm Gabby into loving Christmas in the same way he's charmed his way into her life, or is he just another person who'll end up disappointing her?

Crikey a Bodyguard

She's got the brains, he's got the muscle …

When Kelly Bridge's parents insist on employing a bodyguard for her protection, she's not happy. Okay, so maybe not every woman is on the cusp of developing a vaccine against a potential biological terrorist attack – but crikey, it's not like she's a celebrity!

Ben Jacobs flunked spectacularly out of school, so he knows his new client Dr Kelly Bridge spells trouble for him. But on a conference trip to Rome he finds things are worse than he thought. Not only is he falling for the brilliant scientist, he's also become horribly aware she's in grave danger. As they go on the run, dodging bullets and kidnappers, can he resist his feelings and keep her safe?

Available as an eBook on all platforms.
Visit www.choc-lit.com for details.

Introducing Choc Lit

We're an independent publisher creating
a delicious selection of fiction.
Where heroes are like chocolate – irresistible!
Quality stories with a romance at the heart.

See our selection here:
www.choc-lit.com

We'd love to hear how you enjoyed *Oh Crumbs*. Please
visit **www.choc-lit.com** and give your feedback or
leave a review where you purchased this novel.

Choc Lit novels are selected by genuine readers like yourself.
We only publish stories our Tasting Panel want to see in
print. Our reviews and awards speak for themselves.

**Could you be a Star Selector
and join our Tasting Panel?**
Would you like to play a role in choosing which novels
we decide to publish? Do you enjoy reading women's
fiction? Then you could be perfect for our Tasting Panel.

Visit here for more details...
www.choc-lit.com/join-the-choc-lit-tasting-panel

Keep in touch:
Sign up for our monthly newsletter Spread for all the latest
news and offers: www.spread.choc-lit.com. Follow us
on Twitter: @ChocLituk and Facebook: Choc Lit.

Where heroes are like chocolate – irresistible!